Praise for
New York Times and *USA TODAY* bestselling author
Brenda Jackson

"Brenda Jackson writes romance that sizzles
and characters you fall in love with."
—*New York Times* and *USA TODAY* bestselling author
Lori Foster

"Jackson's trademark ability to weave
multiple characters and side stories together
makes shocking truths all the more exciting."
—*Publishers Weekly*

"There is no getting away from the sex appeal and
charm of Jackson's Westmoreland family."
—*RT Book Reviews* on *Feeling the Heat*

"Jackson's characters are wonderful, strong,
colorful and hot enough to burn the pages."
—*RT Book Reviews* on *Westmoreland's Way*

"The kind of sizzling, heart-tugging story
Brenda Jackson is famous for."
—*RT Book Reviews* on *Spencer's Forbidden Passion*

"This is entertainment at its best."
—*RT Book Reviews* on *Star of His Heart*

BRENDA JACKSON

is a die "heart" romantic who married her childhood sweetheart, Gerald, and still proudly wears the "going steady" ring he gave her when she was fifteen. Their marriage of forty-one years produced two sons, Gerald Jr. and Brandon, of whom Brenda is extremely proud. Because she's always believed in the power of love, Brenda's stories always have happy endings, and she credits Gerald for being her inspiration.

A *New York Times* and *USA TODAY* bestselling author of more than one hundred romance titles, Brenda is a retiree from a major insurance company and now divides her time between family, writing and travel. You may write Brenda at P.O. Box 28267, Jacksonville, Florida 32226, by email at authorbrendajackson@gmail.com or visit her website at www.brendajackson.net.

NEW YORK TIMES AND USA TODAY BESTSELLING AUTHOR

BRENDA JACKSON

THE SECRET AFFAIR
&
BACHELOR UNDONE

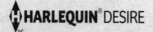 HARLEQUIN® DESIRE

ISBN-13: 978-0-373-83807-3

The Secret Affair & Bachelor Undone

Please Recycle This Product is Recyclable

Recycling programs
for this product may
not exist in your area.

Printed in U.S.A.

HARLEQUIN®
www.Harlequin.com

CONTENTS

Dear Reader,

It is hard to believe that *The Secret Affair* is my twenty-eighth Westmoreland novel. Time most certainly flies when you're having fun, and I hope you're getting as much enjoyment out of reading about this dynamic family as I am in writing about them.

Holding center stage is Aidan, identical twin to Adrian from *The Real Thing*. From the very beginning the twins were a challenge to their family, but we've watched them grow up and mature. They now see life differently than they did as teens. But the one thing that holds true is that Aidan is a Westmoreland man who will go after what he wants.

And he wants Jillian Novak.

Jillian was first introduced some books back when her older sister Pamela married Dillon Westmoreland. Pam and Dillon are clueless that a romance has been bubbling under their very noses. And that's Aidan and Jillian's secret. Aidan is ready to publicly claim the woman he loves, but Jill is having some misgivings. Find out how Aidan convinces Jill in the most passionate way that true love can't be hidden forever.

I hope you enjoy this story about Aidan and Jillian.

Happy reading!

Brenda Jackson

THE SECRET AFFAIR

* * *

To the man who will always and forever be
the love of my life, Gerald Jackson, Sr.

Special thanks to Dr. Dorothy M. Russ of
Meharry Medical College for your assistance in
providing information on medical schools and
residency programs.

In whom are hid all the treasures
of wisdom and knowledge.
—*Colossians* 2:3

THE DENVER WESTMORELAND FAMILY TREE

Raphel and Gemma Westmoreland

Stern Westmoreland (Paula Bailey)

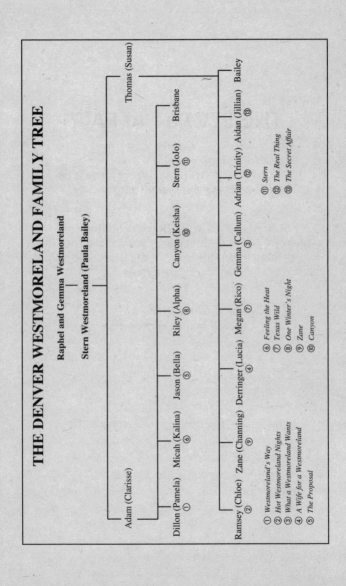

Adam (Clarisse)

Dillon (Pamela) ① Micah (Kalina) ⑥ Jason (Bella) ⑤ Riley (Alpha) ⑧ Canyon (Keisha) ⑩ Gemma (Callum) ③ Stern (JoJo) ⑪ Brisbane

Thomas (Susan)

Ramsey (Chloe) ② Zane (Channing) ⑨ Derringer (Lucia) ④ Megan (Rico) ⑦ Adrian (Trinity) Aidan (Jillian) ⑫ Bailey ~

① Westmoreland's Way
② Hot Westmoreland Nights
③ What a Westmoreland Wants
④ A Wife for a Westmoreland
⑤ The Proposal

⑥ Feeling the Heat
⑦ Texas Wild
⑧ One Winter's Night
⑨ Zane
⑩ Canyon

⑪ Stern
⑫ The Real Thing
⑬ The Secret Affair

PROLOGUE

JILLIAN NOVAK STARED across the table at her sister, not believing what she'd just heard.

Jillian placed the glass of wine she'd been holding on the table, barely keeping the drink from spilling. "What do you mean you aren't going with me? That's crazy, Paige. Need I remind you that you're the one who planned the trip?"

"A reminder isn't needed, Jill, but please understand my dilemma," Paige said in a rueful tone, her dark brown eyes shaded with regret. "Getting a part in a Steven Spielberg movie is a dream come true. You can't imagine what I was feeling—happiness at being chosen one minute, and then disappointment the next, when I found out that shooting starts the same week I was supposed to be on the cruise with you."

"Let me guess, your happiness overpowered your disappointment, right?" Jillian felt a pounding pressure in her head and knew why. She had been looking forward to the Mediterranean cruise—for many reasons—and now it appeared she wouldn't be going.

"I'm sorry, Jill. You've never gone on a cruise and I know it's one of the things on your bucket list."

Paige's apology only made Jillian feel worse. She'd made her sister feel awful for making a choice Jillian would have made herself if given the chance. Reaching across the table, she grabbed Paige's hand.

"I'm the one who should be apologizing, Paige. I was only thinking of myself. You're right. Getting that part in the movie is a dream come true and you'd be crazy not to take it. I'm truly happy for you. Congratulations."

A bright smile spread across Paige's lips. "Thanks. I wanted so much for us to spend time together on the cruise. It's been ages since me, you, Pam and Nadia have had sister time."

Nadia, a senior in college, was their youngest sister. At twenty-one she was two years younger than Paige and four years younger than Jillian. Pamela, their oldest sister—who Jillian, Nadia and Paige were convinced was the best older sister anyone could ever have—was ten years older than Jillian. A former actress, Pam had given up the glitter of Hollywood to return home to Gamble, Wyoming, and raise them when their father died. Now Pam lived in Denver. She was married, the mother of two and the CEO of two acting schools, one in Denver and the other in Gamble. Paige had followed in Pam's footsteps and pursued an acting career. She lived in Los Angeles.

With Pam's busy schedule, she'd said accompanying them on the cruise would have been close to impossible. Nadia had wanted to go but finals kept her from doing so. Jillian had wanted sister time with at least one of her siblings. And now that she had completed medical school, she needed those two weeks on the cruise as a getaway before starting her residency. But there was another reason she wanted to take that two-week cruise.

Aidan Westmoreland.

It was hard to believe it had been a little over a year

since she'd broken things off with him. And every time she remembered the reason she'd done so her heart ached. She needed a distraction from her memories.

"You okay, Jill?"

Jillian glanced up at Paige and forced a smile. "Yes, why do you ask?"

"You zoned out on me just now. I was talking and you appeared to be a million miles away. I noticed you haven't been yourself since I arrived in New Orleans. More than once you've seemed preoccupied about something. Is everything okay?"

Jillian waved off Paige's words. The last thing she wanted was for her sister to start worrying and begin digging. "Yes, everything is okay, Paige."

Paige didn't look convinced. "Um, I don't know. Maybe I should forget about being in that movie and go on that cruise with you after all."

Jillian picked up her wineglass to take a sip. "Don't be silly. You're doing the right thing. Besides, I'm not going on the cruise."

"Why not?"

Jillian was surprised at her sister's question. "Surely you don't expect me to go without you."

"You need a break before starting your residency."

Jillian rolled her eyes. "Get real, Paige. What would I do on a two-week cruise by myself?"

"Rest, relax, enjoy the sights, the ocean, the peace and quiet. And you might luck up and meet some nice single guy."

Jillian shook her head. "Nice single guys don't go on cruises alone. Besides, the last thing I need right now is a man in my life."

Paige laughed. "Jill, you haven't had a guy in your

life since you dated Cobb Grindstone in your senior year at Gamble High. I think what's missing in your life is a man."

Jillian bristled at her sister's words. "Not hardly, especially with my busy schedule. And I don't see you with anyone special."

"At least I've been dating over the years. You haven't. Or, if you have, you haven't told me about it."

Jillian schooled her expression into an impassive facade. She'd never told Paige about her affair with Aidan, and considering how it had ended she was glad she hadn't.

"Jill?"

She glanced up at her sister. "Yes?"

A teasing smile spread across Paige's lips. "You aren't keeping secrets, are you?"

Jill knew Paige had given her the perfect opportunity to come clean about her affair with Aidan, but she wasn't ready. Even after a year, the pain was still raw. And the last thing Jillian needed was for Paige to start probing for more information.

"You know the reason I don't have a man in my life is because of time. My focus has been on becoming a doctor and nothing else." Paige didn't have to know that a few years ago Aidan had wiggled his way past that focus without much effort. That had been a mistake that cost her.

"That's why I think you should go on that cruise without me," Paige said. "You've worked hard and need to rest and enjoy yourself for a change. Once you begin your residency you'll have even less time for yourself—or anything else."

"That's true," Jillian said. "But—"

"No buts, Jillian."

Jillian knew that tone. She also knew that whenever Paige called her by her full name she meant business. "If I were to go on that cruise alone I'd be bored stiff. You're talking about two weeks."

Paige gave her a pointed look. "I'm talking about two weeks that I believe you need. And just think of all the fabulous places you'll get to see—Barcelona, France, Rome, Greece and Turkey." Now it was Paige who reached out to take hold of Jillian's hand. "Look, Jill, there *is* something going on with you, I can feel it. Whatever it is, it's tearing you apart. I picked up on it months ago, the last time I came to visit you."

A wry smile touched Paige's lips when she added, "Perhaps you *are* keeping secrets. Maybe there's some doctor in medical school that caught your eye and you're not ready to tell me about him. One who has blown your mind and you don't know how to handle the intensity of such a relationship. If that's the case, I understand. All of us at some time or another have issues we prefer to deal with alone. That's why I believe two weeks on the open seas will be good for you."

Jillian drew in a deep breath. Paige didn't know how close she was to the truth. Her problem *did* center on some doctor, but not one attending medical school with her.

At that moment the waitress returned with their meal, and Jillian appreciated the interruption. She knew Paige would not be happy until Jillian agreed to go on the cruise. She'd heard what Paige had said—Paige knew something was bothering Jillian. It would only be a matter of time before Pam and Nadia knew as well, if they didn't already. Besides, Jillian had already taken those two weeks off. If she didn't go on the cruise, the family would expect her to come home and spend that time with them. She couldn't do that. What if Aidan came home unexpectedly while she was there? He was the last person she wanted to see.

"Jill?"

Jillian drew in another deep breath and met Paige's gaze. "Okay, I'll do it. I'll go cruising alone. Hopefully, I'll enjoy myself."

Paige smiled. "You will. There will be plenty for you to do and on those days when you feel like doing nothing, you can do that, too. Everybody needs to give their mind a rest once in a while."

Jillian nodded. Her mind definitely needed a rest. She would be the first to admit that she had missed Aidan—the steamy hot text messages, the emails that made her adrenaline surge and the late-night phone calls that sent heat sizzling through her entire body.

But that had been before she'd learned the truth. Now all she wanted to do was get over him.

She sighed deeply while thinking that Paige was right. Jillian needed that cruise and the time away it would give her. She would go on the cruise alone.

DR. AIDAN WESTMORELAND entered his apartment and removed his lab coat. After running a frustrated hand down his face, he glanced at his watch. He'd hoped he would have heard something by now. What if…

The ringing of his cell phone made him pause on his way to the kitchen. It was the call he'd been waiting for. "Paige?"

"Yes, it's me."

"Is she still going?" he asked, not wasting time with chitchat.

There was a slight pause on the other end and in that short space of time knots formed in his stomach. "Yes, she's still going on the cruise, Aidan."

He released the breath he'd been holding as Paige continued, "Jill still has no idea I'm aware that the two of you had an affair."

Aidan hadn't known Paige knew the truth, either, until she'd paid him a surprise visit last month. According to her, she'd figured things out the year Jillian had entered medical school. She'd become suspicious when he'd come home for his cousin Riley's wedding and she'd overheard him call Jillian *Jilly* in an intimate tone. Paige had been concerned this past year when she'd noticed Jillian seemed troubled by something that she wouldn't share with Paige.

Paige had talked to Ivy, Jillian's best friend, who'd also been concerned about Jillian. Ivy had shared everything about the situation with Paige. That prompted Paige to fly to Charlotte and confront him. Until then, he'd been clueless as to the real reason behind his and Jillian's breakup.

When Paige had told him of the cruise she and Jillian had planned and had suggested an idea for getting Jillian on the cruise alone, he'd readily embraced the plan.

I've done my part and the rest is up to you, Aidan. I hope you can convince Jill of the truth.

Moments later he ended the call and continued to the kitchen where he grabbed a beer. Popping the top, he leaned against the counter and took a huge gulp. Two weeks on the open seas with Jillian would be interest-

ing. But he intended to make it more than just interesting. He aimed to make it productive.

A determined smile spread across his lips. By the
time the cruise ended there would be no doubt in Jillian's mind that he was the only man for her.

Moments later, he tossed the empty can in the recycle
bin before heading for the shower. As he undressed, he
couldn't help but recall how his secret affair with Jillian had begun nearly four years ago....

CHAPTER ONE

Four years earlier

"So, how does it feel to be twenty-one?"

Jillian's breath caught in her throat when Aidan Westmoreland's tall frame slid into the seat across from her. It was only then that she noticed everyone had gone inside. She and Aidan were the only ones on the patio that overlooked a beautiful lake.

This birthday party had been a huge surprise and Aidan's attendance even more so since he rarely came home from medical school. She couldn't imagine he'd come home just for her birthday. With her away at college most of the time as well, their paths rarely crossed. She couldn't recall them ever holding what she considered a real conversation during the four years she'd known him.

"It feels the same as yesterday," she said. "Age is just a number. No big deal."

A smile touched the corners of his lips and her stomach clenched. He had a gorgeous smile, one that complemented the rest of him. If there was such a thing as eye candy he was certainly it. She had the hots for him big-time.

Who wouldn't have the hots while sitting across from this hunk of sexiness? If his lips didn't grab you then his eyes certainly would. They were deep, dark and penetrating. Jillian's heart missed beats just looking into them.

"Just a number?" He chuckled, leaning back in his chair, stretching long legs in front of him. "Women might think that way but men think differently."

He smelled good. When did she start noticing the scent of a man?

"And why is that, Aidan?" she asked, picking up her glass of lemonade to take a sip. It suddenly felt hotter than usual. It had nothing to do with the temperature and everything to do with her body's heated reaction to him.

She watched him lift a brow over those striking dark eyes. A feral smile edged his lips as he leaned forward. "Are you sure I'm Aidan and not Adrian?"

Oh, yes she was sure he was Aidan. She'd heard about the games he and his identical twin would play on unsuspecting souls, those who couldn't tell them apart. "I'm sure."

It was Aidan and not Adrian who stirred her in places she'd rather not think about at the moment.

He leaned in even closer. So close she could see the pupils in his dark eyes. "And how are you so certain?" he asked.

Was she imagining things or had the tone of his voice dropped to a husky murmur? It was rumored that he was a big flirt. She had seen him in action at several Westmoreland weddings. It was also a fact that he and his twin were womanizers and had developed quite a reputation at Harvard. She could certainly see why women were at their beck and call.

"Because I am," she replied. And that's all she intended to say on the matter.

There was no way she would tell him the real reason, that from the moment her brother-in-law Dillon had introduced her to Aidan, before he'd married Pam, she had developed a full-blown crush. She'd been seventeen at the time, a senior in high school. The only problem was the crush hadn't lessened much since.

"Why?"

She glanced back up at Aidan. "Why what?"

"Why are you so certain? You still haven't said."

She inwardly sighed. Why couldn't he leave it alone? She had no intention of telling him. But since she had a feeling he wouldn't let up, she added, "The two of you sound different."

He flashed another sexy smile, showing the dimples in his cheeks. Her hormones, which always acted out of control around him, were erratic now. "Funny you say that. Most people think we sound a lot alike."

"Well, I don't think that."

There was no way she could think that when it was Aidan's voice, and not Adrian's, that stroked her senses. Deciding it was time to take charge of the conversation to keep his questions at bay, she inquired, "So how is medical school going?"

He didn't let on that he suspected her ploy, and as she took another sip of her lemonade, he began telling her what she had to look forward to in another year or so. Becoming a neurosurgeon had been a lifelong dream of hers ever since her mother died of a brain infection when Jillian was seven.

Aidan told her about the dual residency program at hospitals in Portland, Maine, and Charlotte, North Carolina, that he planned to pursue after completing medical school. His dream was to become a cardiologist. He was excited about becoming a doctor and she could hear it in his voice. She was thrilled about becoming a doctor one day as well, but she had another year left before she finished her studies at the University of Wyoming.

While he talked, she nodded as she discreetly gave him a slow, appreciative appraisal. The man was too handsome for words. His voice was smooth as silk, with just enough huskiness to keep her pulse rate on edge. Creamy caramel skin spread across the bridge of a hawkish nose, sharp cheekbones, a perfect sculptured jaw and a mouth so sensual she enjoyed watching it in motion. She could imagine all the things he did with that mouth.

"Have you decided where you're going for medical school, Jillian?"

She blinked. He had asked her a question and was waiting on an answer. And while he waited she saw that sexy mouth ease into another smile. She wondered if he'd known she was checking him out.

"I've always wanted to live in New Orleans so working at a hospital there will be at the top of my list," she said, trying to ignore the eyes staring at her.

"And your second choice?"

She shrugged. "Not sure. I guess one in Florida."

"Why?"

She frowned. Why was he quizzing her? "I've never been to Florida."

He chuckled. "I hope that's not the only reason."

Her frown deepened. "Of course that's not the only reason," she said defensively. "There are good medical schools in Louisiana and Florida."

He nodded. "Yes, there are. How's your grade point average?"

"Good. In fact my GPA is better than good. I'm at the top of my class. In the top ten at least."

Getting there hadn't been easy. She'd made a lot of sacrifices, especially in her social life. She couldn't recall the last time she'd gone out on a date or participated in any school activities. But she was okay with that. Pam was paying a lot of the cost for her education and Jillian wanted to make her sister proud.

"What about the entrance exam—the MCAT—and admission essays? Started on them yet?"

"Too early."

"It's never too early. I suggest you prepare for them during your free time."

Now it was her turn to smile. "Free time? What's that?"

The chuckle that erupted from his throat was smooth and sexy and made her pulse thump. "It's time you should squeeze in regardless of whether you think you can or not. It's essential to know how to manage your time wisely, otherwise you'll get burned-out before you even get started."

She grudgingly wondered what made him an expert. Then she pushed her resentment aside. He *was* giving her sound advice and he had gone where she had yet to go. And from what she'd heard, he was doing pretty well at it. He would graduate from Harvard Medical School at the top of his class and then enter a dual residency program that any medical student would die for. He would get the chance to work with the best cardiologists in the United States.

"Thanks for the advice, Aidan."

"You're welcome. When you get ready to knock them out of the way, let me know. I'll help you."

"You will?"

"Sure. Even if I have to come to you to do it."

She lifted a brow. *He would come to her?* She couldn't imagine him doing such a thing. Harvard was in Boston and that was a long way from her university in Laramie, Wyoming.

"Hand me your phone for a second."

His request jarred her thoughts back into focus. "Why?"

"So I can put my numbers into it."

Jillian drew in a deep breath before standing to pull her cell phone from the back pocket of her jeans. She handed it to him and tried to ignore the tingling sensation that flowed through her when their hands touched. She watched him use deft fingers to key in the numbers. Surgeon's fingers. Long, strong, with precise and swift movements. She wondered how those same fingers would feel stroking her skin. She heated just thinking about it.

Moments later his phone rang, interrupting her thoughts. It was then that she realized he'd called himself to have her number, as well. "There," he said, handing her phone back to her. "You now have my number and I have yours."

Was she jumping to conclusions or did his words hold some significance? "Yes, we have each other's numbers," she agreed softly, shoving the assumption out of her mind.

He stood, glancing at his watch. "Adrian and I are meeting up with Canyon and Stern in town for drinks and to shoot pool, so I best get going. Happy birthday again."

"Thanks, Aidan."

"You're welcome."

He walked away but when he got to the French doors he turned and looked back at her, regarding her through his gorgeous dark eyes. The intensity of his gaze made her stomach quiver and another burst of heat swept through her. She felt something…passion? Sexual chemistry? Lust? All three and more, she decided. She'd thought all the Westmoreland males she'd met since Pam married Dillon were eye candy, but there was something about Aidan that pulled at everything female inside of her.

She cleared her throat. "Is anything wrong?" she asked when the silence began to stretch.

Her question seemed to jar him. He frowned slightly before quickly forcing a smile. "Not sure."

As he opened the French door to go inside, she wondered what he meant by that.

Why, of all the women in the world, have I developed this deep attraction for Jillian Novak?

The first time he'd noticed it was when they'd been introduced four years ago. He'd been twenty-two, and she only seventeen, but still a looker. He'd known then that he would have to keep his distance. Now she was twenty-one and still had the word *innocent* written all over her. From what he'd heard, she didn't even have a boyfriend, preferring to concentrate on her studies and forgo a love life.

And speaking of life, Aidan was fairly certain he loved every part of his, especially his family. So why was he allowing himself to be attracted to Pam's sister? He didn't want to cause any trouble for Dillon.

Pam Novak was a jewel and just what Dillon needed. Everyone had been shocked when Dillon announced he had met a woman who he intended to marry. That had been the craziest thing Aidan had ever heard.

Dillon, of all people, should have known better. Hadn't his first wife left him when he'd refused to send the youngest four members of the Westmoreland family—namely him, Adrian, Bane and Bailey—to foster care? What had made Dillon think Pam would be different? But it didn't take Aidan, his siblings and cousins long to discover that she *was* different.

As far as Aidan was concerned, she was everything they'd *all* needed; she knew the value of family. And she had proven it when she'd turned her back on a promising acting career to care for her three teenaged sisters when her father passed away.

To say the Westmorelands had undergone a lot of family turmoil of their own was an understatement. It all started when Aidan's parents and uncle and aunt died in a plane crash, leaving his cousin Dillon in charge of the family, along with Aidan's oldest brother, Ramsey, as backup. Dillon and Ramsey had worked hard and made sacrifices to keep the family together—all fifteen of them.

Aidan's parents had had eight children: five boys—Ramsey, Zane, Derringer and the twins, Aidan and Adrian—and three girls—Megan, Gemma and Bailey. Uncle Adam and Aunt Clarisse had had seven sons: Dillon, Micah, Jason, Riley, Canyon, Stern and Brisbane.

It hadn't been easy, especially since he, Adrian, Brisbane and Bailey had been under the age of sixteen. And

Aidan would admit the four of them had been the most challenging of the bunch, getting into all sorts of mischief, even to the point that the State of Colorado ordered they be put in foster homes. Dillon had appealed that decision and won. Lucky for the four youngest Westmorelands, Dillon had known their acts of rebellion were their way of handling the grief of losing their parents. Now Aidan was in medical school; Adrian was working on his PhD in engineering; Bane had joined the navy and Bailey was taking classes at a local university while working part-time.

Aidan's thoughts shifted back to Jillian, although he didn't want them to. The birthday party yesterday had been a surprise, and the shocked look on her face had been priceless—adorable and a total turn-on. If he'd had any doubt about just how much he was attracted to her, that doubt had been dispelled when he saw her.

She had walked out onto the patio expecting a going-away party for his sister Gemma, who had married Callum and was moving to Australia. Instead it had been a surprise birthday party for her. After shedding a few happy tears, which he would have loved to lick away, she had hugged Pam and Dillon for thinking of her on her twenty-first birthday. From what he'd heard, it was the first time Jillian had had a party since she was a little kid.

While everyone had rushed over to congratulate her, he had hung back, checking her out. The sundress looked cute on her and it was obvious she wasn't the seventeen-year-old he'd met four years ago. Her face was fuller, her features stunning and her body...

Where had those curves come from? There's no way he would have missed them before. She was short compared with his six-foot-two-inch height. He figured she stood no taller than five feet three inches in bare feet. And speaking of her feet, her polished toes, a flaming red, had been another turn-on. Pam might not want to hear it, but her sister was Hot with a capital *H*.

When he realized he had been the only one who hadn't wished her a happy birthday, he was about to do so when his phone rang. He had slipped off the patio to take the call from a friend from college who was trying to fix him up on a blind date for next weekend.

When he returned to the patio after finishing his call, everyone else had gone inside to watch a movie or play cards, and she'd been alone. She would never know how hard it had been for him to sit across from her without touching her. She looked good and smelled good, as well.

Jillian Novak had definitely caught his eye.

But Dillon and Pam would pluck out that same eye if he didn't squash what he was feeling.

Everybody knew how protective Pam was when it came to her sisters. Just like everyone knew Aidan wasn't one to take women seriously. And he didn't plan to change his behavior now. So the best thing for him to do while he was home for the next three days was to keep his distance from Jillian as he'd always done.

So why did I get her phone number and give her mine, for crying out loud?

Okay, he reasoned quickly, it had been a crazy moment, one he now regretted. The good thing was he doubted she would ever call him for help and he would make it a point never to call her.

That was a good plan, one he intended to stick to. Now, if he could only stop thinking about her that would be great. Glancing down at the medical journal he was supposed to be reading, he tried to focus on the words. Within a few minutes he'd read one interesting article and was about to start on another.

"Will you do me a *big* favor?"

Aidan glanced up to stare into the face of his sister Bailey. She used to be the baby in the Denver Westmoreland family but that had changed now that Dillon and Pam had a son, and Aidan's brother Ramsey and his wife, Chloe, had a daughter.

"Depends on what the favor is?"

"I promised Jill that I would go riding with her and show her the section of Westmoreland Country that she hasn't seen yet. Now they've called me to come in to work. I need you to go with Jillian instead."

"Just show her another day," he said, quickly deciding that going horseback riding with Jillian wasn't a smart idea.

"That was my original plan but I can't reach her on her cell phone. We were to meet at Gemma Lake, and you know how bad phone reception is out there. She's already there waiting for me."

He frowned. "Can't you ask someone else?"

"I did but everyone is busy."

His frown deepened. "And I'm not?"

Bailey rolled her eyes. "Not like everyone else. You're just reading a magazine."

He figured there was no use explaining to Bailey that his reading was important. He just so happened to be reading about a medical breakthrough where the use of bionic eyes had been tested as a way to restore sight with good results.

"Well, will you do it?"

He closed the medical journal and placed it aside. "You're positive there's no one else who can do it?"

"Yes, and she really wants to see it. This is her home now and—"

"Her home? She's away at school most of the time," he said.

"And so are you, Adrian, Stern and Canyon, and this is still your home. So what's your point?"

He decided not to argue with her. There were times when his baby sister could read him like an open book and he didn't want her to do that in this instance. It wouldn't take her long to figure out the story written on his pages was all about Jillian.

"Fine. I'll go."

"Act a little enthused, will you? You've been kind of standoffish with Jillian and her sisters since Dillon married Pam."

"I have not."

"You have, too. You should take time to get to know them. They're part of the family now. Besides, you and Jill will both become doctors one day so already you have a common interest."

He hoped like hell that would remain their only common interest. It was up to him to make sure it did. "Whatever," he said, standing and walking toward the door, pausing to grab his Stetson off the hat rack.

"And, Aidan?"

He stopped before opening the door and turned around, somewhat annoyed. "What now?"

"Try to be nice. You can act like a grizzly bear at times."

That was her opinion. Deciding not to disagree with her, because you could never win with Bailey, he walked out of the house.

CHAPTER TWO

JILLIAN HEARD THE sound of a rider approaching and turned around, using her hand to shield her eyes from the glare of the sun. Although she couldn't make out the identity of the rider, she knew it wasn't Bailey.

The rider came closer and when her heart began pounding hard in her chest, she knew it was Aidan. What was he doing here? And where was Bailey?

Over breakfast she and Bailey had agreed to go riding after lunch. Because the property was located so far from Denver's city limits and encompassed so much land, the locals referred to it as Westmoreland Country. Although Jillian had seen parts of it, she had yet to see all of it and Bailey had volunteered to show it to her.

Dropping her hand to her side, Jillian drew in a deep breath as Aidan and his horse came closer. She tried not to notice how straight he sat in the saddle or how good he looked sitting astride the horse. And she tried not to gawk at how his Stetson, along with his western shirt, vest, jeans and boots, made him look like a cowboy in the flesh.

When he brought the horse to a stop a few feet from where she stood, she had to tilt her head all the way back to look up at him. "Aidan."

He nodded. "Jillian."

His irritated expression and the cutting sound of his

voice made her think he was upset about something. Was she trespassing on a particular part of Westmoreland land where she had no business being?

Thinking she needed to give him an explanation, she said, "I'm waiting for Bailey. We're going riding."

"Yes, those *were* your plans."

She lifted a brow. "Were?"

He nodded. "Bailey tried reaching you but your phone is out of range. She was called in to work and asked that I take her place."

"Take her place?"

"Yes, take her place. She indicated you wanted to tour Westmoreland Country."

"I did, but..."

Penetrating dark eyes held hers. "But what?"

She shoved both hands into the pockets of her jeans. There was no way she could tell him that under no circumstances would she go riding anywhere with him. She could barely be around him for a few minutes without becoming unglued...like she was becoming now.

The reason she had placed her hands in her pockets was because they were already sweaty. And then there was that little ball of fire in her stomach that always seemed to burst into flames whenever he was around. Aidan Westmoreland oozed so much sexiness it was driving her to the edge of madness.

"Jillian?"

She blinked when he said her name. The sound of his voice was like a caress across her skin. "Yes?"

"But what? Do you have a problem with me being Bailey's replacement?"

She drew in a deep breath. She couldn't see him being anyone's replacement. It was easy to see he was his own man, and what a man he was. Even now, the weight of his penetrating gaze caused a heated rush to cross her flesh. So, yes, she had a problem with him being Bailey's replacement, but that was something she definitely wouldn't tell him.

"No, I don't have a problem with it," she lied without even blinking. "However, I would think that you do. I'm sure you have more to do with your time than spend it with me."

He shrugged massive shoulders. "No, in fact I don't, so it's not a problem. Besides, it's time for us to get to know each other better."

Why was her body tingling with awareness at his words? She was sure he didn't mean them the way they sounded, but she thought it best to seek clarification. "Why should we get to know each other better?"

He leaned back in the saddle and she couldn't help noticing the long fingers that held the reins. Why was she imagining those same fingers doing things to her, like stroking her hair, splaying up and down her arms, working their way across her naked body? She tried to downplay the shiver that passed through her.

"Dillon married Pam four years ago, and there's still a lot I don't know about you and your sisters," he said, bringing an end to her fantasizing. "We're all family and the Westmorelands are big on family. I haven't been home to get to know you, Paige and Nadia."

With him naming her sisters his earlier statement felt less personal. It wasn't just about her. She should be grateful for that but for some reason she wasn't. "Because of school I haven't been home much, either, but we can get to know each other another time. It doesn't have to be today," she said.

She doubted she could handle his closeness. Even the masculine scent of him was overpowering.

"Today is just as good a day as any. I'm leaving to go back to Boston tomorrow. There's no telling when our paths will cross again. Probably not until we come home for Christmas or something. We might as well do it now and get it over with."

Why did she get the feeling that getting to know her was something he felt forced to do? She took offense at that. "Don't do me any favors," she all but snapped at him while feeling her pulse pound.

"Excuse me?" He seemed surprised by her remark.

"There's no need to get *anything* over with. It's obvious Bailey roped you into doing something you really don't want to do. I can see the rest of Westmoreland Country on my own," she said, untying her horse and then mounting it.

When she sat astride the mare she glanced back over at him. "I don't need your company, Aidan."

He crossed his arms over his chest and she could tell by the sudden tensing of his jaw that he hadn't liked her comment. She was proven right when he said, with a degree of smoldering intensity that she felt through her clothes, "I hate to tell you this, Jillian Novak, but you have my company whether you want it or not."

AIDAN STARED HARD into Jillian's eyes and couldn't help but feel they were waging a battle. Of what he wasn't sure. Of wills? Of desire? Passion? Lust? He rubbed his hand down his face. He preferred none of those things but he had a feeling all of them were fighting for the number one spot right now.

He all but saw steam coming from her ears and figured Jillian didn't like being ordered around.

"Look," he said. "We're wasting time. You want to see the land and I have nothing better to do. I apologize if I came across a little gruff earlier, but by no means did I want to insinuate that I am being forced into showing you around or getting to know you."

There was no need to tell her that Bailey had asked him to be nice to Jillian and her sisters. He'd always been cordial and as far as he was concerned that was good enough. Getting too close to Jillian wasn't a good idea. But then, he was the one who had suggested she call him if she needed help preparing for medical school. He now saw that offer had been a mistake. A big one.

She studied him for a moment and he felt something deep in his gut. It was a lot stronger than the kick in his groin he'd experienced when he'd watched her swing her leg over the back of the horse to mount it. He'd taken a long, explosive breath while fighting the sexual hunger that had roared to life inside of him. Even now, with those beautiful full lips of hers frowning at him, a smoldering spike of heat consumed him. One way he knew he could put a stop to this madness was to get her out of his system, since she seemed to have gotten under his skin.

But the way he would do that wasn't an option...not if he loved his life.

"You're sure about this?"

Hell no, he wasn't sure about anything concerning her. Maybe the main reason behind his attraction to her, in addition to her striking beauty, was that he truly didn't know her that well. Maybe once he got to know her he'd discover that he didn't like her after all.

"Yes, I'm sure about this, so come on," he said, nudging his horse forward to stand beside hers. "There's a lot to see so I hope you're a fairly good rider."

She gave him a smile that made him appreciate the fullness of her mouth even more. "Yes, I'm a fairly good rider."

And then she took off, easing her horse into a canter. He watched in admiration as she flawlessly jumped the horse over a flowing creek.

He chuckled to himself. She wasn't a fairly good rider; she was an excellent one.

JILLIAN SLOWED HER pace and glanced over her shoulder to see Aidan make the same jump she had. She couldn't help but be impressed at his skill, but she shouldn't be surprised. She'd heard from Dillon that all his brothers and cousins were excellent horsemen.

In no time, he'd caught up with her. "You're good," he said, bringing his horse alongside hers. The two animals eased into a communal trot.

"Thanks," she said, smiling over at him. "You're not bad yourself."

He threw his head back and laughed. The robust sound not only floated across the countryside, but it floated across her, as well. Although she'd seen him smile before, she'd never seen him amused about anything.

"No, I'm not bad myself. In fact there was a time I wanted to be a bronco rider in the rodeo."

For some reason she wasn't surprised. "Dillon talked you out of it?"

He shook his head, grinning. "No, he wouldn't have done such a thing. One of Dillon's major rules has been for us to choose our own life goals. At least that was his rule for everyone but Bane."

She'd heard all about Aidan's cousin Brisbane Westmoreland, whom everyone called Bane. She'd also heard Dillon had encouraged his baby brother to join the military. He'd said Bane could do that or possibly go to prison for the trouble he'd caused. Bane had chosen the navy. In the four years that Pam had been married to Dillon, Jillian had only seen Bane twice.

"So what changed your mind about the rodeo?" she asked when they slowed the horses to a walk.

"My brother Derringer. He did the rodeo circuit for a couple of summers after high school. Then he got busted up pretty bad. Scared all of us to death and I freaked out. We all did. The thought of losing another family member brought me to my senses and I knew I couldn't put my family through that."

She nodded. She knew about him losing his parents and his aunt and uncle in a plane crash, leaving Dillon—the oldest at the time—to care for all of them. "Derringer and a few of your cousins and brothers own a horse-training business right?"

"Yes and it's doing well. They weren't cut out to work in the family business so after a few years they left to pursue their dreams of working with horses. I try to help them out whenever I come home but they're doing a great job without me. Several of their horses have won important derbies."

"Ramsey resigned as one of the CEOs as well, right?" she asked of his oldest brother.

He glanced over at her. "Yes. Ramsey has a degree in agriculture and economics. He'd always wanted to be a sheep farmer, but when my parents, aunt and uncle died in that plane crash he knew Dillon would need help at Blue Ridge."

Jillian knew that Blue Ridge Land Management was a Fortune 500 company Aidan's father and uncle had started years ago. "But eventually he was able to pursue his dream, right?"

Aidan nodded. "Yes. Once Dillon convinced Ramsey he could handle things at the corporation without him. Ramsey's sheep ranch is doing great."

She nodded. She liked Ramsey. In fact, she liked all the Westmorelands she had gotten to know. When Pam married Dillon, the family had welcomed her and her sisters with open arms. She'd discovered some of them were more outgoing than the others. But the one thing she couldn't help but notice was that they stuck together like glue.

"So how did you learn to ride so well?" he asked.

"My dad. He was the greatest and although I'm sure he wanted at least one son, he ended up with four girls. He felt we should know how to do certain things and handling a horse was one of them," she said, remembering the time she'd spent with her father and how wonderful it had been for her.

"He evidently saw potential in me because he made sacrifices and sent me to riding school. I competed nationally until he got sick. We needed the money to pay for his medicine and doctor bills."

"Do you regret giving it up?" he asked.

She shook her head. "No. I enjoyed it but making sure Dad got the best care meant more to me…more to all of us…than anything." And she meant it. There had been no regrets for any of them about giving up what they'd loved to help their father.

"Here we are."

She looked around at the beauty of the land surrounding her, as far as her eyes could see and beyond. Since Dillon was the oldest, he had inherited the main house along with the three hundred acres it sat on. Everyone else, upon reaching the age of twenty-five, received one hundred acres to call their own. Some parts of this area were cleared and other parts were dense with thick foliage. But what took her breath away was the beautiful waterway that branched off into a huge lake. Gemma Lake. She'd heard it had been named after Aidan's great-grandmother.

"This place is beautiful. Where are we exactly?"

He glanced over at her and smiled. "My land. Aidan's Haven."

Aidan's Haven, she immediately decided, suited him. She could see him building his home on this piece of land one day near this huge waterway. Today he looked like a cowboy, but she could see him transforming into a boat captain.

"Aidan's Haven. That's a nice name. How did you come up with it?"

"I didn't. Bailey did. She came up with all the names for our one-hundred-acre plots. She chose names like Stern's Stronghold, Zane's Hideout, Derringer's Dungeon, Ramsey's Web and Megan's Meadows, just to name a few."

Jillian had visited each of those areas and all the homes that had been built on the land were gorgeous. Some were single-story ranch-style designs, while others were like mansions with several floors. "When do you plan to build?"

"Not for a while yet. After medical school I'll probably work and live somewhere else for a while since I have six years of residency to complete for the cardiology program."

"But this will eventually be your home."

A pensive look appeared on his face. "Yes, Westmoreland Country will always be my home."

She'd always thought she would live in Gamble, Wyoming. Although she knew she would leave for college, she figured she would return one day and work in the hospital there before setting up a practice of her own. After all, she had lived there her entire life; all her friends were there. But after Pam married Dillon things changed for her, Paige and Nadia. They were close to their oldest sister and decided to leave Wyoming and make their homes close to Pam's. It had worked out well for everyone. Nadia was in her last year of high school here in Colorado and Paige was in California attending UCLA.

"What about you? Do you ever plan to return to Gamble, Wyoming, to live, Jillian?"

Again, she wondered why her stomach tightened whenever he said her name. Probably had something to do with that deep, husky voice of his.

"No, I don't plan to return to Gamble. In fact, Nadia and Paige and I talked a few weeks ago and we plan to approach Pam about selling the place. She would have done so already, but she thinks we want to keep it as part of our legacy."

"You don't?"

"Only because we've moved on and think of Denver as home now. At least Nadia and I do. Paige has made a life for herself in Los Angeles. She's hoping her acting career takes off. We're hoping the same thing for her. Pam has done so much for us already and we don't want her to feel obligated to pay more of our college tuition and expenses, especially when we can use the money from the sale of the house to do so."

He nodded. "Let's take a walk. I want to show you around before we move on to Adrian's Cove."

He dismounted and tied his horse to a nearby tree. Then he turned to help her down. The moment he touched her, awareness of him filled her every pore. From the look in his eyes it was obvious that something similar was happening to him.

This was all new to her. She'd never felt anything like this before. And although her little lovemaking session with Cobb Grindstone on prom night had appeased her curiosity, it had left a lot to be desired.

As soon as her feet touched the ground, she heard a deep moan come from Aidan's throat. Only then did it become obvious that they'd gotten caught up in a carnal attraction that was so sharp it took her breath away.

"Jillian..."

He said her name again and, like all the other times, the deep, husky sound accentuated his sexiness. But before she could respond, the masculine hand planted around her waist nudged her closer and then his mouth lowered to hers.

CHAPTER THREE

ALL SORTS OF feelings ripped through Aidan, making him totally conscious of the woman whose lips were locked to his. Deep in the center of his being he felt a throb unlike any he'd ever felt before—an intense flare of heat shooting straight to his loins.

He knew he had to stop. This wasn't any woman. This was Jillian Novak, Pam's sister. Dillon's sister-in-law. A woman who was now a part of the Westmoreland family. All that was well and good, but at the moment the only thing his mind could comprehend was that she had desire clawing at his insides and filling his every cell with awareness.

Instead of yielding to common sense, he was captivated by her sweet scent and her incredible taste, and the way her tongue stroked his showed both boldness and innocence. She felt exquisite in his arms, as if she belonged there. He wanted more. He wanted to feel her all over, kiss her all over. Taste her. Tempt her with sinful enticements.

The need for air was the only reason he released her lips, but her flavor made him want to return his mouth to hers and continue what they'd started.

The shocked look in her eyes told him she needed time to comprehend what had just happened between them. She took a step back and he watched as she took a deep breath.

"We should not have done that."

Aidan couldn't believe she had the nerve to say that while sultry heat still radiated off her. He might have thought the same thing seconds ago, but he couldn't agree with her now. Not when his fingers itched to reach out and pull her back into his arms so he could plow her mouth with another kiss. Dammit, why did her pouty lips look so inviting?

"Then why did we do it?" he countered. He might have made the first move but she had definitely been a willing participant. Her response couldn't lie. She had enjoyed the kiss as much as he had.

"I don't know why we did it, but we can't do it again."

That was easy for her to say. "Why not?"

She frowned at him. "You know why not. Your cousin is married to my sister."

"And?"

She placed her hands on her hips, giving him a mind-boggling view of her slim waistline. "And we can't do it again. I know all about your womanizing reputation, Aidan."

Her words struck a nerve. "Do you?"

"Yes. And I'm not interested. The only thing I'm interested in is getting into medical school. That's the only thing on my mind."

"And the only thing on mine is getting out of medical school," he countered in a curt tone. "As far as Dillon being married to Pam, it changes nothing. You're still a beautiful woman and I'm a man who happens to notice such things. But since I know how the situation stands between us, I'll make sure it doesn't happen again."

"Thank you."

"You're welcome. Glad we got that cleared up. Now I can continue showing you around."

"I'm not sure that's a good idea."

He watched her and when she pushed a lock of hair away from her face, he again thought how strikingly beautiful she was. "Why not? You don't think you can control yourself around me?" he asked, actually smiling at the possibility of that being true.

Her look of anger should have warned him, but he'd never been one to heed signs. "Trust me, that's definitely not it."

"Then there's no reason for me not to finish showing you around, is there, Jillian? Besides, Bailey will give me hell about it if I don't. There's a lot of land we still have to cover so let's get started."

He began walking along the bank of the river and figured that after cooling off Jillian would eventually catch up.

JILLIAN WATCHED AIDAN walk ahead and decided to hang back a moment to reclaim her common sense. Why had she allowed him to kiss her? And why had she enjoyed it so much?

The man gave French kissing a whole new definition, and she wasn't sure her mouth would ever be the same.

No one had ever kissed her like that before. No one would have dared. To be honest, she doubted anyone she'd ever kissed would know how. Definitely not Cobb. Or that guy in her freshman year at Wyoming University, Les, that she'd dropped really quickly when he wanted to take her to a hotel and spend the night on their first date. He might have been a star on the school's football team, but from the couple of times they had kissed, compared to what she'd just experienced with Aidan, Les had definitely dropped the ball.

But then, regardless of how enjoyable Aidan's kiss had been, she was right in what she'd told him about not repeating it. She had no business getting involved with a guy whose favorite sport was messing around. She knew better. Honestly, she didn't know what had come over her.

However, she knew full well what had come over him. More than once she'd overheard Dillon express his concern to Pam that although the twins were doing well at Harvard, he doubted they would ever settle down into serious relationships since they seemed to enjoy being womanizers. That meant Aidan's interest in her was only because of overactive testosterone. Pam had warned Jillian numerous times about men who would mean her no good, and her oldest sister would be highly disappointed if Jillian fell for the ploy of a man like Aidan. A man who could take away her focus on becoming a doctor just to make her his plaything.

Feeling confident she had her common sense back on track, she began walking. Aidan wasn't too far ahead and it wouldn't take long for her to catch up with him. In the meantime she couldn't help but appreciate his manly physique. His faded jeans emphasized masculine thighs, a rock-solid behind, tight waist and wide shoulders. He didn't just walk, he swaggered, and he did it so blatantly sexily, it increased her heart rate with every step he took.

Moments later he slowed and turned around to stare at her, pinning her with his dark gaze. Had he felt her ogling him? Did he know she had been checking out his rear big-time? She hoped not because his front was just as impressive. She could see why he was in such high demand when it came to women.

"You coming?"

I will be if you don't stop looking at me like that, Jillian thought, getting closer to where he stood. She felt the heat of his gaze on every inch of her. She came to a stop in front of him. She couldn't take looking into his eyes any longer so she glanced around. In addition to the huge lake there were also mountains surrounding the property. "You have a nice mountain view in this spot and can see the lake from here," she said.

"I know. That's why I plan to build my house right here."

She nodded. "Have you designed it yet?"

"No. I don't plan on building for several more years, but I often come here and think about the time when I will. The house will be large enough for me and my family."

She snapped her head around. "You plan on getting married?"

His chuckle was soft but potent. "Yes, one day. That surprises you?"

She decided to be honest. "Yes. You do have a reputation."

He leaned one broad shoulder against a Siberian elm tree. "This is the second time today that you've mentioned something about my reputation. Just what have you heard about me?"

She took a seat across from him on a huge tree stump. "I heard what hellions you, Adrian, Bailey and Bane used to be."

He nodded solemnly. "Yes, we were that. But that

was a long time ago, and I can honestly say we regretted our actions. When we grew older and realized the
impact we'd had on the family, we apologized to each
one of them."

"I'm sure they understood. You were just children
and there was a reason you did what you did," she said.
She'd heard the full story from Pam. The deaths of their
parents, and aunt and uncle, had been the hardest on
those youngest four. Everyone had known that their
acts of rebellion were their way of handling their grief.

"Sorry I mentioned it," she said, feeling bad that
she'd even brought it up.

He shrugged. "No harm done. It is what it is. It seems
the four of us got a reputation we've been trying to live
down for years. But I'm sure that's not the reputation
of mine that you were really referring to."

No, it wasn't. "I understand you like women."

He chuckled. "Most men do."

She raised a brow, not in the least amused. "I mean
you really like them, but you don't care about their feelings. You break their hearts without any concern for the
pain it might cause."

He studied her for a long moment. "That's what you
heard?"

"Yes. And now you want me to believe that you're
seriously considering settling down one day, marrying
and having a family?"

"Yes. One doesn't have anything to do with the other.
What I do now in no way affects any future plans. I
need to clarify something. I don't deliberately set out
to break any woman's heart. I tell any woman I date
the truth up front—my career as a doctor is foremost.
However, if she refuses to take me at my word and as-

sumes that she can change my mind, then it's not my fault when she finds out otherwise."

"So in other words…"

"In other words, Jillian, I don't intentionally set up any woman for heartbreak or lead her on," he answered curtly.

She knew she should probably leave well enough alone and stop digging, but for some reason she couldn't help herself. "However, you do admit to dating a *lot* of women."

"Yes, I admit it. And why not? I'm single and don't plan to get into a committed relationship anytime soon. And contrary to what you believe, I don't date as many women as you might think. My time is pretty limited these days because of medical school."

She could imagine. How he managed to date at all while in medical school was beyond her. He was definitely into multitasking. She'd discovered most relationships demanded a lot of work and it was work she didn't have time for. Evidently he made things easy by not getting serious with any woman. At least he'd been honest about it. He dated women for the fun of it and didn't love any of them.

"I have one other question for you, Aidan," she said, after drawing in a deep breath.

"What's your question?"

"If all of what you said is true, about not getting serious with any woman, then why did you kiss me?"

Now that was a good question, one he could answer but really didn't want to. She did deserve an answer, though, especially after the way he had plowed her mouth earlier. She was twenty-one, five years younger than him.

And although she'd held her own during their kiss, he knew they were worlds apart when it came to sexual experience. Therefore, before he answered her, he needed to ask a few questions of his own.

"Why did you kiss me back?"

He could tell by her expression that she was surprised by his counterquestion. And, as he'd expected, she tried to avoid giving him an answer. "That's not the issue here."

He couldn't help but smile. Little did she know it *was* the issue, but he would touch on that later. "The reason I kissed you, Jillian, is because I was curious. I think you have a beautiful pair of lips and I wanted to taste them. I wanted to taste you. It's something I've wanted to do for a while."

He saw her jaw drop and had to hold his mouth closed for a second to keep from grinning. She hadn't expected him to answer her question so bluntly or to be so direct. That's something she needed to know about him. He didn't sugarcoat anything. *Straightforward* could be his middle name.

"So now that you know my reason for kissing you, what was your reason for kissing me back?"

She began nibbling on her bottom lip. Watching her made him ache, made him want to take hold of those lips and have his way with them again.

"I—I was…"

When she didn't say anything else, he lifted a brow. "You were what?"

Then she had the nerve to take her tongue and lick those same lips she'd been nibbling on moments ago. "I was curious about you, too."

He smiled. Now they were getting somewhere. "I can

understand that. I guess the reason you asked about the kiss is because I told you I'm not into serious relationships when it comes to women. I hope you don't think a deep kiss constitutes a serious relationship."

From the look on her face, which she quickly wiped off, that's exactly what she'd thought. She was more inexperienced than he'd assumed. He wondered just how inexperienced she was. Most twenty-one-year-old women he knew wore desire, instead of their hearts, on their sleeves.

"Of course I knew that."

If she knew that then why were they having this conversation? If she thought he was looking for something serious just because he'd kissed her then she was so far off the mark it wasn't funny.

"How many boyfriends have you had?"

"Excuse me?"

No, he wouldn't excuse her. There were certain things she needed to know. Things experience had nothing to do with. "I asked how many boyfriends you've had. And before you tell me it's none of my business, I'm asking for a reason."

She lifted her chin in a defiant pose. "I can't imagine what reason you would have for needing to know that."

"So you can protect yourself." He thought she looked both adorable and sexy. From the way her curly hair tumbled down her shoulders to the way the smoothness of her skin shone in the sunlight.

She lifted a brow. "Against men like you?"

"No. Men like me would never mislead you into thinking there was anything serious about a kiss. But there are men who would lead you to think otherwise."

She frowned. "And you don't think I can handle myself?"

He smiled. "Not the way I think you should. For some reason you believe you can avoid kisses until you're in a serious relationship and there are certain kisses that can't be avoided."

He could tell by her expression that she didn't believe him. "Take the kiss we shared earlier. Do you honestly think you could have avoided it once I got started?" he asked her.

Her frown deepened. "Yes, of course I could have."

"Then why didn't you?"

She rolled her eyes. "I told you. The only reason I allowed you to kiss me, and the only reason I participated, is because I was curious."

"Really?"

She rolled her eyes again. "Really. Truly."

"So, you're not curious anymore?"

She shook her head. "Nope, not at all. I wondered what kissing you was like and now I know."

Deciding to prove her wrong and settle the matter once and for all, he moved away from the tree and walked toward her.

Figuring out his intent, she stood with a scowl on her face. "Hold it right there, Aidan Westmoreland. Don't you dare think you're going to kiss me again."

When he reached her, he came to a stop directly in front of her and she refused to back up. Instead she stood her ground. He couldn't help but admire her spunk, although in this case it would be wasted.

"I do dare because I don't just think it, Jillian, I know it. And I also know that you're going to kiss me back. *Again.*"

CHAPTER FOUR

JILLIAN DOUBTED SHE'D ever met a more arrogant man. And what was even worse, he had the nerve to stand in front of her with his Stetson tipped back and his legs braced apart in an overconfident stance. How dare he tell her what she would do? Kiss him back? Did he really believe that? Honestly?

She tilted her head back to glare up at him. He didn't glare back, but he held her gaze in a way that was unnerving. And then his eyes moved, slowly raking over her from head to toe. Was that desire she felt rushing through her body? Where had these emotions inside of her come from? Was she getting turned on from the way he was looking at her? She tried to stiffen at the thought but instead she was drawn even more into the heat of his gaze.

"Stop that!"

He lifted a brow. "Stop what?"

"Whatever you're doing."

He crossed his arms over his chest. "So, you think I'm responsible for the sound of your breathing? For the way your nipples have hardened and are pressing against your shirt? And for the way the tip of your tongue is tingling, eager to connect with mine?"

Every single thing he'd pointed out was actually happening to her, but she refused to admit any of them. She crossed her arms over her own chest. "I have no idea what you're talking about."

"Then I guess we're at a standoff."

"No, we're not," she said, dropping her hands to her sides. "I'm leaving. You can play this silly game with someone else."

She turned to go and when his hand reached out and touched her arm, sharp spikes of blood rushed through her veins, filling her pores, drenching the air she was breathing with heated desire. And what on earth was that hunger throbbing inside of her at the juncture of her thighs? And what were those slow circles he was making on her arm with his index finger? She expelled a long deep breath and fought hard to retain control of her senses.

Jillian wanted to snatch her arm away but found she couldn't. What kind of spell had he cast on her? Every hormone in her body sizzled, hissed and surged with a need she'd never felt before. She couldn't deny the yearning pulsing through her even if she wanted to.

"You feel it, don't you, Jillian? It's crazy, I know, and it's something I can't explain, but I feel it each and every time I'm within a few feet of you. As far as I'm concerned, Pam and Dillon are the least of our worries. Figuring out just what the hell is going on between us should be at the top of the agenda. You can deny it as long as you want, but that won't help. You need to admit it like I have."

She did feel it and a part of her knew there was real danger in admitting such a thing. But another part knew he was right. With some things it was best to admit there was a problem and deal with it. Otherwise, she would lay awake tonight and regret not doing so.

His hand slowly traveled up her arm toward her lips. There he cradled her mouth in the palm of his hands. "And whatever it is has me wanting to taste you and has you wanting to taste me. It has me wanting to lick your mouth dry and you wanting to lick mine in the same way."

He paused a moment and when he released a frustrated breath she knew that whatever this "thing" was between them, he had tried fighting it, as well. But he had given up the fight and was now ready to move to the next level, whatever that was.

"I need to taste you, Jillian," he said.

As much as she wished otherwise, there was a deep craving inside of her to taste him, too. Just one more time. Then she would walk away, mount her horse and ride off like the devil himself was after her. But for now she needed this kiss as much as she needed to breathe.

She saw him lowering his head and she was poised for the exact moment when their mouths would connect. She even parted her lips in anticipation. His mouth was moving. He was whispering something but instead of focusing on what he was saying, her gaze was glued to the erotic movement of his lips. And the moment his mouth touched hers she knew she had no intention of turning back.

NOTHING COULD HAVE prepared Aidan for the pleasure that radiated through his body. How could she arouse him like no other woman could? Instead of getting bogged down in the mystery of it all, he buried his fingers in her hair, holding her in place while his mouth mated hungrily with hers.

And she was following his lead, using her tongue

with the same intensity and hunger as he was using his. It was all about tasting, and they were tasting each other with a greed that had every part of his body on fire.

He felt it, was in awe of it. In every pore, in every nerve ending and deep in his pulse, he felt it. Lowering his hand from her hair he gently gripped her around the waist and, with their mouths still locked, he slowly maneuvered her backward toward the tree he'd leaned against earlier. When her back rested against the trunk, her thighs parted and he eased between them, loving the feel of his denim rubbing against hers.

Frissons of fire, hotter than he'd ever encountered, burned a path up his spine and he deepened the kiss as if his life depended on him doing so. Too soon, in his estimation, they had to come up for air and he released her mouth just as quickly as he'd taken it.

He tried not to notice the thoroughly kissed look on her face when she drew in a deep breath. He took a step back so he wouldn't be tempted to kiss her again. The next time he knew he wouldn't stop with a kiss. He wouldn't be satisfied until he had tasted her in other places, as well. And then he would want to make love to her, right here on his land. On the very spot he planned to build his house. Crap! Why was he thinking such a thing? In frustration, he rubbed a hand down his face.

"I think we need to move on."

Her words made him look back at her and an ache settled deep in his stomach. She was beautiful and desire escalated through him all over again. Giving in to what he wanted, he took a step forward and lowered his mouth to hers, taking a sweep of her mouth with his tongue. His groin swelled when she caught his tongue and began sucking on it.

He broke off the kiss and drew in a ragged breath. "Jillian! You're asking for trouble. I'm within two seconds of spreading you on the ground and getting inside of you." The vision of such a thing nearly overpowered his senses.

"I told you we should go. You're the one who kissed me again."

He smiled. "And you kissed me back. Now you understand what I meant when I said there are some kisses that can't be avoided. You didn't want me to kiss you initially, but then you did."

She frowned slightly. "You seduced me. You made me want to kiss you."

His smile widened. "Yes, to both."

"So this was some sort of lesson?"

He shook his head. "Not hardly. I told you I wanted to taste you. I enjoyed doing so."

"This can't become a habit, Aidan."

"And I don't intend to make it one, trust me. My curiosity has more than been satisfied."

She nodded. "So has mine. Are you ready to show me the other parts of Westmoreland Country?"

"Yes. We're headed for Adrian's Cove next and then Bailey's Bay and Bane's Ponderosa."

He backed up to give her space and when she moved around him, he was tempted to reach out and pull her back into his arms, kiss her some more, until he got his fill. But he had a feeling that getting his fill would not be possible and that was something he didn't want to acknowledge.

"So, how did the tour go with Aidan yesterday?"

Jillian glanced up from her breakfast when Bailey

slid into the chair next to her. Pam had shared breakfast with Jillian earlier before leaving for the grocery store, and had asked her the same thing. It had been hard to keep a straight face then and it was harder to do so now.

"It went well. There's a lot of land in Westmoreland Country. I even saw the property you own, Bailey's Bay."

Bailey smiled. "I can't claim ownership until I'm twenty-five so I have a couple years left. But when I do, I plan to build the largest house of them all. It will even be bigger than this one."

Jillian thought that would be an accomplishment because Dillon and Pam's house was huge. Their house was three stories and had eight bedrooms, six bathrooms, a spacious eat-in kitchen, a gigantic living room, a large dining room with a table that could seat over forty people easily, and a seven-car garage.

"I can't wait to see it when you do." Jillian liked Bailey and had from the first time she'd set foot in Westmoreland Country to attend Pam's engagement party. And since there was only a couple years' difference in their ages, with Bailey being older, they had hit it off immediately. "What happens if you meet and marry a guy who wants to take you away from here?"

"That won't happen because there's not a man alive who can do that. This is where I was born and this is where I'll die."

Jillian thought Bailey sounded sure of that. Hadn't Jillian felt the same way about her home in Wyoming at one time? Although it hadn't been a man that had changed her mind, it had been the thought of how much money Pam would be paying for three sisters in college.

BRENDA JACKSON   57

Although her older sister had married a very wealthy man, it still would not have been right.

"Besides," Bailey said, cutting into her thoughts. "I plan to stay single forever. Having five bossy brothers and seven even bossier male cousins is enough. I don't need another man in my life trying to tell me what to do."

Jillian smiled. When she'd heard the stories about all the trouble Bailey used to get into when she was younger, Jillian had found it hard to believe. Sitting across from her was a beautiful, self-confident woman who seemed to have it going on. A woman who definitely knew what she wanted.

"I hope Aidan was nice and didn't give you any trouble."

Jillian lifted a brow. "Why would you say that?"

Bailey shrugged. "Aidan has his moods sometimes."

"Does he?"

"Yes, but if you didn't pick up on them then I guess he did okay."

No, she hadn't picked up on any mood, but she had picked up on his sensual side. And he had definitely picked up on hers. She was still in a quandary as to exactly what had happened yesterday. It was as if she'd become another person with him. She'd discovered that being kissed senseless wasn't just a cliché but was something that could really happen. Aidan had proven it. Even after brushing her teeth twice, rinsing out her mouth and eating a great breakfast Pam had prepared, the taste of him was still deeply embedded on her tongue. And what was even crazier was that she liked it.

Knowing Bailey was probably expecting a response,

she said. "Yes, he was okay. I thought he was rather nice."

Bailey nodded. "I'm glad. I told him he needed to get to know you and your sisters better since he's rarely home. And we're all family now."

All family now. Bailey's words were a stark reminder of why what happened yesterday could never be repeated. They weren't just a guy and a girl who'd met with no connections. They had deep connections. Family connections. And family members didn't go around kissing each other. Why of all the guys out there did she have to be attracted to one with the last name Westmoreland?

"So, besides Bailey's Bay where else did he take you?"

To heaven and back. The words nearly slid from Jillian's lips because that's where she felt she'd actually been. Transported there and back by a kiss. Amazing. Pulling her thoughts together, she said, "First, we toured Aidan's Haven."

"Isn't it beautiful? That's the property I originally wanted because of the way it's surrounded by Gemma Lake. But then I realized it would have been too much water to deal with. I think the spot where Aidan plans to build his house is perfect, though, and will provide an excellent view of the lake and mountains, no matter what room of the house you're in."

Jillian agreed and eradicated the thought from her mind that Aidan's wife and kids would one day live there. "I also saw Adrian's Cove. That piece of property is beautiful, as well. I love the way it's surrounded by mountains."

"Me, too."

"And from there we visited Bailey's Bay, Canyon's Bluff and Stern's Stronghold."

"Like the names?"

Jillian smiled. "Yes, and I heard they were all your idea."

"Yes," Bailey said, grinning. "Being the baby in the family has its benefits. Including the opportunity to play musical beds and sleep at whatever place I want. I was living with Dillon full-time, but after he married I decided to spread myself around and check out my brothers', sisters' and cousins' abodes. I like driving them crazy, especially when one of my brothers or cousins brings his girlfriend home."

Jillian couldn't help but laugh. Although she wouldn't trade her sisters for the world, it had to be fun having older brothers and male cousins to annoy.

"What's so funny?"

Jillian's heart skipped a beat upon hearing that voice and knowing who it belonged to. Aidan leaned in the kitchen doorway. Wearing a pair of jeans that rode low on his hips and a muscle shirt, he looked too sexy for her peace of mind. She couldn't help studying his features. It was obvious he'd just gotten out of bed. Those dark eyes that were alert and penetrating yesterday had a drowsy look. And she couldn't miss the dark shadow on his chin indicating he hadn't shaved yet. If he looked like that every morning, she would just love to see it.

"I thought you'd already left to return to Boston," Bailey said, getting up and crossing the room to give him a hug. Jillian watched the interaction and a part of her wished she could do the same.

"I won't be leaving until tomorrow."

"Why did you change your plans?" Bailey asked, surprised. "Normally, you're in a rush to get back."

Yes, why? Jillian wondered as well and couldn't wait for his answer.

"Because I wasn't ready to go back just yet. No big deal."

"Um," Bailey said, eyeing her brother suspiciously, "I get the feeling it is a big deal and probably has to do with some woman. I heard you, Adrian and Stern didn't get in until late last night."

Jillian turned her gaze away from Bailey and Aidan and took a sip of her orange juice. The spark of anger she suddenly felt couldn't be jealousy over what Bailey had just said. Had Aidan kissed Jillian senseless, then gone somewhere last night and kissed someone else the same way? Why did the thought of him doing that bother her?

"You ask too many questions, Bay, and stay out my business," Aidan said. "So, what's so funny, Jillian?"

Jillian drew in a deep breath before turning back to Aidan. "Nothing."

Bailey chuckled. "In other words, Aidan, stay out of *her* business."

Jillian heard his masculine grunt before he crossed the room to the coffeepot. The kitchen was huge, so why did it suddenly feel so small now that he'd walked in? And why did he have to walk around with such a sexy saunter?

"Well, I hate to run but I promised Megan that I would house-sit for a few hours so I'm headed for Megan's Meadows. Gemma is decorating the place before leaving for Australia and is sending her crew over to hang new curtains."

Megan and Gemma were Bailey and Aidan's sisters, whom Jillian liked tremendously. Megan was a doctor of anesthesiology at one of the local hospitals and Gemma was an interior designer who owned Designs by Gem.

Bailey turned to Jillian. "You're here until tomorrow, right?"

"Yes."

"Then maybe Aidan can show you the parts of Westmoreland Country that you missed yesterday."

Jillian could feel Aidan's gaze on her. "I wouldn't want to put him to any trouble."

"No trouble," Aidan said. "I don't have anything else to do today."

Bailey laughed. "Until it's time for you to go and hook up with the woman who's the reason you're staying around an extra day."

"Goodbye, Bay," Aidan said in what Jillian perceived as an annoyed tone.

Bailey glanced over her shoulder at him while departing. "See you later, Aidan. And you better not leave tomorrow before telling me goodbye." She swept out of the kitchen and Jillian found herself alone with Aidan.

She glanced over at him and saw him leaning back against the counter with a cup of coffee in his hand, staring at her.

She drew in a deep breath when Aidan asked, "How soon can we go riding?"

CHAPTER FIVE

AIDAN COULDN'T HELP staring into Jillian's eyes. He thought she had the most beautiful eyes of any woman he'd ever seen. And that included all those women who'd thrown themselves at him last night.

"I'm not going anywhere with you, Aidan. Besides, I'm sure the reason you changed your plans to remain in Denver another day has nothing to do with me."

Boy was she wrong. It had everything to do with her. He had spent three hours in a nightclub last night surrounded by beautiful women and all he could think about was the one he considered the most beautiful of all. Her.

A possibility suddenly hit him. Was she jealous? Did she actually believe that crap Bailey had just spouted about him changing his schedule because of some woman? He didn't know whether to be flattered or annoyed that she, or any woman, thought they mattered enough that they should care about his comings and goings. But in all honesty, what really annoyed him was that she *was* beginning to matter. And the reason he had decided to hang in Denver another day was because of her.

Instead of saying anything right away, for fear he might say the wrong thing, he turned and refilled his coffee cup. Then he crossed the room and slid into the chair across from her. Immediately, he sensed her nervousness.

"I don't bite, Jillian," he said, before taking a sip of coffee.

"I hope not."

He couldn't help but smile as he placed his cup down. He reached out and closed his fingers around her wrist. "Trust me. I prefer kissing you to biting you."

She pulled her hand back and nervously glanced over her shoulder before glaring at him. "Are you crazy? Anyone could walk in here!"

"And?"

"And had they heard what you just said they would have gotten the wrong impression."

He leaned back in his chair. "What do you think is the *right* impression?"

Her hair was pulled back in a ponytail and he was tempted to reach out, release the clasp and watch the waves fall to her shoulders. Then he would run his fingers through the thick, black tresses. He could just imagine the light, gentle strokes on her scalp and the thought sent a sudden jolt of sexual need through him.

"I don't want to make any impression, Aidan. Right or wrong."

Neither did he. At least he didn't think he did. Damn, the woman had him thinking crazy. He rubbed a frustrated hand down his face.

"It was just a kiss, nothing more."

He looked over at her. Why was he getting upset that she thought that way when he should be thinking the same thing? Hadn't he told her as much yesterday?

"Glad you think that way," he said, standing. "So let's go riding."

"Didn't you hear what I said?"

He smiled down at her. "You've said a lot. What part in particular are you asking about?"

She rolled her eyes. "I said I'm not going anywhere with you."

His smile widened. "Sure you are. We're going riding because if we don't, Bailey will think it's because I did something awful and got you mad with me. And if she confronts me about it, I will have to confess and tell her the truth—that the reason you wouldn't go riding with me is because you were afraid I might try to kiss you again. A kiss you can't avoid enjoying."

She narrowed her gaze at him. "You wouldn't."

"Trust me, I would. Confessing my sins will clear my conscience but will they clear yours? I'm not sure they would since you seem so wrapped up in not making any right or wrong impressions."

She just sat there and said nothing. He figured she was at a loss for words and this would be the best time for him to leave her to her thoughts. "Let's meet at the same place where we met yesterday in about an hour," he said, walking off to place his cup in the dishwasher.

Before exiting the kitchen he turned back to her and said, "And just so you know, Jillian, the reason I'm not leaving today to return to Boston has nothing to do with some woman I met at the club last night, but it has everything to do with you."

It HAS EVERYTHING to do with you.

Not in her wildest dreams had Jillian thought seven little words could have such a huge impact on her. But they did. So much so that an hour later, she was back in the same place she'd been yesterday, waiting on Aidan.

She began pacing. Had she lost her mind? She wasn't sure what kind of game he was playing but instead of putting her foot down and letting him know she wanted no part of his foolishness, somehow she got caught, hook, line and sinker.

And all because of a kiss.

She would have to admit, it had been more than just a kiss. The fact that he was a gorgeous man, a man she'd had a secret crush on for four years, probably had a lot to do with it. But she'd always been able to separate fact from fiction, reality from fantasy, good from bad. So what was wrong with her now? An association with Aidan would only bring on heartache because not only was she deceiving her sister and brother-in-law, and no doubt the entire Westmoreland family, but she was deceiving herself, as well. Why would she want to become involved with a man known as a womanizer?

But then, she really wasn't involved with him. He was taking her riding, probably he would try to steal a few kisses and then nothing. Tomorrow he would return to Boston and she would return to Wyoming and it would be business as usual. But she knew for her it wouldn't be that simple.

She turned when she heard his approach. Their gazes connected and a luscious shiver ran through her body. He rode just like he had yesterday and looked basically the same. But today something was different. Now she knew he had the mouth of a very sensual man. A mouth he definitely knew how to use.

"I was hoping you would be here," he said, bringing his horse to a stop a few feet from her.

"Did you think I wouldn't after what you threatened to do?"

"I guess not," he said, dismounting.

"And you have no remorse?"

He tipped his Stetson back to gaze at her. "I've heard confession is good for the soul."

"And just what would it have accomplished, Aidan?"

"Putting it out there would have cleared your conscience, since it obviously bothers you that someone might discover I'm attracted to you and that you're attracted to me."

She started to deny what he'd said about her being attracted to him, but decided not to waste her time. It was true and they both knew it. "A true gentleman never kisses and tells."

"You're right. A true gentleman doesn't kiss and tell. But I don't like the thought of you cheapening what happened yesterday, either."

She placed her hands on her hips and leaned in, glaring at him. "How is it cheapening it when the whole thing meant nothing to you anyway?"

JILLIAN'S QUESTION STUNNED Aidan. For a moment he couldn't say anything. She had definitely asked a good question, and it was one he wasn't sure he could answer. The only response he could come up with was that the kisses should not have meant anything to him, but they had. Hell, he had spent the past twenty-four hours thinking about nothing else. And hadn't he changed his plans so that he could stay another day just to spend more time with her?

She was standing there, glaring at him, with her arms crossed over her chest in a way that placed emphasis on a nice pair of breasts. Full and perfectly shaped. He could just imagine running his hands over them, teasing the nipples before drawing them in his mouth to…

"Well?"

She wanted an explanation and all he wanted to do was erase the distance separating them, take her into his arms and kiss that glare right off her face. Unfortunately, he knew he wouldn't stop there. Whether she knew it or not, Jillian Novak's taste only made him want more.

"Let's ride," he said, moving toward his horse. Otherwise, he would be tempted to do something he might later regret.

"Ride?" she hissed. "Is that all you've got to say?"

He glanced back over at her as he mounted his horse. "For now."

"None of this makes any sense, Aidan," she said, mounting her own horse.

She was right about that, he thought. None of it made any sense. Why was she like a magnet pulling him in? And why was he letting her?

They had ridden a few moments side by side in total silence when she finally broke it by asking, "Where are we going?"

"Bane's Ponderosa."

She nodded. "Has he built anything on it?"

"No, because legally it's not his yet. He can't claim it until he's twenty-five."

"Like Bailey. She told me about the age requirement."

"Yes, like Bailey."

He wished they could go back to not talking. He needed the silence to figure out what in the hell was happening to him. She must have deciphered that he was not in a talkative mood because she went silent again.

Aidan glanced over at her, admiring how well she handled a horse. He couldn't help admiring other things, as well. Such as how she looked today in her jeans and western shirt, and how the breasts he had fantasized about earlier moved erotically in rhythm with the horse's prance.

"There is a building here," Jillian said, bringing her horse to a stop.

He forced his eyes off her breasts to follow her gaze to the wooden cabin. He brought his horse to a stop, as well. "If you want to call it that, then yes. Bane built it a while back. It became his and Crystal's secret lovers' hideaway."

"Crystal?"

"Yes. Crystal Newsome. Bane's one and only."

Jillian nodded. "She's the reason he had to leave and join the navy, right?"

Aidan shrugged. "I guess you could say that, although I wouldn't place the blame squarely on Crystal's shoulders. Bane was as much into Crystal as Crystal was into Bane. They were both sticks of dynamite waiting to explode."

"Where is she now?"

"Don't know. I'm not sure if Bane even knows. He never says and I prefer not to ask," Aidan said, getting off his horse and tying it to the rail in front of the cabin.

He moved to assist her from her horse and braced himself for the onslaught of emotions he knew he would feel when he did so.

"You don't have to help me down, Aidan. I can manage."

"I'm sure you can but I'm offering my assistance anyway," he said, reaching his arms up to her.

For a minute he thought she would refuse his offer, but then she slid into his embrace. And as expected the moment they touched, fire shot through him. He actually felt his erection throb. He didn't say anything as he stared into her face. How could she arouse him to this degree?

"You can let go of me now, Aidan."

He blinked, realizing her feet were on the ground yet his arms were still around her waist. He tried to drop his arms but couldn't. It was as if they had a mind of their own.

Then, in a surprise move, she reached up and placed her arms around his neck. "This is crazy," she whispered in a quiet tone. "I shouldn't want this but I'm not thinking straight."

He shouldn't want it, either, but at that moment nothing could stop him. "We're leaving tomorrow. When we get back to our respective territories we can think straight then."

"What about right now?" she asked, staring deep into his gaze.

"Right now all I want to do is taste you again, Jillian. So damn bad."

She lifted her chin. "Then do it."

He doubted she knew what she was saying because her lips weren't the only thing he wanted to taste. He lowered his mouth to hers, thinking that she would find that out soon enough.

AT THAT PARTICULAR MOMENT, Jillian couldn't deny herself the enjoyment of this kiss even if her life had depended on it.

She was getting what she wanted in full force—Aidan Westmoreland–style.

She stood with her arms wrapped around his neck and their lips locked, mesmerized, totally captivated, completely enthralled. How his tongue worked around in her mouth was truly remarkable. Every bone, every pore and every nerve ending responded to the way she was being thoroughly kissed. When had she become capable of such an intense yearning like this, where every lick and suck of Aidan's tongue could send electrical waves through her?

"Let's go inside," he whispered, pulling back from the kiss while tonguing her lips.

"Inside?" She could barely get the question past the feeling of burning from the inside out.

"Yes. We don't need to be out here in the open."

No they didn't. She had gotten so caught up in his kiss that she'd forgotten where they were. But instead of saying they shouldn't even be kissing, in the open or behind closed doors, she didn't resist him when he took her hand and tugged her toward the cabin.

Once the door closed behind them she looked around and was surprised at how tidy the place was. Definitely not what she'd expected. It was a one-room cabin with an iron bed. The colorful bedspread matched the curtains and coordinated with the huge area rug.

She turned to Aidan. "This is nice. Who keeps this place up?"

"Gemma promised Bane that she would and of course she had to put her signature on it. Now that she's getting married and moving to Australia, Bailey will take over. This place is important to Bane. He spends time here whenever he comes home."

Jillian nodded. "How's he doing?"

Aidan shrugged. "Okay now. It was hard for him to buckle down and follow authority, but he has no other choice if he wants to be a SEAL."

She'd heard that was Bane Westmoreland's goal. "So no one usually comes out this way?" She needed to know. There would be no turning back after today and she needed to make sure they didn't get caught.

"Rarely, although Ramsey uses this land on occasion for his sheep. But you don't have to worry about anyone showing up if that's what you're worried about."

She turned to face him. "I don't know why I'm doing this."

He touched her chin and tilted her head back to meet his gaze. "Do you want me to tell you?"

"Think you got it all figured out?"

He nodded. "Yes, I think I do."

"Okay then, let's hear it," she said, backing up to sit on the edge of the bed.

He moved to sit down on a nearby stool. "We're attracted to each other."

She chuckled slightly. "Tell me something I don't know, Aidan."

"What if I say that we've sort of gotten obsessed with each other?"

She frowned. "*Obsessed* is too strong a word, I think. We've only kissed twice."

"Actually three times. And I'm dying for the fourth. Aren't you?"

She knew she had to be honest with him and stop denying the obvious. "Yes, but I don't understand why."

He got up from the stool and stood. "Maybe it's not for us to understand, Jillian."

"How can you say that? How do you think our family would react if they knew we were carrying on like this behind their backs?"

He slowly crossed the room to stand in front of where she sat. "We won't know how they'd react because you're determined to keep this a secret, aren't you?"

She tilted her head to look up at him. "Yes. I couldn't hurt Pam that way. She expects me to stay focused on school. And if I did get involved with a guy, I'm sure she wouldn't want that guy to be you."

He frowned. "And what is so bad about getting involved with me?"

"I think you know the answer to that. She thinks of us as one big family. And there's your reputation. But, like you said, we'll be leaving tomorrow and going our separate ways. What's happening between us is curiosity taking its toll on our common sense."

"That's what you think?" he asked, reaching out and taking a lock of her hair between his fingers.

"Yes, that's what I think." She noticed something in the depths of his eyes that gave her pause—but only for a second. That's all the time it took for her gaze to lower from his eyes to his mouth.

She watched as he swept the tip of his tongue across his lips. "I can still taste you, you know," he said in a low, husky tone.

She nodded slowly. "Yes, I know." Deciding to be honest, she said, "And the reason I know is because I can still taste you, as well."

CHAPTER SIX

AIDAN WISHED JILLIAN hadn't said that. After their first kiss, he'd concluded she had enjoyed it as much as he had. When they'd gone another round he'd been sure of it. Just like he was sure that, although her experience with kissing had been at a minimum, she was a fast learner. She had kept up with him, stroke for stroke. And now, for her to confess that she could still taste him, the same way he could still taste her, sent his testosterone level soaring.

He took a step closer, gently pulled her to her feet and wrapped his arms around her waist. He truly didn't understand why the desire between them was so intense but he accepted that it was. The thought of Dillon and Pam's ire didn't appeal to him any more than it did to her, but unlike her, he refused to believe his cousin and cousin-in-law would be dead set against something developing between him and Jillian.

But he didn't have to worry because *nothing* was developing between them. They were attracted to each other; there was nothing serious about that. He'd been attracted to women before, although never to this degree, he would admit. But after today it would be a while before they saw each other again since he rarely came home. This would be a one-and-done fling. He knew for certain that Pam and Dillon would definitely *not* like the thought of that. They would think he'd taken advantage of her. So he agreed they did not need to know.

"I won't sleep with you, Aidan."

Her words interrupted his thoughts. He met her gaze. "You won't?"

"No. I think we should get that straight right now."

He nodded slowly. "All right. So what did you have in mind for us to do in here?" To say he was anxious to hear her answer was an understatement.

"Kiss some more. A lot more."

Evidently she didn't think an intense kissing match could lead to other things, with a loss of control topping the list. "You think it will be that simple?"

She shrugged. "No. But I figure if we both use a reasonable degree of self-control we'll manage."

A reasonable degree of self control? Jillian had more confidence in their abilities than he did. Just being here with her was causing a hard pounding in his crotch. If only she knew just how enticing she looked standing in front of him in a pair of jeans and a white button-up blouse that he would love to peel off her. Her hair was pinned up on her head, but a few locks…like the one he'd played with earlier…had escaped confinement.

"Is there a problem, Aidan?"

He lifted a brow. "Problem?"

"Yes. You're stalling and I'm ready now."

He fought to hide his grin. Was this the same woman who only yesterday swore they would never kiss again? The same woman who just that morning had refused to go riding with him? Her enthusiasm caused something within him to stir, making it hard to keep his control in check. His body wouldn't cooperate mainly because her scent alone was increasing his desire for her.

And she thought all they would do was some heavy-duty kissing?

Deciding not to keep her waiting any longer, he slanted his mouth over hers.

WHEN HAD SHE needed a man's kiss this much? No, *this* much, she thought, leaning up on her toes to become enmeshed in Aidan's kiss even more. Jillian felt his arms move from around her waist to her backside, urging her closer to the fit of him, making her feel his hard erection pressing against her middle. She shouldn't like how it felt but she did.

The tips of her nipples seemed sensitized against his solid chest. When had she become this hot mass of sexual desire?

When he intensified the kiss even more, she actually heard herself moan. Really moan. He was actually tasting her. Using his mouth to absorb hers as if she was a delectable treat he had to consume. She was losing all that control she'd told him they had to keep and she was losing it in a way she couldn't define.

When he groaned deep in his throat and deepened the kiss even more, it took all she had to remain standing and not melt in a puddle on the floor. Why at twenty-one was she just experiencing kisses like these? And why was she allowing her mind to be sacked with emotions and sensations that made it almost impossible to breathe, to think, to do anything but reciprocate? Their tongues tangled greedily, dueling and plowing each other's mouths with a yearning that was unrelenting.

When she noticed his hands were no longer on her

backside but had worked their way to the zipper of her jeans, she gasped and broke off the kiss, only to be swept off her feet into Aidan's strong arms.

Before she could ask what he was doing, he tumbled them both onto the huge bed. She looked up into his dark eyes as he moved his body over hers. Any words she'd wanted to say died in her throat. All she could do was stare at him as intense heat simmered through her veins. He leaned back on his haunches and then in one quick movement, grasped her hips and peeled the jeans down to her knees.

"What—what are you doing?" she managed to ask, while liquid fire sizzled down her spine. She was lying there with only bikini panties covering her.

He met her gaze. "I'm filling my entire mouth with the taste of you." And then he eased her panties down her legs before lifting her hips and lowering his head between her thighs.

The touch of his tongue had her moaning and lifting her hips off the bed. He was relentless, and he used his mouth in a way that should be outlawed. She wanted to push his head away, but instead she used her arms to hold him in place.

And then she felt a series of intense spasms spread through her entire body. Suddenly, he did something wicked with his tongue, driving her wild. She screamed as a flood of sensations claimed her, tossing her into an earth-shaking orgasm. Her very first. It was more powerful than anything she could have imagined.

And he continued to lap her up, not letting go. His actions filled her with more emotions, more wanting, more longing. Her senses were tossed to smithereens. It took a while before she had enough energy to breathe through her lungs to release a slow, steady breath. She wondered if she had enough energy to even mount her horse, much less ride away from here.

Aidan lifted his head and slowly licked his lips, as if savoring her taste, while meeting her eyes. "Mmm, delicious."

His words were as erotic as she felt. "Why? Why did you do that?" she asked, barely able to get the words out. She felt exhausted, totally drained. Yet completely and utterly satisfied.

Instead of giving her an answer, he touched her chin with the tip of his thumb before lowering his lips to hers in an open-mouth kiss that had fire stirring deep in her stomach. Tasting herself on his lips made her quiver.

When he finally released her lips, he eased back on his haunches and gazed down at her. "I did it because you have a flavor that's uniquely you and I wanted to sample it."

She lifted her hips off the bed when he pulled her jeans back up. Then he shifted his body to pull her into his lap. She tilted her head back to look at him. "What about when we leave here tomorrow?"

"When we leave tomorrow we will remember this time with fondness and enjoyment. I'm sure when you wake up in your bed in Wyoming and I wake up in mine in Boston, we will be out of each other's systems."

She nodded. "You think so?"

"Yes, I'm pretty sure of it. And don't feel guilty about anything because we haven't hurt anyone. All we did was appease our curiosity in a very delectable way."

Yes, it had been most delectable. And technically, they hadn't slept together so they hadn't crossed any lines. She pulled away from him to finish fixing her clothing, tucking her shirt back into her jeans.

"Um, a missed opportunity."

She glanced over at him. "What?"

"Your breasts. I had planned to devour them."

At that moment, as if on cue, her breasts began to ache. Her nipples felt tight, sensitive, pulsing. And it didn't help matters when an image of him doing that very thing trickled through her mind.

"We need to go," she said quickly, knowing if they remained any longer it would only lead to trouble.

"Do we?"

He wasn't helping matters by asking her that. "Yes. It's getting late and we might be missed." When he made no attempt to move, she headed for the door. "I can find my way back."

"Wait up, Jillian."

She stopped and turned back to him. "We don't have to go back together, Aidan."

"Yes, we do. Pam knows of our plans to go riding together."

Color drained from Jillian's face. "Who told her?"

"I ran into her when I was headed to the barn and she asked where I was headed. I told her the truth."

At the accusation in her expression, he placed his hands in the back pockets of his jeans. "Had I told her I was going someplace else and she discovered differently, Jillian, she would have wondered why I had lied."

Jillian nodded slowly upon realizing what he said made sense. "What did she say about it?"

"Nothing. In fact I don't think she thought much about it at all. However, she did say she was glad you were about to start medical school and she would appreciate any advice I could give you."

Jillian swallowed tightly. He'd given her more than advice. Thanks to him, she had experienced her first orgasm today. "Okay, we'll ride back together. I'll just wait outside."

She quickly walked out the door. He'd claimed what they'd done today would get them out of each other's systems. She definitely hoped so.

WHEN THE DOOR closed behind Jillian, Aidan rubbed a hand down his face in frustration. He couldn't leave Denver soon enough. The best thing to do was put as much distance between him and Jillian as possible. She felt uncomfortable with the situation and now he was beginning to feel the same. However, his uneasiness had nothing to do with Dillon and Pam finding out what they'd been up to, and everything to do with his intense attraction to Jillian.

Even now he wanted to go outside, throw her over his shoulders and bring her back inside. He wanted to kiss her into submission and taste her some more before making nonstop love to her. How crazy was that?

He'd never felt this much desire for any woman, and knowing she was off-limits only seemed to heighten his desire for her. And now that he'd gotten an intimate taste of her, getting her out of his system might not be as easy as he'd claimed earlier. Her taste hadn't just electrified his taste buds, it had done something to him that was unheard of—he was no longer lingering on the edge of wanting to make love to her but had fallen off big-time.

Every time his tongue explored her mouth, his emotions heated up and began smoldering. And when he lapped her up, he was tempted to do other things to her, as well. Things he doubted she was ready for.

Drawing in a deep breath, he straightened up the bedcovers before heading for the door. Upon stepping outside, he breathed in deeply to calm his racing heart. She stood there stroking his horse and a part of him wished she would stroke him the same way. He got hard just imagining such a thing.

He didn't say anything for a long moment. He just stood there watching her. When his erection pressed uncomfortably against his zipper, he finally spoke up. "I'm ready to ride."

She glanced over at him and actually smiled when she said, "You have a beautiful horse, Aidan."

"Thanks," he said, walking down the steps. "Charger is a fourth-generation Westmoreland stallion."

She turned to stroke the horse again and didn't look up when he came to stand next to her. "I've heard all about Charger. I was warned by Dillon to never try to ride him because only a few people could. It's obvious you're one of those people."

Aidan nodded. "Yes, Charger and I have an understanding."

She stopped stroking Charger to look at him. "What about you and me, Aidan? Do we have an understanding?"

He met her gaze, not sure how he should answer that. Just when he thought he had everything figured out about them, something would happen to make his brains turn to mush. "I assume you're referring to the incidents that have taken place between us over the past two days."

"I am."

"Then, yes, we have an understanding. After today, no more kissing, no more touching—"

"Or tasting," she interjected.

Saying he would never again taste her was a hard one, but for her peace of mind and for his own, he would say it. "Yes, tasting."

"Good. We're in agreement."

He wouldn't exactly say that, but for now he would hold his tongue—that same tongue that enjoyed dueling with hers. "I guess we need to head back."

"Okay, and I don't need your help mounting my horse."

In other words, she didn't want him to touch her. "You sure?"

"Positive."

He nodded and then watched her move away from his horse to get on hers. As usual, it was a total turn-on watching her. "I want to thank you, Aidan."

He took his gaze away from the sight of her legs straddling the horse to look into her face. "Thank me for what?"

"For introducing me to a few things during this visit home."

For some reason that made him smile. "It was my pleasure." And he meant every word.

CHAPTER SEVEN

"You're still not going home, Jillian?"

Jillian looked up from eating her breakfast to see her roommate, Ivy Rollins. They had met in her sophomore year when Jillian knew she didn't want to live in the dorm any longer. She had wanted an apartment off campus and someone to share the cost with her. Ivy, who had plans to attend law school, had answered the ad Jillian placed in the campus newspaper. They'd hit it off the first time they'd met and had been the best of friends since. Jillian couldn't ask for a better roommate.

"I was home last month," she reminded Ivy.

"Yes, but that was a couple of days for your birthday. Next week is spring break."

Jillian didn't want to be reminded. Pam had called yesterday to see if Jillian would be coming home since Nadia had made plans to do so. Paige, who was attending UCLA, had gotten a small part in a play on campus and needed to remain in Los Angeles. Guilt was still riding Jillian over what she and Aidan had done. She hated deceiving her sister about anything. "I explained to Pam that I need to start studying for the MCAT. She understood."

"I hate leaving you, but—"

"But you will," Jillian said, smiling. "And that's fine. I know how homesick you get." That was an understatement. Ivy's family lived in Oregon. Her parents, both chefs, owned a huge restaurant there. Her two older brothers were chefs as well and assisted her parents. Ivy had decided on a different profession than her parents and siblings, but she loved going home every chance she got to help out.

"Yes, I will," Ivy said, returning her smile. "In fact I leave in two days. Sure you'll be okay?"

"Yes, I'll be fine. I've got enough to keep me busy since I'm sitting for the MCAT in two months. And I need to start working on my essays."

"It's a bummer you'll be doing something other than enjoying yourself next week," Ivy said.

"It's okay. Getting into medical school is the most important thing to me right now."

A few hours later Jillian sat at the computer desk in her bedroom searching the internet. She had tossed around the idea of joining a study group for the MCAT and there appeared to be several. Normally, she preferred studying solo but for some reason she couldn't concentrate. She pushed away from the computer and leaned back in her chair knowing the reason.

Aidan.

It had been a little over a month since she'd gone home for her birthday, and Aidan had been wrong. She hadn't woken up in her bed in Wyoming not thinking of him. In fact she thought of him even more. All the time. Thoughts of him had begun interfering with her studies.

She got up and moved to the kitchen to grab a soda from the refrigerator. He should have been out of her system by now, but he wasn't. Memories of him put her to sleep at night and woke her up in the morning. And then in the wee hours of the night, she recalled in vivid detail his kisses, especially the ones between her legs.

Remembering that particular kiss sent a tingling sensation through her womanly core, which wasn't good. In fact, nothing about what she was going through was good. Sexual withdrawal. And she hadn't even had sex with Aidan, but she hadn't needed sex to get an orgasm. That in itself showed the magnitude of his abilities.

Returning to her bedroom she pushed thoughts of him from her mind. Sitting back down at her desk, she resumed surfing the net. She bet he hadn't even given her a thought. He probably wasn't missing any sleep thinking of her, and he had probably woken up his first day back in Boston with some woman in his bed. Why did that thought bother her?

She had been tempted to ask Pam if she'd heard from Aidan, but hadn't for fear her sister would wonder why Jillian was inquiring about Aidan when she hadn't before.

Jillian turned around when she heard a knock on her bedroom door. "Come in."

Ivy walked into the room, smiling. "I know you have a lot to do but you've been in here long enough. Come grab a bite to eat at the Wild Duck. My treat."

Ivy wasn't playing fair. She knew the Wild Duck was one of Jillian's favorite eating places. They had the best hamburgers and fries. "You've twisted my arm," she said, pushing away from the desk.

Ivy chuckled. "Yeah. Right."

Jillian stood, thinking she did need a break. And maybe she could get Aidan off her mind.

"HOW ARE YOU DOING, Dr. Westmoreland?"

Aidan smiled over at the doctor who'd transferred in to the medical school during the weekend that he'd gone home. He really should ask her out. Lynette Bowes was attractive, she had a nice figure, and she seemed friendly enough. At times almost too friendly. She enjoyed flirting with him and she'd gone so far as to make a few bold innuendos, which meant getting her into his bed probably would be easy. So what was he waiting on?

"I'm fine, Dr. Bowes, and how are you?"

She leaned over to hand him a patient's chart, intentionally brushing her breasts against his arm. "I would be a lot a better if you dropped by my apartment tonight," she whispered.

Another invite. Why was he stalling? Why wasn't he on top of his game as usual? And why was he thinking that the intimate caress she'd purposely initiated just now had nothing on the caresses he'd experienced with Jillian?

"Thanks, but I have plans for tonight," he lied.

"Then maybe another night?"

"I'll let you know." He appreciated his cell phone going off at that moment. "I'll see you later." He made a quick escape.

Later that night while at home doing nothing but flipping TV channels, he couldn't help wondering what the hell was wrong with him. Although he'd asked himself that question, he knew the answer without thinking.

Jillian.

He'd assumed once he was back in Boston and waking up in his own bed that he would eradicate her from his mind. Unfortunately, he'd found out that wasn't the case. He thought about her every free moment, and he even went to bed thinking about her. And the dreams he had of her were double X-rated. His desire for her was so bad that he hadn't thought twice about wanting anyone else.

And it hadn't helped matters when he'd called home earlier in the week and Dillon mentioned that Jillian wasn't coming home for spring break. She told Pam she had registered to take the MCAT and needed the time to study and work on her admissions essays. He applauded her decision to make sacrifices to reach her goal, but he was disappointed she hadn't reached out to him like he'd suggested. He'd made a pretty high score on the MCAT and could give her some study pointers. He'd even keyed his contact information into her phone.

Yet she hadn't called to ask him a single question about anything. That could only mean she didn't want his help and had probably pushed what happened between them to the back of her mind. Good for her, but he didn't like the fact that she remained in the center of his.

Tossing the remote aside he reached for his cell phone to pull up her number. When her name appeared he put the phone down. They'd had an agreement, so to speak. An understanding. They would put that time in Denver behind them. It had been enjoyable but was something that could not and would not be repeated. No more kissing, touching...or tasting.

Hell, evidently that was easy for her to do, but it was proving to be downright difficult for him. There were nights he woke up wanting her with a passion, hungering to kiss her, touch her and taste her.

The memories of them going riding together, especially that day spent in Bane's cabin...every moment of that time was etched in Aidan's mind, making his brain cells overload.

Like now.

When he'd pulled down her jeans, followed by her panties, and had buried his head between her legs and tasted her...the memory made his groin tighten. Need for Jillian clawed at him in a way that made it difficult to breathe.

Aidan stood and began pacing the floor in his apartment, trying to wear down his erection. He paused when an idea entered his mind. He had time he could take off and he might as well do it now. He'd only been to Laramie, Wyoming, a couple of times, and maybe he should visit there again. He would take in the sights and check out a few good restaurants. And there was no reason for him not to drop in on Jillian to see how she was doing while he was there.

No reason at all.

THREE DAYS LATER, Jillian sat at the kitchen table staring at the huge study guide in front of her. It had to be at least five hundred pages thick and filled with information to prepare her for the MCAT. The recommendation was that students take three months to study, but since she was enrolled in only one class this semester she figured she would have more time to cram and could get it done in two months. That meant she needed to stay focused. No exceptions. And she meant none.

But her mind was not in agreement, especially when she could lick her lips and imagine Aidan doing that very same thing. And why—after one month, nine days and twenty minutes—could she still do that? Why hadn't she been able to forget about his kisses and move on? Especially now when she needed to focus.

The apartment was empty and felt lonely without Ivy. It was quiet and just what she needed to get some serious studying done. She had eaten a nice breakfast and had taken a walk outside to get her brain and body stimulated. But now her mind wanted to remember another type of stimulation. One that even now sent tingles through her lower stomach.

She was about to take a sip of her coffee when the doorbell sounded. She frowned. Most of her neighbors were college students like her, and the majority of them had gone home for spring break. She'd noticed how vacant the parking lot had looked while out walking earlier.

Getting up from the kitchen table she moved toward the front door. She glanced through her peephole and her breath caught. Standing on the other side of her door was the one man she'd been trying not to think about.

Shocked to the core, she quickly removed the security chain and unlocked the door. Opening it, she tried to ignore the way her heart pounded and how her stomach muscles trembled. "Aidan? What are you doing here?"

Instead of answering, he leaned down and kissed her. Another shock rammed right into the first. She should have pushed him away the moment their mouths connected. But instead she melded her body right to his and his arms reached out to hold her around the waist. As soon as she was reacquainted with his taste, her tongue latched onto his and began a sensuous duel that had her moaning.

In all her attempts at logical thinking over the past

month, not until now could she admit how much she'd missed him. How much she'd missed this. How could a man engrain himself inside a woman's senses so deeply and thoroughly, and so quickly? And how could any woman resist this particular man doing so?

She heard the door click and knew he'd maneuvered her into her apartment and closed the door behind him. Noticing that, she almost pulled back, and she would have had he not at that moment deepened the kiss.

This had to be a dream. Was that why the room felt as if it was spinning? There was no way Aidan was in Laramie, at her apartment and kissing her. But if this was a dream she wasn't ready to wake up. She needed to get her fill of his taste before her fantasy faded. Before she realized in horror that she was actually kissing the short and bald mailman instead of Aidan. Had her fascination with him finally gotten the best of her?

The thought had her breaking off the kiss and opening her eyes. The man standing across from her with lips damp from their kiss was definitely Aidan.

She drew in a deep breath, trying to slow the beat of her heart and regain control of her senses.

As if he'd known just what she was thinking, he said, "It's really me, Jillian. And I'm here to help you study for your MCAT this week."

She blinked. *Help her study?* He had to be kidding.

AIDAN WANTED NOTHING more than to kiss the shocked look off Jillian's face. But he knew that before he could even think about kissing her again he had a lot of explaining to do since he'd gone back on their agreement.

"I talked to Dillon a few days ago and he mentioned you wouldn't be coming home for spring break and the reason why. So I figured I could help by giving you a good study boost."

She shook her head as if doing so would clear her mind. Looking back at him, she said, "There's no way you could have thought that. And what was that kiss about? I thought we had an understanding."

"We did. We still do. However, based on the way you responded to my kiss just now, I think we might need to modify a few things."

She lifted her chin. "There's nothing for us to modify."

That response irritated him to the core. "Do you think I want to be here, Jillian? I have a life in Boston, a life I was enjoying until recently. Ever since the kisses we shared on your birthday, I've done nothing but think about you, want you, miss you."

"That's not my fault," she snapped.

"It is when you're not being honest with yourself. Can you look me in the eyes and tell me that you haven't thought of me? That you haven't been wanting me? And be honest for once because if you deny it then you need to tell me why your kiss just now said otherwise."

He watched as she nervously licked her tongue across her lips and his gut clenched. "Tell me, Jillian," he said in a softer tone. "For once be honest with me and with yourself."

She drew in a long breath as they stared at each other. After several tense moments passed between them, she said, "Okay, I have been thinking of you, missing you, wanting you. And I hated myself for doing so. You're a weakness I can't afford to have right now. It's crazy. I know a lot of guys around campus. But why you? Why do I want the one guy I can't have?"

Her words softened his ire. She was just as confused and frustrated as he was. "And why do you think you can't have me?"

She frowned. "You know why, Aidan. Pam and Dillon would be against it. In their eyes, we're family. And even if you were a guy she would approve of, she would try to convince me not to get involved with you and to stay focused on becoming a doctor."

"You don't know for certain that's how she would feel, Jillian."

"I do know. When Pam was in college pursuing her dream of becoming an actress, I asked her why she didn't date. She told me that a woman should never sacrifice her dream for any man."

"I'm not asking you to sacrifice your dream."

"No, but you want an involvement during a time when I should be more focused than ever on becoming a doctor."

"I want to help you, not hinder you," he stressed again.

"How do you think you can do that?"

At least she was willing to listen. "By using this week to introduce you to study techniques that will help you remember those things you need to remember."

She nervously licked her tongue across her lips again. "It won't work. I won't be able to think straight with you around."

"I'll make sure you do. I'm not asking to stay here, Jillian. I've already checked into a hotel a mile or so from here. I'll arrive every morning and we'll study until evening, taking short breaks in between. Then we'll grab something to eat and enjoy the evening. Afterward, I'll bring you back here and then leave. Before going to bed you should review what was covered that day, making sure you get eight hours of sleep."

She looked at him as if he was crazy. "I can't take time from studying to enjoy the evening. I'll need to study morning, noon and night."

"Not with me helping you. Besides, too much studying will make you burned out, and you don't want to do that. What good is studying if that happens?"

When she didn't say anything, he pushed harder. "Try my way for a couple of days and if it doesn't work, if you feel I'm more of a hindrance than a help, I'll leave Laramie and let you do things your way."

As she stared at him, not saying anything, he could feel blood throb through his veins. As usual she looked serious. Beautiful. Tempting. He wanted her. Being around her would be hard and leaving her every night after dinner would be harder. He would want to stay and make love to her all through the night. But that wasn't possible. No matter how hard it would be, he needed to keep his self-control.

"Okay," she finally said. "We'll try it for a couple of days. And if it doesn't work I intend for you to keep your word about leaving."

"I will." He had no intention of leaving because he intended for his plan to work. He had aced the MCAT the first time around, with flying colors. Once he'd gotten his act together as a teenager, he'd discovered he was an excellent test taker, something Adrian was not. Determined not to leave his twin behind, he'd often tutored Adrian, sharing his study tips and techniques with his brother. Aidan had also done the same with Bailey once she was in college. Unfortunately, he'd never gotten the chance to share his techniques with Bane since his cousin hadn't been interested in anything or anyone but Crystal.

"Now let's seal our agreement," he said.

When she extended her hand, he glanced at it before pulling her into his arms again.

HE WAS TAKING advantage again, Jillian thought. But she only thought that for a second. That was all the time it took for her to begin returning his kiss with the same hunger he seemed to feel. This was crazy. It was insane. It was also what she needed. What she'd been wanting since leaving Denver and returning to Laramie.

Kissing was something they enjoyed doing with each other and the unhurried mating of their mouths definitely should be ruled illegal. But for now she could handle this—in the safety of her living room, in the arms of a man she thoroughly enjoyed kissing—as long as it went no further.

But what if it did? He'd already shown her that his definition of kissing included any part of her body. What if he decided he wanted more than her mouth this time? Her hormones were going haywire just thinking of the possibility.

He suddenly broke off the kiss and she fought back a groan of disappointment. She stared up at him. "Okay, where's the study guide?" he asked her.

She blinked. Her mind was slow in functioning after such a blazing kiss. It had jarred her senses. "Study guide?"

He smiled and caressed her cheek. "Yes, the MCAT study guide."

"On my kitchen table. I was studying when you showed up."

"Good. And you'll study some more. Lead the way."

AIDAN LEANED BACK in his chair and glanced over at Jillian. "Any questions?"

She shook her head. "No, but you make it seem simple."

He smiled. "Trust me, it's not. The key is to remember that you're the one in control of your brain and the knowledge that's stored inside of it. Don't let retrieving that information during test time psych you out."

She chuckled. "That's easy for you to say."

"And it will be easy for you, as well. I've been there, and when time allows I tutor premed students like yourself. You did well on the practice exam, which covers basically everything you need to know. Now you need to concentrate on those areas you're not so sure about."

"Which is a lot."

"All of them are things you know," he countered. He believed the only reason she lacked confidence in her abilities was because the idea of failing was freaking her out. "You don't have to pass on the first go-round. A lot of people don't. That's why it's suggested you plan to take it at least twice."

She lifted her chin. "I want to ace it on the first try."

"Then do it."

Aidan got up from his chair and went over to the coffeepot sitting on her kitchen counter. He needed something stronger than caffeine, but coffee would have to do. He'd been here for five hours already and they hadn't stopped for lunch. The key was to take frequent short breaks instead of one or two long ones.

She had taken the online practice exam on verbal reasoning and he thought she'd done well for her first time. He'd given her study tips for multiple-choice exams and gone over the questions she had missed. Personally, he thought she would do fine, although he thought taking the test in two months was pushing it. He would have suggested three months instead of two.

"Want some coffee?" he asked, pouring himself a cup.

"No, I'm okay."

Yes, she definitely was. He couldn't attest to her mental state with all that she'd crammed into that brain of hers today, but he could definitely attest to her physical one. She looked amazing, even with her hair tied back in a ponytail and a cute pair of reading glasses perched on her nose. He was used to seeing her without makeup and preferred her that way. She had natural beauty with her flawless creamy brown skin. And she looked cute in her jeans and top.

He glanced at his watch. "Jillian?"

She glanced up from the computer and looked over at him. "Yes?"

"It's time to call it a day."

She seemed baffled by his statement. "Call it a day? I haven't covered everything I wanted to do today."

"You covered a lot and you don't want to overload your brain."

She stared at him for a moment and then nodded and began shutting down her computer. "Maybe you're right. Thanks to you, I did cover a lot. Definitely a lot more than I would have if you hadn't been here. You're a great tutor."

"And you're a good student." He glanced at his watch again. "What eating places do you have around here?"

"Depends on what you have a taste for."

He had a taste for her, but knew he had to keep his promise and not push her into anything. "A juicy steak."

"Then you're in luck," she said, standing. "There's a great steak place a few blocks from here. Give me a few minutes to change."

"Okay." He watched her hurry off toward her bedroom.

When she closed the door behind her, he rubbed a hand down his face. Jillian was temptation even when she wasn't trying to be. When he'd asked about her roommate she'd told him that Ivy had gone home for spring break. That meant...

Nothing. Unless she made the first move or issued an invitation. Until then, he would spend his nights alone at the hotel.

CHAPTER EIGHT

JILLIAN GLANCED ACROSS the table at Aidan. It was day three and still hard to believe that he was in Laramie, that he had come to give her a kick-start in her studying. Day one had been frustrating. He'd pushed her beyond what she thought she was ready for. But going to dinner with him that night had smoothed her ruffled feathers.

Dinner had been fun. She'd discovered he enjoyed eating his steaks medium rare and he loved baked potatoes loaded with sour cream, bacon bits and cheddar cheese. He also loved unsweetened tea and when it came to anything with chocolate, he could overdose if he wasn't careful.

He was also a great conversationalist. He engaged her in discussions about everything—but he deemed the topic of medical school to be off-limits. They talked about the economy, recent elections, movies they had enjoyed, and about Adrian's plans to travel the world a few years after getting his PhD in engineering.

And Aidan got her talking. She told him about Ivy, who she thought was the roommate from heaven; about Jillian's decision two years ago to move out of the dorm; and about her first experience with a pushy car salesman. She told him about all the places she wanted to visit one day and that the one thing she wanted to do and hadn't done yet was go on a cruise.

It occurred to her later that it had been the first time she and Aidan had shared a meal together alone, and she had enjoyed it. It had made her even more aware of him as a man. She'd had the time to look beyond his handsome features and she'd discovered he was a thoughtful and kind person. He had been pleasant, treating everyone with respect, including the waitress and servers. And each time he smiled at her, her stomach clenched. Then he would take a sip of his drink, and she would actually envy his straw.

After dinner they returned to her apartment. He made her promise that she would only review what they'd covered that day and not stay up past nine, then he left. But not before taking her into his arms and giving her a kiss that rendered her weak and senseless— to the point where she was tempted to ask him to stay longer. But she fought back the temptation. Knowing she would see him again the next day had made falling asleep quick and easy. For the first time in a long time, she had slept through the night, though he'd dominated her dreams.

He arrived early the next morning with breakfast, which she appreciated. Then it was back to studying again. The second day had been more intense than the first. Knowing they couldn't cover every aspect of the study guide in one week, he had encouraged her to hit the areas she felt were her weakest. He gave her hints on how to handle multiple-choice questions and introduced her to key words to use when completing her essays.

For dinner they had gone to the Wild Duck. She had been eager to introduce him to her favorite place. A dinner of hamburgers, French fries and milk shakes had been wonderful. Afterward they went to Harold's

Game Hall to shoot pool, something she had learned to do in high school.

When he'd brought her home, like the night before, he took her in his arms and kissed her before he left, giving her the same instructions about reviewing what they'd covered that morning and getting eight hours of sleep. Again, she'd slept like a baby with him dominating her dreams.

She enjoyed having him as a study coach. Most of the time she stayed focused. But there were a few times when she felt heat simmering between them, something both of them tried to ignore. They managed it most of the time but today was harder than the two days before.

Aidan was tense. She could tell. He had arrived that morning, like yesterday, with breakfast in hand. Since he believed she should study on a full stomach and not try eating while studying, they had taken their meal outside to her patio. It had been pleasant, but more than once she'd caught him staring at her with a look in his eyes that she felt in the pit of her stomach.

He wasn't as talkative today as he'd been the past two days, and, taking a cue from his mood, she hadn't said much, either. On those occasions when their hands had accidentally touched while he'd been handing her papers or turning a page, she wasn't sure who sizzled more, her or him.

That's why she'd made up her mind about how today would end. She wanted him and he wanted her and there was no reason for them to suffer with their desires any longer. She'd fallen in love with him. After this time together, she could admit that now. That little crush she'd had on him for years had become something more. Something deeper and more profound.

The thought of Pam and Dillon finding out was still an issue that plagued her. However, since Aidan didn't feel the same way about her that she felt about him, she was certain she would be able to convince him to keep whatever they did a secret. He was doing that now anyway. He'd told her that neither Pam nor Dillon knew where he was spending this week. That meant Jillian and Aidan were already keeping secrets from their family, and she would continue to do so if it meant spending more time with him.

That night they went to a restaurant she had never visited because of its pricey menu. The signature dishes had been delicious and the service excellent. But the restaurant's setting spoke of not only elegance but also romance. Rustic wood ceilings with high beams, a huge brick fireplace and a natural stone floor. Beautiful candles adorned the tables and even in the dim light, each time she glanced over at Aidan he was looking back at her.

Getting through dinner hadn't been easy. They conversed but not as much as they had the previous two nights. Was she imagining things or did his voice sound deeper, huskier than usual? His smiles weren't full ones but half smiles, and just as sexy.

Like he'd done the previous two nights, he walked through her apartment, checking to make sure everything was okay. Then he gave her orders to only review what she'd studied that morning and get into bed before nine because at least eight hours of sleep were essential.

And then, as had become his habit, he pulled her into his arms to kiss her goodbye. This was what she had anticipated all day. She was ready for Aidan's kiss. Standing on tiptoe she tilted her open mouth toward him, her tongue ready. He closed his full mouth over hers and their tongues tangled, almost bringing her to her knees.

The kiss lasted for a long, delectable moment. It was different than any they'd shared before and she'd known it the moment their mouths fused. It was hot, heavy and hungry. He wasn't letting up or backing down—and neither was she.

Jillian felt herself being lifted off her feet and she immediately wrapped her legs around his waist while he continued to ravish her mouth in a way that over-whelmed her and overloaded her senses. His hunger was sexual and greedy. She could tell he was fighting hard to hold it together, to stay in control, to keep his sanity in check. But she wasn't. In fact, she was delib-erately trying to tempt him every way that she could.

She felt the wall at her back and knew he'd maneu-vered them over to it. He broke off the kiss and stared at her, impaling her with the flaming fire in his eyes. "Tell me to stop, Jillian," he said. "Because if you don't do it now, I won't be able to stop later. I want to tongue you all over. Lick every inch of your body. Taste you. Make love to you. Hard. Long. Deep. So tell me to stop now."

Her pulse jumped. Every single cell in her body siz-zled with his words. Hot sparks of passion glowed in his gaze and when a powerful burst of primal need slammed through her she didn't want to escape.

"Tell me to stop."

His plea made the already hot sexual tension be-tween them blaze, and she knew of only one way to put out the fire.

"Stop, Aidan!"

His body went still. The only thing that moved was the pulse throbbing in his throat. He held her gaze and she was convinced she could hear blood rushing through both of their veins.

When she felt him about to untangle her legs from around his waist and lower her feet to the floor, she said, "Stop talking and do all those things you claim you're going to do."

She saw the impact of her words reflected in his eyes. While he seemed incapable of speaking, she released her arms from around his neck and tugged at his shirt, working her hands beneath to touch his bare chest. She heard the groan from deep in his throat.

"If you don't take me, Aidan Westmoreland, then I'll be forced to take you."

THAT WAS THE last thing Aidan had expected her to say. But hearing her say it intensified the throbbing need within him. His crotch pounded fiercely and he knew of only one way to remedy that. But first...

He lowered her to her feet as a smile tugged at his lips. Only for a moment, he gazed down at her shirt, noticing the curve of her breasts beneath the cotton. In an instant, he tugged the shirt over her head and tossed it aside.

He drew in a deep breath when his eyes settled on her chest, specifically her skin-tone colored bra. Eager beyond belief, he touched her breasts through the lace material. When his fingers released the front clasp, causing the twin globes to spring free, the breath was snatched from his lungs.

Mercy. He eased the bra straps from her shoulders to remove it completely from her body and his mouth watered. Her breasts were one area that he hadn't tasted yet, and he planned on remedying that soon.

Deciding he wanted to see more naked flesh, he lowered to his knees and slid his fingers beneath the elastic waistband of her skirt to ease it down her legs. She stepped out of it and he tossed it aside to join her shirt and bra. His gaze raked the full length of her body, now only covered by a pair of light blue bikini panties. His hands actually trembled when he ran them down her legs. He felt as if he were unveiling a precious treasure.

She stepped out of them as she'd done her skirt and she stood in front of him totally naked. He leaned back on his haunches while his gaze raked her up and down, coming back to her center. He was tempted to start right there, but he knew if he did that, he wouldn't get to taste her breasts this time, either, and he refused to miss the chance again.

Standing back on his feet, Aidan leaned and lowered his head. He captured a nipple between his lips, loving how the tip hardened in his mouth as his tongue traced circles around the rigid bud. She purred his name as she cradled the back of his head to hold his mouth right there.

He continued to taste her breasts, leaving one and moving to the other, enjoying every single lick and suck. Her moans fueled his desire to possess her. To make love to her. And what he loved more than anything else was the sound of her moaning his name.

Aidan eased his lips from her breasts and moved his mouth slowly downward, tasting her skin. As he crouched, his mouth traced a greedy path over her stomach, loving the way her muscles tightened beneath his lips.

A slow throbbing ache took hold of his erection as he eased down to his knees. This was what he'd gone to

bed craving ever since he'd first tasted her between her
thighs. He'd fallen asleep several nights licking his lips
at the memory. Her feminine scent was unique, so irre-
sistibly Jillian, that his tongue thickened in anticipation.

Knowing she watched him, he ran his hands up and
down the insides of her legs, massaged her thighs and
caressed the area between them. His name was a whisper on her lips when he slid a finger inside of her. He
loved the feel of her juices wetting him. He stroked her.

Hungry for her taste, he withdrew his finger and
licked it. He smiled before using his hands to spread
her feminine core to ready her for an open-mouth kiss.

JILLIAN RELEASED A DEEP, toe-curling moan the moment
Aidan latched his hot tongue onto her. She grabbed
his head to push him away, but he held tight to her legs
while his tongue went deep, thrusting hard. Then she
pressed herself toward his mouth.

She closed her eyes and chanted his name as spasms
ripped through her, making her thighs tremble. He refused to let go, refused to lift his mouth, as sensations
overtook her. Her body throbbed in unexpected places
as an orgasm shook her.

When the last spasm speared through her, she felt
herself being lifted into strong arms. When she opened
her eyes, Aidan was entering her bedroom. He placed
her on the bed, leaned down and kissed her, sending
rekindled desire spiking through her.

When he ended the kiss and eased off the bed, she
watched as he quickly removed his clothes. She could
only lie there and admire his nakedness. He was a fine
specimen of a man, both in and out of clothes. Just as
he'd appeared in her dreams. Thick thighs, muscular

legs and a huge erection nested in a patch of thick, curly black hair.

How will I handle that? she asked herself when he pulled a condom packet from his wallet and quickly sheathed himself. He took his time and she figured it was because he knew she was watching his every move with keen interest.

"You have done this before, right?" he asked her.

"What? Put on a condom? No. One wouldn't fit me."

He grinned over at her. "Funny. You know what I'm asking."

Yes, she knew what he was asking. "Um, sort of."

He lifted a brow. "Sort of?"

She shrugged slightly. "I'm not a virgin, if that's what you're asking," she said softly. "Technically not. But…"

"But what?"

"I was in high school and neither of us knew what we were doing. That was my one and only time."

He just stood there totally naked staring at her. She wondered why he wasn't saying anything. What was he thinking? As if he'd read her mind, he slowly moved toward her, placed his knee on the bed and leaned toward her. "What you missed out on before, you will definitely get tonight. And, Jillian?"

She swallowed. He'd spoken with absolute certainty and all she could do was stare back at him. "Yes?"

"This will not be your only time with me."

Her body reacted to his words and liquid heat traveled through her body. He hadn't spoken any words of love but he'd let her know this wasn't a one-time deal with them.

She didn't have time to dwell on what he'd said. He pulled her into his arms and kissed her. She closed her eyes and let herself be liquefied by the kiss. Like all the other times he'd used his expertise to make everything around her fade into oblivion, the kiss was the only thing her mind and body could comprehend. His hands were all over her, touching her everywhere. She released a deep moan when she felt his knees spreading her legs.

"Open your eyes and look at me, Jillian."

She slowly opened her eyes to look up at the man whose body was poised above hers. He lifted her hips and his enlarged sex slid between her wet feminine folds. He thrust forward and her body stretched to accommodate his size. Instinctively, she wrapped her legs around him and when he began to move, she did so, as well.

She continued to hold his gaze while he thrust in and out of her. Over and over he would take her to the edge just to snatch her back. Her inner muscles clamped down on him, squeezing and tightening around him.

As she felt new spasms rip through her, he threw his head back and let out a roar that shook the room. She was glad most of her neighbors had gone away for spring break; otherwise they would know what she was doing tonight.

But right now, all she cared about was the man she loved, and how he was making her feel things she'd never felt before.

He kissed her again. Their tongues dueled in another erotic kiss and she couldn't help but remember the words he'd spoken earlier.

This will not be your only time with me.

She knew men said words they didn't mean to women

they were about to sleep with, and she had no reason to believe it was any different with Aidan.

Besides, considering that she needed to stay focused on her studies, it was a good thing he wasn't serious.

AIDAN WATCHED THE naked woman sleeping in his arms and let out a frustrated sigh. This was not supposed to happen.

He wasn't talking about making love because there was no way such a thing could have been avoided. The sexual tension between them had been on overload since the day he'd arrived at her apartment and neither of them could have lasted another day.

What was *not* supposed to happen was feeling all these unexpected emotions. They had wrapped around his mind and wouldn't let go. And what bothered him more than anything else was that he knew he was not confusing his emotions with what had definitely been off-the-charts sex. If he hadn't known before that there was a difference in what he felt for Jillian, he definitely knew it now.

He had fallen in love with her.

When? How? Why? He wasn't sure. All he knew, without a doubt, was that it had happened. The promise of great sex hadn't made him take a week's vacation and travel more than fifteen hundred miles across five states to spend time with her. Sex hadn't made him become her personal test coach, suffering the pains of being close to her while maintaining boundaries and limits. And sex definitely had nothing to do with the way he felt right now and how it was nearly impossible for him to think straight.

When she purred softly in her sleep and then wig-

gled her backside snugly against his groin he closed
his eyes and groaned. It had been great sex but it had
been more than that. She had reached a part of him no
woman had reached before.

He'd realized it before they'd made love. He'd known
it the minute she told him she'd only made love once
before. As far as he was concerned that one time didn't
count because the guy had definitely done a piss-poor
job. The only orgasm she'd ever experienced had been
with Aidan.

But in the days he'd spent studying with her he'd
gotten to know a lot about her. She was a fighter, determined to reach whatever goals she established for
herself. And she was thoughtful enough to care that
Pam not bear the burden of the cost of sending Jillian
to medical school. She was even willing to sell her family home.

And he liked being with her, which posed a problem since they lived more than a thousand miles apart.
He'd heard long-distance affairs could sometimes be
brutal. But he and Jillian could make it work if they
wanted to do so. He knew how he felt about her but he
had no idea how she felt about him. As far as he knew,
she wasn't operating on emotion but out of a sense of
curiosity. She'd said as much.

However, the biggest problem of all, one he knew
would pose the most challenge to the possibility of anything ever developing between them was her insistence
on Pam and Dillon not knowing about them.

Aidan didn't feel the same way and now that he loved
her, he really didn't want to keep it a secret. He knew
Dillon well enough to know that if Aidan were to go
to his cousin and come clean, tell Dillon Aidan had

fallen in love with Jillian, Dillon would be okay with it. Although Aidan couldn't say with certainty how Pam would feel, he'd always considered her a fair person. He believed she would eventually give her blessing…but only if she thought Jillian was truly in love with him and that he would make Jillian happy.

There were so many unknowns. The one thing he did know was that he and Jillian had to talk. He'd given her fair warning that what they'd shared would not be one and done. There was no way he would allow her to believe that her involvement with him meant nothing, that she was just another woman to him. She was more than that and he wanted her to know it.

She stirred, shifted in bed and then slowly opened her eyes to stare at him. She blinked a few times as if bringing him into focus—or as if she was trying to figure out if he was really here in her bed.

Aidan let her know she wasn't seeing things. "Good morning." He gently caressed her cheek before glancing over at the digital clock on her nightstand. "You woke up early. It's barely six o'clock."

"A habit I can't break," she said, still staring at him. "You didn't leave."

"Was I supposed to?"

She shrugged bare shoulders. "I thought that's the way it worked."

She had a lot to learn about him. He wouldn't claim he'd never left a woman's bed in the middle of the night, but Jillian was different.

"Not for us, Jillian." He paused. "We need to talk."

She broke eye contact as she pulled up in bed, holding the covers in place to shield her nakedness. Aidan thought the gesture amusing considering all they'd done last night. "I know what you're going to say, Aidan. Although I've never heard it before, Ivy has and she told me how this plays out."

She'd made him curious. "And how does it play out?"

"The guy lets the woman know it was just a one-night stand. Nothing personal and definitely nothing serious."

He hadn't used that particular line before, but he'd used similar ones. He decided not to tell her that. "You weren't a one-night stand, Jillian."

She nodded. "I do recall you mentioning that last night wouldn't be your only time with me."

He tightened his arms around her. "And why do you think I said that?"

"Because you're a man and most men enjoy sex."

He smiled. "A lot of women enjoy it, as well. Didn't you?"

"Yes. There's no need to lie about it. I definitely enjoyed it."

A grin tugged at Aidan's lips. His ego appreciated her honesty. "I enjoyed it, as well." He kissed her, needing the taste of her.

It was a brief kiss and when he lifted his lips from hers, she seemed stunned by what he'd done. He found that strange considering the number of times they had kissed before.

"So, if you don't want to say last night was a one-night stand, what is it you want to talk about?" she asked.

He decided to be just as honest as she had been, and

got straight to the point. "I want to talk about me. And you. Together."

She raised a brow. "Together?"

"Yes. I've fallen in love with you."

CHAPTER NINE

JILLIAN WAS OUT of the bed in a flash, taking half the blankets with her. She speared Aidan with an angry look. "Are you crazy? You can't be in love with me. It won't work, especially when I'm in love with you, too."

Too late she'd realized what she'd said. From the look on Aidan's face, he had heard her admission. "If I love you and you love me, Jillian, then what's the problem?"

She lifted her chin. "The problem is that we can't be together the way you would want us to be. I was okay with it when it was one-sided and I just loved you and didn't think you could possibly return the feelings, but now—"

"Hold up," Aidan said, and her eyes widened when he got off the bed to stand in front of her without a stitch of clothes on. "Let me get this straight. You think it's okay for me to sleep with you and not be in love with you?"

She tossed her hair back from her face. "Why not? I'm sure it's done all the time. Men sleep with women they don't love and vice versa. Are you saying you love every woman you sleep with?"

"No."

"Okay then."

"It's not okay because you're not any woman. You're the one that I *have* fallen in love with."

Why was he making things difficult? Downright complicated? She had to make him understand. "I could deal with this a lot better if you didn't love me, mainly because I would have known it wasn't serious on your end."

"And that would not have bothered you?"

"Not in the least. I need to stay focused on my studies and I can't stay focused if I know you feel the same way about me that I feel about you. That only complicates things."

He stared at her as if he thought she was crazy. In a way she couldn't very much blame him. Most women would prefer falling in love with a man who loved them, and if things were different she would want that, too. But the time wasn't right. Men in love made demands. They expected a woman's time. Her attention. All her energy. And being in love required that a woman give her man what he wanted. Well, she didn't have the time to do that. She was in medical school. She wanted to be a doctor.

And worse than anything, an Aidan who thought he loved her would cause problems. He wouldn't want to keep their relationship a secret. He was not a man to be kept in the closet or denied his right to be seen with her. He would want everyone to know they were together and that was something she couldn't accept.

"I still can't understand why you think me loving you complicates things," Aidan said, interrupting her thoughts.

"Because you wouldn't want to keep our affair a secret. You'll want to tell everyone. Take me out anyplace you want. You wouldn't like the thought of us sneaking around."

"No, I wouldn't." He gently pulled her into his arms. She would have pushed him away if he hadn't at that moment tugged the bedcovers from her hands leaving her as naked as he was. The moment their bodies touched, arousal hit her in the core. She was suddenly reminded of what they'd done last night and how they'd done it. From the way his eyes darkened, she knew he was reliving those same sizzling memories.

"Jillian."

"Aidan."

He drew her closer and closed his mouth over hers. She was lost. For a long while, all she could do was stand there feeling his body plastered to hers, feeling his erection pressed against her, feeling the tips of her nipples poking into his chest while he kissed her. Frissons of fire raced up her spine.

And when she felt herself being maneuvered toward the bed, she was too caught up in desire to do anything about it. The same urgency to mate that had taken hold of him had fused itself to her. As soon as her back touched the mattress she slid from beneath him and pushed him back. She had flipped them and was now on top of him. He stared up at her with surprise in his eyes.

She intended to play out one of her fantasies, one of the ways they'd made love in her dreams—with her on top. But first she needed him to know something. "I take the Pill…to regulate my periods. And I'm safe," she whispered.

"So am I."

She maneuvered her middle over his engorged shaft, which stood straight up. Every hormone inside her body sizzled as she eased down onto him, taking him inside inch by inch. He was big, but like last night her body stretched to accommodate his size.

"Look at me, Jillian." Obeying his command, she held his gaze.

"I love you, whether you want me to or not and it's too late for you to do anything about it."

She drew in a deep breath and continued to ease him inside of her, not wanting to dwell on the problems love could cause. They would talk again later. But for now, this was what she wanted. This was what she needed. And when she had taken him to the hilt, she moved, riding him the way she'd been taught to ride years ago. From the look reflected in the depths of his eyes, she was giving him a ride he would remember for a long time.

She liked the view from up here. Staring down at him, seeing his expression change each time she shoved downward, taking him deeper. His nostrils flared. His breathing was choppy. Was that a little sweat breaking through on his brow?

Riding him felt good. Exhilarating. He definitely had the perfect body to be ridden. Hard, masculine and solid. She had her knees locked on each side of his strong thighs. Her inner muscles clenched, gripping him in a hold that had him groaning deep in his throat.

She loved the sound. Loved being in control. Loved him. The last thought sent her senses spiraling, and when he shouted her name and bucked his entire body upward, she felt his massive explosion. He drenched her insides with thick semen. And she used her muscles to squeeze out more.

Perspiration soaked her head, her face, their bodies…but she kept on riding. When another explosion hit him, she nearly jerked them both off the bed when she screamed in pleasure.

He held her tight and she held him and she wished she never had to let him go.

AIDAN PUSHED A damp curl out of Jillian's eyes. She was sprawled on top of him, breathing deeply. He figured she had earned the right to be exhausted. He'd never experienced anything so invigorating or stimulating in his entire life.

"Don't ask me not to love you, Jillian," he finally found the strength to say softly, and the words came straight from his heart. For the first time in his life, he'd told a woman he loved her and the woman wished that he didn't.

When he felt her tears fall on his arm, he shifted their bodies so he could look at her. "Is me loving you that bad?"

She shook her head. "No. I know it should be what I want but the timing… There is so much I still have to do."

"And you think I'd stop you from doing them?"

"No, but I'd stop myself. I'd lose focus. You would want to be with me and I would want to be with you. In the open. I know you don't understand why I can't do that, but I can't."

She was right, he didn't understand. He believed she was all wrong about how Dillon and Pam, or the entire Westmoreland family, would handle them hooking up. He doubted it would be a big deal. But it didn't matter what he thought. She thought otherwise and that's what mattered.

"What if I agree to do what we're doing now? I mean, keeping things between us a secret."

She lifted her head. "You would agree to that, Aidan? I'm not talking about a few weeks or a few months. I'm talking about until I finish medical school. Could you really wait that long?"

That was a good question. Could he? Could he be around Jillian at family gatherings and pretend nothing was going on between them? And what about the physical distance between them? She wasn't even sure what medical school she would attend. Her two top choices were Florida and New Orleans, both hundreds of miles away from Boston, Maine or North Carolina.

And what about his family and friends? Like Adrian, Aidan had quite a reputation around Harvard. What would his friends think when he suddenly stopped pursuing women? They would think he'd lost his ever-loving mind. But he didn't care what anyone thought.

It didn't matter. Wherever Jillian was, he would get to her, spend time with her and give her the support she needed to be the doctor she wanted to be.

What Jillian needed now more than anything was for him not to place any pressure on her. Her focus should be on completing the MCAT and not on anything else. Somehow he would handle the distance, he would handle his family and friends and their perceptions.

He held her gaze. "Yes, I can wait. No matter how long it takes, Jillian. Because you're worth waiting for."

Then he tugged her mouth down to his for another one of their ultrapassionate, mind-blowing kisses.

CHAPTER TEN

The present

"THIS IS CAPTAIN STEWART MARCELLUS," a deep voice boomed through the intercom in Jillian's cabin. "My crew and I would like to welcome you aboard the Princess Grandeur. For the next fourteen days we'll cruise the Grand Mediterranean for your enjoyment. In an hour we'll depart Barcelona for full days in Monte Carlo and Florence and two days in Rome. From there we'll sail to Greece and Turkey. I invite you to join me tonight at the welcome party, which kicks off two weeks of fun."

Jillian glanced around her cabin. *A suite.* This was something she definitely hadn't paid for. She and Paige had planned to share a standard stateroom, definitely nothing as luxurious and spacious as what she'd been given. When she'd contacted the customer service desk to tell them about the mistake, she was told no mistake had been made and the suite was hers to enjoy.

No sooner had she ended the call than she'd received a delivery—a bouquet of beautiful mixed flowers and a bottle of chilled wine with a card that read, "Congratulations on finishing medical school. We are proud of you. Enjoy the cruise. You deserve it. Your family, The Westmorelands."

Jillian eased down to sit on the side of the bed. *Her family.* She wondered what the Westmorelands would think if they knew the truth about her and Aidan. About the affair the two of them had carried on right under their noses for three years.

As she stood to shower and get dressed for tonight's festivities, she couldn't help remembering what that affair had been like after they'd confessed their love for each other. Aidan had understood and agreed that it was to be their secret. No one else was supposed to know—unless the two of them thought it was absolutely necessary.

The first year had been wonderful, in spite of how hard it had been to engage in a long-distance love affair. Even with Aidan's busy schedule juggling dual residencies, he'd managed to fly to Laramie whenever he had a free weekend. And because their time together was scarce, he'd make it special. They would go out to dinner, see a movie, or if it was a weekend she needed to study, they would do that, too. There was no way she would have passed the MCAT the first time around without his help. She had applied to various medical schools and when she was notified of her acceptance into the one she wanted in New Orleans, Aidan had been the first person with whom she'd shared her good news. They had celebrated the next time he'd come to Laramie.

It was during that first year that they agreed to bring Ivy in on their secret. Otherwise, her roommate would have been worried when Jillian went missing because she was staying with Aidan at the hotel.

Jillian had fallen more and more in love with Aidan during that time. Although she'd had a lot to keep her busy, she missed him when they were apart. But he'd made up for it when he came to town. And even though they'd spent a lot of time in bed making love, their relationship wasn't just about sex. However, she would have to say that the sex was off the chain, and the sexual tension between them was still so thick you could cut it with a knife. Ivy could attest to that and had teased Jillian about it all the time.

It was also during that first year that their control had been tested whenever they went home for holidays, weddings or baby christenings. She would be the first to admit she had felt jealous more than a few times when Aidan's single male cousins, who assumed he was still a player on the prowl, would try setting him up with other women.

Everything had gone well between them as they moved into their second year together. Aidan had helped her relocate to New Orleans after she bid a teary goodbye to Ivy. Jillian leased a one-bedroom efficiency apartment not far from the hospital where she would be working. It was perfect for her needs, but lonely.

It was during the third year that it became harder for Aidan to get away. The hospitals demanded more of his time. And her telephone conversations with him had been reduced from nightly to three times a week. She could tell he was frustrated with the situation. More than once he'd commented that he wished she would have applied to a medical school closer to Maine or North Carolina.

Jillian tried to ignore his attitude but found that difficult to do. Although Aidan didn't say so, deep down she knew the secrecy surrounding their affair was getting to him. It had begun to get to her, as well. And when it seemed Aidan was becoming distant, she knew she had to do something.

When Ivy came to visit Jillian in New Orleans one weekend, she talked to her best friend about the situation. Even now Jillian could remember that time as if it was yesterday…

"So, how is Aidan?" Ivy asked, after placing her order with their waitress.

Jillian had to fight back tears. "Not sure. We haven't talked in a few days and the last time we did, we had an argument."

Ivy raised a brow. "Another one?"

"Yes." She'd told Ivy about their last argument. He'd wanted her to fly to Maine for the weekend for his birthday. She had been excited about doing so until she'd checked her calendar and discovered that was the same weekend of her clinicals. Something she could not miss. Instead of understanding, he'd gotten upset with her and because of his lack of understanding, she'd gotten upset with him. Their most recent argument had started because he told her his twin now knew about them. He'd gotten angry when she'd accused him of breaking his promise and telling Adrian. He'd explained that he didn't have to tell his brother anything. He and his twin could detect each other's moods and feelings sometimes.

"I'm tired of arguing with him, Ivy, and a part of me knows the reason our relationship is getting so strained."

Ivy nodded. "Long-distance romances are hard to maintain, Jillian, and I'm sure the secrecy surrounding your affair isn't helping."

"Yes, I know, which is why I've made a few decisions."

Ivy lifted a brow. "About what?"

Jillian drew in a deep breath. "I've decided to tell Pam about us. The secrecy has gone on long enough. I believe my sister will accept the fact that I'm now an adult and old enough to decide what I want to do in my life and the person I want in it."

"Good for you."

"Thanks. I know she's been concerned about Aidan's womanizing reputation, but once she realizes that I love him and he loves me, I believe she will give us her blessing."

Jillian took a sip of her drink and continued, "But before I tell Pam, I'm flying to Maine to see Aidan. Next weekend is his birthday and I've decided to be there to help him celebrate."

"What about your clinicals?"

Jillian smiled. "I went to my professor and told her I desperately needed that weekend off. She agreed to work with me and arrange for me to do a makeup the following weekend."

"That was nice of her."

"Yes, it was. She said I was a good student, the first to volunteer for projects and my overall attendance is great. So now I'm set to go."

Ivy grinned. "Did you tell Aidan?"

"No. I'm going to surprise him. He mentioned that since I wouldn't be there to celebrate with him that he would sign up to work that day and then hang around his place, watch TV and go to bed early."

"On his birthday? That's a bummer."

"Yes, and that's why I plan to fly there to help him celebrate."

"You're doing the right thing by being there. I think it's wonderful that you're finally letting your sister know about you and Aidan. When she sees how much he adores you she will be happy for the two of you."

A huge smile touched Jillian's lips. "I believe so, too."

JILLIAN STEPPED OUT on the balcony to look at the ocean as she recalled what happened after that. She had been excited when she'd boarded the plane for Portland, Maine. She couldn't wait to tell Aidan of her decision to end the secrecy surrounding their affair and to celebrate his birthday with him.

Due to stormy weather in Atlanta, her connecting flight had been delayed five solid hours and she didn't arrive in Portland until six that evening. It had been another hour before she'd arrived at his apartment complex, anxious to use the door key he'd given her a year ago for the first time.

The moment she'd stepped off the elevator onto his floor she knew a party was going on in one of the apartments. Loud music blasted and boisterous voices made her ears ache. She hadn't known all the noise was coming from Aidan's apartment until she'd reached the door, which she didn't have to unlock since it was slightly ajar.

Jillian walked in and looked around. The place was crowded and there were more women in attendance than men. The women were wearing outfits that probably wouldn't be allowed out on the streets.

Jillian wondered what had happened to Aidan's decision to come home from work, watch TV and go to bed.

It seemed he'd decided to throw a party instead and it was in full swing. In the center of the room Aidan sat in a recliner while some scantily dressed woman gave him a lap dance. And from the look on his face, he was enjoying every single minute of it. Some of the guys on the sidelines, who she figured must be Aidan's friends, were egging on both him and the woman, which prompted the woman to make the dance even more erotic.

When the woman began stripping off her clothes, starting with the barely-there strap of material covering her breasts, Jillian was shocked. She knew she'd seen enough when the woman's breasts all but smothered Aidan's face while she wiggled out of her panties.

Not able to watch any longer, a shaken Jillian had left, grateful Aidan hadn't even noticed her presence. What hurt more than anything was that he'd appeared to be enjoying every single minute of the dance. Aidan Westmoreland had seemed in his element. She couldn't help wondering if they had stopped with the dance or if he and the woman had ended up doing other things later.

When he'd called her a few days later he hadn't mentioned anything about the party at his apartment and she hadn't said anything about being there to witness what had gone on. And when she asked how he'd spent his birthday, he angered her even more when he gave her a smart aleck answer, asking, "Why do you care when you didn't care enough to spend it with me?"

He was wrong. She had cared enough. But he hadn't cared enough to tell her the truth. It was then that she'd made the decision to end things between them, since it was apparent that he missed his life as a womanizer. When he called later in the week and made another excuse for not flying to New Orleans to see her as he'd planned, she decided that would be a good time to break things off with him. She would give him his freedom, let him go back to the life he missed.

Deciding the less drama the better, she told him the secrecy of their affair was weighing her down, making her lose focus, and she couldn't handle it any longer. She didn't tell him the true reason she'd wanted to end things.

Her declaration led to a huge argument between them. When he told her he was flying to New Orleans to talk to her, she told him she didn't want to see him. Then she ended the conversation.

He had called several times to talk to her but she'd refused to answer and eventually blocked his number. She knew that was the reason for the angry looks he'd given her when she'd attended the last couple of Westmoreland weddings. The last time she'd seen him was a few months ago at Stern's ceremony.

There had been no reason to tell Pam about the affair that had been a secret for so long, so she hadn't. The last thing Jillian needed was for her sister to remind her that just like a tiger couldn't change its stripes neither could a womanizer change his ways.

It had been a year since their breakup. At times she felt she had moved on, but other times she felt she had not. It was so disappointing and painful to think about the future they could have been planning together now that she'd finished medical school, if only things had worked out the way she'd hoped they would.

Jillian wiped the tears from her eyes, refusing to shed any more for Aidan. She was on this cruise to have fun and enjoy herself, and she intended to do just that.

"YES, ADRIAN?"

"I'm glad I was able to reach you before ship left port. I just want to wish you the best. I hope everything works out the way you want with Jill."

Aidan hoped things worked out the way he wanted, as well. "Thanks."

Like Paige, Adrian and Aidan's cousin Stern had figured out something was going on between him and Jillian a couple of years ago. "I will do whatever I have to do to get her back. When this ship returns to port, my goal is to have convinced Jillian to give me another chance."

"Well, Trinity and I are cheering for you."

"Thanks, bro." Trinity was Adrian's fiancée and the two would be getting married in a couple of months.

After ending his phone call with Adrian, Aidan crossed the suite to step out on the balcony. Barcelona was beautiful. He had arrived three days ago and taken a tour of what was considered one of the busiest ports in the Mediterranean. He had eaten at the finest restaurants, some in magnificent buildings etched deep with history. He had walked through the crowded streets wishing Jillian had been by his side. Hopefully when they returned to this port in fourteen days she would be.

He could just imagine what Jillian had assumed when she'd seen that woman giving him a lap dance last year. He had worked that day, as he'd told her he would, but he hadn't known about the surprise birthday party a few of his fraternity brothers had thrown for him.

And he definitely hadn't known about the lap dancer or the other strippers they'd invited until the women arrived. He couldn't get mad at his frat brothers for wanting to make his birthday kind of wild. All they knew was that for the past few years, the man who'd once been one of the biggest womanizers in Boston had taken a sabbatical from women. They'd had no idea that the reason for his seemingly boring lifestyle was because he was involved in a secret affair with Jillian.

So, thinking he'd been working too hard for too long and hadn't gotten in any play time, they thought they were doing him a favor. He would admit that after a few drinks he'd loosened up. But at no time had he forgotten he was in love with Jillian. The lap dance had been just for fun, and after the party all the women had left.

Yes, he'd made a mistake by not mentioning the party to Jillian. And he would be the first to admit his attitude had been less than desirable for the last year of their relationship. But he knew why. He'd had the best of intentions when he thought he could keep their secret without any problems, but as time went on, he'd become impatient. While she hadn't wanted anyone to know about them, he had wanted to shout the truth from the highest mountain.

It hadn't helped matters when some of his siblings and cousins began falling in love and getting married. It seemed as if an epidemic had hit Westmoreland Country when five of his relatives got married in a two-year period. And some had been relatives he'd thought would never marry. It had been hard being around his happily married kinfolk without wanting to have some of that happiness for himself. He would admit he'd spent too many months angry with himself, with Jillian, with the world. But at no time did he doubt his love for her.

Nothing had changed his feelings. He was still in love with her, which was why he was here. To right a wrong and convince her that she was the only woman he wanted.

He knew he had his work cut out for him. But he intended to stay the course and not fail in his task. She wouldn't appreciate seeing him and she probably wouldn't like it when she found out about Paige's involvement. Or Ivy's for that matter. If Ivy hadn't told Paige the truth, he would still be angry, thinking the reason Jillian had broken up with him was because they were at odds regarding the secret of their affair.

He went back inside when he heard the cabin phone ring. He picked it up. "Yes?"

"I hope you find your quarters satisfactory."

Aidan smiled. That was an understatement. "It's more than satisfactory, Dominic."

This ship was just one of many in a fleet owned by Dominic Saxon. Dominic was married to the former Taylor Steele, whose sister Cheyenne was married to Aidan's cousin, Quade Westmoreland. Once Aidan discovered Jillian had booked her cruise on one of Dominic's ships, his friend had been all too eager to assist Aidan in getting back the woman he loved. Years ago Dominic had found himself in a similar situation.

"Taylor sends her love and we're all rooting for you. I know how misunderstandings can threaten even the most solid relationships, and I think you're doing the right thing by going after her," Dominic said. "I'm going to give you the same advice a very smart woman—my mother—gave me when I was going through my troubles with Taylor. *Let love guide you to do the right thing.* I hope the two of you enjoy the cruise."

"Thanks for the advice, and as for enjoying the cruise, I intend to make sure that we do."

After ending his call with Dominic, Aidan glanced around the cabin. Thanks to Dominic, Aidan had been given the owner's suite. It was spacious with a double balcony. There were also separate sleeping quarters with a king-size bed and a seventy-inch flat-screen television and a second wall-to-wall balcony. The sitting area contained a sofa that could convert into a double bed, another wall television and a dining area that overlooked yet another balcony. Other amenities he appreciated were the refrigerator, wet bar and huge walk-in closet. The bathroom was bigger than the one he had in his apartment, with both a Jacuzzi tub and a walk-in shower. He could just imagine him and Jillian using that shower together.

He walked back out on the balcony to see that people had gathered on the docks to watch the ship sail, waving flags that represented all the countries they would visit on the cruise. He expected Jillian to attend the welcome party tonight and so would he. Aidan couldn't wait to see Jillian's face when she discovered he was on board with her and would be for the next fourteen days.

He headed for the bathroom to shower.

Tonight couldn't get here fast enough.

"WELCOME, SEÑORITA, MAY we assist with your mask?"

Jillian lifted a brow. "Mask?"

The tall crewman dressed in a crisp white uniform smiled down at her. "*Si*. Tonight's theme is a Spanish masquerade ball," he said, offering a red feathered mask to her.

She took it and slid it across her face. It was a perfect fit. "Thanks."

"Your name?" he asked.

"Jillian Novak."

"Señorita Novak, dinner will be served in a half hour in the Madrid Room; someone will come escort you to your table."

"Thanks."

She entered the huge lounge that had beautiful rosettes hanging from the ceiling and several masquerade props in the corners of the room for picture taking. Flamenco dancers encouraged participation in the middle of the floor and several men dressed as dashing bullfighters walked around as servers. When a woman wearing a gorgeous *quinceañera* gown offered her a beautiful lace fan, Jillian smiled and took it.

"Would the señorita like a glass of rioja?"

"Yes, thanks," she responded to one of the servers.

Jillian took a sip and immediately liked the taste. It wasn't too tart or tangy but was an excellent blend of fruits. As she sipped her wine she looked around the room. It was crowded and most of the individuals were coupled off. Immediately, she felt like a loner crashing a party, but forced the feeling away. So what if there were a lot of couples and she had no one? She'd known it would be like this but had made the decision to come anyway.

"Excuse me, señorita, but someone asked me to give you this," the woman wearing the *quinceañera* gown said, while handing her a single red rose.

"Who?" Jillian asked, curiously glancing around.

The woman smiled. "A *very* handsome man." And then she walked off.

Jillian felt uneasy. What kind of *very* handsome man would come cruising alone? She'd seen a movie once where a serial killer had come on a cruise ship and stalked single women. No one had known just how many women he'd killed and thrown overboard until the end of the cruise. For crying out loud, why was she remembering that particular movie now?

She drew in a deep breath knowing she was letting her imagination get the best of her. The man was probably someone who'd seen her alone and wanted to state his interest by giving her a rose. Romantic but a total waste of his time. Even the woman's claim that he was *very* handsome did nothing for Jillian since she wasn't ready to get involved with anyone. Even after a full year, she compared every man to Aidan. That was the main reason she hadn't dated anyone since him. On the other hand, she would bet any amount of money Aidan was dating someone and probably hadn't wasted any time doing so.

She drew in a deep breath, refusing to let her mind go there. Why should she care in the least what Aidan was doing or who he was doing it with? Deciding not to think of an answer for that one, she glanced around the room, curiosity getting the best of her. She tried to find any single men but all she saw were the bullfighters serving drinks.

Jillian glanced at her watch. She'd deliberately arrived a little late so she wouldn't have long to wait for dinner. She'd grabbed breakfast on the run to catch her plane and because she'd come straight from the Barcelona airport to the ship, she had missed lunch altogether.

After taking another sip of her wine, she was about to check her watch again when suddenly her skin heated. Was that desire floating in her stomach? Why? And for who? This was definitely odd.

Jillian searched the room in earnest as a quiver

inched up her spine. Declining a server's offer of another drink, she nearly dismissed what was happening as a figment of her imagination when she saw him. A man wearing a teal feathered mask stood alone on the other side of the room, watching her. So she watched back, letting her gaze roam over him. Was he the one who'd given her the rose? Who was he? Why was she reacting to him this way?

As she studied him she found him oddly familiar. Was she comparing the man to Aidan to the point where everything about him reminded her of her ex? His height? His build? The low cut of his hair?

She shook her head. She was losing it. She needed another drink after all. That's when the man began walking toward her. She wasn't going crazy. She didn't know the when, how or why of it, but there was no doubt in her mind that the man walking toward her—mask or no mask—was Aidan. No other man had a walk like he did. And those broad shoulders...

He was sex appeal on legs and he walked the part. It was a stroll of self-confidence and sinful eroticism. How could he have this effect on her after a full year? She drew in a deep breath. That's not the question she should be asking. What she wanted to know was why he was on the same cruise with her. She refused to believe it was a coincidence.

Her spine stiffened when he came to a stop in front of her. Her nostrils had picked up his scent from five feet away and now her entire body was responding. Sharp, crackling energy stirred to life between them. And from the look in his eyes he felt it, as well. Hot. Raw. Primal.

She didn't want it. Nor did she need that sort of sexual attraction to him again. She blew out a frustrated breath. "Aidan, what are you doing here?"

AIDAN WASN'T SURPRISED that she had recognized him with the mask on. After all, they'd shared a bed for three solid years so she should know him inside out, clothes or not…just like he knew her. Case in point, he knew exactly what she was wearing beneath that clingy black dress. As little as possible, which meant only a bra and thong. And more than likely both were made of lace. She had the figure to handle just about anything she put on—or nothing at all. Frankly, he preferred nothing at all.

"I asked you what you're doing here."

He noted her voice had tightened in anger and he figured it best to answer. "I've always wanted to take a Mediterranean cruise."

She rolled her eyes. "And you want me to believe you being here is a coincidence? That you had no idea I was here on this cruise ship?"

"That's not what I'm saying."

"Then what *are* you saying, Aidan?"

He placed his half-empty wineglass on the tray of a passing waiter, just in case Jillian was tempted to douse him with it. "I'll tell you after dinner."

"After dinner? No, you will tell me *now*."

Her voice had risen and several people glanced over at them. "I think we need to step outside to finish our discussion."

She frowned. "I think not. You can tell me what I want to know right here."

In anger, she walked into the scant space separating them and leaned in close, her lips almost brushing his. That was too close. His bottom lip tingled and his heart beat like crazy when he remembered her taste. A taste he'd become addicted to. A taste he'd gone a year without.

"I wouldn't bring my mouth any closer if I were you," he warned in a rough whisper.

She blinked as if realizing how close they were. Heeding his warning, she quickly took a step back. "I still want answers, Aidan. What are you doing here?"

He decided to be totally honest with her. Give her the naked truth and let her deal with it. "I came on this cruise, Jillian, with the full intention of winning you back."

CHAPTER ELEVEN

JILLIAN STARED AT Aidan as his words sank in. That's when she decided it would be best for them to take this discussion to a more private area after all. She removed her mask. "I think we need to step outside the room, Aidan."

When they stepped into a vacant hallway, she turned to him. "How dare you assume all you had to do was follow me on this cruise to win me back?"

He pulled off his mask and she fought back a jolt of desire when she looked into his face. How could any man get more handsome in a year's time? Yes, she'd seen him a couple of times since their break-up, but she had avoided getting this close to him. He appeared to have gotten an inch or so taller, his frame was even more muscular and his looks were twice as gorgeous.

"I have given it some thought," he said, leaning back against a railing.

"Evidently, not enough," she countered, not liking how her gaze, with a mind of its own, was traveling over him. He was wearing a dark suit, and he looked like a male model getting ready for a photo shoot—immaculate with nothing out of place.

"Evidently, you've forgotten one major thing about me," she said.

"What? Just how stubborn you are?" he asked, smiling, as if trying to make light of her anger, which irritated her even more.

"That, too, but also that once I make up my mind about something, that's it. And I made up my mind that my life can sail a lot more calmly without you." She watched his expression to see if her words had any effect, but she couldn't tell if they had.

He studied her in silence before saying, "Sorry you feel that way, Jillian. But I intend to prove you wrong."

She lifted a brow. "Excuse me?"

"Over the next fourteen days I intend to prove that your life can't sail more calmly without me. In fact, I intend to show you that you don't even like calm. You need turbulence, furor and even a little mayhem."

She shook her head. "If you believe that then you truly don't know me at all."

"I know you. I also know the real reason you broke things off with me. Why didn't you tell me what you *thought* you saw in my apartment the night of my birthday party?"

She wondered how he'd found out about that. It really didn't matter at this point. "It's not what I *thought* I saw, Aidan. It's what I saw. A woman giving you a lap dance, which you seemed to enjoy, before she began stripping off her clothes." Saying it made the memory flash in her mind and roused her anger that much more.

"She was a paid entertainer, Jillian. All the ladies there that night were. Several of my frat brothers thought I'd been living a boring and dull life and decided to add some excitement into it. I admit they might have gone a little overboard."

"And you enjoyed every minute of it."

He shrugged. "I had a few drinks and—"

"You don't know what all you did, do you?"

He frowned. "I remember fine. Other than the lap dance and her strip act…and a couple other women stripping…nothing else happened."

"Wasn't that enough?" she asked, irritated that he thought several naked women on display in his apartment were of little significance. "And why didn't you tell me about the party? You led me to believe you'd done just as you said you were going to do—watch TV and go to bed."

He released a deep breath. "Okay, I admit I should have told you and I was wrong for not doing so. But I was angry with you. It was my birthday and I wanted to spend it with you. I felt you could have sacrificed a little that weekend to be with me. I hadn't known you changed your mind and flew to Portland."

He paused a moment and then continued, "I realized after we'd broken up just how unpleasant my attitude had been and I do apologize for that. I was getting frustrated with the secrecy surrounding our affair, with my work and how little time I could get off to fly to New Orleans to spend with you."

As far as Jillian was concerned, his attitude had been more than unpleasant; it had become downright unacceptable. He wasn't the only one who'd been frustrated with their situation. She had, too, which was the reason she had decided to confess all to Pam.

"Now that you're finished with medical school, there's no reason to keep our secret any longer anyway," he said, interrupting her thoughts.

She frowned. "And I see no reason to reveal it. Ever," she said. "Especially in light of one very important fact."

"And what fact is that?"

"The fact that we aren't together and we won't ever be together again."

IF SHE FIGURED that then she was wrong.

They *would* be together again. He was counting on it. It was the reason he'd come on the cruise. The one thing she had not said was that she no longer loved him. And as long as she had feelings for him then he could accomplish anything. At this point, even if she claimed she didn't love him, he would have to prove her wrong because he believed she loved him just as much as he loved her. Their relationship was just going through a few hiccups, which he felt they could resolve.

"If you truly believe that then you have nothing to worry about," he said.

She frowned. "Meaning what?"

"Meaning my presence on this ship shouldn't bother you."

She lifted her chin. "It won't unless you become a nuisance."

A smile spread across his face. "Nuisance? I think not. But I do intend to win you back, like I said. Then we can move on with our lives. I see marriage and babies in our future."

She laughed. "You've got to be kidding. Didn't you hear what I said? We won't be getting back together, so we don't have a future."

"And you're willing to throw away the last three years?"

"What I've done is make it easy for you."

He lifted a brow. "To do what?"

"Go back to your womanizing ways. You seemed to

be enjoying yourself so much at your birthday party I wouldn't think of denying you the opportunity."

He crossed his arms over his chest. "I gave up my so-called womanizing ways when I fell in love with you."

"Could have fooled me with your lap dancer and all those strippers waiting their turn."

"Like I said, I didn't invite them."

"But you could have asked them to leave."

He shrugged. "Yes, I could have. But you're going to have to learn to trust me, Jillian. I can see where my attitude leading up to that night might have been less than desirable, but at no time have I betrayed you with another woman. Do you intend to punish me forever for one night of a little fun?"

"I'm not punishing you, Aidan. I'm not doing anything to you. I didn't invite you on this cruise. You took it upon yourself to…"

Her words trailed off and she gazed at him suspiciously before saying, "Paige and I were supposed to go on this cruise together and she had to back out when she had a conflict, which is why I came alone. Please tell me you had nothing to do with that."

He'd known she would eventually figure things out but he had hoped it wouldn't be this soon. "Okay, I won't tell you."

She was back in his face again. "You told Paige about us? Now she knows I was duped by a womanizer."

Her lips were mere inches from his again. Evidently, she'd forgotten his earlier warning. "I am not a womanizer, and I didn't tell her anything about us. She figured things out on her own. Ivy told Paige about the lap dance and Paige told me. And I appreciate her doing so."

From Jill's expression he could tell that although he

might appreciate it, she didn't. "I am so upset with you right now, Aidan. You are—"

Suddenly he pulled her into his arms. "You were warned."

Then he captured her mouth with his.

PUSH HIM AWAY. *Push him away. Push him away,* a voice inside of Jillian's head chanted.

But her body would not obey. Instead of pushing him away, she leaned in closer, wrapping her arms around his neck.

Had it been a year since she had enjoyed this? A year since she'd had the taste of his tongue inside her mouth? Doing all those crazy things in every nook and cranny? Making liquid heat she'd held at bay shoot straight to the area between her legs?

How could any woman deal with a master kisser like him? She would admit that during the past year she had gone to bed dreaming of this but the real thing surpassed any dream she'd ever had.

The sound of voices made them pull apart. She drew in a deep breath, turning her back to him so she could lick her lips without him seeing her do so. That had been one hell of a kiss. Her lips were still electrified.

She turned back around and caught him tracing his tongue across his own lips. Her stomach clenched. "I think you have it all wrong, Aidan," she managed to say.

"After that kiss, I'd say I got it all right."

"Think whatever you like," she said, walking away.

"Hey, where're you going? The Madrid Room is this way."

She stopped and turned. "I'll order room service."

Jillian continued walking, feeling the heat of his gaze on her back.

AIDAN WATCHED HER walk away, appreciating the sway of her hips. He drew in a deep breath. He loved the woman. If there was any doubt in her mind of that—which there seemed to be—he would wipe it out.

Turning, he headed toward his own cabin, thinking room service sounded pretty good. Besides, he had shocked Jillian's senses enough for today. Tomorrow he planned to lay it on even thicker. She had warned him not to be a nuisance. He smiled at the thought. He wouldn't be a nuisance, just totally effective.

Tonight they had talked, although he seemed to annoy her and he'd found her somewhat infuriating. But at least they knew where they both stood. She knew he was aware of the real reason she'd ended things between them. He had to convince her that his life as a womanizer was definitely behind him, that he had no desire to return to that life again.

He would admit getting rid of the lap dancer that night hadn't been easy. Somehow she'd figured it would be okay to hang around after the party was over. She'd been quick to let him know there wouldn't be an overtime charge. He had countered, letting her know he wasn't interested.

When Aidan reached his suite, he saw the elephant made of hand towels on his bed. Cute. But not as cute as the woman he intended to have back in his arms.

JILLIAN CHECKED THE time as she made a call to Paige. It was around ten in the morning in L.A., so there was no reason her sister shouldn't answer the phone. Paige was definitely going to get an earful from her.

"Why are you calling me? Aren't rates higher on the high seas?" Paige asked, answering on the fourth ring.

Jillian frowned. "Don't worry about the cost of the rates. Why didn't you tell me you knew about me and Aidan?"

"Why hadn't you told *me* so I wouldn't have to tell you? And don't say because it was supposed to be a secret."

"Well, it was. How did you figure it out?"

"Wasn't hard to do. Both of you started getting sloppy with it. Aidan slipped and called you Jilly a couple of times, and I caught you almost drooling whenever he walked into the room."

"I did not."

"You did, too. Besides, I knew you had a crush on him that first time we met the Westmoreland family at Pam's engagement party. You kept me up all night asking, 'Isn't Aidan cute, Paige? Isn't he cute?'"

Jillian smiled as she remembered. She had been so taken with Aidan. Although he and Adrian were identical twins it had been Aidan who pushed her buttons. "Well, no thanks to you he's here and he wants me back."

"Do you want him to get you back?"

"No. You didn't see that lap dance. I did."

"Didn't have to see it because I've seen one before. I know they can get rather raunchy. But it was a birthday party. His. Thrown by his friends and the lap dancer and the strippers were entertainment."

"Some entertainment," she mumbled. "He enjoyed

it. You should have seen the look on his face when the woman shoved her girls at him."

"Please. He's a man. They enjoy seeing a pair of breasts. Anytime or anyplace. Will it make you feel better if I get the Chippendales dancers for your next birthday party?"

"This isn't funny, Paige."

"You don't hear me laughing. If anything, you should hear me moaning. Can you imagine a lap dance from one of those guys? If you can't, I can. And my imagination is running pretty wild right now."

Jillian shook her head. "Before I let you go, there's one more thing. Did you really get a part in a Spielberg movie?"

"No."

"So you lied."

"I was acting, and I evidently did a great job. It sounds like you have some serious decisions to make about Aidan. But don't rush. You have fourteen days. In the meantime, enjoy the cruise. Enjoy life. Enjoy Aidan. He plans on getting you back. I'd like to be there to watch him try. I've got my money on him, by the way."

"Sounds like you have money to lose. Goodbye, Paige." Jillian clicked off the phone, refusing to let her sister get in the last word, especially if it would be a word she really didn't want to hear.

Regardless of what Paige said, her sister hadn't been there to witness that lap dance. She hadn't seen that salacious grin on Aidan's face while looking up at the half-naked woman sprawled all over him. There was no doubt in Jillian's mind that he'd enjoyed every minute of it. He had wanted those women there; otherwise, he would have asked them and his friends to leave. And although he claimed otherwise, how could she be certain one of those women didn't spend the night with him; especially since he didn't tell Jillian anything about the party, even when she had asked? She of all people knew what a healthy sexual appetite Aidan had, and they hadn't seen each other in more than three months. And at the time, that had been the longest amount of time they'd been apart.

Before getting in bed later that night, Jillian checked the ship's agenda. Tomorrow was a full day at sea and she refused to stay locked in her cabin. This was a big ship and chances were she might not run into Aidan. She knew the odds of that were slim; especially when he admitted his only reason for coming on the cruise was to win her back. Well, he could certainly try.

She could not deny it had felt good to be kissed by him tonight. Pretty damn good. But there was more to any relationship than kisses. Even the hot, raw, carnal kind that Aidan gave. And when he took a mind to kiss her all over...

She drew in a deep breath, refusing to let her thoughts go there. He would probably try using his sexual wiles to win her back. And she intended to be ready to disappoint him.

CHAPTER TWELVE

"Good morning, Jillian."

Jillian glanced up from the book she was reading to watch Aidan slide onto the lounger beside her. She was on the upper deck near the pool. Why had she thought he would never find her here?

"Good morning," she grumbled and went back to her reading. Although she had gone to bed fairly early, she hadn't gotten a good night's sleep. The man stretched on the lounger beside her had invaded her dreams not once or twice, but all through the night.

"Had breakfast yet?"

She glanced away from her book to look over at him. "Yes." She remembered the pancakes and syrup she'd enjoyed. "It was tasty."

"Um, bet it wasn't tasty as you. Want to go back to my cabin and be my breakfast?"

His question caused a spark of heat to settle between her thighs. Something she definitely didn't need after all those erotic dreams she'd had. "You shouldn't say something like that to me."

"You prefer I say it to someone else?"

She narrowed her gaze. "Do whatever you want. At breakfast I happened to notice a group of women on the cruise. All appeared single. I think I overheard one say they're part of some book club."

"You want me to go check out other women?"

"Won't matter to me. Need I remind you that we aren't together?"

"And need I remind you that I'm working on that? And by the way, I have a proposition for you."

"Whatever it is, the answer is no."

He chuckled. "You haven't heard it."

"Doesn't matter."

"You certain?"

"Positive."

He smiled over at her. "Okay then. I'm glad. In fact, you've made my day by not accepting it. I'm happy that you turned it down."

She stared over at him and frowned. "Really? And just what was this proposition?"

In a warm, teasing tone, he said. "I thought you didn't want to hear it."

"I've changed my mind."

He nodded. "I guess I can allow you to do that." He shifted and sat up. She tried not to notice the khaki shorts he wore and how well they fit the lower half of his body. Or how his muscle shirt covered perfect abs.

He took her hand, easing her into the same sitting position he was in, as if what he had to say was something he didn't want others around them to overhear.

"Well?" she asked, trying to ignore the tingling sensation in the hand he touched.

"You're aware the only reason I came on this cruise was to get you back, right?"

She shrugged. "So you say."

A smile touched the corners of his lips. "Well, I thought about a few of the things you said last night and I wanted to offer you a chance to make some decisions."

She lifted a brow. "Like what?"

"Like whether or not I should even pursue you at all. I don't want to be that nuisance you insinuated I could be. So my proposition was that I just leave you alone and wait patiently for you to come to me. I hope you know what that means since you just turned it down."

She would not have turned it down had she heard him out, and he knew it. Unfortunately, she could guess what the consequences would be and she had a feeling she wasn't going to like it. "What does that mean, Aidan?"

He leaned in closer to whisper in her ear. His warm breath felt like a soft, sensuous lick across her skin. "I want you so bad, Jillian, that I ache. And that means I'm not giving up until you're back in my bed."

She immediately felt a pounding pulse at the tips of her breasts. She leaned back to stare at him and the razor-sharp sensuality openly displayed in his gaze almost made her moan.

"And before you ask, Jillian, the answer is no. It isn't just about sex with me," he murmured in a low, husky tone. "It's about me wanting the woman I love both mentally and physically. You're constantly in my mind but physically, it's been over a year."

She drew in a deep breath and felt the essence of what he'd said in every single nerve ending in her body. It had been over a year. With Aidan she'd had a pretty active sex life, and although there were periods of time when they were apart, they always made up for any time lost whenever they were together.

"Your needing sex is not my problem," she finally said.

"Isn't it?" he countered. "Can you look me in the eyes and say that you don't want me as much as I want you? That you didn't dream about us making love last night? Me being inside you. You riding me? Hard. My tongue inside your mouth…and inside a lot of other places on your body?"

She silently stared at him but her entire body flared in response to the vivid pictures he'd painted in her mind. Unlike Paige, Jillian wasn't an actress and couldn't lie worth a damn. But on that same note she would never admit anything to him. That would give him too much power. "I won't admit to anything, Aidan."

"You don't have to," he said, with a serious smile on his face. "And it's not about me needing sex but me needing you." He paused a moment as if giving his words time to sink in. "But this leads to another proposition I'd like to make."

She'd set herself up for this one. "And what is the proposition this time?"

He leaned in closer. "That for the remainder of the cruise you let your guard down. Believe in me. Believe in yourself. And believe in us. I want you to see I'm still the man who loves you. The man who will always love you. But that's something you have to believe, Jillian. However, at the end of the cruise, if for whatever reason, you still don't believe it or feel that the two of us can make a lifetime commitment, then when we dock back in Barcelona, we'll agree to go our separate ways."

She broke eye contact with him to glance out at the ocean. Today was a rather calm day outside but inside she was in a state of turmoil. He was asking a lot of her and he knew it. His proposition meant forgetting the very reason she broke up with him. That would definitely be easy on him if she did. Was that why he'd come up with this latest proposition?

Jillian turned her gaze back to him. "You want me to just forget everything that's happened, Aidan? Especially the incident that caused our breakup?"

"No, I don't want you to forget a single thing."

His answer surprised her. "Why?"

"Because it's important that the two of us learn from any mistakes we've made, and we can't do that if we safely tuck them away just because doing so will be convenient. We should talk about them openly and honestly. Hopefully, we'll be able to build something positive out of the discussions. You're always harping a lot on the things I did. What about you, Jillian? Do you think you were completely blameless?"

"No, but—"

"I don't want to get into all that now, but have you ever noticed that with you there's always a *but* in there somewhere?"

She frowned at him. "No, I never noticed but obviously you have." Was it really that way with her? As far as sharing the blame, she could do that. But she hadn't been the one getting a lap dance.

"My proposition is still on the table," he said. "I've been completely honest with you on this cruise, Jillian. I've been up-front with my intentions, my wants and my desires."

Yes, he had. Every opportunity he got. And she knew that he would have her on her back in a flash if she were to let him. Jillian inclined her head to look deeper into his eyes. "And you promise that at the end of the cruise if things don't work out the way we think they should that you will go your way and I'll go mine?"

He nodded slowly. "It would be difficult, but yes. I want you to be happy and if being happy for you means not having me in your life then that's the way it will be. It will be your decision and I would like to have that decision the night before we return to Barcelona."

She digested what Aidan said. He'd laid things out, with no fluff. She knew what, and who, she would be dealing with. But she also knew that even if she decided she didn't want him in her life romantically, he could never be fully out of it; their families were connected. How could they manage that?

"What about the family?" she asked. "Paige, Stern and Adrian know our secret. If things don't work out between us it might have an effect on them."

"We will deal with that if it happens. Together. Even if we're no longer lovers, there's no reason we can't remain friends. Besides, are you sure there aren't others in the family besides those three who know? It's my guess others might suspect something even if they haven't said anything."

She shrugged. "Doesn't matter who knows now. I had planned on telling Pam anyway."

Surprise flashed in his eyes. "You had?"

"Yes."

"When?"

"After I talked to you about it, which I had planned to do when I flew into Portland for your birthday."

"Oh."

She released a sigh. Evidently the one thing he hadn't found out was that she'd intended to release him from their secret. "Afterward, when things didn't work out between us, I saw no need for me to tell Pam anything. In fact, I felt the less she knew about the situation, the better."

Aidan didn't say anything for a moment and neither did Jillian. She figured he was thinking how that one weekend had changed things for them. He finally broke the silence by asking, "So, what's your answer to my proposition?"

Jillian nibbled at her bottom lip. Why couldn't she just turn him down, walk away and keep walking? She knew one of the reasons was that her mind was filled with fond memories of the good times they'd shared. It hadn't been all bad.

Would it be so dreadful if she were to give his proposition a try? What did she have to lose? She'd already experienced heartbreak with him. And a year of separation hadn't been easy. Besides, she couldn't deny that it would feel good to be with him out in the open, without any kind of secrecy shrouding them. Whenever he'd come to Laramie, she'd always been on guard, looking over her shoulder in case she ran into someone who knew Pam. And he did have a good point about the remaining days on the cruise testing the strength of a relationship between them.

She met his gaze. "Yes. I accept your proposition and I will hold you to your word, Aidan."

LATER THAT NIGHT, as Aidan changed for dinner, he couldn't help remembering Jillian's words.

"Fine, baby, hold me to my word," he murmured to himself as he tucked his white dress shirt into his pants. "That's the way it should be. And that's the way it will be."

Today had gone just the way he'd wanted. After she'd agreed to his proposition he'd been able to talk her into going with him to the Terelle Deck so he could grab breakfast. She'd sat across from him while he ate a hefty portion of the pancakes and syrup she'd recommended. They had chosen a table with a beautiful view of the ocean, and he liked the way the cool morning breeze stirred her hair. More than once he'd been tempted to reach across the table and run his fingers through it.

After breakfast he had talked her into joining him in the Venus Lounge where a massive bingo game was under way. They had found a table in the back and she'd worked five bingo cards while he worked three. In the end, neither of them had won anything but the game had been fun.

Later they had gone to the art gallery to check out the paintings on display and after that they'd enjoyed a delicious lunch in the Coppeneria Room. After she mentioned her plans to visit the spa, he'd taken a stroll around the ship. The layout was awesome and the entire ship was gorgeous. Tomorrow morning before daybreak they would arrive in Monte Carlo, France, and from there, Florence, Italy. He'd never been to France or Italy before but Adrian had, and according to his twin both countries were beautiful. Aidan couldn't wait to see them for himself.

He smiled as he put on his cuff links. Being around Jillian today had reminded him of how much she liked having her way. In the past he had indulged her. But not this time. While on this cruise he had no intention of letting her have her way. In fact, he planned to teach her the art of compromising. That was the main reason he had suggested she drop by his cabin to grab him for dinner instead of the other way around. Although she hadn't said anything, he could tell she hadn't liked the idea.

He turned from the mirror at the sound of a knock

on his door. She was a little early but he had no problem with that. Moving across the suite, he opened the door, and then stood there, finding it impossible to speak. All he could do was stare at Jillian. Dressed in a red floor-length gown that hugged every curve, her hair wrapped on top of her head with a few curls dangling toward her beautiful face, she looked breathtaking. His gaze scanned the length of her—head to toe.

Pulling himself together, he stepped aside. "Come in. You look very nice."

"Thank you," she said, entering his suite. "I'm a little early. The cabin steward arrived and I didn't want to get in his way."

"No problem. I just need to put on my tie."

"This suite is fantastic. I thought my suite was large but this one is triple mine in size."

He smiled over at her. "It's the owner's personal suite whenever he cruises."

"Really? And how did you get so lucky?"

"He's a friend. You remember my cousin Quade who lives in North Carolina, right?"

"The one who has the triplets?"

"Yes, he's the one. Quade and the ship's owner, Dominic Saxon, are brothers-in-law, married to sisters—the former Steeles, Cheyenne and Taylor."

Jillian nodded. "I remember meeting Cheyenne at Dillon and Pam's wedding. The triplets were adorable. I don't recall ever meeting Taylor."

"I'll make sure you meet Taylor and Dominic if you ever come to visit me in Charlotte." He'd deliberately chosen his words to make sure she understood that if a meeting took place, it would be her decision.

After putting on his tie, he turned to her, trying not to stare again. "I'm all set. Ready?"

"Whenever you are."

He was tempted to kiss her but held back. Knowing him like she did, she would probably expect such a move. But tonight he planned to keep her on her toes. In other words, he would be full of surprises.

"HI, AIDAN!"

Jillian figured it would be one of those nights when the group of women sharing their table chorused the greeting to Aidan. It was the book-club group. She should have known they would find him. Or, for all she knew, he'd found them.

"I take it you've met them," she whispered when he pulled out her chair.

"Yes, earlier today, while taking my stroll when you were at the spa."

"Evening, ladies. How's everyone doing?" Aidan asked the group with familiarity, taking his seat.

"Fine," they responded simultaneously. Jillian noticed some were smiling so hard it made her wonder how anyone's lips could stretch that wide.

"I want you all to meet someone," Aidan was saying. "This is Jillian Novak. My significant other."

"Oh."

Was that disappointment she heard in the voices of the six women? And what happened to those huge smiles? Well, she would just have to show them how it was done. She smiled brightly and then said, "Hello, everyone." Only a few returned her greeting, but she didn't care because she was reflecting on Aidan's introduction.

My significant other.

Before their breakup they had been together for three years and this was the first time he'd introduced her to anyone because of their secret. It made her realize that, other than Ivy, she'd never introduced him to anyone, either.

The waiter came to take their order but not before giving them a run-down of all the delectable meals on the menu tonight. Jillian chose a seafood dinner and Aidan selected steak.

She discreetly checked out the six women engaging in conversation with Aidan. All beautiful. Gorgeously dressed. Articulate. Professional. Single.

"So, how long have the two of you been together?" asked one of the women who'd introduced herself earlier as Wanda.

Since it appeared the woman had directed the question to Aidan, Jillian let him answer. "Four years," he said, spreading butter on his bread. Jillian decided not to remind him that one of those years they hadn't been together.

"Four years? Really?" a woman by the name of Sandra asked, extending her lips into what Jillian could tell was a plastered-on smile.

"Yes, *really,*" Jillian responded, knowing just what the chick was getting at. After four years Jillian should have a ring on her finger. In other words, she should be a wife and not a significant other.

"Then I guess the two of you will probably be tying the knot pretty soon." It was obvious Wanda was digging for information. The others' ears were perked up as if they, too, couldn't wait to hear the response.

Jillian tried not to show her surprise when Aidan

reached across the table and placed his hand over hers. "Sooner rather than later, if I had my way. But I'll be joining the Cardiology Department at Johns Hopkins in the fall, and Jillian's just finished medical school, so we haven't set dates yet."

"You're both doctors?" Sandra asked, smiling.

"Yes," both Aidan and Jillian answered at the same time.

"That's great. So are we," Sandra said, pointing to herself and the others. "Faye and Sherri and I just finished Meharry Medical School a couple of months ago, and Wanda, Joy and Virginia just completed pharmacy school at Florida A&M."

"Congratulations, everyone," Jillian said, giving all six women a genuine smile. After having completed medical school she knew the hard work and dedication that was required for any medical field. And the six had definitely attended excellent schools.

"And congratulations to you, too," the women said simultaneously.

Jillian's smile widened. "Thanks."

AIDAN GLANCED DOWN at the woman walking beside him as they left the jazz lounge where several musicians had performed. Jillian had been pretty quiet since dinner. He couldn't help wondering what she was thinking.

"Did you enjoy dinner?" he asked.

She glanced up at him. "Yes, what about you?"

He shrugged. "It was nice."

"Just nice? You were the only male seated at a table with several females, all gorgeous, so how was it just nice?"

"Because it was," he said, wondering if this conversation would start a discussion he'd rather not have with her. But then, maybe they should have it now. They *had* agreed to talk things out. "So what did you think of the ladies at our table tonight?"

She stopped walking to lean against a rail and look at him. "Maybe I should be asking what you thought of them."

He joined her at the rail, standing a scant foot in front of her. "Pretty. All seven of them. But the prettiest of them all was the one wearing the red dress. The one named Jillian Novak. Now, she was a total knockout. She put the *s* in sexy."

Jillian smiled and shook her head, sending those dangling curls swinging. "Laying it on rather thick, aren't you, Aidan?"

"Not as long as you get the picture."

"And what picture is that?"

"That you're the only woman I want. The only one who can get blood rushing through my veins."

She chuckled. "Sounds serious, Dr. Westmoreland."

"It is." He didn't say anything for a minute as he stared at her. "Do you realize that this is the first time you've ever referred to me as Dr. Westmoreland?"

She nodded. "Yes, I know. Just like I realized tonight at dinner that it was the first time you'd ever introduced me during the time we were together."

"Yes. There were times when I wished I could have."

But you couldn't, she thought. *Because of the secret I made you keep.*

"But I did tonight."

"Yes, you did fib a little. Twice in fact," she pointed out.

He lifted a brow. "When?"

"When you said I was your significant other."

"I didn't fib. You are. There's no one more significant in my life than you," he said softly.

JILLIAN COULDN'T SAY anything after that. How could she? And when the silence between them lengthened, she wondered if he was expecting her to respond. What *could* she say? That she believed him? Did she really?

"And what was the other?" he asked, finally breaking the silence.

"What other?" she asked him.

"Fib. You said there were two."

"Oh. The one about the amount of time we've been together. You said four years and it was three," she said as they began walking again.

"No, it was four. Although we spent a year apart it meant nothing to me, other than frustration and anger. Nevertheless, you were still here," he said, touching his heart. "During every waking moment and in all my dreams."

She glanced away from him as they continued walking only to glance back moments later. "That sounds unfair to the others."

"What others?"

"Any woman you dated that year."

He stopped walking, took her hand and pulled her to the side, back over to the rail. He frowned down at her. "What are you talking about? I didn't date any women last year."

She searched his face and somehow saw the truth in his words. "But why? I thought you would. Figured you had."

"Why?" Before she could respond he went on in a

mocking tone, "Ah, that's right. Because I'm a womanizer."

Jillian heard the anger in his voice, but yes, that was the reason she'd thought he'd dated. Wasn't that the reason she had ended things between them as well, so he would have the freedom to return to his old ways? She drew in a deep breath. "Aidan, I—"

"No, don't say it." He stiffened his chin. "Whatever it is you're going to say, Jillian, don't." He glanced down at his watch and then his gaze moved back to her face. "I know you prefer turning in early, so I'll see you back to your cabin. I think I'll hang out a while in one of the bars."

She didn't say anything for a moment. "Want some company?"

"No," he said softly. "Not right now."

Suddenly, she felt a deep ache in her chest. "Okay. Don't worry about seeing me to my cabin. You can go on."

"You sure?"

She forced a smile. "Yes, I'm sure. I know the way."

"All right. I'll come get you for breakfast around eight."

If you can still stand my company, she thought. "Okay. I'll see you in the morning at eight."

He nodded and, with the hurt she'd brought on herself eating away at her, she watched Aidan walk away.

CHAPTER THIRTEEN

AIDAN FORCED HIS eyes open when he heard banging
coming from the sitting area.

"What the hell?" He closed his eyes as sharp pain
slammed through his head. It was then that he remembered last night. Every single detail.

He had stopped at the bar, noticed it was extremely
crowded and had gone to his room instead. He'd ordered
room service, a bottle of his favorite Scotch. He'd sat
on the balcony, looking out over the ocean beneath the
night sky and drinking alone, nursing a bruised heart.
He didn't finish off the entire bottle but he'd downed
enough to give him the mother of all headaches this
morning. What time was it anyway?

He forced his eyes back open to look at the clock on
the nightstand. Ten? It was ten in the morning? Crap!
He'd promised Jillian to take her to breakfast at eight.
He could only imagine what she'd thought when he was
a no-show. Pulling himself up on the side of the bed he
drew in a deep breath. Honestly, did he care anymore?
She had him pegged as a player in that untrusting mind
of hers, so what did the truth matter?

"Mr. Aidan," called the cabin steward, "do you want
me to clean your bedroom now or come back later?"

"Come back later, Rowan."

When Aidan heard the door close, he dropped back

in bed. He knew he should call Jillian, but chances were she'd gotten tired of waiting around and had gone to breakfast without him. He could imagine her sitting there eating pancakes while all kinds of insane ideas flowed through her head. All about him. Hell, he might as well get up, get dressed and search the ship for her to put those crazy ideas to rest.

He was about to get out of bed when he heard a knock at the door. He figured it was probably the guy coming around to pick up laundry, so he slipped into his pajama bottoms to tell the person to come back later.

He snatched open the door but instead of the laundry guy, Jillian stood there carrying a tray of food. "Jillian? What are you doing here?"

She stared at him for a moment. "You look like crap."

"I feel like crap," he muttered, moving aside to let her in. She placed the tray on his dining table. His head still pounded somewhat, but not as hard as the way his erection throbbed while staring at her. She was wearing a cute and sexy shorts set that showed what a gorgeous pair of legs she had. And her hair, which had been pinned atop her head last night, flowed down her shoulders while gold hoop earrings dangled from her ears. Damn, he couldn't handle this much sexiness in the morning.

She turned around. "To answer your question as to why I'm here, you missed breakfast so I thought I'd bring you something to eat."

He closed the door and leaned against it. "And what else?"

She lifted a brow. "And what else?"

"Yes. What other reason do you have for coming here? Let me guess. You figured I brought a woman here last night and you wanted to catch me in the act? Right? Go ahead, Jillian, search my bedroom if you like. The bathroom, too, if that suits your fancy. Oh, and don't forget to check the balconies in case I've hidden her out there until after you leave."

Jillian didn't say anything for a long minute. "I guess I deserved that. But—"

He held his hand to interrupt her. "Please. No buts, Jillian. I'm tired of them coming from you. Let me ask you something. How many men did you sleep with during the year we weren't together since you think I didn't leave a single woman standing?"

She narrowed her gaze at him. "Not a single one."

He crossed his arms over his chest. "Why?"

She lifted a chin. "Because I didn't want to."

"Why didn't you want to? You had broken things off with me and we weren't together. Why didn't you sleep with another man?"

JILLIAN KNEW SHE'D screwed up badly last night and she could hardly wait until morning to see Aidan so she could apologize. When he didn't show up at eight as he'd promised, she would admit that for a quick second she'd thought he might have been mad enough to spend the night with someone else. But all it had taken to erase that thought was for her to remember how he'd looked last night when he told her the reason why he'd introduced her as his significant other.

There's no one more significant in my life than you.

And she believed him. His reason for not sleeping with another woman during the year they'd been apart was the same reason she hadn't slept with another man.

"Jillian?"

She met his gaze. He wanted an answer and she would give him one. The truth and nothing but the truth.

"Sleeping with another man never crossed my mind, Aidan," she said softly. "Because I still loved you. And no matter what I saw or imagined you did with that lap dancer, I still loved you. My body has your imprint all over it and the thought of another man touching it sickens me."

She paused and then added, "You're wrong. I didn't come here thinking I'd find another woman. I came to apologize. I figured the reason you didn't come take me to breakfast was because you were still mad at me. And after last night I knew that I deserved your anger."

"Why do you think you deserve my anger?"

"Because everything is my fault. You only kept our affair a secret because I asked you to, begged you to. Last night when I got to my room, I sat out on the balcony and thought about everything. I forced myself to see the situation through someone else's eyes other than my own. And you know what I saw, Aidan?"

"No, what did you see, Jillian?"

She fought back tears. "I saw a man who loved me enough to take a lot of crap. I never thought about what all the secrecy would mean. And then the long distance and the sacrifices you made to come see me whenever you could. The money you spent for airplane fare, your time. I wasn't the only one with the goal of becoming a doctor. It's not like you didn't have a life, trying to handle the pressure of your dual residency."

She paused. "And I can just imagine what your friends thought when all of a sudden you became a saint for no reason. You couldn't tell them about me, so I can understand them wanting to help get your life back on track with those women. That was the Aidan they knew. And unfortunately that was the Aidan I wanted to think you missed being. That night I showed up at the party, I should have realized that you were just having the fun you deserved. Fun you'd denied yourself since your involvement with me. I should have loved you enough and trusted you enough to believe that no matter what, you wouldn't betray me. That I meant more to you than any lap dancer with silicone boobs."

He uncrossed his arms. "You're right. You do mean more to me than any lap dancer, stripper, book-club member or any other woman out there, Jillian," he said in a soft tone. "And you were wrong to think I missed my old life. What I miss is being with you. I think we handled things okay that first year, but during those second and third years, because of trying to make that dual residency program work and still keep you at the top of the list, things became difficult for me. Then in the third year, I was the one with focusing issues. It became harder and harder to keep our long-distance affair afloat and stay focused at work. And the secrecy only added more stress. But I knew if I complained to you about it, that it would only stress you out and make you lose focus on what you needed to do.

"You were young when we started our affair. Only twenty-one. And you hadn't dated much. In all honesty, probably not at all, because I refuse to count that dude you dated in high school. So deep down I knew you weren't quite ready for the type of relationship I wanted. But I loved you and I wanted you and I figured everything would work out. I knew how challenging medical school could be and I wanted to make your life as calm as possible. I didn't want to be the one to add to your stress."

He paused. "But it looks like I did anyway. I tried to make the best of it, but unfortunately sometimes when we talked, I was in one of my foul moods because of stress. I would get an attitude with you instead of talking to you about it. At no time should I have made you feel that you deserved my anger. I apologize. I regret doing that."

"It's okay," Jillian said, pulling out a chair. "Come sit down and eat. Your food is getting cold."

She watched him move away from the door. When he reached the table, she skirted back so he could sit down. When he sat, he reached out, grabbed her around the waist and brought her down to his lap.

"Aidan! What do you think you're doing?"

He wrapped both arms around her so she wouldn't go anywhere. "What I should have done last night. Brought you back here and put you in my lap, wrapped my arms around you and convinced you that I meant everything I said about your value to me. Instead I got upset and walked away."

She pressed her forehead to his and whispered, "Sorry I made you upset with me last night."

"I love you so much, Jillian, and when I think you don't believe just how much I love you, how much you mean to me, I get frustrated and wonder just what else I have to do. I'm not a perfect man. I'm human. I'm going to make mistakes. We both are. But the one thing I won't do is betray your love with another woman. Those days are over for me. You're all the woman I'll ever need."

She leaned back from him to look in his eyes. "I believe you, Aidan. I won't lie and say I'll never get jealous, but I can say it'll be because I'm questioning the woman's motives, not yours."

And she really meant that. When he hadn't come down for breakfast she had gone into the Terelle Dining Room to eat alone. She ran into the book-club ladies and ended up eating breakfast with them and enjoying herself. Once Aidan had made it clear last night that he was not available, they had put a lid on their man-hunter instincts. Jillian and the six women had a lot in common, since they were all recent medical-school graduates, and they enjoyed sharing their experiences over breakfast. They invited her to join them for shopping at some point during their two days in Rome and she agreed to do that.

She shifted in Aidan's lap to find a more comfortable position.

"I wouldn't do that too many times if I were you," he warned in a husky whisper.

A hot wave of desire washed over her. He was looking at her with those dark, penetrating eyes. The same ones that could arouse her as no man ever had...or would. "Why not?"

If he was going to give her a warning, she wanted him to explain himself, although she knew what he meant.

"Because if you keep it up, *you* might become my breakfast."

The thought of that happening had the muscles between her legs tightening, and she was aware that every hormone in her body was downright sizzling. "But you like pancakes and syrup," she said innocently.

A smile spread across his lips. "But I like your taste better."

"Do you?" she asked, intentionally shifting again to lean forward so that she could bury her face in the hollow of his throat. He was shirtless and she loved getting close to him, drinking in his scent.

"You did it again."

She leaned back and met his gaze. "Did I?"

"Yes."

She intentionally shifted in his lap when she lowered her head to lick the upper part of his chest. She loved the salty taste of his flesh and loved even more the moan she heard from his lips.

"It's been a year, Jillian. If I get you in my bed today it will be a long time before I let you out."

"And miss touring Monte Carlo? The ship has already docked."

"We have time." He suddenly stood, with her in his arms, and she quickly grabbed him around the neck and held on. He chuckled. "Trust me. I'm not going to let you fall." He headed for the bedroom.

"Now to enjoy breakfast, the Aidan Westmoreland way," he said, easing her down on the bed. He stood back and stared at her for a long moment. "I want you so much I ache. I desire you so much I throb. And I will always love you, even after drawing my last breath."

For the second time that day, she fought back tears. "Oh, Aidan. I want, desire and love you, too. Just as much."

He leaned down and removed her shoes before removing every stitch of her clothing with a skill only he had perfected. When she lay there naked before him, he slid his pj's down his legs. "Lie still for a minute. There's something I want to do," he instructed in a throaty tone.

That's when Jillian saw the bottle of syrup he'd brought into the bedroom with them. She looked at the bottle and then looked up at him. "You are kidding, right?"

"Do I look like I'm kidding?" he asked, removing the top.

She swallowed. No, he definitely didn't look as if he was kidding. In fact he looked totally serious. Too serious. "But I'm going to be all sticky," she reasoned. All she could think about was how glad she was for the bikini wax she'd gotten at the spa yesterday.

"You won't be sticky for long. I plan to lick it all off you and then we'll shower together."

"Aidan!" She squealed when she felt the thick liquid touch her skin. Aidan made good on his word. He dripped it all over her chest, making sure there was a lot covering her breasts, around her navel and lower still. He laid it on thick between her legs, drenching her womanly core.

And then he used his tongue to drive her insane with pleasure while taking his time to lick off all the syrup. The flick of his tongue sent sensuous shivers down her spine, and all she could do was lie there and moan while encased in a cloud of sensations.

He used his mouth as a bearer of pleasure as he laved her breasts, drawing the nipples between his lips and sucking on the turgid buds with a greed that made her womb contract. She wasn't sure how much more she could take when his mouth lowered to her stomach. She reached down and buried her fingers in his scalp as his mouth traced a hungry path around her navel.

Moments later he lifted his head to stare at her, deliberately licking his lips. They both knew where he was headed next. The look on his face said he wanted her to know he intended to go for the gusto.

And he did.

Jillian screamed his name the moment his tongue entered her, sending shockwaves of a gigantic orgasm through her body. His hot and greedy tongue had desire clawing at her insides, heightening her pulse. And when she felt another orgasm coming on the heels of the first, she knew it was time she took control. Otherwise, Aidan would lick her crazy.

With all the strength she could muster she tried to shift their bodies, which was hard to do since his mouth was on her while his hands held tight to her hips. When she saw there was no way she could make Aidan budge until he got his fill, she gave in to another scream when a second orgasm hit.

He finally lifted his head, smiled at her while licking his lips and then eased his body over hers. "I told you I was going to lick it all off you, baby."

Yes, he had. Then his engorged erection slid inside of her. All she recalled after that was her brain taking a holiday as passion overtook her, driving her over the edge, bringing her back, then driving her to the edge again.

He thrust hard, all the way to the hilt and then some. He lifted her hips and set the pace. The bed springs were tested to their maximum and so was she. She released a deep moan when he pounded into her, making her use muscles she hadn't used in a year. And then he slowed and without disconnecting their bodies, eased to his knees. He lifted her legs all the way to his shoulders and continued thrusting.

"Aidan!"

He answered with a deep growl when the same explosion that tore through her ripped through him, as well. She could feel his hot, molten liquid rush through her body, bathing her womb. But he didn't stop. He kept going, enlarging inside her all over again.

She saw arousal coiling in the depth of his eyes. They were in it for the long haul, right now and forever. And when his wet, slick body finally eased down, he pulled her into his arms, wrapped the strength of his legs over hers and held her close. She breathed in his scent. This was where she wanted to be. Always.

Hours later, Jillian stirred in Aidan's arms and eased over to whisper in his ear. "Remind me never to let you go without me for a full year again."

He grinned as he opened his eyes. "One year, two months and four days. But I wasn't counting or anything, mind you."

She smiled. "I'll take your word for it." She eased up to glance over at the clock. Had they been in bed five hours already? "We need to shower."

"Again?"

She laughed out. "The last time doesn't count."

"Why?"

She playfully glared over at him. "You know why."

He'd taken her into the shower to wash off any lingering stickiness from the syrup. Instead he ended up making love to her again. Then he'd dried them both off and had taken her to the bed and made love to her again several times, before they'd both drifted off to sleep.

"I guess we do need to get up, shower and dress if we want to see any of Monte Carlo."

"Yes, and I want to see Monte Carlo."

"I want to see you," he said, easing back and raking his gaze over her naked body. "Do you know how much I missed this? Missed you?"

"The same way I missed you?"

"More," he said, running his hand over her body.

She couldn't ignore the delicious heat of the fingers touching her. "I doubt that, Dr. Westmoreland."

"Trust me."

She did trust him. And she loved him so much she wanted everyone to know it. "I can't wait until we return to Denver for Adrian's wedding."

He looked down at her. "Why?"

"So we can tell Pam and Dillon."

He studied her expression. "Are you ready for that?"

"More than ready. Do you think they already know?"

"It wouldn't surprise me if they did. Dillon isn't a dummy. Neither is Pam."

"Then why haven't they said anything?"

He shrugged. "Probably waiting for us to tell them."

She thought about what he'd said and figured he might be right. "Doesn't matter now. They will find out soon enough. Are you ready?"

"For another round?"

"No, not for another round. Are you ready to take a shower so we can get off this ship for a while?"

He pulled her into his arms. "Um, maybe. After another round." And then he lowered his mouth to hers.

CHAPTER FOURTEEN

"I HOPE YOU'RE not punishing me for what happened the last two days, Jillian."

Jillian glanced up at Aidan and smiled. "Why would I do that?" she asked as they walked the streets of Rome, Italy. She'd never visited a city more drenched in history. They would be here for two days and she doubted she could visit all the places she wanted to see in that time. She would have to make plans to come back one day.

"Because it was late when we finally got off the ship to tour Monte Carlo, and the same thing happened yesterday when we toured Florence. I have a feeling you blame me for both."

She chuckled. "Who else should I blame? Every time I mentioned it was time for us to get up, shower and get off the ship, you had other ideas."

He smiled as if remembering several of those ideas. "But we did do the tours. We just got a late start."

Yes, they had done the tours. For barely three hours in Monte Carlo. They had seen all they could in a cab ride around the city. Then yesterday, at least they had ridden up the most scenic road in Florence to reach Piazzale Michelangelo. From there they toured several palaces and museums before it was time to get back to the ship.

She had made sure they had gotten up, dressed and were off the ship at a reasonable time this morning for their tour of Rome. Already they had walked a lot, which was probably the reason Aidan was whining.

"What's the complaint, Aidan? You're in great shape." She of all people should know. He hadn't wasted time having her belongings moved into his suite where she had spent the night…and got very little sleep until dawn. But somehow she still felt energized.

"You think I'm punishing you by suggesting that we walk instead of taking a taxi-tour?" she asked as they crossed one of the busy streets.

"No. I think you're punishing me because you talked me out of renting that red Ferrari. Just think of all the places I could have taken you while driving it."

She chuckled. "Yes, but I would have wanted to get there in one piece and without an accelerated heart rate."

He placed his arms around her shoulders. "Have you forgotten that one day I intend to be one of the most sought-after cardiologists in the world?"

"How could I forget?" she said, smiling. She was really proud of him and his accomplishments. Going through that dual residency program was what had opened the door for him to continue his specialty training at Johns Hopkins, one of the most renowned research hospitals in the country.

Last night, in between making love, they had talked about their future goals. He knew she would start her residency at a hospital in Orlando, Florida, in the fall. The good thing was that after a year of internship, she could transfer to another hospital. Because he would be working for at least three years at John Hopkins, she would try to relocate to the Washington, D.C., or Maryland area.

A few hours later they had toured a number of places, including the Colosseum, St. Peter's Basilica, the Trevi Fountain and the Catacombs. While standing in front of the Spanish Steps, waiting for Aidan to return from retrieving the lace fan she'd left behind in the church of Trinità dei Monti, she blinked when she saw a familiar man pass by.

Riley Westmoreland? What was Aidan's cousin doing in Rome?

"Riley!" she yelled out. When the man didn't look her way, she figured he must not have heard her. Taking the steps almost two at a time, she hurriedly raced after him.

When she caught up with him she grabbed his arm. "Riley, wait up! I didn't know you—"

She stopped in midsentence when the man turned around. It wasn't Riley. But he looked enough like him to be a twin. "I'm so sorry. I thought you were someone else."

The man smiled and she blinked. He even had Riley's smile. Or more specifically, one of those Westmoreland smiles. All the men in the family had dimples. And like all the Westmoreland men, he was extremely handsome.

"No problem, signorina."

She smiled. "You're Italian?" she asked.

"No. American. I'm here on business. And you?"

"American. Here vacationing." She extended her hand. "I'm Jillian Novak."

He nodded as he took her hand. "Garth Outlaw."

"Nice meeting you, Garth, and again I'm sorry that I

mistook you for someone else, but you and Riley West-moreland could almost be twins."

He chuckled. "A woman as beautiful as you can do whatever you like, signorina. No need to apologize." He grasped her hand and lifted it to his lips. "Have a good day, beautiful Jillian Novak, and enjoy the rest of your time in Rome."

"And you do the same."

He turned and walked away. She stood there for a minute, thinking. He was even a flirt like those West-morelands before they'd married. And the man even had that Westmoreland sexy walk. How crazy was that?

"Jillian?" She turned when she heard Aidan call her name.

"I thought you were going to wait for me on the steps," he said when he reached her.

"I did but then I thought I saw Riley and—"

"Riley? Trust me, Riley would not be in Rome, especially not with Alpha expecting their baby any day now."

"I know, but this guy looked so much like Riley that I raced after him. He could have been Riley's twin. I apologized for my mistake and he was nice about it. He was an American, here on business. Said his name was Garth Outlaw. And he really did favor Riley."

Aidan frowned. "Outlaw?"

"Yes."

"Um, that's interesting. The last time we had our family meeting about the investigation Rico is handling, I think he said something about tracing a branch of the Westmoreland roots to a family who goes by the last name of Outlaw."

"Really?"

"That's what I recall, but Dillon would know for sure. I'll mention it to him when we return home. That information might help Rico," Aidan said as they walked back toward the Spanish Steps.

Rico Claiborne, a private investigator, was married to Aidan's sister Megan. Jillian was aware that Rico's PI firm had been investigating the connection of four women to Aidan's great-grandfather, Raphel Westmoreland. It had been discovered during a genealogy search that before marrying Aidan's great-grandmother Gemma, Raphel had been connected to four other women who'd been listed as former wives. Rico's investigation had confirmed that Raphel hadn't married any of the women, but that one of them had given birth to a son that Raphel had never known about. Evidently, Jillian thought, at some point Rico had traced that son to the Outlaw family.

"Ready to head back to the ship?" Aidan asked, interrupting her thoughts.

She glanced back at her watch. "Yes, it's getting kind of late. You can join me and the book-club ladies when we go shopping tomorrow if you'd like."

He shook his head. "No thanks. Although it's a beautiful city, I've seen enough of Rome for now. But I will bring you back."

She lifted a brow. "You will?"

"Yes."

"When?"

"For our honeymoon. I hope." Aidan then got down on one knee and took her hand in his. "I love you, Jillian. Will you marry me?"

Jillian stared at him in shock. It was only when he tugged at her hand did she notice the ring he'd placed there. Her eyes widened. "Oh, my God!" Never had she seen anything so beautiful.

"Well?" Aidan asked, grinning. "People are standing around. We've gotten their attention. Are you going to embarrass me or what?"

She saw that people had stopped to stare. They had heard his proposal and, like Aidan, they were waiting for her answer. She could not believe that here in the beautiful city of Rome, on the Spanish Steps, Aidan had asked her to marry him. She would remember this day for as long as she lived.

"Yes. Yes!" she said, filled with happiness. "Yes, I will marry you."

"Thank you," he said, getting back to his feet and pulling her into his arms. "For a minute there you had me worried."

The people around them cheered and clapped while a smiling Aidan pulled Jillian into his arms and kissed her.

AIDAN WALKED DOWN the long corridor to his suite. Jillian had sent him away an hour ago with instructions not to return until now because she would have a surprise waiting for him when he got back. He smiled thinking she had probably planned a candlelit dinner for their last day on the cruise.

It was hard to believe their two weeks were up. To-morrow they would return to Barcelona. After two days in Rome they had spent two days at sea before touring Athens, Greece. While there they had taken part in a wine-tasting excursion and visited several museums. From there they had toured Turkey, Mykonos and Malta.

Now they were headed back to Barcelona and would arrive before daybreak.

He couldn't help the feeling of happiness that puffed out his chest when he thought of being an engaged man. Although they hadn't set a date, the most important thing was that he had asked and she had said yes. They talked every day about their future, and although they still had at least another year before she could join him in Maryland, they were okay with it because they knew the day would come when they would be together.

They decided not to wait until they went home for Adrian's wedding to tell the family their news. Some would be shocked, while others who knew about their affair would be relieved that their secret wasn't a secret any longer. They would head straight to Denver tomorrow when the ship docked.

He chuckled when he thought about Jillian's excitement over her engagement ring. The book-club ladies had definitely been impressed as well, ahhing and ooh-ing every night at dinner. Jewelry by Zion was the rave since Zion was the First Lady's personal jeweler. Jillian hadn't known that he knew Zion personally because of Aidan's friendship with the Steele family, who were close personal friends of Zion. Zion had designed most of his signature custom jewelry collection while living in Rome for the past ten years. Thanks to Dominic, Aidan had met with Zion privately on board the ship in the wee hours of the morning while Jillian slept, when they first docked in a port near Rome. Zion had brought an attaché case filled with beautiful rings—all originals hand-crafted by Zion. When Aidan had seen this one particular ring, he'd known it was the one he wanted to put on Jillian's finger.

When Aidan reached his suite's door, he knocked, to let her know he had returned.

"Come in."

Using his passkey, he opened the door and smiled upon seeing the lit candles around the room. His bride-to-be had set the mood for a romantic dinner, he thought, when he saw how beautifully the table was set.

Closing the door behind him he glanced around the dimly lit suite but didn't see Jillian anywhere. Was she in the bedroom waiting on him? He moved in that direction and then felt a hand on his shoulder. He turned around and his breath caught. Jillian wore a provocative black lace teddy that showed a lot of flesh. Attached to the teddy were matching lace garters and she wore a pair of stilettoes on her feet. He thought he hadn't seen anyone as sexy in his entire life and he couldn't help groaning in appreciation.

She leaned close, swirled the tip of her tongue around his ear and whispered, "I'm about to give you the lap dance of your life, Aidan Westmoreland."

The next thing he knew he was gently shoved in a chair. "And remember no touching, so put your hands behind your back."

He followed her instructions, mesmerized beyond belief. Her sensual persona stirred his desire. His pulse kicked up a notch, followed immediately by a deep throbbing in his erection. "And just what do you want me to do?" he asked in a low voice.

She smiled at him. "Just enjoy. I plan to do all the work. But by the time I finish, you will be too exhausted to move."

Really? Him? Too exhausted to move? And she would be the one doing all the work? He couldn't wait for that experience. "Now will you keep your hands to yourself or do I need to handcuff you?" she asked him.

He couldn't help smiling at the thought of that. Did she really have handcuffs? Would she be that daring? He decided to find out. "I can't make any promises, so you might want to handcuff me."

"No problem."

The next thing he knew she'd whipped out a pair of handcuffs, slapped them on his wrists and locked them with a click to the chair. *Damn*. While he was taking all this in, he suddenly heard music coming from the sound system in the room. He didn't recognize the artist, but the song had a sensual beat.

While sitting there handcuffed to the chair, he watched as Jillian responded to the music, her movements slow, graceful and seductive. She rolled her stomach and then shimmied her hips and backside in a sinfully erotic way. He sat there awestruck, fascinated, staring at her as she moved in front of him. He felt the rapid beat of his heart and the sweet pull of desire as his erection continued to pulsate.

Although he couldn't touch her, she was definitely touching him—rubbing her hands over his shirt, underneath it, through the hair on his chest, before taking her time unbuttoning his shirt and easing it from his shoulders.

"Have I ever told you how much I love your chest, Aidan?" she asked him in a sultry tone.

"No," he answered huskily. "You never have."

"Well, I'm telling you now. In fact, I want to show you just how much I like it."

Then she crouched over him and used her tongue to lick his shoulder blades before moving slowly across the span of his chest. He would have come out of his chair had he not been handcuffed to it. She used her tongue in ways she hadn't before and he heard himself groaning out loud.

"You like that?" she asked, leaning close to his mouth, and licking there, as well. "Want more? Want to see what else you've taught me to do with my tongue?"

He swallowed. Oh, yes, he wanted more. He wanted to see just what he'd taught her. Instead of answering, he nodded.

She smiled as she bent down to remove his shoes. Reaching up, she unzipped his pants and he raised his hips as she slid both his pants and briefs down his legs. She smiled at him again.

"You once licked me all over, Aidan, and you seemed to have enjoyed it. Now I'm going to do the same to you and I intend to enjoy myself, as well."

Moistening her lips with a delicious-looking sweep of her tongue, she got down on her knees before him and spread his legs. Then she lowered her head between his thighs and took him into her mouth.

As soon as she touched him, blood rushed through his veins, sexual hunger curled his stomach and desire stroked his gut. Her mouth widened to accommodate his size and she used her tongue to show that with this, she was definitely in control. He watched in a sensual daze as her head bobbed up and down while she fanned the blaze of his desire.

He wanted to grab hold of her hair, stroke her back, caress her shoulders but he couldn't. He felt defenseless, totally under her control but he loved every single minute of it. When he couldn't take any more, his body jerked in one hell of an explosion and she still wouldn't let go.

"Jillian!"

He wanted her with an intensity that terrified him. And when she lifted her head and smiled at him, he knew what it meant to love someone with every part of your heart, your entire being and your soul.

While the music continued to play, she straightened and began stripping for him, removing each piece of clothing slowly, and teasing his nostrils before tossing it aside. Sexual excitement filled his inner core as he inhaled her scent. When she was totally naked, she began dancing again, touching herself and touching him. He'd never seen anything so erotic in his entire life.

When she curled into his lap and continued to dance, the feel of her soft curves had him growling, had his erection throbbing again, harder. "Set me free," he begged. He needed to touch her now. He wanted his hands in her hair and his fingers inside her.

"Not yet," she whispered in a purr that made even more need wash over him. Then she twisted her body around so her back was plastered to his chest then she eased down onto his manhood and rode him.

Never had she ridden him this hard and when she shifted so they faced each other, the feel of her breasts hitting his chest sent all kinds of sensations through him.

"Jillian!"

He screamed her name as an orgasm hit him again, deep, and he pulled the scent of her sex through his nostrils. He leaned forward. Although he couldn't touch her, he could lick her. He used his tongue to touch her earlobe and her face. "Uncuff me, baby. Please. Uncuff me now."

She reached behind him and he heard the click that released him. When his hands were free he stood, with her in his arms, and quickly moved toward the bedroom.

"You're the one who was supposed to be exhausted," she mumbled into his chest.

"Sorry, it doesn't quite work that way, baby." And then he stretched her out on the bed.

He straddled her, eased inside her and thrust, stroking her, wanting her to feel his love in every movement. This was erotic pleasure beyond compare and her inner muscles clenched him, held him tight and tempted him to beg again.

His thrusts became harder, her moans louder and the desire he felt for her more relentless than ever. And when he finally exploded, he took her along with him as an earth-shattering climax claimed them both. They were blasted into the heavens. Jillian Novak had delivered the kind of mindless pleasure every man should experience at least once in his lifetime. And he was glad that he had.

Moments later, he eased off her and pulled her into his arms, entwining her legs with his. He kissed the side of her face while she fell into a deep sleep.

Their secret affair was not a secret any longer and he couldn't wait to tell the world that he'd found his mate for life. And he would cherish her forever.

EPILOGUE

"So, YOU THOUGHT you were keeping a secret from us," Pam said, smiling, sitting beside her husband on the sofa as they met with Aidan and Jillian.

"But we didn't?" Jillian asked, grinning and holding Aidan's hand.

"For a little while, maybe," Dillon replied. "But when you fall in love with someone, it's hard to keep something like that hidden, especially in *this* family."

Jillian knew exactly what Dillon meant. It seemed the bigger secret had been that she and Aidan had wanted to keep their relationship a secret. No one in the family knew who else knew, so everyone kept their suspicions to themselves.

"Well, I'm glad we don't have to hide things anymore," Aidan said, standing, pulling Jillian up with him and then wrapping his arms around her shoulders.

"You mean you don't have to *try* and hide things," Pam corrected. "Neither of you were doing such a good job of pretending. And when the two of you had that rift, Dillon and I were tempted to intervene. But we figured if it was meant for the two of you to be together, you would be, without our help."

Jillian looked down at her ring. "Yes, we were able to get our act together, although I will have to give Paige some credit for bailing out of the cruise. Aidan and I needed that time together to work things out."

"And I guess from that ring on your finger, the two of you managed to do that," Dillon said.

Aidan nodded as he smiled down at Jillian. "Yes, we did. The thought of a year-long engagement doesn't bother us. After Jillian's first year at that hospital in Orlando, Florida, she'll be able to transfer to one near me. That's when we plan to tie the knot."

"Besides," Pam said, smiling, "the year gives me plenty of time to plan for the wedding without feeling rushed. These Westmoreland weddings are coming around fast, but trust me, I'm not complaining."

Dillon reached out and hugged his wife. "Please don't complain. I'm elated with each one. After Adrian gets hitched next month and Aidan is married in a year, all we'll have to be concerned with is Bailey and Bane."

The room got quiet as everyone thought about that. Only two Westmorelands were left single, and those two were known to be the most headstrong of them all.

"Bay says she's never getting married," Aidan said, grinning.

"So did you and Adrian," Dillon reminded him. "In fact, I don't think there's a single Westmoreland who hasn't made that claim at some point in time, including me. But all it takes is for one of us to find that special person who's our soul mate, and we start singing a different tune."

"But can you see Bay singing a different tune?" Aidan asked.

Dillon thought about the question for a minute, drew in a deep breath and then shook his head. "No."

Everyone laughed. When their laughter subsided

Pam smiled and said, "There's someone for everyone, including Bailey. She just hasn't met him yet. In other words, Bailey hasn't met her match. But one day, I believe that she will."

The following month

"ADRIAN WESTMORELAND, YOU may kiss your bride."

Aidan, serving as best man, smiled as he watched his twin brother take the woman he loved, Dr. Trinity Matthews Westmoreland, into his arms to seal their marriage vows with one hell of a kiss. Aidan spotted Jillian in the audience sitting with her sisters and winked at her. Their day would be coming and he couldn't wait.

A short while later, Aidan stole his twin away for a few minutes. The wedding had been held in Trinity's hometown of Bunnell, Florida, at the same church where their cousin Thorn had married Trinity's sister Tara. The weather had been beautiful and it seemed everyone in the little town had been invited to the wedding, which accounted for the packed church of more than eight hundred guests. The reception was held in the ballroom of a beautiful hotel overlooking the Atlantic Ocean.

"Great job, Dr. Westmoreland," he said, grinning at Adrian.

Adrian chuckled. "I intend to say the same to you a year from now, Dr. Westmoreland, when you tie the knot. I'm glad the cruise helped, and that you and Jillian were able to work things out."

"So am I. That had to be the worst year of my life when we were apart."

Adrian nodded. "I know. Remember I felt your pain whenever you let out any strong emotions."

Yes, Aidan did remember. "So where are you headed for your honeymoon?"

"Sydney, Australia. I've always wanted to go back, and I look forward to taking Trinity there with me."

"Well, the two of you deserve a lifetime of happiness," Aidan said, taking a sip of his champagne.

"You and Jillian do, as well. I'm so glad the secret is a secret no longer."

Aidan's smile widened. "So am I. And on that note, I'm going to go claim my fiancée so you can go claim your bride."

Aidan crossed the span of the ballroom to where Jillian stood with her sisters Paige and Nadia, and his sister Bailey. He and Jillian would leave Bunnell in the morning and take the hour-long drive to Orlando. Together they would look for an apartment for her close to the hospital where she would be working as an intern. He had checked and discovered that flights from the D.C. area into Orlando were pretty frequent. He was glad about that because he intended to pay his woman plenty of visits.

Aidan had told Dillon about Jillian's chance meeting with a man by the name of Garth Outlaw while in Rome and how she'd originally thought he was Riley. Dillon wasn't surprised that any kin out there would have the Westmoreland look due to dominant genes. He had passed the information on to Rico. The family was hoping something resulted from Jillian's encounter.

"Sorry, ladies, I need to grab Jillian for a minute," he said, snagging her hand.

"Where are we going?" Jillian asked as he led her toward the exit.

"To walk on the beach."

"Okay."

Holding hands, they crossed the boardwalk and went down the steps. Pausing briefly, they removed their shoes. Jillian moaned when her feet touched the sand.

"What are you thinking about, baby?" Aidan asked her.

"I'm thinking about how wonderful I feel right now. Walking in the sand, being around the people I love, not having to hide my feelings for you. And what a lucky woman I am to have such a loving family and such a gorgeous and loving fiancé."

He glanced down at her. "You think I'm gorgeous?"

"Yes."

"You think I'm loving?"

"Definitely."

"Will that qualify me for another lap dance tonight?"

Jillian threw her head back and laughed, causing the wind to send hair flying across her face. Aidan pushed her hair back and she smiled up at him.

"Dr. Westmoreland, you can get a lap dance out of me anytime. Just say the word."

"Lap dance."

She leaned up on tiptoes. "You got it."

Aidan then pulled her into his arms and kissed her. Life couldn't get any better than this.

* * * * *

BACHELOR UNDONE

PROLOGUE

SPENDING HER VACATION in New York during the month of December was not on Darcelle Owens's list of things to do, which was why she was in a cab headed for JFK International Airport. She loved living in the Big Apple, but when forecasters had predicted the city's coldest winter ever, she was glad she had plans to get the hell out of Dodge.

Jamaica, here I come, she thought relaxing back in her seat. While her coworkers would be battling the snow, she planned to be lying half-naked on the beach under the heat of the Jamaican sun. And then at night, she'd become a sophisticated hooch and let her hair down, party and even do a little man-hunting. She deserved it after working her tail off the past two years.

She had the whole month of December off and would have loved to spend the entire time in Jamaica. But her parents expected her to come home for Christmas, as usual. She got a chill in her bones just thinking of returning to Minneapolis for even a little while.

She'd always hated cold weather and would have headed south to attend college if her parents hadn't convinced her of how much money they could save not having to pay out-of-state tuition. When she talked to her mother just that morning, it was twenty below zero. *Brrrr.*

And then her best friend Ellie Lassiter expected her to spend a few days with her at her lake house in North Carolina before Ellie and her husband Uriel's New Year's Eve bash.

Darcy planned to keep her family and Ellie happy, but first she intended to relax in the warm weather for at least three weeks.

Darcy cringed when she heard the chime of a text message on her cell phone. How dare her younger brother Prescott teach their mother how to text! Darcy bet between her, Prescott and her older brother Jonas that their mother, Joan Owens, sent out over one hundred text messages a day. Okay, maybe she was exaggerating a tad bit, but it would seem about that number.

Checking her phone, Darcy smiled when she saw the message hadn't come from her mother after all. It was from Ellie.

Behave yourself in J. Have fun. E

Darcy chuckled and quickly texted back. Can't behave myself and have fun, too. LOL.

Got Bruce with you? the responding text asked.

Darcy's smile widened. Bruce was the name she'd given her little sex toy. Nope. Left Bruce behind this time. I hope to get lucky and find someone who's looking to have some fun. Looking forward to relaxing, reading and replacing Bruce with the real thing.

She wasn't surprised when within seconds of sending that message her cell phone rang. Of course it was Ellie. "Yes, El?"

"And just what do you mean by that?" her best friend asked.

Darcy threw her head back and laughed. "Just what I said. It's time Bruce goes into retirement. He's earned it."

"Girl, you're awful."

"No, I'm not. If I was awful, I wouldn't have gone without being in a relationship for two years. If it hadn't been for Bruce and my romance novels, I don't know what I would have done to keep sane."

And that was so true. She had moved from Minneapolis after taking a job as a city planner for New York City. Over the past two years, she had been working day and night trying to prove the city hadn't made a mistake by hiring an outsider.

She had worked hard and hadn't taken any time off other than the recognized holidays, which was why she had accumulated so much vacation time. And now she intended to enjoy it. It was the end of the year, and her boss had warned her to "use it or lose it." The only thing she planned to lose was two years of abstinence.

"Chill, El," she said when there was silence on the other end. "I'm taking plenty of condoms with me if that makes you happy."

She glanced up and saw the elderly cabdriver looking at her in the rearview mirror. *Oops.* She couldn't do anything but smile. She lowered her head and whispered into the phone. "Look, you're going to get me in trouble, El. The cabbie heard my remark about condoms and is looking at me funny. Like he thinks I'm a loose woman or something."

"Nobody's fault but your own for saying what you did."

"It's the truth."

"Whatever. Go and have your fun, but be careful,

stay safe and you better have a lot to tell me when you get back."

Darcy felt giddy all the way to her toes. "Trust me, I will. I intend to become one of the heroines in those romance novels I enjoy reading so much. And I got this hot pink bikini with the word *seduction* written all over it."

Darcy then clicked off the phone and glanced out the cab's window. It had started snowing. She drew in a deep breath thinking she couldn't get to Jamaica fast enough.

YORK ELLIS, FORMER NYPD officer and present-day security expert, felt adrenaline flow through his veins. It was always that way at the start of a new case, and from the sound of things, this one would be a challenge. As far as he was concerned, anything would top the last case he had protecting the horse who'd won the Kentucky Derby when rumors of a horse-napping had begun circulating.

He glanced across his desk at Malcolm Overstreet, renowned director and screenwriter. Malcolm was there to represent a group of New York filmmakers whose movies were getting put on the black market before they got the chance to be released to theaters. This was causing the filmmakers enormous loss of profits and almost forcing them into bankruptcy. In this case, the actual movie footage was being sold while the production was still in process. Certain scenes were even appearing on the internet.

On top of that, idle threats had been made against the making of a controversial movie. Malcolm wanted

York's firm to find out who was behind the bootlegging as well as handle the security for the movie.

York had enough people working for him to do the latter, and as far as finding out who was involved in advance footage being released to the public, he figured with the right plan in place that should be easy enough.

"Have you ever considered the possibility this might be an inside job?" he asked Malcolm. He could tell from the man's expression that he hadn't.

"We have good people working for our production company," Malcolm said. "If we lose money, they lose money."

Not necessarily, York thought. "When does the movie continue shooting?" he asked.

"Next week in Jamaica," Malcolm responded.

York nodded as he jotted down a few notes. He knew the film was a controversial biography on the life of Marcus Garvey, the black civil rights activist from Jamaica. And he knew it would depict a side of Garvey that some didn't want told—which was the reason for the heightened security while they were on the island. "Has any current cast or crew member worked on your last couple of movies?"

"Yes, we usually hire the same crew for all our productions. Some of them have been with us for years, and it's hard to imagine them being a part of anything illegal."

"What about your cast?"

"Johnny Rush is my leading man as Garvey, and Danielle Simone is my leading lady as his love interest. But you can scratch them off the list," Malcolm said confidently.

York lifted a brow. "Why are you so sure?"

"Their egos. Both are too vain to want their work anywhere other than the big screen, trust me. They think having their work out on the black market is an insult to their talent. In fact, the only way they would agree to work with Spirit Head Productions again is if we assured them their work will not be undermined and hit the streets before a premier date."

"What about Damien Felder?" York asked, glancing down at the papers on his desk. "I've noticed his name has shown up on probably every production you've done."

Malcolm nodded. "You can mark Damien's name off the list as well. He's my line producer, and a cut in our profits slashes into his bank account as well. He has nothing to gain from our movies appearing on the black market. If another one of our movies gets bootlegged, we'll be filing for bankruptcy."

Malcolm then leaned forward. "I believe whoever is behind things will try and get the footage sometime while my cast and crew are shooting the final scenes in Jamaica. And I want you to make sure that doesn't happen, York. My partners and I are sick and tired of losing money that way. It's not fair not only to us but to every person who has a stake in the production."

The man paused and then added, "And then there's this threat on Rush. Some think he fabricated things for publicity, but we can't take any chances."

York closed his notepad. Malcolm and his group were heavy hitters who could open the doors to even more business for York's security firm. But more importantly, it was the principle of the thing. Someone was breaking the law and cutting into the profits—actually outright stealing them—and they were profits they didn't deserve.

He knew one of the main reasons Malcolm had come to him was because Malcolm was a friend of his father's. Malcolm had also attended Morehouse College as a young man along with York's father and five godfathers before getting a graduate degree from Columbia University Film School. "I understand, and I intend to fly to Jamaica immediately and find out who is behind things."

Malcolm lifted a brow. "Will it be that easy?"

York met the man's gaze with an intense look. "No, but once I establish my cover, I'll be a regular on set and I can keep an eye on what's going on. And the six men and three women working for me are the best of the best. Rest assured, whoever is behind this has messed with one of your productions for the last time."

CHAPTER ONE

DARCY STOOD ON the balcony and glanced out at the beach. It was hard to believe this was her third day in Jamaica and she was just getting out of her hotel room today for the first time. She, who rarely got sick, had gotten a stomach virus her first day and had stayed in her hotel room in bed. What a bummer of a way to start off her vacation.

The good thing was that today she was feeling like her old self again, and she intended to spend as much time outside as she possibly could. She had lost two valuable days, but from here on out it was full steam ahead.

When she had checked in, the hotel clerk had given her a list of the hotel's activities for the week, and tonight they would be hosting a classy beach party. Her health had improved just in time. A party was the last thing she wanted to miss.

She turned away from the window and crossed the room to glance at herself in the full-length mirror. She had purchased the wide-brimmed straw hat from a gift shop at the airport, and the sundress she was wearing had caught her eye the moment she'd seen it at Macy's over the summer. At the time, a trip to Jamaica had been just a fancy, and in a way, it was hard to believe she was actually here.

Instead of donning a bikini and lying on the beach today, she thought she would take a tour of the island and get some sightseeing in. She had purchased a new digital camera and intended to put it to good use. And she definitely intended to do some shopping. When she had visited Jamaica a few years ago—a college graduation present from her parents—she had purchased several pieces of jewelry that had been handcrafted by an island woman. Darcy intended to see if the small shop near the pier was still there. There were several more pieces she would love to add to her collection.

She glanced around the room. Since she would be here for three weeks she'd decided to get one of the residential suites, and she loved it. It was huge and spacious, and although it was costing her a pretty penny, it was worth it. Besides, she deserved it.

The furniture in the sitting area was elegant and the decor colors of cream, yellow, mint green and plum perfectly reflected an island theme. Floor-to-ceiling windows lined one wall and provided a balcony view of the water.

French doors led from the sitting room directly into the bedroom, which had its own balcony. There was nothing like waking up to the beauty of the Caribbean Sea. But it was the bathroom that she'd found simply breathtaking. It had a dressing room area and a closet large enough to camp out in if the need arose. Then there was the humongous Jacuzzi tub that could hold several couples if you were inclined to get that kinky… which she wasn't. She wasn't into sharing of any kind when it came to relationships.

Grabbing her purse off the table, she headed for the door. It was a beautiful day, and she planned to spend

as much of it as she could outside. Then she would return and take a shower and a nap before getting ready
for the party tonight.

YORK WALKED ALONG the pier. It hadn't taken any time to
get his game plan in place and head toward the island.
Jamaica was beautiful, but unlike all the other times he
came to the island, he was here for business.

Regardless of what Malcolm thought, every member
of the cast and crew was a suspect. His team had divided
the list, and every single person was being checked out.
He was hoping it wouldn't take long to expose the cul-
prit since he planned to spend the holidays back in the
States. His parents had moved to Seattle a few years
ago and luckily didn't expect everyone to show up on
their doorsteps for the holidays. In fact, as long as he
could remember, once he and his siblings began having lives of their own, his parents would spend the holidays in Toronto, visiting friends they had there. Usually
York would spend a quiet Christmas at home, and those
times he wanted company, he had five sets of godparents he could visit.

Most people knew the story as to how six guys who'd
met and become best friends while attending Morehouse had on graduation day made a pact to stay in
touch by becoming godfathers to each of their children and that the firstborn sons' names would carry
the letters of the alphabet from *U* to *Z*. And that was
how Uriel Lassiter, Virgil Bougard, Winston Coltrane,
Xavier Kane, York Ellis and Zion Blackstone had come
into existence. He was close to his godparents and god-

brothers and couldn't imagine them not being a part of his life.

He checked his watch. A couple of his men had checked in already with their reports, and it was obvious Malcolm didn't know some of his people as well as he thought he did. However, there was nothing to indicate any of them could be suspected of anything other than engaging in a number of illicit affairs.

York glanced around and saw he was the object of several women's attention. He didn't mind, and if he'd had the time, he would even indulge their fantasies. He was well aware that a number of women came to the island alone to get their groove on. They were man-hunters who were only looking for a good time.

He kept walking. He was on assignment, and there wasn't a woman he'd met yet who could make him take his mind off work.

DARCY SQUINTED AGAINST the brightness of the sun while moving from shop to shop in Montego Bay. Reggae music seemed to be playing just about everywhere. Pausing, she pulled out her sunglasses to shield her eyes from the sun. It was hard to believe how bright it shone here when, according to weather reports, it was still snowing in New York.

She stopped at a fruit stand, admiring the basket of strawberries, all plump and ripe, when something out of the corner of her eye caught her attention.

A man.

And boy, what a man he was. She could only see his profile, but even from almost fifteen feet away she could tell he was a fine specimen of the opposite sex. He was in a squatting position, going through a rack of T-shirts that some peddler was trying to sell him.

Darcy tilted the sunglasses a little off her eyes to get a better view, deciding she didn't want to miss anything—especially the way the denim of his jeans managed to stretch tight across his thighs. And the way his shoulders filled the shirt he was wearing.

He stood up a little and his tush—OMG, it was definitely the kind a woman would drool over. She bet they were perfect masculine cheeks, firm and fine.

Her mind began working, and she immediately began seeing him as a hero from one of the romance novels she read. *But which one?* she asked herself, thumping her finger against her chin.

She immediately thought of Jansen Trumble, the bad boy from the spicy novel *Mine Until Morning.* That had been one hot book, and even after reading it at least four or five times, she would give just about anything to have a rumble with Trumble. She settled her sunglasses back on her eyes thinking if she couldn't have the fictional Trumble then a look-alike would have to suffice.

"Miss, would you like to try some of my strawberries? I just rinsed this batch off. I bet you'd like them."

Her attention was pulled momentarily away from the gorgeous hunk when an island woman offered her a tray of fresh strawberries, sill wet from a recent rinsing. "Thanks, I'd love to try one."

She popped a strawberry in her mouth, immediately enjoying the taste when the sweet flavor burst on her tongue. It was wet, juicy and so delicious. That made her glance back over at the man. Now he was standing to his full height as he continued to consider the T-shirts. He was tall, and she could see just how well built he was.

She tilted her head, thinking there was something about him that was oddly familiar, although she had yet to see his features. Like her, he was wearing sunglasses. His were aviators. And even from a distance she could tell he was an American. He had chocolate-colored skin, and his dark hair was cut close to his head.

"Delicious, miss?"

She glanced back at the woman and smiled, remembering they were talking about the strawberries and not the man. "Yes, definitely delicious."

"Would you like another?"

Darcy chuckled. She hadn't intended on being greedy but since the woman asked… "Yes, I'd love another."

She put another strawberry into her mouth, and when she glanced back over at the man, she saw he was staring over at her. Facing him, she immediately recognized him and almost choked on the strawberry in her mouth.

York Ellis!

Even wearing sunglasses she would know him anywhere. The shape of his mouth and his chiseled jaw would give him away each time. What the heck was he doing here?

She felt irritation invade her entire body. Staring into his handsome face did nothing to calm her rising anger. Her best friend was married to one of his godbrothers, so they were usually invited to the same family functions.

She and York always managed to rub each other the wrong way whenever they would run into each other. Things had been that way between them since the time they'd met at Ellie and Uriel's wedding two years ago. During that time, her ex-husband Harold had tried threatening her to take him back. York had tried coming on to her at the reception. She had been in a bad mood at the time and had rebuffed his advances. Evidently he hadn't taken rejection well.

He removed his sunglasses and stood staring across the way at her, evidently as surprised to see her as she was to see him. She felt her body get hot under his intense stare but forced her emotions to stay in check. She certainly couldn't be that hard up for a man that she would be attracted to him.

And this wasn't just any man. It was York Ellis. He was arrogant. Cocky. Too damn sure of himself at times to suit her. So why was she having such a hard time dragging her gaze from him? Why instead was she allowing her eyes to roam all over him, taking in how well he fit his jeans, his shirt? And then, there was his looks…

So, okay, he had a nice-looking mouth, one that was shaped just for kissing and those other scandalous things mouths could do. And his eyes were dark, so compelling and so magnetic. And at the moment, those dark eyes were intent on staring her down.

His half smile told her he knew she was checking him out and evidently found it amusing, considering their history. Anyone who'd ever hung around them knew they had one. He rubbed her the wrong way, and it seemed she always managed to rub him the wrong way as well.

He continued to smile, and she tried to ignore the fact that doing so made the angular plane of his face more pronounced, made dimples slash deep in his cheeks.

This was the first time she ever noticed them. But then this was the first time he'd smiled at her.

But she quickly reminded herself he wasn't smiling at her now. He was smirking at having caught her sizing him up. Good grief! With his arrogance, he'd probably assumed she was interested in him sexually—not on her life and not even if he was the last man on this earth.

But then she couldn't help noticing that he was checking her out as well. His gaze was scanning up and down her body, and in response she could feel the nipples of her breasts press hard against the material of her sundress. She broke eye contact to reach for another strawberry. She needed it.

"All the others are for sale, miss," the woman told her gently.

Darcy couldn't help but chuckle at the woman's game and conceded it had worked. The woman had offered her two free strawberries to taste, knowing she would like them enough to buy the rest. And she was right.

"All right then, I want the entire basket. They are delicious."

The woman's face beamed. "Thank you. Would you like to try any other fruit?"

Darcy figured she might as well—anything to get her mind off the man across the street. Ellie liked York and couldn't figure out why her best friend and one of her husband's godbrothers could not get along. She had constantly told Ellie not to lose any sleep over it. Life wasn't intended for every single person to live together in harmony.

She glanced back at York and saw he was still staring over at her. Data rushed through her brain as to how much she knew about him. He was thirty-four, had gotten a criminology degree from a university in Florida and had been a cop with the NYPD for a few years before going into business for himself as a security expert. Both of his parents were living, and he had a younger sister and brother.

She also knew that he and his six godbrothers had formed the Bachelors in Demand club, with each one vowing to remain single. Now it was down to only four since two had married. Uriel Lassiter had married Ellie and Xavier Kane had married a woman by the name of Farrah earlier in the year.

"Here are your purchases," the woman said, handing her a huge brown paper bag containing the strawberries, mangoes and guineps. Darcy figured her next destination would be the hotel. Seeing York had practically ruined her day. She needed to revamp and get prepared for her night on the beach.

"Here, let me help you with that."

Darcy turned her head at the deep, husky male voice who'd spoken close to her ear at the same time her bag was smoothly taken from her hand. She frowned when she glanced up at a face that was too handsome for his own good. "York, what are you doing here in Jamaica?" She all but snapped the question out at him.

He smiled, and she had to force her gaze from the curve of his mouth when he said, "Funny, I was about to ask you the same thing. Are you sure New York can handle things without you?"

"It will be a struggle, but they'll manage," she responded smartly. They both lived in New York but made it a point not to have their paths cross, which had always been fine with her—definitely preferable. "What about with you? Is the security of the city being tested with you gone?"

"Not at all," he said smoothly. "And you never answered my question as to what you're doing here in Jamaica."

She glared up at him. "Not that it's any of your business but I'm here vacationing for three weeks. I've earned the time off and intend to enjoy myself. And why are you here?"

"Vacationing as well. Funny we picked the same place to unwind and seek out relaxation."

Darcy didn't see anything amusing about it. Being on the same island with him was definitely not how she wanted things to be. It was bad enough that they lived in the same city. "Well, enjoy your vacation, and I can carry my own bag, thank you." She tried tugging her bag from his grip and he held tight.

"Excuse me, but will you let go of my bag?"

Instead of doing so, he asked, "Where are you on your way to?"

She let out a deep, frustrated sigh. "My hotel."

"Which one?"

"The Ritz-Carlton," she said, without thinking.

His smile widened. "Now isn't that a coincidence? So am I."

He had to be joking, she thought. There was no way he could be staying at her hotel. As if he'd read her thoughts, he chuckled and said, "I guess this isn't your lucky day, huh?"

She snatched her bag from him. "You're right, it's not."

She turned and thanked the woman for her purchase and moved to walk away. Why wasn't she surprised when York fell in step beside her? She stopped and turned to him. "And just where do you think you're going?"

"Back to the hotel. Since we're headed the same way, I figure we might as well keep each other company."

"Has it ever occurred to you that I might not want your company?"

His answer was simple. "No, that thought has never occurred to me."

"Like the time you rushed over to my place thinking I was a helpless female in distress?"

He laughed. "Hey, that was Ellie's idea, not mine."

He was right. It had been Ellie's idea. She and Ellie had been talking on the phone late one night when Darcy had heard a noise downstairs. She put Ellie on hold to investigate, not knowing Ellie had panicked and called York, who lived less than a mile away. Ellie had asked him to go to Darcy's house to make sure everything was okay.

It turned out there had been a burglar. Some guy had broken into her house, and she had caught him rummaging through her kitchen drawers. By the time York had gotten there, the guy had discovered just how well she could defend herself when she'd demonstrated the karate skills she'd acquired growing up and taking classes with her brothers.

York, who had arrived before the police, had gotten extremely angry with her, saying she had no business taking on the likes of a burglar. Of course, she had disagreed with him.

"Okay, your showing up at my place might have been El's idea, but you had no right to scold me in front of those police officers."

"You took your life in your hands when you should have called the police," he said, and she could tell from the tone of his voice her actions that night last year was still a sore spot with him.

"Had I waited for the police, the man would have gotten away just to break into someone else's home. I had no intentions of letting him do that."

York frowned. "Does it matter that you could have gotten killed?" Anger laced his every word.

"Could have but I didn't. I had sized up the situation and knew it was one I could handle. Not every woman needs a man for protection, York."

"And evidently you're one of those kinds."

She wasn't sure what he meant by that, but hell yes, she was one of those kinds. She didn't need a man around to protect her. Her first husband had learned that the hard way when he began showing abusive tendencies. "I guess I am," she finally said, smiling as if she was proud of that fact.

She began walking again, convinced he would decide he wouldn't want her company after all. He proved her wrong when he picked up his pace and began walking beside her again. She decided to ignore him. The good thing was that the hotel was less than a block away.

York walked beside Darcy and tried not to keep glancing over at her. She looked cute in her wide-brimmed straw hat and sundress. He had noticed her checking him out, and when she'd removed her sunglasses and he'd seen it was Darcy, he hadn't known whether to be amused or annoyed. She certainly hadn't known who he was at first, just like he hadn't recognized her.

But once she had known it was him, he could immediately see her guard go up. She had intended to put distance between them. At any other time he would let her but not this time. He wasn't sure why, but all he knew was that was how it would be.

"Would the lady like to look at my bracelets?" a peddler asked.

She stopped and so did York. He observed her when she conversed with the man who had several bangle bracelets for her to see.

York continued to watch as the man ardently pitched his goods and was impressed with the way Darcy handled the anxious merchant by not giving in to his outrageous prices. He inwardly chuckled, thinking she definitely had no intentions of paying an exorbitant amount.

She seemed pretty sharp for a twenty-eight-year-old, and he figured she rarely missed anything. It would be hard, if not next to impossible, for a man to run a game on her.

He could vividly recall the first time he'd seen her rushing into the church for Uriel's wedding rehearsal. She'd been late since her plane had had mechanical problems.

Like all the other men, he had simply stared at her— the woman with all that dark brown hair flowing around her shoulders, hazel eyes, striking cocoa-colored features and a body to die for. The last thing he'd expected when he'd tried coming on to her later was to be told she wasn't interested. He would admit it had been a blow to his ego. That incident had been almost two years ago, and if the way she'd been sizing him up moments ago was anything to go by, it seemed she was pretty interested now.

He knew he should let go and move on, but so far he hadn't been able to do that. And whenever he saw her they had a tendency to get on each other's last nerves. If the truth be told, he had a mind to pay her back for rebuffing his advances that day. He could seduce her, make love to her and then walk away and not look back. Yes, that would serve her right.

"Well, that's that," she said, reclaiming his attention. He saw the way her lips quirked in amusement as well as the gleam of triumph shining in her eyes. He gathered she'd made a purchase she was pleased with.

They continued walking again, side by side, and he wondered how long she would continue to ignore him. He decided to stir conversation and asked, "When was the last time you talked to Ellie?" He eased the bag containing her fruit from her hand once again.

Darcy glanced over at York and decided that she would allow him to carry that bag since he seemed hell-bent on doing so anyway. She would keep the bag with the four bracelets she'd purchased from the peddler at a good price. "We're best friends, so I talk to El practically every day," she said. "But she hasn't called since I arrived here. She's going to be busy this week."

"Doing what?"

She wondered if he thought everything was his business. "She's hosting several holiday parties."

"Oh."

"It is the holiday season, you know," she reminded him.

"Yes, I know."

She didn't say anything and for a moment regretted bringing up any mention of the holidays. She'd heard from El that a woman York had been dating and had begun caring deeply about, and who'd been a fellow officer when he'd been a cop with the NYPD, had gotten gunned down on Christmas Day while investigating a robbery. That had been over six years ago. After that, he'd sworn never to get seriously involved with a woman again, especially one in a dangerous profession. She knew all about the Bachelors in Demand club, one he formed along with his bachelor godbrothers who were all intent on staying single men forever. She had met all six of the godbrothers and got along with each of them…except for York.

"So how are your parents?" she asked, deciding to change the subject. She had first met the Ellises at Ellie and Uriel's wedding and had run into them again when another one of Uriel and York's godbrothers, Xavier Kane, had gotten married earlier in the year.

"They're doing fine. I visited with them a couple of months ago." He glanced back over at her. "So what do you plan on doing later?"

She glanced up at him from under the wide-brimmed hat. "I'm resting up for the big beach party the hotel is hosting tonight. I hear it's a real classy black-tie affair. You are going, aren't you?"

"Hadn't planned on it."

"Oh, well." She should have felt relieved that he wouldn't be there, but for some reason she felt a pang of disappointment in her chest. Why was that?

"Behave yourself tonight, Darcy."

She lifted a brow. If he was being cute, she wasn't appreciating it. "Let me assure you, Mr. Ellis, that you don't need to tell me how to behave. And just for the record, I don't plan on taking your advice. The reason

I'm here is to have a good time, and a good time is what I will have—even if it means misbehaving."

He stopped walking and stared at her, and she could see anger lurking in the dark depths of his eyes. She knew it was probably bothering him that she was standing there, facing him and looking nonplussed. Her two brothers were dominating males, so York's personality type was not foreign to her. But that didn't mean she had to tolerate it or him.

She glanced around. They were now standing in the plush lobby of the hotel. "I guess this is where we need to part ways, and hopefully we won't run into each other again anytime soon. You didn't say how long you intend to visit here."

He smiled at her. "No, I didn't say."

And when she saw that he had no intention of doing so either, she released a sigh, took her bag from him and said, "Goodbye, York." She then turned and headed for the bank of elevators.

Darcy drew in a deep breath with every step she took, tempted to glance over her shoulder. But she had a feeling he was still standing there, staring at her, and she didn't want to give him the impression that she'd given him another thought...although she was doing so.

A few moments later, she stepped on the elevator and turned. She'd been right. He was still standing there. And while others joined her on the elevator their gazes held. At that moment, she felt a pang of regret that the two of them had never gotten along. Too bad. She was too set in her ways to make any changes now. Besides, she didn't want to make any changes. For some reason, she much preferred that she and York keep their distance. The man was temptation personified. She could deal with temptation but not when it included an extreme amount of arrogance.

The elevator doors swooshed shut, breaking their eye connection. She released a deep breath, only realizing at that moment she'd been holding it. He was staying in another section of the hotel. It was a humongous place, but their paths might cross again and she would be ready and prepared. She had no intentions of letting York Ellis catch her off guard again.

CHAPTER TWO

DAMN, THE WOMAN was too beautiful for her own good, York thought, watching the elevator door close behind Darcy Owens. Beautiful with a smart mouth, a delectable-looking mouth. More than once he'd been tempted to kiss it shut and to demonstrate just what he could do when his tongue connected with hers.

But then he had to remember that Darcy was too brash and outspoken to suit him. He didn't want a "yes" woman by any means, but he didn't want a woman who would dissect his every word looking for some hidden meaning. For some reason, she couldn't take things at face value when it came to him, and he couldn't understand why.

If he had the time, he would put it at the top of his list to seduce the smart-mouthed Darcy Owens just for the hell of it. If she wanted to misbehave, he could certainly show her what misbehaving was all about. But he had to remember she was the best friend of his godbrother's wife, and Ellie probably wouldn't take too kindly if he seduced her best friend just for the hell of paying her back.

He was about to head over to his side of the hotel when his cell phone rang. He pulled it off his belt and saw it was Wesley Carr, one of the retired police officers that he used as part of his investigative team. It had been his father's idea.

Jerome Ellis had retired a few years ago as a circuit judge. He was a firm believer that retired police officers could better serve as more than just bailiffs at the courthouses. Most had sharp minds and loved the challenge of working on a case. York had taken his father's advice and hired three such men at his firm and never regretted doing so.

"Yes, Wesley, what you got for me?" York asked.

"First of all, are you taking those vitamin supplements I told you about?" Wesley asked.

York shook his head. One of the pitfalls of hiring the men was that they liked to run his life by making sure he got the proper rest, ate healthy and didn't overdo it when it came to women. They claimed all three things would eventually take a toll on a man.

"Yes, I'm taking them, so what do you have?"

"I think Damien Felder might be your man," Wesley said with certainty.

"Why?"

"He has a ton of gambling debts."

York rubbed his chin thoughtfully. "He's a gambler?"

"Of the worst kind. Although he's tried covering his tracks, I was able to trace his ties to the Medina family."

"Damn." The Medina family had their hands into anything illegal they could touch. York hadn't gotten wind of them involved in movie piracy before now, though. Mainly it'd been drugs, prostitution and the transportation of illegal immigrants.

And Roswell Medina's name had been linked to the homicide investigation involving Rhona, the only woman York had ever considered marrying. Like him she had been a police officer and had gotten struck down by a bullet when she had investigated a robbery. The authorities believed the rash of burglaries in Harlem had been organized by Medina but could never prove it.

"I can see them getting interested, if they had the right person on the inside to help them. It's evidently a profitable business," York added.

"Apparently."

He inhaled a deep sigh. He knew Damien Felder would be the one to watch for a while. "I want all the information you can get me on Felder's association with any of the Medinas." He would just love to nail any member of that crime family for something, even if it was for jaywalking.

As he headed back toward his side of the hotel he thought about Darcy and doubted the two of them would be running into each other again any time soon.

Hell, he hoped not.

A TWENTY-PIECE orchestra on the beach.

The hotel had thought of everything, Darcy concluded as she stepped outside. Everyone had been told that tonight's affair was all glitz and glamour, and everyone had dressed to the nines. Men were in tuxes and women were in beautiful gowns. She had decided to wear the short white lace dress and silver sandals she had purchased a few months ago when she had joined Ellie on a shopping spree when she'd visited her best friend in Charlotte.

With a glass of champagne in her hand, Darcy made her way down the white stone steps with towering balustrades on both sides. She could see the beach and see how the water was shimmering beneath the glow of the moon. To her right, tables of food had been set up, and shrimp, lobsters and oysters were being steamed on an open fire.

For those not wanting to get sand in their shoes, a huge wooden deck had been placed on the ground, and several light fixtures provided just the right amount of light to the affair.

She was about to grab another flute of champagne from a passing waiter when she happened to glance across the way and saw a man looking at her. He looked American and she placed his age in his late thirties. And she had to give it to him—he looked like a million bucks in his black tux.

But compared to York there was something lacking. He was handsome, although he wasn't of the jaw-dropping kind like York Ellis. And she would have to be the first to concede that even with all the stranger's handsomeness, she couldn't even conjure up what hero he could represent from those tons of romance novels she had read. She'd had no such problem with York.

She bit down on her lip wondering why she'd just made the comparison. Why had York even crossed her mind? The stranger smiled over at her, and she smiled back before another partier walked up to him and claimed his attention. At least it hadn't been a woman. As she sipped her champagne, she saw him glance over her way, as if assuring himself she was still there—still unattached, possibly still interested.

Deciding not to appear too interested, she began mingling, enjoying the sights and sounds. Moments later, she was leaning against a balustrade watching a group of the island dancers perform. Their movements were so romantic and breathtaking beneath the stars.

"I can tell you are enjoying yourself," a deep, husky male voice said.

The first thought that flashed through her mind was that it wasn't as deep as York's, and it wasn't making her skin feel like it was being caressed. Pushing that observation to the back of her mind, she looked up at the stranger she'd seen earlier and asked, "And just how can you tell?"

"You have that look. And whatever the cause of it, do you mind sharing it because I'm simply bored."

She fought from shaking her head. She had heard that pickup line so many other times, surely the man could have thought of something else. But she could go along with it for now. "Then I guess I need to make sure you enjoy yourself as much as I do."

He smiled, flashing her perfect white teeth. "I would definitely appreciate it." He then held his hand out to her. "I'm Damien Felder, by the way."

She returned his smile. "And I'm Darcy Owens."

"Please to meet you, Darcy. And is that a Midwestern accent I hear?"

"Yes, it is," she replied. "And yours is part southern and part western."

Instead of saying whether her assumption was correct, he took a step closer to her. "Are you staying at this hotel?"

She didn't have to wonder why he was asking. The man was a fast mover, and she had no problem with that if her vibes had been in sync with his. They weren't for some reason. "Yes, I'm at this hotel. What about you?"

"No, my hotel is a few miles from here. I was invited tonight by a friend. But an emergency came up, and he had to leave the island. He encouraged me to come anyway. He thought I would enjoy myself. I hadn't been until I saw you."

She smiled. "Thank you."

"You're welcome. And why would a beautiful woman travel to this island alone?"

She took a sip of her champagne and smiled as she looked up at him. "What makes you think I'm alone?"

A gleam appeared in the depths of his brown eyes. "Because no man with a lick of sense would let you out of his sight for long."

Darcy smiled. The man was full of compliments, although she'd heard most of them before. "I needed a little vacation." And before he could ask her anything else, she decided to ask him a question. "So what brings you to the island?"

"I'm associated with a movie that will be filmed on the island starting tomorrow."

She lifted a brow. "A movie?"

He chuckled. "Yes, one from Spirit Head Productions."

She nodded. She had heard of them. In fact, their main headquarters were in New York. "Let me guess," she said, smiling. "You're the leading man."

From his expression, she could tell he enjoyed getting compliments as much as he enjoyed giving them. "No, I hold an administrative position. I'm a line producer."

"Sounds exciting."

He met her gaze. "It is. How would you like me to give you a tour of the set tomorrow?"

She thought his offer was certainly generous, and she could tell from the way he was looking at her he thought so, too, and expected her to jump at it. So she did, all but clapping her hands in fake excitement. "Oh, that would be wonderful. I'd love to."

"Well then, it's settled. Now how about if I come up to your room tonight so I'll know where to come get you tomorrow."

"I prefer that we meet in the lobby."

She could see the disappointment flash in his eyes. She all but shrugged at the thought. He might eventually share her bed before she left the island, but he would work hard for the privilege. So far she didn't feel a connection to him but was hoping it was just her and not him. For some reason when she looked at him, visions of York entered her mind. And that wasn't good.

"Would you like to take a walk on the beach?"

She smiled. "No. In fact, it's been a tiring day for me. I think I'll call it an early night and go back up to my room now," she said.

"Alone?" he asked.

"Yes, alone. I'm recovering from a flu bug and don't want to overdo it."

"I understand, and I wouldn't want you to overdo it either." He reached into his jacket and pulled out a card. "Here's my business card. Call me when you get up in the morning. Maybe we can share breakfast."

"Thanks, and I will give you a call," she said, taking the card.

"Are you sure you don't need me to walk you back to your room?"

"Thanks for the offer but I'm positive. Good night. I'll see you tomorrow, Damien."

And then she walked off, knowing he was still watching her. She knew he thought he had her within his scope, but he would soon discover that she was the one who had him in hers.

YORK STOOD IN the shadows, behind the orchestra stand, and sipped his wine. He watched the man he'd identified earlier that day as Damien Felder, hitting on Darcy Owens of all people. And from the way the man was still looking at Darcy as she disappeared among the other partiers, he was definitely interested in her. That York could understand. Not only did she have striking features but the dress she was wearing showed a pair of gorgeous legs and a very curvy body.

"Damn." He drew in a deep breath. The man's interest in Darcy was the last thing York needed. Based on the report Wesley had given him earlier, Felder was the last person she should even be talking to. Even Malcolm and his group didn't know half the stuff Damien Felder was involved in, but York didn't plan on sharing any of it with them until he had concrete proof to back it up.

But first he needed to make sure Darcy stayed out of the picture. He had seen the moment Felder had slid his business card into the palm of her hand. Since York could read lips—something he taught himself to do after his sister was born deaf—he knew that Felder had invited her on set tomorrow. He wasn't sure what her response had been since Felder had been the one facing him, while Darcy's back had been to him.

The man had also tried inviting himself up to Darcy's room, which she apparently turned down since she had left the party alone. At least York was grateful for that. He felt a deep pull in his stomach and tried convincing himself that the only reason he was grateful was because he was looking out for her. After all, she was Ellie's best friend, so that was the least he could do. Wanting to keep her out of the picture had nothing to do with the jealousy he'd felt when he'd seen Felder approach her. He assured himself that it hadn't been jealousy, just concern. Besides, too much was at stake with this case, and the last thing he needed was Darcy screwing things up.

He was about to leave when he noticed Felder giving the nod to another woman at the party. He recognized her immediately—Danielle Simone, the leading lady in the movie they were filming. Malcolm was pretty convinced that Danielle was not in any way a part of the black market ring. Now York wasn't so sure when he watched as she walked toward the beach with Felder following her, keeping a careful distance.

Interesting. He couldn't help wonder what that was about. Were the two having a secret affair? His cell phone rang, and he picked it up. It was one of his men who was attending the party undercover. "Yes, Mark, I picked up on the two. Follow them from here, and let me know where they go and what they do."

He clicked off the phone, satisfied his man was on it and wouldn't let the couple out of his sight. York then turned toward the part of the hotel where Darcy's room was located.

DARCY HAD SHOWERED and slipped into the hotel's complimentary bathrobe when she heard a knock on her hotel room door. She frowned, wondering who it could be. It was way past midnight, although she was sure a number of people were still at the party having a good time.

She crossed the room to look out the peephole in the door, and a frown settled around her mouth. *York Ellis.* Why on earth would he visit her room, and most importantly, how did he know her room number? She knew for certain that she had not given it to him.

Knowing he was the only person who could answer that question, she tightened the belt around her robe before taking off the lock and snatching open the door. "York, what on earth are you doing here, and how do you know my room number?"

"We need to talk."

"What?" she asked as she nearly drowned in the dark eyes staring down at her. She'd always thought they were such a gorgeous pair—although she would never admit such a thing to him or anyone else for that matter. She wouldn't even confess it to Ellie. Nor would she ever mention how heat would course through her body whenever he stood this close to her. She'd noticed it that first time they'd met, which was why she had deliberately avoided him. The last thing she had needed at the time was to be attracted to a man after what she'd gone through with her ex-husband.

"I said we need to talk, Darcy."

She stiffened her spine and glared at him. "Why? And you haven't answered my question. How did you get my room number?"

He leaned in the doorway, and her gaze watched his every movement at the same time her nostrils inhaled his manly scent. Her heart skipped a beat when her gaze roamed over him. He looked good in a tux. Had he attended the party when he'd said earlier that day that he wouldn't be doing so?

"I have ways of finding out anything I want to know, Darcy."

The deep huskiness of his voice had her gaze returning back to his. Even leaning in the doorway, he was towering over her. For some reason, her gaze shifted to his hands. This wasn't the first time she had noticed just how large they were. Heat spread throughout her body when she recalled the theory about the size of a man's hands and feet in comparison to another part of his anatomy. Automatically her gaze shifted to his feet.

"Looking for anything in particular?"

She snatched her gaze up to him. He had caught her checking him out again. "No, I was just thinking." That wasn't a total lie. He didn't have to know what she was thinking about. "And as far as you having ways of finding out whatever you want to know…well, that's probably true, but you won't hold a single conversation with me unless you tell me what it's about."

He rubbed his hand down his face as if annoyed with her. "It's about Damien Felder. You were flirting with him at the party tonight."

They were flirting with each other, but his impression of how things had been meant nothing to her. "I thought you weren't going to the party."

"I changed my mind."

"And you know Damien?"

He shook his head. "No, but I know *of* Damien, which is what I want to talk to you about."

There was no denying that York had her curious. "Very well, come in."

She took a step back, and he entered her hotel room and closed the door behind him. He glanced around the room, and when his gaze returned to her, it seemed the intensity in the depths of his eyes was pinning her in place.

She drew in a deep breath, refusing to get caught like a deer in the headlights where he was concerned. So she tightened the sash of her robe around her even more and broke eye contact with him and beckoned him to the sofa. "Have a seat and let's talk."

She watched him move to the sofa while heat spread throughout her body. He looked too darn comfortable for her liking. There was something about the way he was sitting, with his arms spread across the back of the sofa, that made her want to slide down on the sofa with him, ease the tux jacket off his shoulders and run her hands across the broad width of his chest.

Where on earth had those thoughts come from? This was York Ellis, the one man she didn't get along with, the one man who seemed to enjoy rubbing her the wrong way whenever their paths crossed. "What about Damien?" she spoke up and asked, reminding herself the only reason he was sitting on her sofa was because she was interested in what he had to say.

For some reason, the mention of Damien made him lean closer, cause something akin to anger to flash across his features. "You met him tonight."

She heard the censure in his tone and wondered the reason for it. "Yes, and why do you care?"

Evidently her question stumped him. The irritation in his face was replaced by a slow smile, one that didn't quite reach his eyes. "Personally, I don't other than the fact that you're screwing things up for me and my investigation."

She bit down on her lips as she struggled to keep a civil tongue. "What investigation?"

As he sat back, York drew in a deep breath, trying to calm the anger that was flowing through him. And it was anger he could not explain. What she did and who she did it with was her business. He shouldn't care one bit, and he had tried convincing himself that he didn't. But the truth of the matter was that he did. There was no way he would allow her to blindly walk into a dangerous situation.

"I wasn't absolutely up front with you earlier today when I gave my reason for being here on the island."

"You weren't?"

"No. I'm here on a job. My company was hired by a group of moviemakers for security detail on a movie being filmed, the same one Felder is associated with. And while my outfit is doing that, I'm working behind the scenes to protect their interest. Someone is slipping the movies to the black market before their theatrical release."

She lifted a brow. "And what does that have to do with Damien Felder?"

It was hard to explain why a part of him wanted to kiss her and strangle her at the same time. What was there about her that could drive him to such extremes? "I have reason to believe Felder might be involved in some way."

"Do you have any proof?"

"No."

"Then it's merely speculation on your part."

"For now. But he is being watched, and if he is guilty, I would hate for your name to be linked to his."

She glared at him. "And what if your suspicions are wrong? Do you expect me not to enjoy the company of a man because you think he might be involved in some case you're investigating?"

"I was hoping that you would. And as far as me suspecting him, I'm almost sure he's my man. I wouldn't have come to you if I didn't."

Darcy wondered just why he had. They weren't friends, so his concern about her had nothing to do with it. He must have been truthful earlier when he'd said she had the potential of screwing things up for him.

She stood. "Okay, you've warned me. I'll walk you to the door."

He remained sitting. "And what the hell does that mean?" he asked.

The anger in his tone made her lift her chin. "It means just what I said, York. You've warned me. Now you can leave."

"But you will take my advice."

To Darcy, it sounded more like a direct order than a question. "No, I don't plan to take your advice. Unless you have something more concrete than assumptions, I see no reason not to see Damien again. In fact, we've made plans for later today."

He held her gaze, and she could see the fire in his eyes. He was so angry with her that he was almost baring his teeth. He slowly leaned forward in his seat, and in a tone of voice tinged with a growl, he asked, "Why are you being difficult?"

She curved her lips into a smile only because she knew it would get on his last nerve. "Because I want to."

She knew she was being childish. Pretty darn petty, in fact, when for whatever his reason, he had come to warn her about Damien. She had no intentions of telling him that the warning was not needed since she wasn't attracted to Damien and didn't plan on seeing him again after their date that day. And the only reason she was keeping her date with him was because she'd always wanted to check out a movie set, nothing more. Even with Damien's handsome looks, he hadn't done anything for her.

And definitely not in the way the man sitting on her sofa was doing. Even now she was struggling, trying hard to fight the attraction, the magnetic pull, especially since it was an attraction she didn't want or need. And it was an attraction she didn't intend to go anywhere.

"You like rattling me, don't you, Darcy?"

His words pulled her attention back to the present. She figured there was no need to lie. "Yes, I guess I do."

Darcy didn't think there could be anything sexy about a man who merely stood up from sitting on a sofa. But with York, watching his body in movement was enough to cause heat to flare in her center and the juncture of her thighs.

And when he slowly walked toward her, advancing on her like he was the hunter and she his prey, she merely stood her ground. She refused to back up or retreat. And it seemed he had no intentions of halting his approach until he came to a stop in front of her.

"I've heard of stubborn women before, but you have to be the stubbornest."

She glared up at him. "I'll take that as a compliment, York. Now if you don't mind, it's late and you need to leave."

York thought some women had to be born for trouble, and this one standing in front of him was one of them. Against his better judgment, he had come here tonight to give her fair warning and he had done so. If she didn't want to heed to his warnings, there was nothing he could do about it.

He tried to push the thought from his mind that while he'd been sitting on the sofa, whether she knew it or not, he had been fighting desire for her that had all but seeped into his bones. Why on earth would he be attracted to her of all women?

Before he'd come up to her room tonight, he'd been approached by a couple of women who'd all but invited him to their hotel room. One had brazenly offered to give him a blow job right there on the elevator. But he hadn't wanted any of them. He wanted this one. This haughty-looking female, who had blood firing through his veins, who was staring him down and standing in front of him looking as sexy as any woman had a right to look in a bathrobe.

He glared down at her when the room got too quiet for his taste. "Don't say I didn't warn you."

"I won't. Now goodbye, York."

At that moment, something inside of him snapped. She was glaring at him, yet earlier tonight she'd been smiling at Damien Felder. Not only had she been smiling but she'd also flirted with the man. "You like pushing my buttons, don't you, Darcy?"

"Yes," she said, smiling. "Gives me great pleasure."

"No, this is pleasure." And then he reached out, pulled her to him and captured her mouth with his.

CHAPTER THREE

HE WAS RIGHT, Darcy thought, when York began kissing her with a hunger that surprised her. This was pleasure. And it began overwhelming her as sensations tore through her. When she felt those big hands she'd checked out earlier tighten their hold on her, she became wrapped in his heat with every languorous stroke of his tongue. That was all it took for desire to start coiling deep in her body, thickening the blood rushing through her veins. And when she released a surprised gasp, he slid his tongue deeper inside her mouth.

He shifted, and his body pressed hard against her and she felt him—his aroused thickness. His hardness. It was poking her in the belly. A part of her wanted to push him away. But another part wanted to draw him even closer. She knew what part won when a moan flowed from deep within her throat. Instinctively, she eased up on tiptoes to return the kiss with the same demand and hunger he was putting into it. And when her tongue tried battling his for control, his arms tightened even more around her, almost crushing her body to his. Easing upward shifted his aroused part from her belly right to the juncture of her thighs, and immediately she could feel her panties get wet.

York's heart was hammering hard in his chest. He didn't understand why he was kissing Darcy this way, a woman he'd convinced himself that he didn't even like. Evidently his personal feelings toward her had nothing to do with lust, and he was convinced that was what was filling his mind at that moment. That was what had him eating away at her mouth as if it was the last meal he would have. And she was kissing him back with just as much intensity. It seemed as if a floodgate had burst open, and they didn't know how to stop the lusty water from rushing through.

They didn't know or they didn't want *to know?*

At that moment, it didn't matter to him, and he had a feeling it didn't matter to her either. He wanted her, and from the way she was kissing him back, she wanted him as well. And if she didn't let up on his tongue he was certain he was going to lose his mind. He hadn't made love to a woman in a while, and he couldn't recall one being this passionate, this aggressive, this damn hot. He had initiated the kiss, but there was a big question as to who was being seduced.

Suddenly, he pulled back, reached out and ripped the bathrobe off her body. Just as he thought, she was completely naked underneath.

"What do you think you're doing?" she asked, inhaling a deep breath of air.

He glanced over at her while tearing off his own clothes, not believing she had to ask. But just in case she had any intentions of suddenly deciding she didn't want this as much as he did, he stopped short of removing his slacks. Instead he reached out, pulled her to him and captured her mouth once more.

Darcy couldn't help the moan that eased from deep in her throat. Had it really been two years since she'd felt sensations like this? Sure, there'd been Bruce, but York was showing her that when it came to hot sex between a man and woman, there was nothing like the real thing. A sex toy couldn't compare.

She felt everything. The hardness of his erection was pressed against her center, the material of his tux was rubbing against her thigh causing all kinds of sensations to erupt within her. And when she felt those large hands of his stroke the soft skin of her backside, molding her cheeks closer to him, she couldn't do anything but surrender. He had blazed a fire that was consuming them both.

Knowing she was capitulating didn't sit too well with her, but every stroke of his tongue in her mouth was making her appreciate the benefits. The man didn't intend to hold anything back, and she decided at that moment, neither would she.

She'd had all intentions of having an island fling, so there was no stopping her now. Besides, this would be a one-night stand. She would merely use him to take the two-year edge off, since he seemed to know just what he was doing.

He broke off the kiss, and his gaze burned into hers as he kicked off his shoes before easing his pants and briefs down his legs all at once. Her breath got caught in her throat when her gaze lowered. Maybe that saying about the size of feet and hands in comparison to other parts of a man's body wasn't just a theory at all. It was a truth.

Her gaze moved back to his face, and she wasn't sure who made the first move—nor did she care. All she cared about was that she was in his arms again while he kissed her with a madness she felt to her toes. And she was convinced what they were doing was sheer madness. A thought entered her mind that maybe they should slow down and talk about it. Then she decided there was no need to waste time talking.

He tore his mouth from hers, and the look she saw in his eyes indicated his agreement. "I want to get inside you, Darcy."

He couldn't have said it any plainer than that, she thought. She went to him and then spread her hands out across his stomach. His skin felt hot beneath her fingers, and that same heat spread through her when she moved her hands lower. When her hand pressed against the thickness of his muscular thighs, she felt a stirring in the pit of her stomach. The intensity of it was almost frightening.

She was convinced the desire taking over her mind and her body had nothing to do with York per se but with the fact that he was a man. But not just any man. He was a red-hot, good-looking man who had the ability to shoot adrenaline up her spine in very high dosages.

And she couldn't discount the fact that she hadn't slept with a man in almost two years, not since moving to New York. Before then, thanks to her ex-husband, she had washed her hands of men. She found there was too much drama where they were concerned. Bruce had been given to her as a prank gift and she—who'd never considered using a sex toy before—had discovered in time of need he could be her best friend.

But now York was reminding her in a very explosive way that there was nothing like a flesh-and-blood male. Nothing like a real man breathing down your neck, kissing you, touching you, letting you touch him. And at that moment, it didn't matter one iota that the man causing her so much sumptuous turbulence was the one man she thought she didn't even like.

She might have regrets for her actions in the morning, but at that very moment, she wanted him, too. She wanted him inside of her.

Her breaths were coming out in tortured moans when she lowered her hand and touched his erection. Ignoring his masculine growl, she cupped him, loving the feel of his hardness in her hand, loving the heat of it. It was rock hard. Solid. Big. And when she began running her thumb over the shaft's head, wanting to feel the protruding veins beneath her fingertips, she felt him shudder in her hand.

She imagined in the deep recesses of her mind this same solid flesh sliding all the way inside of her and how her muscles would clench it, possess it, milk it for everything it was worth and then some. It had been a long time for her, way too long. She was greedy and wanted it all.

She glanced up at him, met his gaze through desire-glazed eyes and saw the state of his arousal in the dark eyes staring right back at her.

"Condom?" she asked him almost in a moan. When he nodded and made a move to step back, she had to release him and immediately felt the loss.

And then he took time to remove his socks before retrieving a condom packet from his wallet. As if having a woman watch him don a condom was the most natural thing, he proceeded to put on protection.

She was suddenly engulfed in strong arms when York swept her off her feet to carry her to the bedroom.

YORK COULD NOT recall when he'd wanted a woman this much. And why did that woman have to be Darcy Owens? He should find the very thought unsettling, but at the moment too much desire was running through his body to be concerned with emotions he wasn't used to.

He figured there had to be a full moon out tonight, or maybe there was something to that passion fruit he'd had at lunch. Regardless, tomorrow and the days that followed he was certain he would be back on track—revert to his right mind and be ruled by logic and less by lust. He shouldn't have any problems keeping his distance from Darcy during his remaining time on the island.

But at this very moment his thoughts, his actions were ruled by a yearning that had taken over his entire body. Deep down, he knew it was almost two years in the works. He had wanted her the first time he'd seen her at Ellie and Uriel's wedding. He had even warned his other godbrothers to keep their distance. And when she had snubbed him, told him in no uncertain words that she wasn't interested, his attraction had turned to outright dislike. He hadn't taken her rejection well.

That's why one of the most satisfying things for him right now was to know she was as much of a goner as he was. She definitely wasn't rejecting him now. The thought made him smile as he placed her on the bed and then took a step back. Seeing her naked body in the middle of the king-size bed made him more aroused, especially when the mass of dark brown hair looked in total disarray around her shoulders. She looked sexy. She looked hot. She looked as if she was ready for anything he had to give her. And tonight he had plenty.

But she intended to play the vixen. He figured as

much when she deliberately stretched to make her breasts lift at an angle that made them appear ready for his mouth. And her legs slowly opened, showing how ripe, wet and ready she was. A fierce need ripped through him, and he moved back toward the bed. He was well aware of the rules he would be breaking about never losing control when it came to a woman.

He chuckled. It was too late. He'd already lost it. And he would make sure that her payback for driving him over the edge was a night she wouldn't forget. He knew for certain that he wouldn't.

York moved toward the bed, and his main thought was to reconnect his mouth to hers. He pulled her toward him and captured her mouth. There was something about her taste that had him wanting more. But she seemed just as ravenous as he and was returning his stroke lick for lick.

He broke off the kiss and lowered his gaze from her wet lips down her breasts, and he saw how her nipples were hardening to stiff buds right before his eyes. He felt all his senses begin to flash and his tongue all but thicken in his mouth with thoughts of just what he wanted to do with those nipples.

"You want to taste them, York? If so, don't let me stop you."

Her words had him glancing up. She must have seen the intensity in his gaze when he'd been staring at her breasts. He found a woman who spoke her mind in the bedroom pretty refreshing. But then he wasn't surprised that was the tactic an outspoken woman like Darcy would use.

His gaze lowered back to her nipples. Yes, he wanted to taste them. He was getting harder just thinking about all the things he'd liked doing to them with his mouth. But he wouldn't stop at her breasts. He intended to taste every inch of her and felt he should at least warn her.

"Your breasts aren't the only thing I want to taste, Darcy." He didn't feel he had to go into specifics. And just the thought rocked his senses.

York immediately drew a turgid nipple into his mouth and began devouring it with a greed he knew she'd feel all the way to her toes but especially at her center. And speaking of her center…

His hand found its target at the juncture of her thighs, and sensations sizzled through him, making him ache. His fingers spread her apart first, then delved into her heated wetness, and he felt his erection throb in response.

She moaned when he allowed his mouth to pay homage to the other nipple, letting his tongue lap at it a few times before easing it between his lips. He sucked on it while a lusty rush filled him, obliterated his senses and sent a fierce need rushing through his bloodstream.

And when he couldn't hold back any longer, he pulled away from her breasts and went straight to the source of her heat. Lifting her hips, he lowered his mouth to her, intent on licking every inch of her and lapping up her dewy wetness, tasting her until he got his fill. He wanted every lusty cell in his body to be satisfied.

Darcy began trembling the exact moment she felt the heat of York's tongue ease inside of her, and it became nearly impossible to breathe. All she could do was whimper in pleasure. So she did. He knew what he was doing by using his tongue to stroke her. He was so skilled that it had her shaking from head to toe. He felt her shudders and was lapping up every single shiver.

She needed to grab hold of something, and the bed-spread just wouldn't do. So she reached for his head instead. She held him steady, kept him in place, but the feel of his tongue moving inside of her was too much. Her fingers clenched the side of his head the moment her world exploded in a orgasm that detonated every part of her body.

And she heard herself call his name. It was a blazing rush from her lips, a satisfying ache that she felt when his tongue delved deeper, lapped harder. She was transformed into a mass of lusty mush, and it had to be the most exquisite feeling she'd ever encountered. This single act was worth the two years she'd gone without.

When she felt him release her and pull out his tongue, she almost screamed her regret. Watching through passion-glazed eyes, she saw him straddle her, felt the hardness of him replace his tongue to ease inside of her, stretching her to the point where she wondered if they would fit and knowing he would die trying.

As if her body was made just for him, her insides expanded, got wetter, felt slicker. He continued to push his way inside, and she gazed up at him, saw the beads of perspiration on his brow. He lifted her hips, intent on her taking him, receiving him and welcoming him.

When he had reached her hilt, he began moving, stroking her with a rhythm that had every cell in her body, every single molecule responding. The heat of his skin rubbed against her thighs as he thrust back and forth, going deeper and deeper with every stroke. Her clit was on fire, and he wasn't trying to put out the flames. Instead, he was taking the flames higher, sparking every single ember inside of her.

And she clenched him, refusing to let him take without giving. She began milking him and felt her muscles tighten then pull to get the full benefit, maximize the sensual effect of what he was doing to her. The bed was shaking in its frame as he rode her in a way she'd never been ridden before. And his shaft seemed to get bigger and harder inside of her.

Just when she thought she couldn't take any more, she was pushed over the edge, and her body erupted in a colossal explosion. Her fingers dug into the muscles of his shoulders, and the lower part of her lifted off the bed with the massive blast. He growled when he pressed harder into her body, spreading her thighs apart even more.

York was replacing two years of pent-up, half filled, half measured pleasure. Before now what she'd assumed was satisfaction had only been appeasement. This was better than anything she could have imagined from any man or toy. It was beyond her wildest dream—and over the years she'd had plenty of wild dreams. But none could compare to this reality.

He continued to ride her, continued to pound into her, intent on getting in the last stroke, gratifying her every pulsation as well as his own.

"York…"

She heard the sound of his name from her lips as she continued to come, but she couldn't make herself stop as pleasure continued to hold her in its grip. She knew if she never made love to another man again she would have memories of tonight stored away in the back of her mind.

"Darcy…"

The rough and deep sound of his voice rushed over her, made her body respond the way it had never responded to a man before. She looked up into his dark gaze. He had slowed down but not stopped. And then he slowly began easing from her body when all of a sudden he thrust right back in all the way to the hilt. He lowered his head and whispered in her ear in a deep, primitive growl. "I want more."

And in response, she wrapped her legs around him as she felt need coupled with desire rush through her veins, overtake her senses. Tonight she would give him more because giving him more meant she was taking just as much for herself.

DAYBREAK WAS PEEKING through the window blinds when York glanced over his shoulder at Darcy. He slowly eased from the bed, determined not to wake her. Drawing in a deep breath, he tried to regain control of his senses while piecing together everything that had happened last night in this room. He should feel vindicated at having seduced her, but instead he was wondering who had seduced whom.

He'd known before last night there was sexual attraction between them, which was the cause of a lot of their bickering. But he hadn't known until last night just how much he'd wanted her—not just to prove a point or to right what he'd considered a wrong. He refused to think making love to her had anything to do with revenge or getting back at her. And he refused to consider the pleasure had been one-sided. She hadn't shown resistance to anything they'd done in that bed.

And hell, they had done a lot. He hadn't known a woman's skin could taste so luscious or that hazel eyes could turn so many different shades while in the throes of heated passion. Nor had he known that a woman could ride just as hard as a man.

Even when he had fought to keep himself in check and to regain control, he'd found his efforts wasted. Darcy had given him the kind of pleasure he hadn't shared with any woman before her. That said a lot, considering his reputation.

Before leaving her bedroom, he glanced over his shoulder. She was still sleeping, and he understood why. They had made love almost nonstop through the night. One orgasm was followed by another. The pleasure had been too intense to even think about stopping, and she hadn't complained. In fact, she had kept up with him all the way. At that very moment, he didn't see Darcy Owens as a woman with a smart mouth but as a woman who definitely knew how to use that mouth.

She was lying on top of the covers, and he couldn't stop his gaze from roaming over her naked body. Passion marks were visible on her thighs, stomach and around her breasts, and he could immediately recall the exact moment he'd placed each of them there. He shook his head and glanced down at himself. He had a number of passion marks on his body as well. Darcy definitely believed in equal play.

York glanced back at her and felt his body grow hard all over again. He drew in a deep breath and forced his gaze from her or else he'd be tempted to crawl back in bed with her, hold her in his arms and patiently wait until she awakened. Then he would make love to her all over again.

Damn. He was losing control again, becoming undone. Okay, he had enjoyed the Darcy experience, but he needed to regroup and remember the reason he was in Jamaica. And it wasn't to spend his time in Darcy Owens's bed.

But still, he wasn't sure if they understood each other where Damien Felder was concerned. She had started out defying him, and in the end, she still hadn't yielded to his way of thinking. He hoped what they shared last night gave her other ideas on the matter. He truly couldn't see how it couldn't.

And there was another thing he had to consider. He had gotten so into making love to her that he'd done something else he usually didn't do. He had taken risks by not putting on a new condom at the start of each lovemaking session. Although he wanted to believe it was a long shot, what if she was pregnant at this very moment?

Hell, York, don't even go there, man, a part of his mind screamed. *She's probably on the Pill, which means that although you got sloppy this one time, she managed to save the day...or in this case, the night.*

When she shifted her position in the bed he took a step back, feeling the need to put distance between them and knowing it would be best if he wasn't there when she woke up. There was no telling what frame of mind she would be in, and he didn't want her making it seem as though making love was all his idea. Nor did he want to hear that she regretted anything about their time together—especially when he had no regrets.

Once in her living room, he quickly picked up his clothes off the floor and put them on. He glanced at the clock on one of the tables and saw the time was six in the morning. Chances were he would be getting a lot of strange looks when he made his way from one part of the hotel to the other still wearing a tux. But then chances were anyone who saw him would figure out why. Liaisons were a way of life.

He crossed the room to glance into the bedroom once again before leaving. She was still sleeping like a baby, and as much as he wished otherwise, a part of him regretted that he wouldn't be there when she woke up.

CHAPTER FOUR

DARCY STIRRED AWAKE when the sun spilled in through the window to hit her right in the face. But she refused to open her eyes just yet. She expected at any moment to feel York's warm breath on her neck or have his aroused body part—one that she'd gotten to know up close and personal—cuddle close to her backside, right smack against her bare cheeks. And she wouldn't mind it at all if he threw one of his legs over her. Nor would she care if he were to run his fingers through her hair.

But as she continued to lie there all she heard was silence and felt no human contact. Moments ticked by, and she flipped onto her back and glanced over at the empty spot beside her. Had York gotten up to use the bathroom?

Easing out of bed, she went into the bathroom and found it empty. She then strolled to the living room and found it vacant as well. Her bathrobe was tossed across the sofa, and his clothes that had littered the floor last night were gone. That meant he was wearing them.

Disappointment settled in her chest, and for a moment she wondered just what she had expected. York had handled last night for what it had been—a one-night stand. Why had she assumed he would think of it as anything more? Why did she care that he hadn't? And why was she taking it as a personal affront?

Both men and women had meaningless sexual liaisons all the time. She had even caught the plane from New York with plans to have a fling, had even joked with Ellie about it. But that was when she would have been in total control, and the man was to have been a stranger. Someone who wouldn't leave any lingering affects or someone she wouldn't miss once the moments passed. In other words, she hadn't expected York Ellis to be so overpowering, so overwhelming, so doggone good between the sheets that her body still throbbed between her legs.

She slid into her robe as she recalled her actions and behavior of the night. Red-hot embarrassment reddened her cheeks. She had gotten wild and outrageous. She guessed two years of celibacy could do that to you. And she didn't need to look at her body to know there were probably passion marks all over every inch of her skin. And she was certain he was sporting his fair share of the marks as well.

She ran her hands through her hair, frustrated. No matter how good the sex had been, she could literally kick herself for tumbling into bed with York. They didn't even like each other, although it was apparent they'd gotten along pretty well between the sheets. He had made her feel things she hadn't ever felt.

And after each lovemaking session, before they would start all over again, he would hold her tenderly in his arms. She certainly hadn't expected that. There had been something so calming and relaxing to lie there in his arms. And when she had dozed off to sleep that last time, weary after rounds and rounds of lovemaking, she had assumed he would be there whenever she woke up.

Wrong. He had skipped out like a thief in the night. It was hard to explain why she felt so annoyed about it but she was. His actions were probably his M.O. when it came to a woman. Why had she assumed things would be different with her?

Fine, he could continue to handle his business that same way. It meant nothing to her. In fact, now that they'd gotten what they'd undoubtedly wanted from each other, she hoped she didn't run into him again while she was here. He wouldn't be the first man she'd written off.

Her marriage to Harold Calhoun had started out like a storybook romance. They had met in college and had married soon after graduation. But within a year after living under the same roof, she had discovered things about her husband she hadn't known—like the fact that he had a tendency to get abusive at times. The verbal abuse was bad enough, but the first time he'd tried getting physically abusive with her, it had been his last time. He had found out, much to his detriment, that his wife could defend herself so well, he'd been the one hovering in a corner pleading for mercy by the time the authorities had arrived.

She drew in a deep breath and turned toward her bedroom. She then recalled York's words to her about Damien Felder. As far as she was concerned, a man was innocent of any crime until proven guilty. Besides, she doubted had it been Damien who'd slept with her last night he would have left the way York had done, without even a wham, bam, thank you ma'am.

And speaking of Damien…

It was probably too late to join him for breakfast, but she would keep her date with him to let him show her around the movie set. She was a big girl who could handle herself, regardless of what York thought. And frankly, what he thought didn't matter to her.

She would arrange to meet Damien just as she'd planned. She had gotten what she wanted from York, and she was confident he'd gotten what he wanted from her. They were even. Now things could go back to how they'd always been between them.

York GLANCED AROUND the movie set. Today the location was a cottage on the beach where the scene would be shot. The crew and equipment were in place, and the cast was in their individual trailers getting the attention of the hair and makeup artists.

He had been introduced earlier and was told his job was to provide backup security to the production team since they would be filming in several parts of the island, some less than desirable.

Several members of his security group would keep that focus while others worked undercover to identify who was crippling the production in another way. So far Damien Felder hadn't shown up on set, and York hadn't missed the whispered jokes of several crew members as to why. A number were wondering whose bed he'd spent the night in. Evidently, Felder was a known playboy. So far, no one had linked Felder's name with that of the leading lady, and York found that slightly odd since very few secrets survived on a movie set. Someone was working extremely hard to keep their affair a secret. He definitely found that interesting.

"Um, looks like Damien has been busy," someone whispered behind York, and he glanced up to see Damien walk in with Darcy at his side. At that moment,

York discovered firsthand what it meant to see bloodred. What the hell was she doing here with him? Hadn't she listened to anything he'd told her about Felder last night?

And he could tell from the whispers behind him that many assumed she had been Felder's sleeping partner last night. He was tempted to turn around and tell them how wrong they were since she had been his. But just the thought that she was getting whispered about, by those who didn't even know her and who assumed false things about her, pissed him off to the point where he was fighting intense anger within him.

He continued to pretend to peruse documents on a clipboard while watching Felder show Darcy around. It was obvious he was trying to impress her, probably was working real hard to get into her bed tonight or to get her in his. The thought of either happening set York on edge, made him madder.

"Ellis, I need to introduce you to Felder," Bob Crowder, the production manager, said.

York glanced up. "Fine. Let's do it," he said, placing the clipboard aside and trying to keep the hardness from his tone.

They crossed the room to where Felder stood with Darcy by his side near a tray of coffee and donuts. He smelled her before he got within ten feet of her. Aside from the cologne she was wearing, she had a unique feminine scent that could probably drive men wild. He wondered if he was the only man who detected it and quickly realized he had reason to know it so well. Her aroma had gotten absorbed into his nostrils pretty damn good last night.

"Damien, I need to introduce you to the guy who

owns the company we're using for security now," Crowder said, snagging Felder's attention.

Felder turned and gave York a once-over before asking, "What happened to the other company that was hired?"

"Evidently, they didn't work out," York responded before Crowder could. Felder really was in no position to ask questions.

"And you think your outfit will be able to do a better job?" Felder asked.

York smiled, well aware that Darcy was staring at him, listening attentively. At least she hadn't let on that they knew each other, and he was grateful for that. "I *know* we'll do a better job." He figured his response sounded pretty damn confident, overly cocky to an extreme, but that sort of attitude was probably one Felder could relate to.

Felder proved him right when his lips curved into a smile. "Hey, York Ellis. I like you."

It was on the tip of York's tongue to respond that the feeling wasn't mutual. Instead, he said, "My job is not to get you to like me, Felder, but to make sure you and everyone else who're part of this production are safe."

York knew his statement was establishing his persona as a no-nonsense sort of guy. That's what he wanted. He'd heard Felder had a tendency to try and cozy up to those in charge so when he decided to break rules they would look the other way. It was good to let the man know up front he wouldn't allow it and not to waste his time trying to earn brownie points.

He then shifted his gaze from Felder to Darcy. "And you are?"

York knew Felder assumed he was asking for security reasons. Darcy opened her mouth to respond, but Felder beat her to the punch. "She's with me, Ellis, and her name is Darcy Owens. She's my guest."

York nodded as he glanced down at the clipboard in his hand. "Her name isn't on the list, Felder." He could tell from Felder's expression that the man didn't appreciate being called out on breaking one of the production rules about bringing visitors on set.

"I made her an exception," Felder said, smiling.

"There are no exceptions around here," York said, not returning the smile. "In the future, make sure all exceptions are cleared by me first."

He glanced over at Darcy and saw her glaring at him, actually saw a spark of fire in her eyes. He then turned to Crowder. "I need to check on a few other things around here."

"All right, come on," Crowder said, before leading him away. York didn't say anything else to the couple, just merely nodded before walking off.

"HE'S NOT GOING to last around here long," Darcy heard Damien mutter as they watched York leave.

"Why do you say that?" she asked, curious to know. She felt York's annoyance at seeing her as well as his immediate dislike of Damien. It was funny how well she could read him.

"He's trying to throw his weight around much too soon. I'd heard the bigwigs were sending in some new guy to handle security, but I can tell he's not going to work out. I don't like the fact that he questioned anything about you when you were with me."

She shrugged. "I'm sure he was just doing his job."

It wasn't that she was taking up for York's brash behavior but she didn't want to do anything to blow whatever cover he had, although she still wasn't convinced Damien was someone he should be watching. York had his reasons for being here on the island and she had hers. She intended to have a good time and enjoy herself.

Damien gave her a tour of the set while telling her bits and pieces of what scenes they would be shooting. Every once in a while she would glance over to where York was standing and find him staring hard at her. She would stare back. It seemed things were back to normal with them.

At least they were to a degree. Since sharing a bed with him she felt an intimate connection that she didn't want to feel. She could no longer look at his large hands and wonder. Now she knew. She couldn't look at his mouth without remembering all the naughty things his lips and tongue could do. Even from across the room he was emitting a heat that could sear her. Knowing that was the last thing she wanted, she let out a deep sigh.

"What's wrong? Am I boring you?"

She glanced up and forced a smile at Damien. "No, in fact I'm a little overwhelmed by it all. The next time I go to a movie I'm going to appreciate all the behind-the-scenes things it took to bring the movie to the big screen."

"Now you know." He glanced at his watch. "How would you like to have lunch with me? And then I can take you back to your hotel, let you rest up a bit and then we can go out tonight. I heard there's a club that's a hot spot on the island. I would love to take you dancing."

His suggestion sounded good, and there was no reason she shouldn't have lunch with him or go dancing at the club. Her smile widened and she said, "That sounds wonderful. I'd love to."

OUT OF THE corner of his eye, York watched Darcy leave with Felder, and his heart banged against his chest causing a deep, hard thump. What the hell was wrong with him? He had gone above and beyond by warning her about the man, yet she still was with him today. It was as if she'd deliberately ignored what he'd said about Damien Felder.

"Looks like Damien's got another looker."

York turned around slowly to face the production's leading man, Johnny Rush. He'd officially met the man yesterday. "Yeah, looks that way," he said dryly, as if the thought of who Felder was with didn't interest him in the least.

He knew that Malcolm was convinced Rush and Danielle Simone were in no way involved in the bootlegging activity, but as far as York was concerned, there was still a possibility. At least he was suspicious of Simone since she and Felder had met up somewhere last night.

"I wonder where they met."

He studied the man's features. "Is there any reason you want to know?"

Johnny shook his head and chuckled. "No, in fact I'm happy for him. Maybe now he'll leave Danielle alone."

York couldn't help wondering why Rush felt the need to drop that information. Since he wasn't sure, he decided to play it out as much as he could. "I didn't know he and Ms. Simone had something going on."

He saw the frown settle on Johnny's face. "They

don't. Damien thinks he's someone important with this outfit and has been trying to box her into an affair. But she's not interested in him."

York nodded and decided not to say that wasn't the way he'd seen things last night. "And that bothers you?"

The man met his gaze and held it. "Yes, I want Danielle for myself."

The man couldn't get any plainer than that. Again, York wondered what purpose Johnny had for revealing that…unless the man assumed York would develop a roving eye where Danielle Simone was concerned. He decided to quickly squash that idea. "Good luck. I know how it feels when a man truly wants a woman."

Johnny lifted a brow. "Do you?"

"Yes. There's a woman I'm all into back in New York. She's the only woman for me." He said the lie so Johnny wouldn't think he was a threat.

"You engaged?" Johnny asked.

"Not yet. I'm thinking of popping the question around the holidays," York lied further. What he'd just told Johnny was a whopper. There was no way he was thinking about proposing to any woman around the holidays.

"Hey, man, congratulations. I'm thinking about asking Danielle myself around the holidays."

York lifted a brow. "Things are *that* serious between you two?"

Johnny beamed. "Not yet but they will be. I'm working on it now that my divorce is final. She is destined to become the next Mrs. Johnny Rush."

York held his tongue from saying that would probably come as a surprise to Danielle. One of his men had followed Danielle and Felder to their lovers' hideaway on the beach last night. And from the man's report, he had seen enough to let him know the two were involved, and it wasn't all Felder's doing as Johnny assumed.

"Where is Ms. Simone anyway?" York asked, glancing around.

"She overslept. She had a bad migraine yesterday and went to bed early last night."

Like hell she did, York almost said.

"She gets to sleep in because her scene isn't getting filmed today," Johnny added.

York didn't say anything; he just nodded. He'd heard of romantic entanglements on movie sets but he figured the one between the leading man, the leading lady and Damien Felder was a bit outrageous.

"ARE YOU SURE you don't need me to walk you to your room?"

Darcy glanced up at Damien as they stood in the lobby of her hotel. He'd spent most of the day with her, as well as the evening, going to dinner and a club, but now it was late, close to midnight. She had enjoyed herself but if walking her up to her room meant he assumed he would be staying the night then she rather he didn't. "I'm positive."

"All right then. Can I see you again tomorrow?"

She figured she shouldn't let him dominate her vacation, but she'd had a good time with him. He hadn't tried coming on to her and actually seemed to enjoy her company, as well. "I've made plans to have a day of beauty tomorrow. Most of my time will be spent at the spa and then later the hotel is throwing another party. You can come as my guest if you'd like."

He shook his head. "No, I need to fly to Miami tomorrow night for a couple of days since we won't be filming over the weekend. Can I contact you when I return?"

She saw no reason why he couldn't. "Sure, just call the hotel and ask for me. They will connect you to my room."

"All right, no problem."

If he was bothered about her not giving him her contact information, he wasn't showing it. "And thanks for the tote bag," she said. "I've been doing a lot of shopping, and I intend to fill it up with all sorts of goodies."

He smiled. "No problem. I thought you'd like it since it promotes the movie and will be a memento of your day spent on the set."

"Yes, it will be. Good night, Damien, and thanks again for a wonderful day and evening."

"You're welcome." He then leaned over and placed a kiss on her cheek. "I hope to see you when I return. Not that you need one, but do enjoy your day of beauty tomorrow."

"Thanks for the compliment, and I will."

She turned to head toward the bank of elevators when she felt heat in her midsection. She wasn't surprised when she glanced to her right and saw York sitting at one of the restaurant's tables that gave him a good view of the lobby. Their gazes met, and the penetrating dark eyes staring at her made her increase her pace as she moved toward the elevator. Why did his look have such a mesmerizing effect on her? Even before last night, his stare could get next to her, and after last night, the effect was even worse.

She couldn't help noticing he was frowning, and the frown was so deep she could see the fierce lines of displeasure slashing between the darkness of his eyes. Darcy set her jaw, not caring one iota that he was probably pissed with her for not staying away from Damien.

She stepped on the elevator, and when she turned around, she saw he'd left the restaurant and was heading toward the revolving doors, the same ones Damien had left through moments ago. As she watched him cross the lobby, she couldn't help but think that York Ellis was undoubtedly six feet plus of heart-stopping masculinity. She thought he was an awesome sight last night in a tux, but tonight in a pair of jeans and a pullover shirt, he looked hot.

The elevator door closed, and she backed up against the wall to give others room. There was no use wishing last night had never happened, because it had, and as much as she wished otherwise, she had no regrets.

Subconsciously, she took her tongue and ran it across her bottom lip when she remembered the searing kiss they'd shared. She wasn't surprised that York was a good kisser and was convinced she could still taste him on her tongue.

You have it bad, girl. You shouldn't go two years without sex again. She couldn't help laughing out loud at that thought. She quickly wiped the amusement off her face when others in the elevator turned to stare at her as if she had a few screws loose.

Hell, maybe she did, because at that moment she knew if given the chance, she would definitely do York again.

CHAPTER FIVE

DARCY HADN'T EXPECTED to go all out when she'd arrived at the spa that morning, but a few hours later, she was walking out of the place feeling like a brand-new woman. She was definitely more at peace with herself for the time being. In addition to the body massage, she had waded in the serenity fountains, spent time walking through the private herbal gardens and indulged in a mineral bath. It had been a peaceful interlude, an emotional escape and a chance to let her mind just relax and unwind.

She had needed the peaceful diversion since she had spent the majority of the night tossing between the sheets while memories of what she'd shared with York the previous night racked her body. It was one of those times that Bruce would have probably come in handy. But after York, she was convinced she was putting Bruce in permanent retirement.

She hadn't gotten much sleep as memories washed through her, making her body tense, irritable and in a need that could get satisfied only one way and with only one man. She was totally convinced that no other man would be able to make her body hum the way York had.

She glanced at her watch as she entered her hotel room. More than half of the day had passed by already. She felt another presence the moment she entered her hotel room. She glanced around and nearly dropped the shopping bag filled with items she'd purchased at the spa. York was sitting on her sofa as if he had every right to be there waiting on her return.

She closed the door and glared at him. "How did you get in here?"

He smiled. "I have my ways."

She placed her bags on the table. "Breaking and entering now, York?"

"A man has to do what a man has to do."

She crossed her arms over her chest. "Meaning?"

"I came to check on you."

She watched as he rose to his feet, appreciating the way his entire body moved with charismatic precision, fluidity and an agility that not only held her attention but was dousing her with an arousing effect of sensations. He was wearing a pair of khakis and an island shirt. He looked laid-back, too sinfully sexy for his good—as well as for hers.

Knowing she needed to keep their conversation on a straight and narrow path, she asked, "Why would you need to check on me? You saw Damien return me to the hotel last night. And I saw you follow him, so don't pretend that you didn't."

He shrugged as he placed his hands in his pockets. "Why would I pretend? I told you my reason for being here in Jamaica."

Yes, he had. "But why are you inside my hotel room? Why couldn't you call or sit in the lobby and wait for me there?"

He shrugged. "I don't have your phone number, and why sit in a lobby when I can have a comfortable spot in here?"

Her frown deepened. "You could have contacted me through the hotel's operator."

"I did. I called your room several times, but you didn't answer."

"I spent most of the day at the spa. And you've got a lot of nerve being here. What if I'd brought someone back with me?"

She saw a tick in his jaw when he responded. "Then I guess it would not have been his lucky day."

She felt swamped with varying emotions at the subtle threat she'd heard in his voice. She fought them off by refusing to believe her having a fling with another man meant anything to him other than the typical male possession. They make love to you and thought they owned you. But she knew of York's reputation with women. He probably wouldn't know how to be possessive of one.

"I'm going to ask you one more time, York. Why are you in my hotel room?"

"I told you," he said, sinking back down on the sofa. "I wanted to make sure you were okay. Evidently you didn't take my warning about Felder at face value. Why are you still seeing him?"

She crossed her arms over her chest. "Because I want to. He hasn't done anything to me, and I enjoy his company."

She then rubbed a frustrated hand down her face. "Look, York, I understand you have a job to do, which is why I didn't give anything away yesterday while we were on set. I pretended we didn't already know each other. You placed me in an awkward position."

"No, I didn't. You placed yourself in an awkward position by being with Felder in the first place."

Darcy felt a headache coming on and decided she

needed for York to leave. They weren't getting any-where. "No need to rehash anything, York. We don't think the same way about things."

"We seemed to be in accord the other night."

She glared at him. "A real gentleman wouldn't bring that up."

He chuckled, but she could tell the amusement on his face was forced. "And who said I was a gentleman?"

Her chin firmed. "Sorry, my mistake."

She licked her lips to keep her teeth from grinding. She just didn't get it. He was right. In bed, they were of one mind, their dislike of each other tossed to the wayside as they concentrated on something else en-tirely. Something hot and simmering. Pleasure of the most intense kind. However, out of bed they were con-stantly at each other's throats, bickering, biting each other's heads off.

"Don't you think we should consider a truce?" he asked.

"Why?"

"So we could try and get along."

"We get along as much as we need to," she said, wav-ing off his words. "What I think we should do while we're in Jamaica is put distance between us. This island is big enough for the both of us so our paths shouldn't cross too much."

"Distance won't work now. Problem with that, Darcy, is that I've made love to you."

She looked at him confused. "What does that have to do with anything? I'm sure you've made love to a lot of women over the years."

"But I particularly enjoyed making love to you."

She didn't want to admit that she had definitely enjoyed making love with him as well. But she didn't intend to lose any sleep over it. She drew in a deep breath. Who was she fooling? She had lost sleep over it. Last night she had lain awake in a bad way. She had needed him. She had yearned to be touched the same way and in the same places he had touched her the night before.

"I'm glad you enjoyed our romp between the sheets, York, but we need to move past that. When I left New York to come here, you weren't even on my mind. And I'm sure I wasn't on yours. People have flings all the time with no lasting effects."

"That might be true, but I refuse to believe I'm not on your mind right now or that you don't want me again."

She was so taken back by his direct assertion that she was left momentarily stunned. He was right on both accounts, but she would never admit to it. "You're wrong."

She then watched him ease off the sofa. Seeing him do so was a total turn-on once again. She was so filled with sexual awareness of him that she knew he had to know it. He began walking toward her, and her gaze tracked his every movement. No matter what kind of clothes he wore he was striking, and he had the ability to stir emotions deep inside of her. She considered backing up, running for cover, but decided to hold her ground.

"I can prove that I'm right and you know it," he said when he came to a stop in front of her. "You want me to prove it?"

No, she didn't want him to prove it because he would prove her wrong. She figured the best thing to do was to stay on a topic that would keep them at odds with each other. "You don't like Damien," she said.

If the change of subject seemed odd, he didn't let

on. "No, I don't like him," he said easily in a hardened voice.

"Why, York? Because he's showing interest in me?"

York drew in a deep breath while tossing Darcy's question around in his head. In a way, she was right but then in a way she was wrong. He decided to be honest with her. "I had reason to suspect Felder of wrongdoing even before seeing the two of you together. But then I will admit that I don't like the interest he's showing in you or the interest you're returning, especially after our time together the other night."

"It was a one-night stand, York. Don't try to make it into more than it was because jealousy doesn't become you."

He had news for her. It was already more than that, and evidently jealousy *did* become him, although he wished otherwise. And he couldn't understand why it mattered to him. He of all people had never been possessive where lovers were concerned. He enjoyed women and had no problem moving on when boredom set in. But he had a feeling Darcy was a woman a man wouldn't get bored with easily.

He hadn't been able to sleep last night for thinking of her, wanting her. And it hadn't helped matters that he'd followed Felder after he'd left her only to see him meet up with Danielle Simone. York was still trying to figure out that angle. If Felder was so into the leading lady then why was he spending as much time as he could with Darcy? And if Rush was so into Danielle, why hadn't he figured out that something more was going on between her and Felder?

After the accusation Darcy had just thrown at him—that he disliked Felder because he was jealous—she wouldn't believe him if he told her the man was probably just using her as a decoy for some unscrupulous purpose. He might as well keep his mouth shut on the subject until he could prove his theory.

In the meantime, there was a subject he wanted to bring up and decided just to come out and ask. "Are you on the Pill or any other type of birth control?" He knew it was crazy but he had lowered his voice, as if there was someone else in the room besides them.

York could tell from her expression that she was surprised not only with the swift change in subject but also with what he'd asked. "Why do you want to know?"

"Because of the other night." The memories were etched in his mind and with her standing there in a cute sundress that showed what a gorgeous pair of legs she had, he could recall the feel of those same legs wrapped around him.

His gaze raked over her, and he couldn't help but appreciate her feminine curves, small waist and firm and full breasts. The fact that she was a looker wasn't helping matters—or the fact that he'd seen her naked.

Seeing the way he was checking her out made her gaze drill into his. "And if I remember correctly…and I do…you wore a condom each time. I hope you're not about to break the news to me that they were defective or something."

He shook his head. "No, that's not it."

"Then what is it, York?"

He wished she wouldn't ask so many questions. It would really help matters if she just told him what he wanted to know. "I wasn't as careful as I usually am with the condoms," he finally said.

She tilted her head at an angle that pinned him to

the spot. "Yes, I happened to notice, but I was enjoying myself too much to call it to your attention."

He laughed. The woman never ceased to amaze him. She said just what she thought or felt.

"I'm glad you find me amusing, York."

"Only when you say whatever the hell you feel like saying," he said.

She shrugged. "And that's all the time. I do the professional thing at work but when I'm out among friends—or those who might not be friends—I am the real me. What you see is what you get. Now to answer your question…yes, I'm on some sort of birth control but it's not the Pill. So you're safe this time, and I want to think you're also healthy because I am."

"Yes, I am."

"Good, then there's nothing you need to worry about. I came to Jamaica to relax, read and romp. Since sex was on the list, I definitely came prepared."

She then glanced at her watch. "Don't you have somewhere to go?"

"No. So what about that truce?" he asked her, taking a step closer.

Darcy tried not to notice his fascinatingly sexy mouth, a mouth that had nearly driven her insane two nights ago. She wished she didn't have to think about that now but found she couldn't help herself. "You think a truce will work with us?"

A slow smile touched his lips. "It wouldn't hurt."

She wasn't too convinced of that. When she'd left New York, she'd made plans, had such big ideas of how she wanted her three weeks of vacation to start and end. She'd intended to kick up her legs and have some fun. Well, she'd certainly kicked up her legs, right his way.

And he hadn't wasted any time getting between them. "I wouldn't want you to get any ideas."

He chuckled. "About what?"

"What a truce between us means. I didn't come here to have an affair with you."

He flashed her another smile, one that made her body shiver inside. "But you came here intending to have an affair with somebody, right?"

"Yes."

"Then it might as well be me since we've already gotten off to a good start where sex is concerned." He held out his hand. "So, can we agree on a truce? Even if we decide to take sex off the table and never sleep together again?"

She looked at his outstretched hand and asked, "Will you stop accusing Damien of things you're not certain that he's done?"

He frowned. "Why do you keep defending him?"

"And why are you so convinced he's guilty?"

He didn't reply for a moment and then said, "May I suggest we leave Damien out of this for now? This is between me and you."

She narrowed her gaze. "Fine. For now," she said, finally taking his hand. The moment she did so she knew it had been a mistake to agree to a truce with him. Stealing a look at him from beneath her lashes, she saw the smoldering look in his gaze.

She knew she should heed the warning bells that suddenly went off in her head, but she didn't have the strength to do so. The man had the ability to blur the line between reason and desire. She pulled her hand from his when it seemed he was in no hurry to release it.

"Have dinner with me tonight, Darcy."

She lifted a brow. "Dinner? What if we're seen together? Would you want that?"

York responded to Darcy's question with a shake of his head. No, he shouldn't want it but he did. And she had openly admitted she'd come to Jamaica for relaxation, reading and sex. Was Felder someone she'd placed on her to-do list? If that was the case then she could scratch him off. He intended to be the only man she made love to while on the island. A part of him knew that sounded crazy. They'd made love that one time, and it didn't give him any right to possess her. But he couldn't help it for some reason.

He was satisfied with the fact that Felder had caught a plane off the island for a few days, and coincidentally, Danielle Simone had left the island as well. He had men tailing them both, and he wouldn't be surprised to receive a call saying they were together somewhere. He couldn't help wonder where that left good old Johnny-boy. What lie had Danielle told him so he wouldn't suspect anything? And why was Darcy being pulled into their little game? What role did they intend for her to play?

"Since filming has stopped for the weekend the majority of the cast and crew have scattered with plans to return on Monday," he said. "But even if they were here, it wouldn't matter to me if we were seen together. But if it makes you feel better, I know just the place to ensure our privacy."

She shrugged beautiful shoulders. "Doesn't matter to me."

He stared at her. Today her skin appeared smoother than before, and the scent emitting from her skin was different from those other times. The fragrance was just as seductive but reminded him of a flower garden. "You sure? There's still that chance that no matter where we go, we might still be seen by someone. So, if you're so into Felder that it would matter if he finds out we were seen together, then say so. I know some women get all excited by those Hollywood types."

He could tell by the tightening of her lips and the flash that appeared in her eyes that she hadn't liked what he'd said. "I'm not one of them. I only spent yesterday with him, and he seems to be a nice guy. I think you're wrong about him, York."

He rolled his eyes. "Just remember there are a lot of nice guys sitting in jail right now, Darcy."

He checked his watch. "What about if I come back around six?"

For a moment, he thought she wouldn't agree, and then she said, "That's fine. I'll be ready."

"And wear something with an accent on having fun. I plan to take you for a walk on the beach later," he said, dragging in a deep breath as he headed for the door. He needed to get out of there now. It wouldn't take much to pull her into his arms for a repeat of what they'd shared two nights ago.

They would make love again. He was certain of it. That night she had been simply amazing, had met him on every level and then in a surprising move, she had ridden him, given him an orgasm that still made his body tremble just thinking about it. Afterward he had been weak, wrung out and exhausted. And then she had proceeded to arouse him all over again.

When he reached her door, he turned unexpectedly, and the guilty look on her face let him know she had been checking him out from behind. The gaze now looking at him was hot. He could easily change their plans and stay in—order room service, then spend a night between the sheets. They could take turns riding each other like they'd done the other night.

A predatory and primitive urge eased up his spine. He felt great satisfaction in knowing she wanted him as much as he wanted her. "I'll see you at six."

Then he opened the door and walked out.

CHAPTER SIX

THEY WERE JUST going to dinner and taking a walk on the beach later, Darcy said, looking at herself in the bathroom's full-length mirror. No biggie. It meant nothing.

First of all, York wasn't her type. But she would have to admit he had been the best lover she'd ever had. With him, there were no limitations. He was willing to try just about anything, and she'd had a lot of ideas. When you read as many romance novels as she had over the years, you were bound to have a few unique positions stored up in your brain.

She left her bedroom and entered the living room area. York had said he would return at six, and it was a few minutes to that time. She was dressed, so with nothing else to do, she began pacing the floor, feeling hot and restless.

Another first when it came to York. She would have to give him credit as being the first man she'd dated that not only made her aware of her power as a woman but encouraged her to flaunt it, to wrap herself up in her femininity in a way she'd never done before.

Harold had been a total jerk, she could see that now. In the early days, all she'd wanted to do was to please him, both in and out of the bedroom. But he was never satisfied.

When his job began going bad, he wanted to blame his problems on her since she was happy at her job.

Then after he'd gotten laid off he resented that she was working. That was when the abuse began and when the love and respect she'd thought she had for him went plummeting down the toilet. It was then she'd vowed never to be ruled by another man. They were just heartbreak waiting to happen, and she'd learned her lesson. From what she'd heard, York was just as commitment phobic as she was—smart man.

But the one thing she couldn't forget, although she'd tried, was that they'd made love. He wasn't the first man she'd made love to since her divorce, but she had even put affairs on the back burner. In fact, she'd begun to wonder why she'd even bothered getting those injections for birth control when there hadn't been any real action going down in that neck of the woods. But York had reminded her of why it was always important to be prepared for the unexpected.

She hadn't expected to make love to him that night. Nor had she expected him to get so carried away he would get careless. The thought of having some man's child would cross her mind every so often, but she would push it way to the back. She loved kids and wanted some of her own one day. But she knew since she didn't plan to ever marry again that she would venture into the life of a single mother.

The knock on the door made her breath catch in her throat knowing York was standing on the other side. Not surprisingly, he was right on time. She looked down at herself. He'd suggested she wear something for fun; she felt the short tropical-print dress did the trick. It was one she'd purchased on one of her infamous shopping sprees. This was her first time wearing it, and she couldn't wait to see York's reaction to it.

Her insides were churning when she opened the door and saw him standing there. The way his gaze roamed over her from head to toe made her smile at the look of male appreciation in the dark depths of his eyes. She had gotten the reaction she'd wanted and had hoped for.

"Hello, York, you're right on time. It will only take me a second to grab my purse."

She walked over to the table knowing his gaze was following her every step. Usually she didn't wear her dresses this short, but when she'd seen it on a manne-quin while shopping with Ellie one day during her best friend's New York visit, El had convinced her it would look even better on her. And from the way York kept looking at her she had a feeling it did. She heard the door close behind him and knew he'd stepped over the threshold to come into the hotel room.

She turned and saw the deep frown on his face. "Is anything wrong?"

He placed his hands in the pockets of his slacks. "I suggested you wear something for fun. Not something to keep me aroused the rest of the evening."

She tossed her head, sending a mass of hair around her shoulders. She couldn't help the smile that touched her lips. "Poor baby. You'll survive. In fact, I'll make sure that you do." She liked the fact that he spoke his mind just like she spoke hers.

She placed the straps of her purse on her shoulder. "I'm ready."

She'd made the statement, but neither of them made an attempt to move. They just stood there staring at each other. Then he spoke. "Don't think that I don't know what you're up to, Darcy."

She threw him an innocent look. "I have no idea what you're talking about." She then smiled smugly. "But then, maybe I do."

He took his hands out of his pockets and placed them across his chest. "You play with fire, and you're liable to get burned."

She gave him a thoughtful look. She'd already encountered his fire and knew how hot he was capable of getting things. And as long as he was the one doing the burning she wouldn't back down. "Fire doesn't scare me, York."

He shook his head and chuckled. "Maybe it should. Come on, let's get out of here."

She led the way out of the hotel room, figuring he was still enjoying the backside view. "So where are you taking me?" she asked when they reached the elevator.

He smiled down at her. "You'll see."

YORK WAS GLAD there were others on the elevator with them or else he would have been tempted to take her right then and there. Every single cell in his body had to be aroused right now, thanks to the sexiest minidress a woman could wear. And she definitely had the body for it. He could just imagine other men checking her out in this outfit and felt pressure at the top of his head just thinking about it. Now he was glad he'd made the decision to take her to a place where it would be just the two of them.

His lips thinned when he recalled that he had run into Johnny Rush on the way up to Darcy's room. He knew for a fact the man was staying at a hotel a few miles away, so who had he been visiting here at this hotel? If he'd expected to drop in on Danielle Simone, then he'd discovered she was long gone, since Danielle and Felder were together in Miami.

"You've gotten quiet on me, York."

He glanced down at Darcy as he led her through the hotel's glass doors. Just as he'd figured, they'd gotten plenty of attention walking across the lobby. Men had literally stopped what they were doing to stare at her. And he had seen the look of envy in their eyes when they'd gazed at him walking by her side.

"Um, I'm thinking about all the heat you and I seem to stir whenever we're together."

Instead of making a comment, she arched her brows. There was no need for him to elaborate. He was certain that she understood what he was talking about. Even now he was convinced he could still taste the most recent kiss they'd shared.

He studied her underneath his lashes and thought now the same thing he'd thought when he first saw her that day two years ago. She was a whirlwind and could probably have a man falling for her without much effort on her part. You couldn't help but be drawn to her. And now he wanted to get to know the real Darcy Owens— uncensored, up close and personal. He knew she figured since they had slept together that should be the end of it, and maybe under normal circumstances that would be. But as far as he was concerned, the circumstances weren't normal. They shared the same close friends, yet there was a lot about her that he didn't know. He wanted to get to know her better. He *intended* to get to know her better.

It didn't take long for the valet to bring his rental

car to him. Watching her get in the car and ease down on the leather seats in that dress was worth the last few sleepless nights he'd endured thinking about her. She definitely had nice thighs, shapely and perfect for her legs. He wanted her. He had been convinced that a strong-willed woman turned him off, but the one sitting in the car beside him in that short dress turned him on big time.

"Penny for your thoughts," she said when they had driven away from the hotel.

He hadn't said anything for a while, trying to get his thoughts and his libido under control. He glanced over at her and decided to be honest. "I was thinking about making love to you again. I want you."

He did no more than steal a quick glance at her expression before turning his gaze back to the road. He'd seen what he had wanted to see. A mirror image of the desire he felt was reflected in her shocked gaze. He was beginning to understand just how to handle Darcy. She didn't need a man who sugarcoated anything but a man who could dish it out just like she could. She spoke her mind and appreciated a man who did the same.

She was different from the women he usually dated, those who preferred being told what they wanted to hear. And he had no trouble obliging them if he got what he wanted in the end. With Darcy, there was no need to play games or talk in circles. He liked that.

When he braked the car to a stop at the traffic light, on impulse he reached over and traced his fingertips along her thigh, liking the way her skin felt there— soft and smooth. He couldn't help but remember how it felt riding those same thighs and how those thighs had also ridden him.

He glanced over at her and saw fire flaring in the depths of her eyes. It was fire he'd generated, fire he intended to stir into a huge flame, fire he intended to extinguish in his own special way. He returned his hand back to the steering wheel when the traffic light changed.

"What's your sign, York?"

He chuckled. Now she was going to try and figure him out. He really wasn't a complicated sort of guy. He was just a horny one at the moment, thanks to her. He answered merely to amuse her. "Scorpio."

Now it was her turn to chuckle before saying, "I figured as much."

He wasn't into that astrology stuff but was curious as to how she'd figured it. "You need to expound on that."

"No problem." And then she said, "Scorpios are very passionate beings. They crave physical contact. In other words, they love sex."

He wouldn't go so far as to say he loved sex, but he certainly enjoyed it. "And how would you know that?"

"Because I'm a Scorpio."

If her words were meant to make him get hard, they succeeded. The erection already there got even harder, bigger. The thought that she liked sex made him throb. He should have figured that much from when they'd made love. There had been something else about that night that stayed with him. He could tell that it had been a long time since she'd made love to a man. Her body was tight. And if that hadn't been enough to give something away, he couldn't forget that several times in the course of their lovemaking she'd let it slip that it had been a long time for her, which was why she thought she was being so greedy. If she loved sex so much, why had she gone without?

He decided to ask her. "Then why did you go without it for a long time?"

She looked at him as if wondering how he'd known and he said, "That night, you let it slip that it had been a long time for you."

How much time passed before she answered he wasn't sure, but he was certain he'd been holding his breath for her response. Finally she said, "I hadn't meant to tell you that, but I guess I sort of got caught up in the moment."

He smiled remembering. "You did. So did I," he said, not ashamed to admit it.

He could feel the constant thump of his heart in his chest when she said, "Yes, it had been a long time for me."

"Why?"

He thought she would tell him it wasn't any of his business. She certainly had every right to do so. Instead she surprised him by saying, "I decided to take a two-year hiatus. I was starting a new job and needed to stay focused on something other than male body parts. Besides, I had gotten out of one hell of a marriage and refused to even consider getting into a serious relationship."

He brought the car to another stop. He'd heard from Uriel that her ex-husband had been a jerk. "If you like sex so much, how did you survive going without it?"

She shrugged delicate-looking shoulders beneath her spaghetti straps. "I had my ways of keeping myself entertained."

He quickly caught on to what she'd meant. What a

pity. A woman with profound needs should not have had to settle for a substitute.

"We might as well clear things up about something else while we're in a talkative mood, York."

He glanced over at her. "About what?"

"That day we met at Uriel and Ellie's wedding and you tried coming on to me and I was a smart-ass and all but told you to go screw yourself."

He could clearly recall that day, and that's not all she'd said. "Yes? What about it?"

"I was in a bad mood. I had just received a call from my ex that he intended to make my life miserable by moving to New York just to aggravate the hell out of me."

"So you took it out on me?"

"I would have taken it out on anyone with a penis, and you just happened to be the first man who approached me after that phone call."

He remembered she had left the wedding rehearsal for a short while, and when she'd returned he had high-tailed it over to her to see if she wanted to go out with him later that night. Her words had set his face on fire, and he'd walked off intending to never have anything to do with her again.

"I took it out on you, and I apologize."

Her apology was two years in coming, but there was no need for either of them to hold a grudge forever. But still… "Why are you apologizing now, Darcy?"

"Because I think I should. Okay, I admit I should have done so long ago, but every time I ran into you at one of Ellie's functions, you would avoid me like I had a disease or something and it sort of pissed me off."

He frowned as he stared over at her. "And after what

you said to me, you really expected me not to avoid you? You threatened to all but castrate me if I got in your face again."

"Okay, I remember all that, and I'm sorry. Do you accept my apology?"

He drew in a deep breath. It would be silly if he didn't, especially since he knew for a fact she wouldn't harm that particular body part. She'd held it in her hand, had taken it in her mouth. The memory of her doing both was increasing his arousal. "Yes, I accept your apology. It's in the past, so let's leave it there. We've moved beyond that now, haven't we?"

"Yes. Ellie will be glad to hear we're no longer enemies. That bothered her," she said.

He decided not to say that their less than friendly attitude never bothered Uriel. It had taken a while for Darcy to grow on him, as well. It had something to do with a prank Darcy had gotten Ellie to play on Uriel when the two women were in their teens. It had taken Uriel a long time to get over it.

"You and Ellie been best friends a long time?" he asked her.

"Almost forever. She's the sister I never had, and since she was an only child, I got to go a lot of places with her, like to Cavanaugh Lake for the summers."

Since he was godbrother to Uriel, whose parents also owned a place at Cavanaugh Lake, he spent a lot of his summers there as well. He could remember Ellie and her annoying little friend but hadn't known until Ellie and Uriel's wedding that Darcy had been that annoying friend. She had grown into a beautiful woman—not that she'd been an ugly kid or anything but just one not all that noticeable. Besides, she'd been five years younger, and he'd never paid her much attention. Now he did.

"So you're not telling me where we're going?" she asked, glancing over at him.

He smiled. "Not yet. We'll be there in a minute. Just relax. You have nothing to worry about."

DARCY WASN'T TOO sure of that. Just sharing a car with York was pure torture. The man was too virile. When he made such blatant statements as he'd done earlier, he made her remember everything about the night they'd made love.

Being coy was not a part of her makeup, and it seemed it wasn't a part of his either. She liked that, and she hated to admit it—since they had avoided each other for so long—that she kind of liked him, too. He was a Scorpio; so was she. According to their signs when it came to compatibility, a Scorpio and Scorpio match was rated high, the same when it came to sex between a Scorpio and a Scorpio. So it seemed they had that in the bag. After the other night, she had no reason not to believe it. But the ratings weren't so high when it came to communication between two Scorpios. She wondered why. She enjoyed discussing things with York, at least when they stayed away from controversial subjects like Damien Felder. York had his own opinions about the man, and she had hers.

She was glad she'd apologized for her behavior two years ago. Ellie had kept telling her that she should, and like she'd told him, she had tried. But he hadn't given her the opportunity. Even that night when he'd shown up at her place because Ellie had convinced him to come, he had come arguing about it, which set her off again.

"How do you like your job as a city planner?"

She looked over at him. "I like it on those days politics aren't involved." On the days it was, she wanted to quit and do something else. But her job paid her well even with the headaches. And she did enjoy living in New York, especially when the weather was nice. There were so many things to see and do.

"So, did your ex follow you to New York?" he asked her.

"Yes, and he tried making my life a living hell for a couple of months. I ended up getting a restraining order on him. That's the reason Ellie had you rush over to my place that night. She was convinced my intruder was Harold."

Over the next few minutes she engaged in conversation with him and found herself telling him the reason she had gotten a divorce.

She also told him about her job and that she hadn't taken a lot of time off for the two years she'd worked as a city planner and that in addition to much needed R & R, she'd also wanted to escape the cold weather in New York for a while.

And just the opposite, he told her how much he enjoyed New York winters and that he was missing the snowstorm passing through even now. As they talked, it dawned on her just how laid-back he was once you got to know him. She was enjoying the conversation. He was arrogant, true enough, but there was something about his arrogance that she found a total turn-on at times.

And she couldn't dismiss the fact that being with him did something to her, gave her an adrenaline rush like she'd never experienced before. Especially when he was so up front and candid about certain things. She had a feeling how he intended the evening to end. He'd all but spelled it out to her. The thought that he pretty much had sexual ideas that included her didn't bother her in the least. In fact, if truth be told, she was still in awe of their lovemaking the other night. Although at the time she'd figured it was one and done, it still had lingering effects on her.

She couldn't look at her naked body in the mirror without remembering how he'd licked every single inch of it. And her nipples would strain against her top when she recalled how he had sucked the dark pebbles into his mouth and feasted on them. Even now, the memory of his head between her legs had heat rushing all through her.

"What are your plans for the holidays, Darcy?"

She glanced over at him, wondering why he'd want to know and then quickly figured he'd asked for conversational purposes only. "When I leave here, instead of flying back to New York, I'm headed to Minnesota to spend Christmas with my parents and brothers. I've timed it to be with them Christmas Eve and Christmas Day. That's the most I can take of the harsh, cold Minnesota weather. Then on the day after Christmas I'm heading to Cavanaugh Lake to help Ellie with her New Year's Eve bash. She's planning a masquerade party this year."

"That should be interesting and a lot of fun."

She thought so as well and looked forward to the event.

As the car continued to move through the streets of Jamaica, she glanced out the window to take in the sights they passed. They were on the grander side of the island, where the wealthy resided, which was evident by the spacious homes they passed. She knew the houses were owned by wealthy Americans and Europeans who wanted to get away to the tropical island whenever they could. Cheyenne Steele Westmoreland and Vanessa Steele Cody, along with their husbands, owned beautiful homes in this part of the island as well. The two women were first cousins to Donovan Steele, a close friend of Uriel's. She had met most of the Steele family through Ellie at family functions and gatherings.

It had turned dark, and the lights that lined the streets seemed to shimmer across the water. When York turned off the main road and onto a street lined with palm trees on both sides, she studied the homes they passed. *Huge, magnificent* and *beautiful* were just a few words she could use to describe them. And when he pulled into the driveway of one such home, she turned and glanced over at him questioningly.

He smiled. "This is where we'll be spending the evening. I plan to treat you to my own brand of an island feast."

She glanced back at the house and then back at him. "And the owner has no problem with you doing that?" she asked, trying to downplay her excitement at the thought that he wanted to prepare a meal for her.

He chuckled. "Trust me, he won't mind since I know him well."

"Do you?"

"Yes. I own the place. And I want to welcome you, Darcy Owens, to my summer home in Jamaica."

CHAPTER SEVEN

YORK LEANED BACK against the closed door and watched as Darcy moved around his living room. It was as if she was fascinated by each and every thing she saw, whether it was the furniture, the paintings on the wall or the large potted plants he had strategically arranged to get the optimum amount of sun. Then there was the sea view from every window.

He had bought the home when it had been in foreclosure and never regretted doing so. It was his haven, his escape when he'd found himself working too hard and needing playtime. He liked spending time on the water and owned a Jet Ski that he enjoyed taking out every chance he got.

"This place is beautiful, York, and the view of the ocean is simply breathtaking."

"Thanks." He smiled, pleased with her assessment of his home. He was a man who really never cared what others thought of his possessions, but knowing she liked this place filled him with something he'd never felt before. It was then that he realized he had never brought a woman here. Usually his time spent at this place was what he considered as "me" time—his time alone to unwind and enjoy the beach that was literally in his backyard.

He studied her as she continued to look out one of his

floor-to-ceiling windows and thought she was breath-taking, as well. That short dress had practically undone him the moment he'd seen her in it. She was the only woman that could get him wound up to this point, where he was filled with a simmering need that was hard to keep in check. And it didn't help matters to know he'd already sampled her, already knew her taste and scent. Knew how it felt to ride her.

She turned and caught him staring but didn't seem surprised. He had a feeling she was aware of every move he made. He wondered if she was privy to his thoughts as well. If she was, then she knew those thoughts were salacious, indecent at best, highly X-rated. Even now he was wondering what was or wasn't under her dress.

He drew in a long breath when their gazes held, and the silence between them was becoming noticeably long. It wouldn't take much to cross the room, lift that short dress and take her just where she stood.

It was she who finally broke the silence by asking, "How long have you owned the house?"

"A few years. I always wanted a place on the island, and when I heard about it I couldn't pass up the chance to get it. It's my escape from reality. I've been a beach bum here a time or two."

"Why are you staying at the hotel when you have this place?"

He moved away from the door. "I'm on the island working, and I need to be in the thick of things."

"Oh."

He knew his words reminded her of his allegations about Felder. She tilted back her head, stared at him and asked, "Why are you so hell-bent on Damien Felder being guilty?"

"And why are you so hell-bent that he's innocent?"

He could feel a confrontation coming on, and he could deal with that. A verbal sparring with her was always refreshing. But what he didn't like was the thought that they would be arguing about another man—a man who when he wasn't with her was sleeping with another woman. And it was a woman who another man wanted or assumed he had. If that wasn't a mixed-up affair, he didn't know what was. He didn't want Darcy to be a part of such foolishness.

"I like giving people the benefit of the doubt, York."

He rolled his shoulders in a shrug. "That's a nice gesture, but people aren't always what they seem to be."

"I know that," she all but snapped and he had a feeling she wanted to smack him.

"Did Felder make that much of an impression on you, or do you just want to refute what I say just for the hell of it?" he asked, regarding her intently.

She smiled, and he thought back to the first time he had seen her smile…although the smile had not been directed at him. It had been at Uriel and Ellie's wedding, and she'd smiled a lot, genuinely happy for her best friend. And her hazel eyes had sparkled a lot that night, too.

"You shouldn't be so quick to jump to conclusions about people, York," she said, interrupting his thoughts.

"And you think that's what I'm doing?" he asked.

"Don't you?"

"No. And for you to assume I would consider a man guilty of wrongdoing just because he's shown an interest in you is unfair to me."

He knew his comment had given her food for thought when she hung her head to study the grain of the wood on his floor. She lifted her head. "You're right, and I owe you another apology."

"Yes, you do."

She frowned. "You don't have to rub it in."

He began slowly walking toward her, and the frown on her face showed no signs of disappearing. In fact, it deepened, and he thought she looked pretty darn sexy when angry. He came to a stop in front of her and said, "I didn't bring you here to argue with you, Darcy."

She tilted her head at an angle to meet his direct gaze. "And why *did* you bring me here?"

He smiled. "To feed you, for starters. You can have a seat here in the living room and enjoy a view of the water, or you can join me in the kitchen to see what else I can do besides nab the bad guys."

He could tell by the light that lit her eyes that the latter suggestion caught her interest. He was proven right when she said, "I'll join you in the kitchen."

DARCY SAT ON a stool at the breakfast bar and sipped a glass of wine as she watched York in action. She was paying attention to how well he handled himself in the kitchen as he went about chopping vegetables to go with the chicken he'd put in the oven to bake.

But her attention went beyond that. For such a tall, well-built guy, he was quick on his feet as he moved around the huge kitchen. It was obvious that he knew his way around the room, which meant he spent a lot of time in it. A man with decent cooking skills was hard to come by these days. And she liked how he could carry on a conversation with her while preparing their food. He liked giving her pointers about how to keep the chicken moist and the easiest way to chop the vegetables so they could retain their nutritional value under heat.

However, what she enjoyed the most was just sitting there and watching him while memories of their one night together continued to consume her. The man was handsome and well built. And his ruggedly handsome features were definitely a plus in her book. He looked good in jeans, and any woman would appreciate the way his muscle shirt covered his broad shoulders. He was definitely eye candy.

She was fairly certain that with his looks and build York could have his pick of women and probably did. Although he'd never brought one to any of the functions Ellie gave, she knew he dated a lot. She'd heard that right after his lover's death he had quit the NYPD and traveled abroad for a year with another one of his godbrothers by the name of Zion Blackstone. Zion had continued living abroad but York had returned to the States and instead of returning to work as a police officer, he had opened his own security firm with money his grandmother had left for him when she'd died. That had been over five years ago, and now his security business was a successful one, and he had nine employees working for him.

"Tell me about some of the cases your company has handled."

He glanced up at her and smiled. "Why? You thinking about changing professions?"

She chuckled. "Um, you never know. Right now, anything would be more appealing than having to deal with the politics of getting things done. Everyone loves New York, but my job is to make sure they continue to love it. Budget cuts haven't helped things."

"I'm sure they haven't." He then began telling her about one of his cases that involved protecting a well-known celebrity from an overzealous fan. "The woman was eventually arrested," he said.

Darcy nodded. She had her favorite celebrities but couldn't for the life of her imagine herself stalking any of them.

"Everything is almost ready. I can give you a tour of the place while we're waiting for the chicken to finish baking."

"Thanks. I'd like that."

YORK THOUGHT THAT the only thing better than a woman who looked good was one who smelled good as well. And Darcy smelled good. He wasn't sure of what cologne she was wearing tonight, but it was one that made everything inside of him feel primitive and male each time he sniffed it.

She walked beside him as he took her from room to room. It was a big place, but it was cozy enough for him and he made use of every available space. But then he didn't believe in overcrowding. He had hired a private decorator and had been pleased with the results.

As soon as he entered his bedroom and saw his huge bed, he immediately thought of Darcy sharing it with him. And he had a feeling before the night was over, she would. He'd told her on the way here that he wanted her. Nothing had changed. And he'd been aware of how she had been watching him while he'd prepared dinner. Knowing that her eyes had been on him, studying his every move, had made him want her even more.

When they returned to the living room, she sat down on the leather sofa; he sat opposite her on the matching love seat. He watched her cross her legs and clasp her hands together in her lap. The simple gestures turned him on. She had that much of an impact on him without even trying.

And then he watched as she took a sip from her wine glass and remembered just how well she could use that mouth of hers. Suddenly he envisioned Darcy in his bed riding him while he kissed her senseless. He imagined them flipping positions so he could ride her. And just like before, he would ride her hard.

He sat there and listened while she talked, telling him more about her job and then about some of the escapades she and Ellie had gotten into as children. When he asked her about the prank they had once played on Uriel, she told him how she had talked a six-teen-year-old Ellie into kissing Uriel on a dare. Uriel had been in college at the time and hadn't liked it one bit. In fact, it had taken him a while to get over it and his anger had been with Darcy just as much as it had been with Ellie. He could tell by the sparkle in her eyes and the laughter in her voice while she retold the story that she still thought what happened that day had been funny, especially when a furious twenty-one-year-old Uriel had found out he'd been set up by two teenage girls.

York checked his watch before glancing up in time to see her take her last sip of wine. He liked the way the liquid trickled down her throat and remembered how his tongue had licked that part of her. He stood. "Let's get dinner out of the way so we can take a walk on the beach."

She stood as well and returned his smile. "I'm definitely looking forward to that."

MEN, DARCY THOUGHT, glancing across the table at York, could be unpredictable creatures at times. On the drive over, York had all but hinted he would jump her bones the first chance he got. Yet, she had been here for a couple of hours and he had yet to make a move on her. She wondered if he really did have plans for them to take a walk on the beach.

"You've gotten quiet on me, Darcy."

She chuckled, deciding she wouldn't share what she'd been thinking. "Dinner was delicious," she said, slightly pushing away from the table. And she meant it. He had done an outstanding job.

"Ready to spend some time on the beach?"

So he had been serious. "Sure."

He glanced down at her shoes. "Go ahead and take them off. You're going to love the feel of the sand beneath your feet."

"All right."

She kicked off her sandals and watched as he did the same for his own. She noticed he grabbed a blanket off a shelf before leading her out of his back door. It was dark, and she could hear the sound of the sea roaring through her ears, while the scent of salt water filled her nostrils. He took her hand and they began walking to the beach, which was right in his backyard.

When she'd had thoughts of spending three weeks in Jamaica, her plans included meeting a man with whom she would share a walk on the beach. At the time, she hadn't thought the man would be York.

He'd been right. She liked the feel of the sand beneath her feet, and that, combined with the scent of the beach and the knowledge that she had a virile man walking beside her, one whose fingers were entwined with hers, was reminding her of just how much of a woman she was.

It also reminded her of what had happened once already between them and what she looked forward to happening again. Before this trip, she had gone without sex long enough, so wanting to make up for lost time was a strong and healthy urge. Making love to York that night had been like a welcome back to life. She felt good and knew without any doubt that she wanted York again.

"This is a good spot."

They stopped walking, and he released her hand to spread the blanket on the sand. It was dark, but the brightly lit lantern on his back porch provided enough light to see their surroundings. And then there were the stars that dotted the sky overhead and the full moon right in front of them that cast a romantic glow upon where they were. It was like a scene straight out of one of her romance novels. There was nothing better than a romantic night and an ultra-handsome man. A woman couldn't ask for much more.

"That's that," York said, interrupting her thoughts. She saw he had finished spreading the blanket out and had turned toward her. He was standing about five feet away, yet she was able to feel the moment their gazes connected. Desire immediately began oozing through her bloodstream. Her lips suddenly felt dry, and she automatically ran the tip of her tongue over her bottom lip and was well aware his gaze had followed the movement.

She wanted him. He wanted her. It was all about lust. He knew it, and she knew it, as well. The man had haunted her thoughts since making love to her two nights ago. She had tried convincing herself the reason she'd gotten so into him the way she had was because he had been her first in two years. But now she knew that excuse wouldn't fly. It was deeper than that. As a lover, he had not only satisfied her yearning but he had also captivated her mind. No other man had been able to do the latter, not even Harold.

She tilted her head as an intense yearning continued to fill her. Refusing to be denied what she wanted, she sauntered toward York, deciding she had no problem making the first move if things called for that. There was a slight breeze in the air that carried moisture to dampen her skin, and the night air seemed to carry the sound of her footsteps in the sand.

There was something about being out on the beach tonight with York and the way he was standing there not moving, watching her and waiting for her to come to him. Her inner thighs clenched with every step she took, and she breathed in deeply when she came to a stop in front of him.

Later, she would wonder why they were opposites capable of becoming magnets that could attract each other in such a volatile way—and why the need to make love to him on the beach was a *must do* on her list.

He didn't say anything for a long moment. He just stood there and stared at her, letting his gaze roam up and down her as if he could see through her clothes. And then, when she thought she could not take any more of his blatant perusal or the intense yearning filling her to capacity, he reached out and pulled her to him. He pressed her body close to his, letting her feel just how hard and erect he was for her. Her breasts, pressed hard against his chest, began to throb, and she breathed in his scent at the same time she felt a tingling sensation between her thighs.

"I could make love to you out here all night, Darcy."

His words, spoken in a deep, desire-laced voice, inflamed her mind and she nearly released a groan when she felt the erection pressed against her get even larger. The feel of it sent heat rushing through her, and her breathing became labored. Making love on the beach under the stars with a man had always been a fantasy of hers after reading such a scene in a romance novel. Now here she was with York and a burst of desire, the magnitude of which she'd only ever experienced with him, was taking over her senses.

She studied the gaze staring back at her, saw the need that was as deep as her own. She reached out and pressed her hand to his chest and felt the hard, thumping beat of his heart beneath her palm. How could she feel this immediate desire for him and not for Damien?

She wasn't sure just how much time had elapsed while they stood there, with intense desire building between them by the second. Then, not able to handle the anticipation any longer or the forceful longing, she rose up on her tiptoes, leaned in and took that same tip of her tongue she'd used to moisten her lip earlier and ran it along his jaw. She heard the sound of his heavy breathing in her ear. She heard his moan. She felt the hardness of him swell even more against her belly.

"Will your neighbors see us out here?" she whispered as she continued to use the tip of her tongue to lick underneath his ear. She liked the taste of his skin, hot against her tongue.

"No," he said huskily. "They can't see a thing. The

homes on this beach were built to provide ultimate privacy."

"Are you sure?"

"Positive."

Taking his word, she stepped back and began removing her dress. To be honest, even if his neighbors could see anything she was beyond stopping at this point. Modesty was the last thing on her mind. Him getting inside of her and stroking her to a powerful orgasm headed the list right now. The prospect of that happening consumed her thoughts. The breeze whispering in off the water did nothing to cool her heat. It merely intensified it.

She eased her dress up to her waist, and it didn't take long to whip the garment over her head. She hadn't worn a bra, and her thong slid down her legs easily. As the breeze flitted across her naked skin, she knew what this night held for her, and she couldn't downplay her body's excitement or the urges that were taking over her mind and making her want him even more. She was filled with the need for him with every catch of her breath.

York had stood there and watched Darcy strip, and now seeing her without clothes did something to him. He quickly unzipped his jeans and removed them. Then came his briefs and shirt. When he stood before her completely naked, he took the time to sheath a condom over his engorged shaft. His hand nearly trembled with the need for her.

Never had he known a woman quite like her, and in a way, he'd known she would be the one to send his mind in a topsy-turvy. He had hit on her that first time, and when she had rejected his interest, he should have been grateful for her sparing his sanity. Instead he had been resentful. Now he knew it hadn't been meant for them to connect then. But now the field was wide open, and there was no stopping them. It had taken two years for him to accept the intensity of his desire for her, even when he hadn't wanted to crave her to such a degree.

He reached out for her. Instead of lowering her on the blanket, he swept her into his arms and began heading toward the water.

"Where are you taking me, York?"

He glanced down at her and smiled. "You'll see."

And moments later he lowered her naked body into one of those heavyweight vinyl floaters. The inflatable floor cushioned her backside, and he shifted her position to where her legs were spread open. The raft was large enough for more than one person, and he joined her, bracing himself against the side to stare down at her, taking note of the position he'd placed her in, all spread open for him to see. He then took his hand and traced a path up her inner thigh. Then his fingers began inching inside of her, and he studied the emotions that crossed her face when they did.

"You're hot," he said in a deep, husky tone. "You're still tight, and I plan to loosen you up a bit."

"Is that a promise?" she asked, in a whimpering tone.

"Definitely a promise."

And then he shifted positions to straddle her while simultaneously sliding his hands beneath her hips to lift her backside to receive him. His entry inside her was swift, and his heart began thumping hard in his chest when his thrust went to the hilt as he spread her legs farther apart, making them hang off the sides of the raft.

He used his hands to push the raft into the water,

and as soon as they were afloat, he began moving in and out of her. This was crazy, but he wanted her this way. He wanted her here. Making love to a woman on a raft in the water had always been a fantasy of his and now he was doing it here with Darcy—only with Darcy.

It was a new float, one he had purchased recently, one that hadn't ever been in the water. Now he was using it for the first time, officially christening it with her. With the water flapping beneath them, every stroke inside of her made his want that much more intense. The low ache in his belly was being appeased with every thrust.

He wanted to make her his.

Why such a thought had even crossed his mind, had lurked its way into his thoughts, he wasn't sure. All he knew at that moment was that he intended to be the only man to ever make love to her in a raft, on the beach or any place else. There would be no Damien Felder in her future. Anyone who knew York was well aware that once he staked a claim about anything that was that. With every lunge into her body, he was doing more than staking a claim; he was declaring possession.

DARCY MOANED DEEP within her throat when York's thrust became ever more powerful. She had fantasized about making love on the beach, but doing so in a raft in the water hadn't crossed her mind. And with each breath she was taking, York was driving into her, pushing her over the edge. His thrusts were hard and so intense she figured they would tumble out of the raft and into the water, never to be heard from again. But he managed to handle both her and the raft. He might be keeping the watercraft afloat, but her mind and body were drowning in waters so sensual that she had to pull in deep breaths to survive what he was doing.

What if they ended up in one of his neighbors' back-yards or right smack in the middle of the sea? She could see the headlines now. "Man and woman found naked on a raft—bodies can't be pried apart."

That scenario should concern her, but instead she pushed it to the back of her mind. It couldn't compete with the sensations tearing through her. And when York shifted his body slightly and touched an inner part of her that had never been touched before, she screamed. Then an orgasm rammed through her and shook her to the core. The feelings were so intense that he had to grip down on her to keep her body from pushing them both out of the raft and into the water.

He was stroking her into sweet oblivion, and she closed her eyes and threw her head back when she burst into a second orgasm. She moaned his name, and when his mouth captured her to silence the sound, she felt his body buck above her just seconds before he drove even deeper into her.

He released her mouth, and she bit down on her bottom lip to keep from screaming out again. The motion of the water beneath them sent waves pleasure through her. She opened her eyes and saw he was staring down at her and the sound emitting from between his clenched lips could be considered a growl.

"You're mine, Darcy."

The strong tread of York's voice floated through her mind. She heard his words but couldn't fathom why he'd said them or what he meant by them. She quickly figured he had gotten caught up in the moment and to-morrow he wouldn't even remember them.

As he continued to push her into another orgasm, she knew his virility was unlimited, his desire was primitive and his ability to bring her pleasure was unprecedented. Her breathing got shallow as sensual bliss took over her mind and body. Her heart raced so fast she thought she might faint.

Several pleasure-filled moments later, her body calmed, and when she felt him lift off her she felt an intense sense of loss. She was too afraid to look around, too nervous about where they might have drifted.

"You okay, baby?"

His question made her glance up at him, and she saw the stars were still dotting the sky overhead. At least it was still nighttime. She hadn't been sure how much time had passed. When you were in the throes of extreme sexual pleasure, you were destined to forget about time.

She shifted and moved her legs. If they were out in the middle of the sea, she didn't want her legs hanging over the sides. Sharks could be hungry creatures, and she didn't want to be one's meal.

"Where are we?" she asked him.

He smiled. "Out in the water."

She couldn't help returning his smile. "Please tell me we're not near a cruise ship and that you can still see land."

He chuckled, and it was then that she realized just how large the raft was. "No cruise ship on the horizon and yes, we can still see land. I'll have us back to shore in no time."

She felt both relief and excitement upon hearing that. "You sure?"

"Positive."

Believing him, she sat up and let out a deep sigh of

relief when she saw they were probably no more than fifty feet from land. He pulled oars—that she noticed for the first time—from the sides of the raft and began using them.

"Need help?" she asked him.

He smiled over at her, his pupils glimmered with sensuality. "No. I got us out here, and I'll get us back. No problem. Besides, I want you to keep all your energy for later."

She took his words as an indication of what was yet to come. He wasn't through with her yet, and she didn't have a problem with any plans his mind was conjuring up. No small surprise there. He could create an intense yearning within her, a hunger, with just a look. She'd thought it before and still thought it now. She'd never met a man quite like York.

As they got closer and closer to land, she could feel the quickened beat of her heart, and as she watched him handle the oars, she saw as well as felt his strength. His broad chest, belly and hips tightened with every push and pull of the oars, and he was still hard and fully erected. She was entranced with the sight before her. His naked body was a total turn-on and knowing what that body had done to her was unforgettable.

She could tell from the way he was looking at her that he was fully aware of just how much he had satisfied her. No doubt even in the moonlight her face was basking with a heated glow that only the pleasures of lovemaking could cause.

She blinked when the raft hit land and then he was out of it to secure it. Then he was reaching for her, carrying her into his arms toward the blanket. Moments later, he was lowering her onto it. By the time she felt the material against her back, York had spread her thighs and was settling between them. He looked down at her and their gazes held. When he entered her, stretching her again, she knew tonight would be one she would remember for a long time.

CHAPTER EIGHT

HE WAS A bachelor undone, York decided as he eased out of bed the next morning. And the woman who had slept beside him all night was responsible. He glanced over at her as he made his way to the bathroom. After making love to her on the blanket several times under the moonlight, he had carried her inside and they had showered together, washing sand from their bodies. Eventually they made love again.

They had tumbled into bed too exhausted to make love in the place where most normal people did, but just like she had christened his raft he had plans for that bed. He figured she would be sleeping awhile and after washing his face, brushing his teeth and slipping into a pair of jeans he padded barefoot and bare chested out the room and down the stairs.

He checked his phone and saw he'd missed several calls. One was from Rich, the man he had tailing Felder, and the other two were from Uriel. He quickly called Rich back, and a few moments later the man had brought him up to date. Felder and Danielle Simone were still together, and another interesting fact was that the couple had gotten a visit from someone else, a man not yet identified. But that man was now, too, being tailed as well.

When York ended the call with Rich he called Uriel.

"You called?" he asked the moment he heard his god-brother's voice.

"Where the hell are you, Y?"

"I'm in Jamaica working on a case."

"Oh." Then Uriel said, "You probably couldn't care less, but Ellie mentioned that Darcy went to Jamaica on vacation."

"You don't say," he murmured, smiling.

"I do say, so don't be surprised if you run into her."

Evidently Darcy hadn't mentioned to Ellie that she'd seen him on the island, so he wouldn't give anything away. "Thanks for the warning."

"No problem. I called to give you some news."

"What?"

"I got a call from Donovan."

York nodded. Donovan Steele was one of Uriel's closest friends from college. "Yes?"

"He told me that Eli's getting married."

York almost dropped the phone. Eli Steele was one of Donovan's cousins who lived in Phoenix. York and the rest of his godbrothers had gotten to know Eli and his five brothers when they'd traveled as a group to the NASCAR races to support Bronson Scott, Donovan's best friend who was also a mutual friend to everyone.

"He's getting married?" York asked. Eli was the second of the Phoenix Steeles to marry in a year's time. What was surprising was that those Steeles were die-hard bachelors who'd vowed never to marry.

"Yes, he's marrying on Christmas Day. Can you believe that?"

York was finding it hard to believe. Earlier that year, Eli's brother Galen had gotten hitched to some woman he'd known less than a month. It wouldn't be such a shocker if Eli and Galen, along with their other brothers, hadn't been known womanizers. For them to settle down with one woman was more than a surprise. It was a downright shock.

He talked to Uriel a few more moments before finally ending the call. He then called his parents and another one of his men who was following Johnny Rush. He discovered Rush had spent the night at a bar, probably drowning in grief since he didn't know the whereabouts of Danielle Simone.

York placed his phone back on the table and headed for the kitchen, deciding Darcy deserved breakfast in bed.

A POLICE SIREN sounded in the distance and woke Darcy. She opened her eyes to the glare of the bright sunlight shining into the bedroom window and glanced around, immediately remembering where she was and whose bed she was in.

She shifted and immediately felt the tenderness between her legs, which was a blatant reminder of all the lovemaking she'd participated in the night before. Had she really made love on a raft in the sea? And on the beach? Jeez.

And she couldn't forget how they'd come inside later to shower together and ended up doing that and a whole lot more. She recalled how they'd slept during the night with his body spooning hers.

She lay on her side to glance out the window, and all she could see was the beautiful blue-green water. Waking up to such a sight was simply awesome.

She heard movement downstairs and immediately felt the quickened beats of her heart. What had brought her and York to this? Why even now she had to admit that he had to be the most generous of lovers…and the most skilled. The man didn't miss a beat when it came to pleasuring a woman. He had mastered the skills. It was certainly an ingrained talent that some men never gained. After making love with him she doubted she could ever turn to the likes of Bruce again for anything.

And now that she'd apologized for her behavior of two years ago, they were getting along. At least they were when neither of them mentioned Damien Felder. She knew York suspected the man of wrongdoing, but she was of the mind that a man was innocent until proven guilty. All it took was to remember what had happened to her father years ago when Darcy had been in her early teens.

Her father was a high school teacher, and one of his female students had accused him of inappropriate behavior toward her. Matlock Owens was about to lose his job as well as the respect of the community before the young girl tearfully admitted she had lied just to get attention from her parents. The girl and her family, totally embarrassed by what they'd done, had eventually moved away, but it had taken years before the Owens family had gotten over what had been done to them. Darcy, who'd always been a "daddy's girl," had seen firsthand what the false accusations had done to her father and didn't want the same thing to happen to Damien.

She knew York assumed she was defensive of Damien because she was interested in him, but that was not the case. And in a way she shouldn't really care what York thought. But for some reason she did.

"You're awake."

She turned to the sound of York's voice. He was

standing in the doorway with a breakfast tray in his hand. She couldn't help but smile. No man had ever treated her to breakfast in bed before. She pulled up into a sitting position, realizing she was completely naked under the covers. Where were her clothes? She recalled racing into the house naked last night, then remembered they'd left their clothes in a heap near the blanket. They'd probably gotten washed away by now.

As if reading her thoughts, York came into the room and placed the tray on the nightstand. "I got our clothes. I just shook the sand from your dress because I didn't know if it was washable. But everything else I tossed into the washing machine."

She nodded. The thought of him handling her underthings sent flutters all through her. "Thanks."

He then glanced down at the tray. "I wasn't sure what you liked, so I brought you a little bit of everything."

He was right. It was loaded with pancakes, sausage, bacon, scrambled eggs, a bowl of fresh fruit and toast. She felt she gained five pounds just looking at all the food he'd prepared. "Thanks, and I hope you know there's no way I can eat this all by myself. You are planning to join me, right?"

He chuckled. "Right. But I need to go back for the coffee."

It was only after York had left the room that Darcy was able to breathe normally. He needed a shave but that *I-could-use-a-shave* look made him appear even sexier and more rugged. She shook her head. Ellie would never believe that she and York had called a truce long enough to toss between the sheets.

"I'm back."

Darcy glanced over at him as he entered the room.

He was wearing a pair of jeans that rode low on his hips, and he was bare chested. She recalled licking every inch of that broad chest last night. She also remembered licking other parts of him as well. The scorching sensuality of her actions, as well as her risqué behavior, almost entrapped her into a deep-rooted desire that could overtake her if she wasn't careful.

She watched as he placed two cups of coffee beside the breakfast tray. He then proceeded to remove his jeans before crawling back into bed with her. She quickly scooted over and made room for him. But he didn't let her go too far before pulling her close for a kiss.

Dang. No man should be able to kiss that good in the mornings. Such a thing should be outlawed. It was a kiss so arousing that her body tingled.

She was the one who finally pulled back from the kiss knowing if she didn't she would be spread eagle beneath him in no time. And as much as she didn't want to admit it, being with York could be habit-forming, and she'd never wanted to find herself addicted to any man. She was deeply attracted to him; that in itself could make her vulnerable, and she didn't want that.

"I think you need to feed me," she said, lifting a finger to his jaw and rubbing the stubble there as she gazed at his mouth. He had such a beautiful pair of lips, and he definitely knew how to use them to his advantage. She would always have to be a few steps ahead of him, otherwise she would risk getting in too deep. This was a man who—if she wasn't careful and on her toes—would make her want the one thing she swore she would never want with a man again. An exclusive relationship.

He reached for the coffee and handed her a cup. "Be careful, it's hot," he said.

And so are you, she wanted to counter and decided to keep that thought to herself.

He then placed the tray of food between them and began eating off of it. Several times he actually fed pieces of bacon to her. And when he leaned in to nibble a piece of bacon off her lip she thought she would come in a full-blown orgasm then and there.

There was something she needed to ask him about, something that still bothered her although it shouldn't. "York?"

"Yes?"

"That morning after we made love in my hotel room. You left before I woke up. Why?"

He held her gaze. "Had I not left then, Darcy, I might not have left. You had a tendency to make me forget I was on the island for a reason. I had a job to do. My team needed me in place, although I wanted more than anything to stay right in your bed."

She inwardly smiled and didn't want to think how his words had her floating on a cloud of contentment. He *had* wanted to stay with her.

"Any more questions, Darcy?"

She shook her head. "No, not right now."

"Good. What do you want to do today?" he then asked her.

She took a sip of her coffee, surprised by his question. She had assumed he would be taking her back to the hotel after breakfast. She'd figured taking up his time was not an option.

"What do you suggest?" she asked him.

That I-can-think-of-a-number-of-things smile tempted

her to lean over and kiss it off his lips, but she decided to refrain from doing so. "We can go back rafting today," he suggested, reminding her of what they'd done last night. "Or we can stay in, naked, and watch movies," he added.

She chuckled as she took another sip of her coffee. "Sounds interesting."

"Trust me, I can make it as interesting as you want."

She could believe that. "Don't you have work to do today? Need I remind you that you're working on a case?"

He grinned. "Need I remind you that it's the weekend? No filming today and the cast and crew have scattered. I have several men assisting me, and they are keeping tabs on those I need to keep up with."

She couldn't help but wonder if Damien was one of those. She couldn't imagine having her privacy invaded in such a way and pushed the thought to the back of her mind. Otherwise, she would speak her mind and she and York would end up arguing again. "Watching movies sounds good, but I'm not doing so in the nude. The first thing I plan on doing is washing my dress."

"You're a spoilsport, Darcy Owens," he said, chuckling, a pretend pout on his lips.

They continued to eat breakfast, and he mentioned the call he'd gotten from Uriel with the news about Eli Steele. She knew Eli and his brothers through her association with Ellie and Uriel. She glanced over at York after taking another sip of her coffee. "Did you mention to Uriel that we were together?"

He met her gaze and shook his head. "No. I didn't feel it was my place, especially since he didn't mention it, which to me meant you hadn't said anything to Ellie."

She paused in chewing a piece of sausage. "I haven't

talked to Ellie since arriving. I'm due to give her a call, but I prefer not saying anything about us being together. At least not yet. El gets carried away with certain things," she said. *Especially when it's about me and a man.*

"No problem. We will handle our involvement whatever way you prefer."

Our involvement. Were they actually involved? Did their actions on two separate occasions account for an involvement? She couldn't help wondering if an involvement and a fling were basically the same thing. She considered a fling as short term and an involvement as something a little longer.

She continued to eat wondering just how he really saw their affair.

YORK SIPPED ON his coffee in thoughtful silence. He couldn't get the vision out of his mind of him making love to Darcy last night—first on a raft and then later on the blanket he'd spread on the sand. Both times had been simply incredible. And he couldn't forget that night in her hotel room.

While he'd been downstairs preparing breakfast, he had found himself watching the clock, anticipating the moment she would awake. He had never felt possessive when it came to a woman, but he did so with her. He could even recall the exact moment he felt he had made her his.

He wondered how he was going to break the news to her. He'd told her at the time, while they'd been making love, but he doubted she remembered.

He had a gut feeling that Darcy was a woman that didn't want to belong to anyone. But he wanted to prove her wrong. York shook his head thinking something was wrong with him. Here he was on the island and working an important case, and the only thing he wanted to think about was making love to Darcy again. He'd thought that calling for a truce had been a good idea. He hadn't known doing so would entice him to build a relationship with a woman who had built a wall around herself. What he'd told her earlier was true. They were involved, and it was an involvement that he intended to explore to the fullest.

"This is delicious, York."

"Thanks. I enjoy being in the kitchen when I have the time. Usually I don't."

"You travel a lot?"

He glanced over at her and nodded. "Not as much as I used to when I was getting the business off the ground. Now I have people who travel for me. This case was different, though, and I wanted to be in the thick of things. One of the men who invested a lot of money into the movie production is a close friend of my father's. He's been losing a lot of money lately."

When he told her just how much, her eyes widened as if she'd found it hard to believe. "That's a lot of money for anyone to lose on a business deal," she said.

"Yes, it is, and it bothers me to think that it's an inside job."

Darcy didn't say anything, and York knew she was thinking of Felder and whether his accusations about the man could be true. She wouldn't bring him up and neither would he. The man was a touchy subject between them, and it was best his name remained out of their conversation.

And speaking of conversation, he decided to switch things. "Have you ever ridden a Jet Ski?"

She shook her head. "No."

He smiled. "Then that's what we'll do today. I'll teach you how it's done."

"You own one?"

"Yes."

She nodded. "Sounds like fun." She then leaned over and softly kissed his lips. "Thanks for last night, York. It was wonderful."

Yes, what they'd shared had been wonderful, and he intended to spend more of such wonderful times with her.

DARCY COULDN'T HELP but smile as she watched York give her a demonstration on the proper way to use the Jet Ski. It was a beautiful piece of equipment, but then the person showing her how to use it was a beautiful man.

After breakfast they had dressed and he had taken her back to the hotel where she had packed an overnight bag and returned here. They had gone swimming for a while and now he was showing her how to use a Jet Ski, and she was having a great time watching him.

They were still wearing their swimsuits. She was wearing a fuchsia bikini, which he seemed quite taken with when she'd put it on. In fact, he'd seemed quite taken with taking it off her as well. He had stripped her naked, tossed the bikini on shore while they went skinny-dipping.

She smiled remembering that time as she studied him. His swimming trunks showed just what a fine physique he had—tight muscles, firm stomach, and thick muscular thighs. His skin was glistening from the water, and her tongue tingled, tempted to lick him dry.

"Any questions?"

She smiled upon realizing that he had asked her a question. "About what?"

He laughed and shook his head. "About anything I just went over with you."

The only thing she could remember—and rather vividly—was listing parts of his body she found fascinating. But not to give anything away, she said, "No, I don't have any questions."

"So you're ready to try it?"

She wouldn't say that. "Only if we can do it together."

That statement made him grin, and she immediately understood why. They had been practically doing it together most of the morning. Ever since she had let the cat out of the bag that she'd gone without sex for almost two years, he had definitely made himself available without any trouble, and she had readily taken him up on his offers.

After breakfast they'd made love, and when they had gotten to her hotel room after she'd thrown items into her overnight bag, they'd made love again. There was just something about him that pushed thoughts of sex to the forefront of her mind. Their lovemaking sessions were always wild and out of control, unrestrained and uncontrollable. He seemed to enjoy it that way, and so did she.

"What I meant," she decided to clarify, "is to ask if we can ride the Jet Ski together."

"We sure can. It can hold up to three people," he said, smiling over at her.

Darcy nodded. She was about to tell him how

nice the brightly colored Jet Ski was when her cell phone rang.

She recognized the number and felt a deep thump in her chest. She glanced over at York and knew she didn't have to tell him who was calling. She probably had a guilty look on her face, although there was no reason for her to be guilty about anything. She had come to the island to enjoy herself and have fun. York didn't mean any more to her than Damien did.

She knew it was a lie as soon as the thought left her brain. She considered ignoring the call and then decided to go ahead and answer it, knowing full well that York would be listening to her every word. "Yes, Damien?"

"I'll be back on the island Monday night, and I was wondering when I can see you again."

CHAPTER NINE

A FROWN SETTLED around York's lips. Part of his brain tried convincing him that he didn't care, that whatever Darcy did and with whom was her business and that it didn't concern him. But that was a bald-faced lie. It did concern him, not just personally but physically.

He continued to wipe down his Jet Ski while trying to ignore her conversation with Felder. The man was with Danielle Simone, so why was he calling Darcy? He fought to keep his teeth from clenching and had to suck in a deep breath when he was struck by an intense urge to take the phone from her and ask him. The very thought was insane, but the one thing he wasn't feeling at the moment was sane.

Keep your cool, Ellis. Just because you and Darcy have been mating like rabbits every chance you get is no reason to get all possessive and territorial. But then again, maybe you have every right since you did claim her and decided she was yours.

He crouched down to wipe off a lower part of the Jet Ski while thinking he could bet all the tea in China that Darcy wouldn't agree with that assessment. She would probably box his ears if she even knew he had such thoughts and was making such assumptions.

He pretended not to notice when she ended the call. He tried ignoring the moment of awkward silence that

followed and figured he should say something but decided considering how he felt it was best to keep his
mouth shut. He was encountering emotions he'd never
felt before, and he wasn't quite sure how to handle them.
No woman had ever made him feel this way, and quite
honestly, he didn't like it.

"That was Damien."

He glanced over at her without stopping what he was
doing. "I gathered."

She didn't say anything for a moment and neither
did he. A part of him wished he could concentrate on
something else. For the last hour or so, he had been admiring how she looked in the bikini, appreciating her
curvy figure and long legs. Now all he could see was
the color red flash across his eyes.

He knew his attitude wasn't helping matters, but at
the moment, he truly didn't give a damn. Standing less
than five feet away was the woman he had made love
with most of the night—the woman who had somehow
gotten underneath his skin. He broke eye contact with
her and continued his work.

"You have no right to be this way, you know."

Her words did something to him, snapped off the last
of his patience. He rose to his feet and faced her. Instead
of saying anything, he stepped around her and went
inside through the back door. She was watching him
curiously, and he knew eventually she would follow.

Once inside his kitchen, he turned the moment she
swept in behind him. Before she could open her mouth,
he was on her, kissing her. Every part of him was throbbing in both anger and arousal. She evidently didn't
know anything about rights when it came to him. And
he intended to teach her a few things.

God, he wanted her again. He wanted to wipe Damien Felder's name from her memory. He wanted to feel the way their bodies connected when they made love, feel her fingers digging deep in his shoulder blades while he rode her hard, hear her scream his name when she came. Hell, they didn't just have sex together; they had something a lot more remarkable and astonishing.

Instead of pushing him away, she gripped his shoulders and pressed her mouth even closer to him, and he took it with fierce intensity, using his tongue to seduce her to a moan.

And it seemed that she needed the kiss as much as he did when she proceeded to feast hungrily on his mouth. He lifted her up slightly, and she instinctively wrapped her legs around him. Without breaking the kiss, he began walking toward the living room. It was hot outside, but nothing could compare to the temperature he was feeling inside.

York was determined by the time things were over she would know what rights he did have.

THIS WAS MADNESS. When he kissed her, Darcy couldn't form a coherent thought. All she knew was that if she continued to get wrapped up in York she could get hurt, because he was awakening emotions she preferred not feeling.

Darcy felt the back of her legs touch the sofa, but instead of lowering her to the sofa, York scooped her into his arms, headed over to the desk and placed her on it. He kissed her again greedily, and she returned the kiss with the same intensity, urgency and hunger.

Moments later when York broke off the kiss to look at her, all she could do was stare into his eyes, just moments before moving her gaze to his wet lips. Then her gaze moved lower, past his bare chest to the swimming trunks. They were no longer wet, probably from all the heat being generated in that area. He was hard and enlarged, and she couldn't stop herself from reaching out and sliding her fingers inside his swimming trunks.

His erection felt hot to the touch, and she cupped him in her hand and could feel the huge veins along the head of him throbbing. She couldn't stop running her fingers along the side of his thickness, thinking he was getting even larger with each stroke.

He reached down and covered her hand with his and asked huskily, "Do you want this?"

His question was definitely a no-brainer. Yes, she wanted it. Since he asked, he evidently wanted to hear her say it and she had no problem doing so. She said, "Yes, I want it." And then because she wanted to hear his admission as well, she asked, "Do you want me?"

He released her hand and slid his own inside her bikini bottom, and then his fingers began exploring her like they had every right to do so. Instinctively, the moment he touched her feminine mound she spread her legs to give him better access. And when he touched her clit, she moaned deep in her throat.

"Oh, yeah, I want you," he whispered close to her lips and leaned over while his fingers continued to stroke her inside. Her heart pounded fiercely in her chest as sensations began overtaking her.

Every nerve inside her body began tingling. And then he leaned forward and used his teeth to lower her bikini top and bared her breasts. Before she could release a gasp of surprise, his mouth latched onto a nipple and began sucking.

Darcy tossed her head back when she felt unbearably hungry for him. Her body was craving him with an intensity that shocked her.

Suddenly he released her to take a step back, and she was forced to let go of him as well. She drew in a deep breath when he eased his swimming trunks down his legs after removing a condom packet from the pocket. She loved a man who believed in being prepared. She then watched as he sheathed his erection, forcing herself to swallow during the process.

He returned to her, and she assumed he would take her off the desk. Instead, he lifted her hips and proceeded to remove her bikini, tossing both somewhere behind him. "You like undressing me, don't you?" she asked in a trembling voice. They had made love several times before, but with York, she never knew what to expect. There was never a dull moment with him when it came to making love—in or out of the bedroom.

"Yes," was his husky response, and before she could say anything else, he lowered his head to her breasts again.

She moaned and lifted her hand to stroke the side of his face, close to his mouth, and she could feel how hard he was sucking her breasts. It caused a myriad of sensations to invade the area between her legs. He had a way of making her feel desired and wanted.

And then he released her nipple, and before she could move, he lifted her hips just seconds before lowering his head between her legs. The second his tongue touched her clit, sensations rammed through her, and she let out a deep moan. He began tonguing her as if she would be his last meal, as if he was intent on exploring every single inch of her satiny flesh.

"York!"

Instead of answering her, he pulled her body closer to his mouth, and his tongue delved even deeper. She'd never felt this aroused in her entire life. He was doing something with his tongue, drawing little circles inside of her, especially on her G-spot.

She felt an orgasm coming on and tried pushing him away, but just as he'd done the last time he had performed oral sex on her, he remained unmovable, unstoppable. Sensations exploded inside of her, and her entire body shook in extreme pleasure. His mouth closed deeper on her and his tongue continued to lave her clit, and her orgasm seemed endless. A rush of heat infused her, and she couldn't help screaming out his name when more and more explosions shattered her body.

"Damn, you taste good," he said moments later when he raised his head and smiled at her. Before she could give him a response, he had grabbed her by the hips and eased her toward his waiting erection. It felt hot when it brushed against her thigh and when he was easing it inside of her. Immediately, her inner muscles clamped down on his pulsating erection. He went deep and deeper, until she could feel his testicles resting against her flesh. He filled her so completely, so totally, she didn't think he had room to move inside.

He proved her wrong when he began stroking her, easing out and going back in, making sensations rush through her veins and pour into her bloodstream. She was convinced she felt him all the way to her womb, and she knew for certain that her body could feel every hard inch of him.

His strokes seemed urgent, and her inner muscles

began milking him, needing to keep him inside her for as long as she could. The more he pounded into her, the deeper he seemed to go and the more she wanted him. He lifted her hips, held them tight and steady to receive each and every one of his hard thrusts.

"Tell me, Darcy," she heard him say. "Tell me this gives me the right. Tell me."

She bit down on her mouth, not wanting to say the words he wanted to hear. She had made love to other men and would have thrown such a request back in their face. But she knew he was right. No other man had made love to her like York did or could. No other man could make her womanhood contract with such intense pleasure.

But should that alone give him the right to anything when it came to her? Oh, hell, she thought, when he increased his pace and began pounding into her with an intensity that almost left her speechless. To get this type of pleasure she would give him whatever rights he thought he wanted.

"York!"

She screamed his name and felt her entire body tremble when an orgasm tore into her. And she knew at that moment what else she wanted, what else she wanted to feel. If he was demanding rights from her then she wanted what she considered as the ultimate in pleasure.

When he pushed hard inside of her and then retreated to thrust back into her, she shifted her body to ease away slightly. Before he realized what she was doing, she reached out and tugged the condom off his erection and tossed it to the floor. She looked at him and said, "With rights come sacrifices. I want you to let go inside of me. I want to feel your semen."

DARCY DIDN'T HAVE to ask twice. Before she could draw in her next breath, York was back inside of her, skin to skin, and he felt the difference all the way to his toes. Hell, he wanted her to feel his semen as well.

There was something about her that had his erection throbbing mercilessly inside of her. That had pressure building up inside him just for the purpose of exploding inside of her. He began stroking her again, almost nonstop.

"Oh, baby, I'm coming." He leaned forward to claim her mouth the moment his body exploded, blasting hot semen inside of her and rocking his entire body from head to toe. This was lovemaking as it should be, lovemaking as it was for him and Darcy. They had made a deal, and both had delivered. At least he had given her what she wanted, and he intended to get what he wanted—rights with her.

He broke off the kiss and threw his head back when he kept coming. Rocking his hips against her to go deeper, he knew he was branding her in a way that he had never branded a woman before. He knew the first time they'd made love there had been a chance some of his semen might have escaped inside of her, but this time he knew for certain.

He had intentionally flooded her with his seed, not for a baby but because she had asked for it. And he knew at that moment he would just about give Darcy Owens anything she wanted. And when she screamed out her orgasm it triggered another one within him, and he shot off inside of her again.

At that moment he knew that no matter how she felt about it, he would not give Damien Felder the chance to ever touch her this way or any other way.

CHAPTER TEN

DARCY CAME AWAKE and glanced out the window. It was still light outside, which meant it was still the same day. She inhaled the scent of sex. She glanced around the room and saw she was in York's bed, and all she had to do was close her eyes to remember when he had brought her in here.

It had been right after he'd made love to her on the desk. He had gathered her naked body into his arms and taken her into his bedroom where he had placed her in the bed. He had joined her there, stroked her body all over with the pads of his fingers to bring her to another aroused state before straddling her to make love to her again.

His arms tightened around her, and she knew he was awake as well and then he was tugging her closer to him, shifting her on her back and taking possession of her mouth. Only York could kiss her this way and make her want to demand things from a man she'd never demanded before—like his semen.

He released her mouth and stared down at her. "While you were asleep, I've been thinking," he said. His gaze was intense.

She lifted a brow. "About what?"

"Why Damien is so determined to keep you within his reach."

She released a frustrated breath. A part of her wanted to clobber him for bringing up the other man at a time like this, and a part of her wanted to reach up and wrap her arms around his neck to kiss the other man's name from his lips.

"Why are you bringing him up? I gave you rights while we're together on the island. I won't be seeing him or talking to him. Isn't that what you wanted?"

He nodded slowly. "Yes, but there are still unanswered questions in my mind."

"What kind of unanswered questions, York?"

He released a deep sigh and rubbed his hand down his face before sitting up. "My men and I have been keeping close tabs on Felder, and I haven't told you everything."

She lifted a confused brow. "Everything like what?"

"Like the fact that as soon as he parts company with you, he seeks out Danielle Simone or vice versa. Something is going on with those two."

She shrugged. "If you think you were sparing my feelings by not telling me, you were wrong. The thought that he was hitting on her or any other woman for that matter doesn't bother me. He and I never slept together. We didn't as much as share a kiss. In my book, I was doing something that could be considered worse. I was talking to him and making love to you, a man who was having him investigated."

"That might be true, but I still think he sought you out for another reason."

She rolled her eyes. "And what reason is that?"

"To use you as a decoy to get something off this island. Has he given you anything to keep for him?"

"No. I wouldn't take anything from him."

He nodded slowly. "And you're sure he hasn't slipped anything into your purse without your knowledge?"

"No, I keep my purse on me at all times, so he wouldn't have gotten the chance." A frown then marred her forehead when she remembered something. "However, Damien did give me one of those tote bags that promoted the movie before we left the set that day. But it was empty."

"You sure of that?"

"Yes." And then she shook her head and pulled herself up in bed. "At least it felt empty. I didn't look inside of it."

"Where is it now?"

"Back at the hotel."

He was easing out of bed. "Do you mind if I take a look at it?"

Darcy shook her head, not wanting to believe he was starting back up on his mistrust of Damien all over again. "I'm going to ask you one more time, York. Why is it you want to nail everything on Damien? Why are you so convinced he's guilty of anything?"

He didn't answer immediately. Instead, he walked over to the window and glanced out. Moments later, he turned around and said, "A woman who meant a lot to me was killed when she accidentally stumbled into a robbery. Recently I found out one of the men Felder is associated with is someone the authorities believed set things up that night. There was not enough proof to arrest him. If that's true, I might be able to solve two cases, and one is deeply personal."

Darcy didn't say anything for a moment as she absorbed everything he said. She recalled everything Ellie had told her about the woman he was to marry and how she'd gotten killed.

"So what about you?" he asked. "Why are you so hell-bent on believing Felder is innocent?"

She drew in a deep breath. "I believe a person is innocent until proven guilty."

She then told him what had happened with her father while she was growing up. "So you see, York, my father was accused of something he didn't do, and I saw what it did to him. I don't want any part of doing something similar to another human being."

He nodded slowly. "I understand, Darcy, and would love to tell you I might be wrong about Felder but I don't think that I am. He has too many ties to unsavory individuals."

He glanced at his watch. "I want to check out that bag he gave you."

Darcy eased out of bed, met his unwavering gaze and sighed. "Fine. Give me a few minutes to shower and get dressed and then we can leave. But don't be surprised if you discover you're just wasting your time."

It DIDN'T TAKE any time getting back to the hotel. York was well aware that Darcy thought he was wasting his time and that might very well be the case, but he refused to leave any stone unturned. Someone was sneaking footage off the set some way, and he intended to find out if his hunch was right.

York slid his hands into the pockets of his jeans after they entered Darcy's hotel room, and he closed the door behind them. His gaze drifted over her as she moved in the sunlight coming in through the windows. She was wearing a short denim skirt and a cute zebra-print midriff blouse that showed a lot of skin. He could vividly recall how his hands had moved over every inch of her body, touching her, caressing her, igniting heat wherever he touched and eliciting her whimpers and moans.

He had liked the sound of her calling his name. He had liked it even more when she'd reciprocated and touched him all over, making his body quiver beneath the contact of her hands to his flesh.

Since he'd told her what he thought Felder was up to, she had a no-nonsense air about her. At least he now understood why she'd always come to the man's defense. After what had happened to her dad he could understand her trying to defend anyone she felt was being falsely accused. But he hadn't told her everything about Felder. The man had all the reasons for wanting to make a little bit of extra money on the side, even if it was at York's client's expense.

It took him a moment to realize Darcy had said something. "Sorry, could you repeat that?" he asked.

A frown appeared between her neatly arched eyebrows. "I said the tote bag is in the bedroom. I had already packed it up with my stuff since I wouldn't be using it. I'll go and get it."

He thought about following her in that bedroom and decided that wouldn't be a good idea. He might be tempted to toss her on that bed and make love to her, which was definitely something he enjoyed doing. Being around her was pure torture. If her touch didn't get to him then her scent definitely did.

He moved away from the door and crossed the room to the sliding glass doors to look out. If his theory was right then Darcy wasn't in any real danger; however, the thought that anyone, especially Felder, was using her made his teeth clench again.

There was something about her that brought out not only his protective instincts but his possessive instincts as well. A part of him just didn't know what to make of it when he'd never acted this way around other women. He needed to be in better control of his emotions since for the first time ever they seemed to be getting the best of him.

"Here's the bag, and just like I assumed, York, it's empty."

He slowly turned from the window. He tried to focus on the canvas tote bag she was holding in her hand but instead he concentrated on her hands, and he recalled just where those hands had touched him, all the things those hands had done to him.

His gaze roamed over her, and he thought today the same thing he thought every time he saw Darcy. She was a beautiful woman—beautiful and striking. The sunlight highlighted her creamy brown skin and the luster of her dark hair.

He took the tote bag to check for himself. Carrying the bag over to a table, he heard her sigh of frustration when she followed him.

"I hope you don't plan to rip my bag apart trying to find something that's probably not there, York," she said with a degree of agitation in her tone.

He merely glanced over at her and smiled. "If I have to, I'll make sure you get another one." Although he knew he was petty and childish, he didn't like the thought of her stressing out over a bag Felder had given her.

He knew she had gotten really upset with him when

she left his side and sat down on the sofa. He glanced over at her and met her gaze and saw the fire in her eyes. She'd gotten uptight again, and when they got back to his place, he would look forward to loosening her up a bit.

From his pocket he pulled out what to a layman looked like an ink pen. The tip of the pen had a scanning light, and he slowly skimmed it across the bag. He smiled when the tip began blinking. He turned to Darcy and said, "According to this scanner, Darcy, this bag isn't empty."

She was off the sofa in a flash. "That's not possible," she said adamantly as she came to stand beside him, giving him more than a whiff of her luscious scent.

"We'll see," he said as he glanced back down at the tote bag. It looked empty and it felt empty, as well. Evidently there was a secret compartment somewhere in the bag. He flipped it inside out and didn't see anything suspicious. He then began feeling around and still didn't detect anything. Whatever was being hidden was a small object.

Using the scanning pen again, he skimmed it over the bag, and when the light turned red over a certain area York smiled again. Bingo. He glanced back over at her. "Like I said earlier, I'll get you another bag."

With that said, he reached into his back pocket to retrieve a pocketknife and sliced through the seam. "What do we have here?" he asked when two memory cards slid out.

Darcy inched closer, and he noted the surprised expression on her face. Her eyes had widened, and her mouth had fallen open. "I don't believe it," she said in both disbelief and anger.

"Seeing is believing, baby. Now if we had a video camera we could see just what's on here, although I have an idea."

"I have a video camera." With that said, she rushed off toward the bedroom.

He held up the memory cards in his hand to study them. Filming had just begun, so he couldn't imagine anyone collecting too much footage yet.

He looked up when Darcy reentered the room carrying her video camera. "Nice camera," he said, when she handed it over to him.

"Thanks. It was a birthday present from my oldest brother."

He slipped in the memory card, and they watched the screen flare to life. "Whoa!"

Flashed before them was footage of the scenes being shot for Spirit Head Productions. "I don't believe this!" Darcy gasped in anger. "Felder is ripping off the company."

York clicked off the camera. "Looks that way," he said, barely able to contain his anger. "Do you know what would have happened to you if these were found in your possession by anyone?"

He could tell by her expression that she knew the seriousness of the predicament Felder had placed her in. And he could also tell that the more she thought about it the angrier she was becoming.

"I can't wait to see him, and when I do I'll—"

"Say nothing," he said with a dark scowl. "I tried to warn you about him, but you wouldn't take heed to my warning."

She lifted her chin. "I know that, York, and I regret

not doing so, but not saying anything to him is not an option."

"It has to be," he said. "Calm down and think for a minute. Felder believes that you're clueless that he's using you as a decoy to get these back into the States. Now I'm curious as to who is supposed to get these. I'm sure it's probably not anyone you know, so when was he going to get the bag from you? Who is it going to? And who—"

"And you think I give a royal flip about any of that?" she asked, fuming. "If I would have gotten arrested returning from vacation carrying those memory cards I might as well have kissed my job goodbye. I can imagine the article that would have appeared in the papers, the embarrassment it would have caused my family."

"But you would have been innocent."

"Yes, just like my dad had been innocent—but the humiliation almost killed him," she said furiously.

York knew she was taking in the blunt reality of what could have happened and he understood. Now it was imperative that he make her understand something as well. "But you've been spared all of that, Darcy. Think of the next person he might use. Think about how Felder and his accomplices are getting away with it."

He knew his words had gotten to her when she lowered her head to study the floor. Her breathing indicated she was still upset and angry. But at least he had gotten her to start thinking. "Just think about it, Darcy. I'll have a chance to nail this guy and his associates for good."

She lifted her head and met his gaze head-on. "Correction, York. *We'll* have a chance to nail them. I'm the one he's set up to take the fall if anything went wrong."

She didn't say anything for a moment and then added, "But he's counting on nothing going wrong. Now I'm just as curious as you as to who is supposed to take this bag off me. I wouldn't just meekly turn it over to anyone."

York's expression was mixed with wariness and caution. "What do you mean 'we'?"

"Just what I said. In order for you to find out who this bag was meant for and how they plan to get it, I'll need to be a player in all this."

He crossed his arms over his chest and stared down at her. "No, you don't. Now that you know the truth about Felder, I want you to bow out of the picture."

Darcy shook her head. "No, I won't do that. I'm keeping that bag."

"And risk going to jail?"

"Then I guess it will be up to you to make sure I don't," she replied as she brought her face close to his.

That wasn't the only thing close. Her breasts were now pushed up to his chest. Desire as thick as it could get suddenly rushed through his veins. All sorts of scenarios entered his mind of what could go wrong if he went along with what she was proposing. But at that moment, he couldn't think. Lust was taking over, and logical thoughts couldn't compete.

He leaned forward, and he growled close to her lips before he took her mouth with all the hunger he felt.

DARCY KNEW SHE wasn't thinking sensibly. But she hadn't thought sensibly since she'd planned this trip. She had wanted action and a man, and by golly she was getting them both in the form of York Ellis. And the way he was kissing her was making her realize she was one lucky woman.

No man could kiss the way he did. No other male had his taste. And she was totally convinced that no man's tongue could do all the things that his could. He'd told her at breakfast that he thought her mouth was made for kissing. Well, she thought his was, too.

He was kissing her with a sexual tempo, a seductive rhythm that had her moving her body even closer to his. They didn't just fit together, she thought. They fit together perfectly. She could feel the hard tips of her nipples press against the T-shirt he was wearing.

And that wasn't all she was feeling. She knew the moment his hands cupped her backside to make them an even more perfect fit. She liked the way his huge and hard erection was nestled at the juncture of her thighs and the way his breathing sounded while he was kissing her.

Heat rushed through her bloodstream. She wasn't surprised when he lifted up the hem of her jeans skirt and with eager fingers explored underneath.

She moaned deep in her throat when those same fingers came in contact with her thong and moved beyond them to her satiny folds. He dipped his fingers in her wetness, and she gripped his shoulders to keep from tumbling in desire.

She pulled her mouth from his and moaned out his name. "York."

"I want to take you into that bedroom, strip you naked and lick you all over."

His words had her mind, her senses and her entire body spinning. She met the heated gaze. "If you get to do it to me then I get to do it to you. Is that a deal?"

He smiled. "Hell, yeah." He then swept her off her feet and carried her into the bedroom.

DARCY'S HEART POUNDED hard in her chest. She had never made love in this position. She was straddling York's face and he was straddling hers, and the moment his tongue slid inside of her she nearly lost it. Every nerve in her body responded, and when he began feasting on her clit, she moaned deep in her throat.

And that's when she knew she needed to taste him the same way he was tasting her. Her fingers gripped his erection and brought it to her mouth. She began devouring him the same way he was devouring her. She could feel the strength of him throb in her throat, expand in her mouth, thicken around her tongue.

She loved the taste of him, and she loved what he was doing to her, how he was making her feel. Some type of movement that he did with his tongue made her moan out loud. What was he doing to her? To retaliate, she deepened her hold on him, and he rocked his hips against her mouth when she rocked hers against his.

She felt sensations burst to life inside her belly and knew what was about to happen. She sank her mouth deeper on him when her body exploded about the same time that his did. And she applied even more pressure on him to absorb the very essence of him like he was doing with her.

It seemed as if this orgasm for the both of them was endless and they rode it out, satisfying their taste buds as he filled her the way she was filling him.

Moments later, he rolled away from her, and she was forced to let him go. He faced her, then straddled her again and slid into her still wet warmth.

"York."

"Darcy."

And then he began thrusting inside of her. Hard. Penetrating. Deep. With every hard stab, every delicious pounding, she groaned. He was filling her, going deeper and deeper, and her greedy inner muscles were gripping him, clenching him, demanding he give her now what he'd shot into her mouth moments ago.

He lifted his head to stare down at her while the lower part of his body continued to ride her. "Like it?"

"Love it."

He smiled, and that smile coming from York sent pleasure reeling all through her. "You're mine, Darcy."

She heard his words, and for the moment she couldn't argue with him. At that moment, she and every part of her being were his. He was giving her insurmountable pleasure and she felt it from the top of her head to the soles of her feet, and when another explosion took its toll on her, she knew one thing was for certain. She knew she would never play around with a sex toy again. Not when she could have the real thing from York Ellis.

CHAPTER ELEVEN

"York, you are definitely a bad boy."

York smiled as he shifted to his side to gaze down at her. She sounded out of breath, like she could barely get the words out, like she had gotten worn out. He was filled with male pride that he was the reason.

"A bad boy?" he asked, holding her gaze.

"Oh, yes, definitely bad. I've never done anything like that before. In fact, I've never done half the stuff I've done with you. Who makes love on the beach or in a raft for heaven's sake?"

He chuckled. "A man hard up for the woman he's with."

She smiled as if pleased with his answer. "And were you hard up for me?"

"Baby, I'm hard up for you now." He knew there was no way she could not believe what he'd said with the strength of his erection resting against her thigh, throbbing like it hadn't come a few times already.

"Now to get back to the subject we were discussing earlier," she said softly.

He shook his head. "I don't recall us discussing anything."

She gently punched him in his arm. "Liar. If I have to, I will refresh your memory. And speaking of memory, it was about those memory cards."

York didn't say anything for a moment. He had hoped she had somehow forgotten about that but should have known better. He reached down and swept a lock of hair off her forehead and said softly, "Let me handle it, Darcy."

She held his gaze. "I appreciate you wanting to, but I'm the one Felder figured to use. I owe him."

York pulled in a deep breath. He'd heard about a woman scorned, but he had a feeling a woman a man had set out to use would be just as resentful and spiteful. She would also be revengeful, and that's what he didn't have time for. He didn't need her or anyone else getting in the way of him bringing down Felder and whoever he was working for and with. "Darcy, I want you to let me handle it. Let it go."

"I can't."

He heard the seriousness in her voice and realized at that moment she truly couldn't. Then he again remembered what she'd told him about her father. She was a woman wronged, and she intended—come hell or high water—to get even. At that moment, he truly felt sorry for Felder.

But still, York decided to try to appeal on her logical side, to get her to back away from the unknown. He had some names of those Felder might be in cahoots with and expected there might be others. The bootlegged films would bring in a lot of money and would possibly bankrupt the production company. It wasn't fair that many people would lose their jobs due to shameless greed.

"You have got to let me do this, York."

Her words regained his attention, and he glanced down at her, saw the determination in her eyes. "This is not a game, Darcy. It's serious business. You don't know the type of men we're dealing with. You could get hurt." He came short of saying she could lose her life. He thought about Rhonda, how her life had ended and she had been trained to take down the bad guys. But a bullet had stopped her, anyway.

"Yes, but think about it for a moment. They'd singled me out as their fall guy. Supposedly, without my knowledge, they have given me something to pass on to someone. But who? How is the contact supposed to be made? Why was I singled out? All we know is someone is supposed to get those memory cards. But when? I think I should go along pretending that business is usual and see how this plays out. I'm just as capable as any female employee you might bring in. Have you forgotten I can defend myself?"

No, he hadn't forgotten. He knew she was trained in martial arts. And from what he'd heard she was pretty good. But still, karate couldn't stand a chance against a gun aimed at you with a bullet destined to kill you.

He rubbed his hand down his face and then said, "Let me think about this."

She nodded, but again he saw the determined look in her eyes. Regardless of what his decision might be, she'd already made hers. "Did Felder say when he'll be back?" he asked her.

"Yes. He said he was returning Monday and wanted to see me again."

He thought for a second and then said, "That tote bag isn't something you would automatically bring with you, and he knows you'll probably get suspicious if you were asked about it. He plans to get it some other way. And I don't think it will be on this island. I believe he plans for someone to get it from you when you get back to Miami. I think he just wants to keep up with you while you're here on the island. Those videos are worth a lot of money, and he'll want to keep tabs on them."

"Let him."

"Did you ever mention to him how long you'll be on the island?" he asked.

"Yes, that night he took me to dinner and dancing. He also knows that I have a few hours layover in Miami before flying on to Minnesota."

York nodded slowly. "Come on, let's get up, get dressed and go back to my place. We can think some more there."

But it wasn't thinking that he wanted to do. He wanted nothing more than to make love to her again. And more than anything, he wanted to keep her safe from men like Felder. But he knew she wouldn't appreciate his protection. She would see it as a weakness on her part.

He eased his naked body out of bed and glanced around the room for his jeans. "Can I ask you something, York?" he heard her say.

He turned his attention to her. "Yes."

"How do you manage to stay hard for so long? Even when you don't have sex on your mind?"

Of all the things he had expected her to ask, that wasn't it and he couldn't help his quick laugh. But then he really shouldn't be surprised. Darcy did have the tendency to speak her mind. "And what makes you think I don't have sex on my mind?" he countered.

She shrugged beautiful naked shoulders. "I just figured you didn't."

He smiled. "You're lying in bed naked and you think

I don't have sex on my mind? Less than an hour after I got to perform one of my fantasy positions?"

A smile curved her lips. "That was your fantasy position?"

"Yes, but I have several."

She pushed the bedcovers aside exposing her nakedness. "Show me another one. I'm game."

The pulse at the base of his throat was fluttering erratically as he raked his gaze over her. He thought she was simply beautiful whether she was in clothes or out of them. Lying there naked in bed, looking more gorgeous than any woman had a right to look, made him get harder and thicker. He wasn't surprised she noticed that as well.

"You're getting even more aroused, York. There's no need letting a good, hard erection go to waste, is there?"

He truly liked the way she thought. "No, there's not," he said and headed back to the bed.

THEY HAD BEEN back at York's beach house less than ten minutes when Darcy's cell phone rang. York had gone outside to put away the Jet Ski and set up the grill. She smiled when she saw her caller was Ellie. She was glad her friend was not there to see the deep blush that suddenly appeared on her features. If Ellie knew what she'd been doing for the past few days and with whom, she wouldn't believe her.

"Hello."

"Hey, girl, just thought I'd give you a warning. Uriel mentioned at dinner that York is also on the island."

Darcy smiled. Everyone in their inner circles knew of her and York's dislike of each other and would probably be shocked and surprised as hell to discover they liked each other after all. In fact, she would go so far to say they liked each other a lot.

Their last escapade in her hotel room had turned into a sex game for them, one she had enjoyed. She hadn't known there were so many naughty ways to have fun with one's lover.

Lover.

Yes, he was definitely her lover…at least while she was here on the island. She knew once they returned to New York that it would be business as usual, although she doubted she could draw enough energy not to like him again. She liked him way too much now. What woman wouldn't like a man who could make her head spin, her knees go weak and her toes curl? A man who had the ability to dish out multiple orgasms?

"Darcy?"

"Yes?"

"Why aren't you saying anything? I expected you to have sent out a few colorful curse words by now, especially since you and York can't get along."

And under any normal circumstances when it came to York, she would have. But that was before she had discovered a lot more about him, including some things not connected to the bedroom. Over the past couple of days, they had talked a lot over dinner, breakfast and when they weren't busy blowing each other's minds in the bedroom. She believed he was a great brother, as great as her two, and a girl couldn't ask for more than that.

She also believed he was a natural-born protector. That was evident in the way he was still trying to talk her out of any involvement with those memory cards.

And she would even go so far as to admit that once

you got to know him, he was a likable person, a lot of fun to be around and wonderful company. He was well versed on a lot of things. She liked the fact that they shared the same political party, held strong in their belief there was a God and thought no matter how old he got, Prince was the bomb.

"Darcy!"

She snapped to attention. "What?"

"What's the matter with you?" Then in a low voice, Ellie asked, "Did I catch you at a bad time?"

Darcy smiled. "If you're asking if you caught me with my panties off and in bed with a man, then the answer is no. But had you called an hour or so earlier the answer would be a resounding yes!"

"You are protecting yourself, right?"

She swallowed deeply. "Yes, I am protecting myself."

She knew why Ellie was asking. Ellie was the only person who knew how much she enjoyed the feel of a man's release erupting inside of her. That had always been a deep, dark fantasy of hers—one she could never indulge in with a man. It had been okay with her and Harold when they were married, but after her divorce she could never trust any man to go that far with her.

But she trusted York. She believed he was in good health like he believed she was. He had told her he didn't make it a point to make love to a woman without a condom, regardless of whether she was on any type of birth control or not. Too many women out there were looking for some man to become their baby's daddy, and he did not want that status. However, he didn't mind letting go inside of her. In fact, she would probably be safe to say he enjoyed giving it as much as she enjoyed getting it.

"So you've met a man..."

Ellie's statement reclaimed her attention. She decided to be honest. "Yes, I've met a man."

"Is he someone from the islands?" Ellie asked.

"No."

"American?"

"Yes."

"I don't have to ask if he's nice looking," Ellie tacked on.

Darcy smiled. "No, you don't have to ask. And don't bother asking if he's good in bed because he is. And yes, he was well worth my two years of abstinence."

There was a pause on the other end, and then Ellie asked quietly, "Is he someone you can see yourself falling in love with, Darcy?"

At that moment, Darcy's heart sank from her chest right into the pit of her stomach. Ellie's question hit her like a ton of bricks and made her realize something she had tried not to think about. She had come to the island for fun and sex but not love. *Love* had been a word that had gotten torn from the pages of her memory the day she'd divorced Harold. Love was an emotion she hadn't thought about since the day she had refused to take any more of her ex's foolishness, and had come to the realization that she could do bad all by herself and that he wasn't worth the heartache.

But now thanks to Ellie that one word was back, and all the emotions that came with it were staring her right smack in the face. And the sad thing was that she knew the answer to her best friend's question. Yes, York was someone she could see herself falling in love with, and heaven help her, she was almost there. It wouldn't take much to push her over the edge and get her heart screwed up all over again.

She rubbed her hand down her face. How could she have let it happen? When did it happen? Was it too late to pull back and run in the opposite direction?

"You've taken too long to answer, Dar. Should I include another place setting at the New Year's Eve dinner party?"

She closed her eyes, trying to force her body, her mind, her thoughts into denial. York was just her island lover. When they returned to New York, things would go back to how they were before. Her mind could agree with that reasoning but her heart was playing hardball.

Darcy drew in a deep breath, knowing why. She would want to continue to play all those naughty and fun games with him. She couldn't imagine being in the same room with him and not being able to plan their next sexual escapade. And she refused not to be able to kiss him, tangle her tongue with his, suck on it as if she had every right.

Rights.

He wanted rights when it came to her, and hadn't she given them to him to some degree? Did he expect those rights to extend beyond Jamaica? Would it truly bother her if he did expect it? She shook her head knowing it would probably bother her if he didn't.

"Maybe I need to call you back later. Sounds like I've given you a lot to think about," Ellie said, once again interrupting Darcy's thoughts.

"Yes, you have."

"And when you call me back you will let me know if I should add another name to my guest list, right?" Ellie said.

Darcy forced a chuckle. She was one hundred percent certain her lover's name was already on the guest list. But she wasn't ready to tell Ellie that yet. "Yes, I'll let you know then."

Moments later, she hung up the phone. Ellie was right. She had been given a lot to think about.

CHAPTER TWELVE

"IT'S A GOOD THING you discovered those memory cards on Ms. Owens, York," Wesley Carr was saying. "There's a chance she would have cleared security like Felder counted on her doing. But what if she hadn't?"

York leaned against the shed in his backyard and rubbed a hand down his face as he talked to Wesley on his cell phone. That scenario Wesley had just mentioned was one he really and truly didn't want to think about. It would have been hard for her to convince anyone that those memory cards had been planted on her and that she knew nothing about having them.

"I know, Wesley. And she's determined to let Felder think he's using her and has her just where he wants her. I'm just curious to know how he intends to get that tote bag from her."

York released a deep breath. Unknowns were what had his gut twisting when several scenarios flashed across his mind. He didn't like a single one of them since all of them placed Darcy in some sort of danger. And all he had to do was think of what had happened to Rhonda to know he had no intention of letting that happen.

"Where is the tote bag now?" Wesley asked.

"We brought it back from the hotel, and it's here at my place."

"So what's your plan, son?"

York couldn't help but smile. Wesley personified the saying "Once a cop always a cop." "Don't know. But what I do know is that I don't want Darcy Owens placed in any danger."

"And we will work hard to make sure that doesn't happen. You got good men and women working for you."

York knew that to be true. But still…

There had to be that *but* in there somewhere, and he didn't like it. And of course Darcy was trying to make things complicated. She should have taken his advice from the jump and not become involved with Felder. But the stubborn woman refused to do so, and now she had the nerve to want to help him nail the guy. Well, he had news for her. Things would not go down that way. He couldn't take the chance.

"York, you still there?"

It was then that York remembered he had Wesley on the phone. "Yes, Wesley, I'm still here. I'll check in with Marlon to see how things are going with Johnny Rush. He seemed put out that Danielle Simone is missing."

"I guess he would be when it appears that she and Felder have a thing going on right under the man's nose. In my day, a man found the woman he wanted and settled down with her. Nowadays you young people shy away from commitment. Why is that, York?"

York knew he couldn't speak for others, only for himself. "Marriage isn't easy to deal with anymore, Wesley." He then thought about Rhonda. He had planned to ask her to marry him Christmas night. Her untimely death had shown him you couldn't take much for granted. It had also made him vow never to fall for another woman who didn't mind putting herself in a dangerous position.

So why was he falling for Darcy?

And he would admit that he was falling for her big time. It wasn't just the sex, although he would be the first to admit any time he was inside of her was off the chain. But there was a side of her he hadn't gotten to know until recently when he'd begun spending time with her. Besides being sexy, she was witty and fun to be around.

"I'll check in with the others. As you know, Felder and Simone aren't the only ones I'm keeping a close eye on. I have a feeling there are others in this game of deceit. And I think it's time we need to move to plan B. And fast."

A few moments later, York had ended his conversation with Wesley and was about to go back inside his house when he got another call. This one was from his godbrother Zion to say he would be returning to the States for the holidays since Ellie insisted he attend her New Year's party.

They talked a little while, and Zion brought him up to date on how the jewelry business was doing. His hand-made jewelry was now on every woman's wish list, after the president had purchased a few pieces for the first lady. Moments later, he hung up the phone thinking he had left Darcy to her own devices way too long. It was time for him to go check on her. And time to come up with a game plan to get any ideas out of her mind of working with him to bring Felder down.

"SO WHAT'S OUR game plan, York?"

York glanced up from his breakfast and looked

across the table at Darcy. Yesterday they had gone swimming and later he had treated her to grilled trout, a salad, roasted corn on the cob and ice-cold lemonade. As before, she had sat at the kitchen counter and watched him work. She had volunteered to pitch in to help, but he'd convinced her his kitchen was a one-man show and that he preferred she just sit and watch him in action. She had a way of undressing him with her gaze. Usually thinking that any woman found him that interesting would annoy him, but not with Darcy—mainly because he was just as interested in her as she seemed to be in him.

And he'd proven just how much at bedtime. Memories of making love to her were still vibrant in his mind. She had surprised him upon waking up this morning. She had treated him to breakfast…only after treating him to something else. He'd never enjoyed early morning lovemaking so much.

He met her gaze. "Would it matter very much if I said we don't have one?" he responded while twirling his wineglass between his fingers. He had taken her up on her suggestion of swapping orange juice for wine, and he rather enjoyed it.

She gave him a sweet smile, one that didn't fool him for a minute. He'd figured it was only a matter of time for her to recall they still had a bone to pick. "Of course it would matter, York. I thought we agreed that I would be included."

He didn't want to argue with her, but he decided to try once again to make her understand why he couldn't—wouldn't—let her become involved. "We didn't agree to anything." He took a sip of his wine and then said, "I don't want anything to happen to you."

Evidently it was how he'd said it more than what he'd said that gave her pause. For the longest moment, she just stared across the table at him, and he was able to feel the intensity of her gaze. Exactly how had he said it? Then he realized it was with more emotion than he had intended.

Too late he also realized the show of emotions couldn't be helped. Darcelle Owens had literally gotten under his skin in a way no other woman had since Rhonda and in a way he'd vowed that no other woman ever would.

"Tell me about her, York."

He took another sip of his wine and played ignorant. "Tell you about who?"

"The woman you lost that meant so much to you."

There was no reason to ask how she'd heard about Rhonda. Darcy and Ellie were best friends, and somewhere along the way, Ellie had probably heard the story from Uriel, who had shared it with her…at least the parts Uriel knew. But there was so much more that none of his godbrothers knew—like the fact that not only had York lost the woman he had planned to marry but he'd also lost his unborn child. Rhonda had told him a week or so earlier that she was pregnant.

He liked her a lot, but he wasn't sure he had been in love with her—at least not to the extent he figured his godbrothers Uriel and Xavier were with their wives. And he had taken extreme caution each and every time they'd made love. When she'd decided to begin using the Pill, he had thought things were safe enough for him to stop using a condom. She had gotten pregnant when the antibiotics she had been taking for the flu had counteracted her birth control pills.

He had been more than willing to step up to the plate and do the right thing and marry her. However, he was certain he wouldn't have thought of marriage without the pregnancy.

"Why do you want to know anything about Rhonda?" he finally asked, placing his wineglass next to his plate after deciding he needed to be in full control of his senses when engaging in such a conversation with Darcy.

"I just do."

He held her gaze for several long moments—so long that he would not have been surprised if she withdrew her request. Of course she didn't. A part of him was tempted to tell her that her reasoning wasn't good enough, but he decided not to even bother. She had asked a question and expected a response, regardless of whether he wanted to give her one or not. York wondered if it would always be that way with them. Would there ever be a time when they would be on an even keel?

He leaned back in his chair. "Rhonda and I met about seven years ago when she joined the NYPD. I had gotten out of rookie training, and she was just beginning it. We dated off and on for a while, then decided to date exclusively. We'd been at it almost eight months when she was killed."

"And you were about to ask her to marry you?"

"Yes."

She nodded slowly as if she understood everything and then she added, "You loved her that much."

He wasn't sure just what "that much" entailed, but for some reason he felt the need to set the record straight. Why he was doing it with her when he hadn't with anyone else, he wasn't sure. A slow, yet serious smile spread across his lips. Then he simply said, "No."

The room lapsed into a moment of dead silence, and he was certain he didn't hear anything. Not the sound of the waves beating against the shoreline, nor the sound of the clock on the wall ticking and not even the sound of her breathing. The look she gave him beneath silky long lashes would have him squirming in his seat had he not gotten immune to that look by now.

York watched the frown settle around her lips, and he thought that once again she looked annoyed—but not too annoyed not to ask, "And why were you planning to marry her, then?"

The answer was simple. "She was having my baby."

CHAPTER THIRTEEN

DARCY SAT UP straight in her chair, pulled her bathrobe together when it gaped open, probably the same way her mouth did. His girlfriend had been pregnant when she'd gotten killed? Why hadn't Ellie told her that?

Evidently, that question was etched across her face because York said, "The reason Ellie didn't tell you is because she doesn't know. I've never told Uriel. No one knows. In the six years since Rhonda's death, you're the only person I've told."

Darcy wondered how she got so lucky and decided to ask. "Why tell me?"

"Because you asked."

Darcy wondered when she would learn to mind her own business. But then she recalled there was a reason for this line of conversation, and it had to do with him not wanting her to participate in exposing Felder. "I assumed the reason you didn't want me to be a part of exposing Damien is because you'd somehow feel responsible if something happened to me. Do you feel responsible for what happened to the mother of your child?"

He shook his head. "No. What she did for a living didn't bother me. I was a cop as well. I had no reason to feel responsible. We had parted that morning with plans to get together for dinner later that night. I had it all planned, a nice cozy dinner around the fireplace where I would ask her to marry me."

"But you didn't love her?"

He took another sip of his wine. "Evidently, there are several degrees of love. At the time I was in my twenties and thought I was in love but since then after hanging around Uriel and Xavier, I realized I didn't have the intense emotions toward Rhonda as they have toward their wives. If Rhonda hadn't gotten pregnant, there's no telling if the thought of marrying her would have entered my mind."

Darcy nodded. He was being honest with her, and she could appreciate that. She knew all about being in your twenties and thinking love ruled your heart and then finding out you didn't know the difference between lust and love. It had been a rude awakening for her and a period of time from which she thought she would never recover. Sometimes she wondered if she would truly ever fully recover.

"And had she lived?" Darcy heard herself prompting.

He held her gaze. "We would have married and I would have tried to be a good husband and father. But I have reason to believe we would not have made it past the five-year mark. When it came to me, she was too easy, too dead set on letting me have things my way. We rarely argued about anything because she would give in too quickly."

Darcy took a sip of her wine thinking it was just the opposite for them. Was that the reason he was attracted to her? Then what was the reason she was attracted to him besides the obvious—looks, body, his skill in the bedroom or any place you wanted to enjoy sex?

Deciding she needed to make sure he understood

her position about Damien Felder, she said, "I won't be changing my mind about helping out, York."

"You'd only get in the way. Become a distraction."

She lifted both her chin and her brow. "A distraction to who?"

"Me."

She narrowed her gaze. "That sounds like a personal problem."

"It is," he agreed. "But since I can't do anything about it, I have to handle it the best way I can." He leaned closer toward her at the table. "I suggest you agree to do things my way, Darcy."

She leaned closer toward him as well. "And I suggest you do things my way, York."

He didn't as much as blink when he said, "It seems that we have a problem."

She smiled. "Like I said, it's your problem and not mine."

There was something in the way he was looking at her, holding her gaze within his dark, sharp depths, that made her heart rate increase. If his eyes could talk, she knew just what they would be saying. It was evident that he was not pleased with the way things were going. She was not a "yes" girl, and he didn't very much like it. Well, that was too bad. She had no intentions of backing down.

"You know there is a simple solution to this, don't you?" he asked, still holding her gaze.

"Is there?"

"Yes, I can make sure you're out of the picture by holding you here against your will."

She smiled at the thought of that. "You don't look the type who would easily break the law."

"Then I suggest you look again."

She did. What she detected in his body language made her uneasy. "You wouldn't dare."

"You want to bet?"

No, she didn't want to bet. She wanted to leave. Standing slowly, she said, "I want to return to the hotel now."

He remained seated in his chair. His gaze was now speculative. Amused. "Running off so soon?"

She figured it was now or never. He had this way about him that attracted her way too much. Even now she felt her thighs trembling, her panties getting wet. The urge to mate with him was too intense for her comfort. If he thought he could divert her attention with something like sex…well, he was probably right. But she would stand firm and not let him.

"I'm going to get dressed. Are you taking me back or do I get a cab?"

"Neither."

He was serious. "I'm going to start screaming," she warned.

He chuckled. "Baby, you've been screaming a lot since you've been here, anyway."

That was true, but he didn't have to remind her or call her out on it. Her attention was drawn back to him when she heard his chair scraping against the floor, and she backed up when he stood. "Let's stop playing games, York."

"I'm not playing games, Darcy. By now, Damien has gotten word that you happened to meet an overzealous Johnny Rush fan who talked you out of your tote bag. That woman, Patricia Palmer, is an ex-cop and happens to work for me. She left the island with the tote bag in her possession this morning, headed home via a connection in Miami. My men are posted all over the Miami International Airport, along with Miami police, just waiting to see how things are going to go down."

Darcy stared at him, and when she saw he wasn't kidding and that he was dead serious, anger took over her body. "And just how did she get my tote bag?"

He crossed his arms over his chest, looking smug. "I gave it to her last night. She dropped by while you were asleep."

And because he knew how her mind worked, York added, "And no, I did not make love to you to the point of exhaustion for that reason, Darcy. Making love with that much intensity and vigor is normal for us."

She slowly rounded the table and crossed the room to him. "You had no right to give what was mine to someone else," she said, seething between clenched teeth.

"Would you rather I let you keep it and turn it over to the authorities and let you explain what the hell you were doing with it? This was not a game to be played out your way, Darcy. Lives were at risk. These men will kill anyone who gets in the way of what they consider a million-dollar business. I could not take a chance on your life. I had warned you about Felder, but you wouldn't listen."

She lifted her chin and glared at him. "I could have handled him."

Did she not hear a single thing he said? Was she *that* stubborn? At that moment, something inside him snapped. Did she think she was indestructible? A damn superwoman? Someone with nine lives or something?

She had the nerve to step closer, get in his face. "You used me."

He rolled his eyes. "If that's what you want to think, go right ahead. But when you calm down you'll realize what I did was keep you alive."

"I don't see it that way."

"One day you will."

And before she could utter another word, he captured her mouth with his, went at it with a hunger that even surprised him. He knew she was mad, and it would probably take a long time for her to get over things. He'd heard that she could hold a grudge like nobody's business. But he'd had to take his chances. At least she was alive and wasn't in any danger.

Her heart was beating just as fast and intense as his, and he released her mouth long enough to draw in air that was drenched with her scent—an indication that she wanted him as much as he wanted her. Their gazes connected. At that moment, heat surged between them, so strong it nearly singed his insides.

He was definitely undone.

Without any type of control, he reached out and his hands ripped the silk gown off her body. He tossed the shreds of torn fabric to the floor. He was about to take her like she'd probably never been taken before. She was in his blood, in his mind. And heaven help him, the woman had somehow wiggled her way into his heart. And she had the nerve to assume that he would let her walk blindly into a dangerous situation?

He opened his mouth to say something and couldn't. What could he say? An admission of love probably wouldn't ring true to her ears right now anyway. So he would speak in a way that they communicated so well, with their bodies. Whenever they were inside each other they were of one mind, like two peas in a pod.

And Lord knew he needed to get all inside that luscious pod of hers.

Time passed that was measured by the beats of their hearts, a thrumming sound that enlarged his erection with every single tick of the clock. And then he growled, a primitive sound that rented the air, as he lowered his gaze to her naked body and saw everything he wanted, everything he needed, every single thing he loved and desired.

He unzipped his jeans and quickly stepped out of them, flung them aside. He reached out and drew her into his arms and hungrily captured her mouth once again and began mating with it in a frenzy that he felt down to his gut.

He felt the moment tension flowed from her shoulders, the moment she forgot all about her anger for the time being to concentrate on their kiss. It was just as fiery and passionate as all the others. He sank his fingers in her hair, felt her scalp and he deepened the kiss. It was as if he couldn't get enough of her, and the more he got, the more he wanted.

It seemed her hunger was just as intense as his was for her. She had taken him in her hand, was stroking his head and he felt his erection get larger beneath her fingers. She broke the kiss to breathe against his moist lips. "Hurry, York. I want you now!"

He heard the hunger in her voice. She might still be mad at him, but at the moment she would put her anger aside for this. So would he. There would be a lot to talk about later. And they would talk. Their future depended on an in-depth discussion and whether she wanted to accept it or believe it, they had a future. He now knew how it felt to love a woman to the point where you felt it in every bone in your body, and the need to become one with her was as vital as breathing.

She twisted out of his arms. "You're taking too long."

The moment her feet touched the floor she fell to her knees and took him into her mouth. And he let out a groan that nearly pierced the back of his throat. Immense heat surged in his testicles, and he felt them about to burst. He knew what she was doing. She wanted as much juice from him as his body could produce, and she was making sure there would be plenty by drawing out the lust in him.

If only she knew. There was no longer lust—only love.

When he felt his body almost explode in her mouth, he held back. And then without warning he dropped down on his knees and turned her around so that her back was pressed against his chest, her backside snug against his erection. And then his fingers felt around for her, felt the moist heat of her feminine mound, and like radar, the head of his erection found her and he eagerly thrust inside her.

"Hold on, baby. I'm going to ride you good," he whispered hotly, close to her ear, and she threw her head back and moaned with every single thrust into her body. He cradled her hips tight into the breadth of his thighs while he pounded into her and she begged for more.

He reached around her and let his fingers caress the tips of her breasts, cupped them in his hands and kneaded them to his heart's content. Her nipples were firm, erect, like pebbles in his hands. And he knew at that moment he would never, ever get enough of her and that Darcy Owens would be a permanent fixture in his life.

DARCY FELT YORK in every part of her body each time he pounded into her and then withdrew only to thrust back. He had her thighs spread wide, and she could feel the heat of his chest on hers. He was riding her in a way she'd never been ridden before, driving her insane with pleasure. And when she was to the point of detonating he would slowly ease out of her and in one hard thrust, find his way back in. Over and over again.

He was literally breaking her down with a need she only knew about since meeting him. She was desperate to have him, to feel him come inside of her, drench her with his release. Intense pleasure was thrumming, bursting to life in her feminine core, making her whimper, moan, and she knew soon he would have her screaming.

He thrust deeper inside of her, and she wondered how that was possible. It was as if his shaft had grown in length to accommodate her needs and desires. And then she felt her body buck into an explosion, detonate in rapture and she screamed. It seemed her scream torched something within him, and he rammed into her even deeper, just seconds before exploding.

"Yes! Yes! Yes!" She felt the essence of him spill into her, flood her in a thick, heated bath of release. It did something to her, and she sucked in a deep breath; with it came the scent of mingled bodies, tantalizing sex. This was pleasure beyond anything they had ever shared, and she knew that as much as she enjoyed it that this would be it for them. The end. He had deliberately kept her with him last night for a reason. It had nothing to do with wanting her but all to do with solving his case.

But she was convinced that now, at this moment, he

needed her. And she hoped he realized that when she left and would refuse to see him again. This was more than a parting gift. This would fuel his thoughts of what he would never have again.

She pushed the thoughts out of her mind when he kept going for another round and her body was in full agreement when another orgasm swept through her the same time it did him. She gloried in the feel of his hardness exploding into her once again, and she knew at that moment that she loved him. She loved every part of him, but because of what he'd done, her love would not be enough to consider forgiving him.

YORK WASN'T SURE what woke him up, but he opened his eyes and glanced at the clock on his nightstand. It was almost two in the afternoon. He closed his eyes wanting to remember every detail of what had happened between him and Darcy after breakfast. He smiled as he recalled every luscious detail of them making love—doggy style—on his kitchen floor, showering together afterward before falling into his bed and making love again.

He opened his eyes knowing the time had come for them to talk. He needed to explain why he could not have let her take part in exposing Felder. She meant too much to him, and there was no way he could have put her at any risk. He loved her.

His phone rang, and he quickly eased out of bed and glanced over his shoulder. The place where Darcy had lain was empty. He figured she had probably gotten hungry and had gone downstairs to grab something to eat. After all, it was way past lunchtime.

He grabbed for the phone and recognized the number. "Yes, Wesley?"

"Mission accomplished."

He smiled knowing what that meant. Once again, his men had done an outstanding job. He had wanted to be there, right in the thick of things, but he had been needed here to keep his woman out of trouble, out of harm's way. "I need full details. Give me a minute to get downstairs to my office, and I'll call you right back."

He hung up the phone and glanced around and immediately knew something was wrong. Darcy's overnight bag, the one that had been sitting next to his dresser, was gone. He quickly went into the bathroom and found his vanity cleaned of her belongings. It was as if she'd never been there.

Grabbing a robe, like a madman he tore out of the room and rushed down the stairs. But the house was empty. He moved back to the kitchen and saw the note she had scribbled and left on the front of his refrigerator. She had written the message with red lipstick.

You got what you wanted. Now stay away from me!

Fuming, he snatched the paper off his refrigerator and crushed it in his hands before tossing it in a nearby trash can. He growled deep in his throat. "Like hell I will."

CHAPTER FOURTEEN

"IF YOU THINK finally getting around to admitting you had an affair with York in Jamaica will exonerate you from spending New Year's with me then you are wrong, Darcelle Owens."

Darcy rolled her eyes as she stood at the window in her New York house. It was two days after Christmas. If her parents had been surprised that she had shown up on their doorstep a few days earlier than planned, they didn't let on. And she knew her brothers had been itching to ask why her eyes were so swollen and her nose was red. Instead, they did what they usually did when she was a kid and would fly into the house crying from a boo-boo. They would cuddle her and try to kiss her hurt away.

And for a while she was able to get York Ellis out of her mind but not out of her heart. Instead of leaving her parents' home the day after Christmas as planned to head to Cavanaugh Lake, she had returned home to New York, determined to spend New Year's alone. She was not surprised that Ellie wasn't happy with that decision. Even after confessing and telling her friend everything, she wasn't budging.

"Did you hear everything I said, El?"

"Yes, I heard you. I saw York on Christmas Day in

Phoenix when everyone flew in for Eli Steele's wedding. He didn't give anything away."

That meant out of sight, out of mind. She hadn't expected anything other than that anyway. She wouldn't be surprised if Ellie mentioned he had brought someone. She wouldn't ask for fear of finding out something she didn't want to know, something that would break her heart even more.

"Besides, Darcy," Ellie broke into her thoughts and said, "I heard on the news about that case his company busted. From what I understand it was pretty dangerous, so I'm glad he kept you from getting involved."

Darcy frowned. "I could have handled my own."

"Are you listening to me? Those men would not have hesitated to hurt you if you tried to disrupt their plan."

But still…

"He used me," she said, determined for her best friend to see her point. She needed some sympathy here.

"And I'm sure you used him as well, so get over it, Dar, and catch a plane here."

She nibbled on her bottom lip. "I'm not ready to see him, and chances are he'll be there."

"Yes, he will be. But that shouldn't stop you from coming as well. It will be business as usual since you and York have always avoided each other anyway." There was a pause, then Ellie said, "Unless there is more to it than what you're telling me."

Darcy continued nibbling on her lip. "More like what?"

"Your true feelings for him. You sound more like a woman in love than a woman upset for not getting her way."

Darcy frowned. "I'm not in love with York!" Maybe

if she said it enough times she would be able to convince herself of that.

"Um, if you say so. Look, I need to get out of here and go to the grocery store, but I'll call you later. The weather around the lake is beautiful. You don't know what you're missing."

Darcy wiped a tear that had just fallen from her eye. "Yes, I do." *I won't be seeing York again anytime soon.*

"Is there a message you want me to give York when I see him?" Ellie asked.

"Of course not. He means nothing to me. I just don't like being played."

"Well, it sounds to me you're getting played confused with protected. I'll talk to you later, Darcy."

She heard the phone click in her ear and shook her head. What did Ellie know? She loved a man who loved her back. Some women had all the luck. Not ready to start her day yet, she tightened her robe around her and headed toward the kitchen to grab something for breakfast.

Since she'd planned to be away for the holidays, she hadn't put up a tree this year. But she had decorated the fireplace with garland and had even hung out the stocking her secretary's eight-year-old daughter had made for her last Christmas.

With a cup of hot chocolate and small plate of crescent rolls, she went back to the living room to enjoy her breakfast alone. Turning on the television, she saw that more arrests had been made in the case York and his people had cracked, including members of the Medina family. She even caught a quick glimpse of a handcuffed Damien being led away by authorities. Feeling

even more depressed she turned off the television and
finished her breakfast.

An hour or so later after cleaning up the kitchen,
watering her plants and rearranging items in her cabi-
nets, she decided she would take a nap. She might as
well since she still had her nightgown on underneath
her robe. She would treat this as a lazy day. She was
headed toward her bedroom when her doorbell sounded.
She figured it was her neighbor who'd been kind enough
to collect her mail while she was gone.

Darcy glanced out the peephole and caught her
breath. York!

Mixed emotions flooded her. On one hand, she was
tempted to pinch herself to make sure what she was
seeing was real. On the other hand, she wanted to open
the door just to slam it in his face. It had been over a
week since that morning when she had slipped out of
bed to flee the island, needing to put as much distance
between them as she possibly could.

Over a week.

And she hadn't heard from him. But she had to admit
she had warned him to stay away from her. However,
when did men like York do what they were told? And
why was he here now? And why was a part of her glad
that he was?

He rang the doorbell again, and she drew in a deep
breath. "I can handle this," she muttered under her
breath as she slowly removed the chain off the door.
"And I can handle him," she added to assure herself as
she slowly turned the knob.

The moment she flung the door wide and his gaze
connected with his, she knew she'd assumed wrong. She
couldn't handle him. He was standing there, leaning in

her doorway. Her nose inhaled his cologne that mingled
was the scent of primitive man. He was dressed in a
pair of snug-fitting jeans and a blue pullover sweater,
looking like the man he was, the man who'd captured
her heart.

The man she loved.

"DARCY."

York studied the woman standing in front of him.
Had it really been eight days since he'd seen her, eight
days since he'd made loved to her, heard her scream?
Even with that little annoying frown forming around
her mouth, she looked beautiful. She looked as if she'd
raked her fingers instead of a comb through her hair.
It was tossed in disarray around her shoulders, and the
early morning sun gave it a sun-kissed luster.

"Why are you here, York?"

That question was simple enough. "I came for you."

She looked surprised. "For me?"

"Yes."

She crossed her arms over her chest, and the gesture
uplifted her breasts. Her cleavage looked good, and he
bet her nipples looked even better. His tongue seemed
to thicken at the thought of being wrapped around one.

"Didn't you get my note? The one I left on your refrigerator?"

He shrugged. "Yes, I got it."

"And?"

"And I figured you were mad when you wrote it."

An angry tint suddenly appeared on her cheeks, and
she just stared at him. York suspected that she was probably wondering what would be the best way to throt-
tle him.

"Yes, I was mad when I wrote it and I'm still mad."

He held her gaze. "Then I suggest you get over it." And before she could pick up her mouth that had nearly dropped to the floor, he took the opportunity to walk past her into her house.

"Wait a minute. I didn't invite you in, York."

He glanced over his shoulder. "You didn't have to."

She slammed the door with enough force to make the room shake. "Now, you listen here."

He turned around. "No, you listen here," he said back at her. "I've given you eight days, and I refuse to give you any more."

"Y-you g-gave me," she stuttered in anger.

"Yes. I would have come after you right away but I figured you needed to cool off and think things through. That gave me time to wrap up the case and attend Eli's wedding since I knew you'd already made plans to spend the holidays with your own family. But I talked to Uriel last night, and he mentioned you had changed your mind about coming to the lake."

"Not that it's any of your business, but I have," she said, lifting her chin.

"Then you need to rethink that decision." He knew if she had something handy to throw at him, she would.

She crossed the room, and he could see flames bursting in her eyes. "Just who the hell do you think you are?"

He couldn't help the smile that touched his lips. "York Celtic Ellis," he said, moving to cover the distance separating them. "The last man you slept with. The only man you'll be sleeping with from here on out." When he came to a stop in front of her, he said in an even huskier voice, "I'm also the man who loves you more than life itself."

She nearly stumbled backward. "No."

He advanced forward. "Hell, yes. You might not ask for my love, probably don't even want it, but you got it, lock, stock and barrel."

"No."

"Why are you in denial, Darcy? There was no way in hell I would let you go into danger of any kind. Now I understand what true love is. I know what it truly is to love a woman."

DARCY STARED AT HIM, nearly frozen in shock at his words. She had to take a few moments to inhale and slowly exhale to fight the emotions that tried overtaking her. Did he know what he was saying? Did he understand the full impact?

She studied his features and saw the intensity in the dark eyes staring back at her. Yes, he knew and understood. She felt the sincerity of his gaze all the way to her bones when he lowered his voice to say, "I hadn't planned on loving any woman this much. I honestly didn't think that I could. You proved me wrong, Darcy."

His words propelled her to move, take a step closer to him. "How wrong?"

"Very wrong. But in my heart I know I did the right thing keeping you out of that mess with Felder."

In her heart, she knew the same thing. She could finally admit that. Not only had he and the people who worked for him exposed the persons behind the black marketing of those movies but they were able to establish a strong connection between the death of York's former girlfriend and the Medinas.

For a moment she couldn't say anything. She just stood there and stared at him, and she knew Ellie had been right. Her stubbornness wouldn't let her see what was quite obvious. He hadn't played her but had protected her.

She inched a little closer to him and heard his sharp intake of breath when a hardened nipple protruding through her silk robe came into contact with his chest. Electric energy flared between them and sent a jolt to the juncture of her thighs. She could feel every beat of his heart. If her move surprised him, he didn't let on. Instead, he was watching her with those dark eyes as if waiting to see what she would do next.

Darcy didn't give him long to wait. She wrapped her arms around his neck and then leaned in closer to bring her lips just a breath away from his sensual mouth. "And I love you, too, York. So very much," she whispered.

By the way his brow arched, she could tell that he was surprised by that, and from the immediate curve of his lips she knew her admission had pleased him.

"But don't think for one minute that I'm a pushover," she warned.

"Such a thing never crossed my mind," he responded, wrapping his arms around her waist.

And then he leaned in to kiss her, and she didn't hesitate in kissing him back. The hunger was immediate, the desire apparent. She needed to be his woman, the one to whom he'd declared his love. She relayed it in her kiss with a relentless attack on his mouth. When he lifted her up into his arms and wrapped her legs around him, she knew it was just the beginning.

He broke off their kiss and stared at her. "Marry me."

She smiled. It wasn't a request. Instead, it sounded

more like a demand. Would he never learn? "I'll think about it."

She let out a sharp gasp when he jousted her up and all but tossed her across his shoulders like a sack of potatoes. "York, put me down!"

"Soon enough."

It was a short walk from her kitchen to her living room, where he gently placed her down on the sofa and joined her. She couldn't help but laugh as she stared up into his love-filled eyes. And just to think she had fled New York three weeks ago because of the cold, and now she was back in the city surrounded by intense heat.

"There's nothing to think about, baby. I refuse to spend any more time without you, so plan a wedding."

She knew he was dead serious and deciding they needed to spend their time doing things other than arguing. She asked, "Would a Valentine's Day wedding be soon enough?"

"Yes, if I have to wait that long."

She smiled up at him as she reached up to entwine her arms around his neck. "I'll just have to make sure it's a pleasurable wait."

And then she pulled his mouth down to hers.

EPILOGUE

YORK SMILED DOWN at his beautiful bride thinking she had kept her word and it had been a pleasurable wait. But as of an hour ago, the waiting had come to an end. Darcelle Owens was now Darcelle Ellis and he couldn't be happier. However, a quick glance across the room at his remaining three single godbrothers showed they were just the opposite.

He inwardly smiled thinking sooner or later they would get over it. But then again, in a way he knew just how they felt. If anyone would have told him months ago he was headed for the altar he would not have believed them.

"Do you mind if I have a dance with my daughter-in-law?"

York chuckled as he glanced over at his father. His parents, like everyone else, had been shocked at his wedding announcement. "Sure, Dad. That will give me some time to go over and smooth three of your godsons' ruffled feathers."

His father laughed. "Good luck."

York placed a kiss on Darcy's lips. "I'll be back in a minute, sweetheart."

"I'll be waiting," she said, grinning up at him.

He couldn't help the smile that touched his lips. Darcy had been a beautiful bride and he would never forget how she'd looked walking down the aisle on her father's arms in her beautiful wedding gown. He was convinced the memory would remain in his heart forever.

York came to a stop in front of Winston, Zion and Virgil. He was glad to see all three of them, as well as Uriel and Xavier who were on the dance floor with their wives.

"So the traitor has decided to say a few words, has he?" Winston Coltrane asked in a clipped voice.

York nodded, smiling. He couldn't help it. He was definitely a happy man. "Don't hate, guys. Appreciate."

"Appreciate what?" Virgil asked, frowning. "The fact that another member of the Bachelors in Demand club has defected? I see no reason to jump for joy at that. I hope you know what you've done."

York glanced over his shoulder at his wife and couldn't help the way his gaze lingered on her awhile as she danced with his father. He then turned back to his three godbrothers. "Yes, I know what I've done, and honestly, I don't expect the three of you to understand things yet. But I have a feeling you will one day. Trust me when I say I have no regrets in getting married."

"But you and Darcy never got along," Winston reminded him.

"Yes, but we definitely get along now," York replied.

"I guess you're out of the club," Zion said, shaking his head smiling. "And to think you were the president."

Yes, he'd been the president, and a staunch supporter of bachelorhood. "Sorry, guys, but I got a feeling one of you will be next. Probably in less than a year from now," York said grinning.

Virgil frowned. "Marriage has turned you into a fortune teller, Y?"

"No, just a happy man who wants to spread the cheer. I'll see you guys around…after my honeymoon."

Moments later he returned to Darcy and pulled her into his arms. She tilted her head back and glanced up at her husband. "They still don't look too happy with you."

He brushed a kiss across her lips. "I've been where they are before. In fact, I'm the one who delivered the news to Uriel at his wedding that he was no longer in the club. Not that he cared."

York sighed and added, "Winston, Virgil and Zion see the club's members dwindling and can't help wondering what the hell is going on. That's three of us that have taken the plunge and three still remaining as bachelors."

She nodded. "What do you think they'll do?"

He tightened his arms around her waist. "Fight love like hell when it comes knocking on their doors. But in the end they will be what I had become."

"And what is that?"

"A bachelor undone by a gorgeous woman destined to be my soul mate. You can't fight love. And I can't wait to see when they find that out."

Darcy glanced over at the three men, and thought she couldn't wait to see as well. That would definitely be interesting. She then glanced back at the man she had married just hours ago. York was her hero and the man who would always have her heart. Forever.

* * * * *

YOU HAVE JUST READ A

 HARLEQUIN®

Desire

BOOK

If you were taken by the strong, **powerful hero** and are looking for the ultimate destination for **provocative and passionate romance,** be sure to look for all six Harlequin® Desire books every month.

"It would be better for you if I was here full-time," Keaton said.

"How do you figure?"

"Have you considered what will happen if Grace is up all night? If I'm here we can take turns getting up with her." He could see Lark was weakening. "It makes sense."

"Let me sleep on it tonight?" She held out her hands for the baby.

"Sure."

Only, Lark never got the chance to sleep. Neither did Keaton. Shortly after Grace finished eating, she began to fuss. During the second hour of the baby's crying, Keaton searched for advice on his tablet.

"She's dry, fed and obviously tired. Why won't she sleep?"

"Because it's her first day out of the NICU and she's overstimulated."

"How about wrapping her up?" he suggested. "Says here that babies feel more secure when they're swaddled." He cued up a video and they watched it. The demonstration looked straightforward, but the woman in the video used a doll, not a real baby.

"We can try it." Lark went to the closet and returned with two blankets of different sizes. "Hopefully one of these will do the trick."

When she was done, Lark braced her hands on the dining room table and stared down at the swaddled baby. "This doesn't look right."

Keaton returned to the video. "I think we missed this part here."

Grace was growing more upset by the second and she'd managed to free her left arm.

"Is it terrible that I have no idea what I'm doing?" Lark sounded close to tears. It had been a long, stressful evening.

"Not at all. I think every first-time parent feels just as overwhelmed as we do right now."

"Thank you for sticking around and helping me."

"We're helping Grace."

The corners of her lips quivered. "Not very well, as it happens."

And then, because she looked determined and hopeless all at once, Keaton succumbed to the impulse that had been threatening to break free all week. He cupped her cheek, lowered his head and kissed her.

Don't miss BECAUSE OF THE BABY...
by Cat Schield
Available January 2015
wherever Harlequin® Desire books and ebooks are sold.

HARLEQUIN®

Desire

Powerful heroes…scandalous secrets…burning desires.

Use this coupon to save

$1.00

on the purchase of any
Harlequin® Desire book.

Six new titles available every month wherever
books are sold, including most bookstores,
supermarkets, drugstores and discount stores.

Save $1.00

on the purchase of any Harlequin® Desire book.

Coupon expires February 28, 2015. Redeemable at participating retail outlets
in the U.S. and Canada only. Limit one coupon per customer.

52612116

Canadian Retailers: Harlequin Enterprises Limited will pay the face value of this coupon plus 10.25¢ if submitted by customer for this product only. Any other use constitutes fraud. Coupon is nonassignable. Void if taxed, prohibited or restricted by law. Consumer must pay any government taxes. Void if copied. Millennium I Promotional Services ("M1P") customers submit coupons and proof of sales to Harlequin Enterprises Limited, P.O. Box 3000, Saint John, NB E2L 4L3, Canada. Non-M1P retailer—for reimbursement submit coupons and proof of sales directly to Harlequin Enterprises Limited, Retail Marketing Department, 225 Duncan Mill Rd., Don Mills, Ontario M3B 3K9, Canada.

5 65373 00076 2   (8100)0 11996

U.S. Retailers: Harlequin Enterprises Limited will pay the face value of this coupon plus 8¢ if submitted by customer for this product only. Any other use constitutes fraud. Coupon is nonassignable. Void if taxed, prohibited or restricted by law. Consumer must pay any government taxes. Void if copied. For reimbursement submit coupons and proof of sales directly to Harlequin Enterprises Limited, P.O. Box 880478, El Paso, TX 88588-0478, U.S.A. Cash value 1/100 cents.

® and TM are trademarks owned and used by the trademark owner and/or its licensee.
© 2014 Harlequin Enterprises Limited

BJINC1214COUP